Karen Hawkins is the *New York Times* bestselling author of some of the funniest and freshest Scottish historical romances. When not stalking hot Australian actors, getting kicked out of West Virginia thanks to the antics of her extended family, or adding to her considerable shoe collection, Karen is getting chocolate on her keyboard while writing her next delightfully fun and sexy historical romance. Find her online at www.karenhawkins. com, follow her on Twitter @TheKarenHawkins, and on Facebook at www.facebook.com/AuthorKarenHawkins.

Karen Hawkins' glittering romances are...

'Fast, fun, and sexy . . . the perfect read' Christina Dodd, *New York Times* bestselling author

'Delightfully humorous, poignant, and satisfying' *Romantic Times*

'Always fun and sexy . . . a sure delight' Victoria Alexander, *New York Times* bestselling author

'Fast-paced, robust . . . filled with wit' *Night Owl Reviews*

'Charming and witty' *Publishers Weekly*

'Spiced by a chemistry that practically leaps off the pages' *Coffee Time Romance & More*

'Beautifully written . . . filled with passion, zest, and humor' *Addicted to Romance*

'Truly warm and funny' *Cherry Picks Romance*

'Completely captivating, wonderfully written, and ripe with romance with a legend so captivating you'll believe every word' *Romance Junkies*

By Karen Hawkins

Princes Of Oxenburg Series
The Prince Who Loved Me
The Prince And I
The Princess Wore Plaid (enovella)
Mad For The Plaid

Duchess Diaries Series
Princess In Disguise (enovella)
How To Capture A Countess
How To Pursue A Princess
How To Entice An Enchantress

KAREN HAWKINS

THE OXENBURG PRINCES

Mad for the Plaid

headline
ETERNAL

Published by arrangement with Pocket Books,
a division of Simon & Schuster, Inc.

First published in Great Britain in 2016
by HEADLINE ETERNAL
An imprint of HEADLINE PUBLISHING GROUP

1

Cataloguing in Publication Data is available from the British Library

ISBN 978 1 4722 2905 2

Offset in 11.33/15.85 pt Palatino LT Std by Jouve (UK), Milton Keynes

Printed and bound in Great Britain by CPI Group (UK) Ltd, Croydon, CR0 4YY

MIX
Paper from
responsible sources
FSC® C104740

Headline's policy is to use papers that are natural, renewable and recyclable
products and made from wood grown in well-managed forests and other
controlled sources. The logging and manufacturing processes are expected
to conform to the environmental regulations of the country of origin.

HEADLINE PUBLISHING GROUP
An Hachette UK Company
Carmelite House
50 Victoria Embankment
London EC4Y 0DZ

www.headlineeternal.com
www.headline.co.uk
www.hachette.co.uk

To Hot Cop, who instinctively recognizes when I need
hugs, a laugh, or a cup of coffee.
You know what I'm like without those,
and love me anyway.
Thank you.

Acknowledgments

Many thanks to my soon-to-be-retired editor, Micki Nuding, who found me in her slush pile one fateful day in 1998. I still remember where I was at the exact moment she called to say she'd read my submission and loved it. (FYI: I was standing in a pile of dirty laundry— it wasn't pretty.)

It's been a long, fun, rewarding ride and I'm so, so grateful for all the time, effort, and care you put into my books over the years. Micki, I'm going to miss you!

Mad for the Plaid

Prologue

To: His Royal Highness
Prince Nikolai Romanovin of Oxenburg
Holyroodhouse, Edinburgh

Your Highness,

As you may recall, two weeks ago you escorted the Grand
Duchess Natasha Nikolaevna to Castle Leod for her visit
with my grandmother, the Dowager Countess Cromartie.
I'm sorry we did not have the opportunity to meet, but
that is not surprising, as I was informed you stayed less
than ten minutes.

Soon after you left, your grandmother discovered her
black leather travel case was not with her trunks. Her
Grace assures me it is quite important and that she must
have it with all possible haste and thus requests that you
send it at your earliest convenience.

Yours sincerely,
Lady Ailsa Mackenzie
September 12, 1824

To: Lady Ailsa Mackenzie
Castle Leod

Lady Ailsa:

Pray inform my grandmother that the "case" to which she refers is actually a very large and heavy trunk and would take well over a fortnight to ship, by which time her visit will be over. She can do without it.

HRH Nikolai of Oxenburg
September 21, 1824

To: His Royal Highness
Prince Nikolai Romanovin of Oxenburg
Holyroodhouse, Edinburgh

Your Highness,

Once again I am writing on behalf of your grandmother the Grand Duchess Nikolaevna. Her Grace requests (again) that you send her black leather case which contains her favorite lotions as soon as possible (again), for she has great need of them (still). As she has decided to stay another month and perhaps longer, there is now plenty of time to have the case (or trunk, if you insist) delivered.

Yours sincerely,
Lady Ailsa Mackenzie
October 2, 1824

———∞∞∞———

To: *Lady Ailsa Mackenzie*
Castle Leod

Lady Ailsa:

I was not aware Her Grace was staying another month
and (hopefully) longer. I cannot tell you how happy I am
to learn this. Expect that blasted trunk in the next week
or so.

HRH Nikolai
October 11, 1824

———∞∞∞———

To: *His Royal Highness*
Prince Nikolai Romanovin of Oxenburg
Holyroodhouse, Edinburgh

Your Highness,

I regret to inform you that Her Grace's black dressing
case containing her lotions still has not arrived and
your grandmother strongly requests that you send
it immediately. She wishes me to remind you that it
has been one week and two days since your letter was
posted. (On an aside, I did point out that your use of
"next week or so" was obviously a generalization and
that the case would most likely show up before this

letter arrives on your desk, but she will have none of it.) As I'm sure you are aware (as evidenced by your rapid departure on leaving your grandmother on our doorstep), Her Grace tends to be moody when she is upset.

Send the case or trunk or whatever it is as soon as is humanly possible.

Yours sincerely,
Lady Ailsa Mackenzie
October 21, 1824

⚬⚬⚬

To: Lady Ailsa Mackenzie
Castle Leod

Lady Ailsa:

When my men fetched the trunk from Her Grace's bedchamber last week, my men discovered something dripping out of one corner. Upon opening the trunk, we were met with a smell I cannot describe, even though it still lingers throughout the house like a deadly mist.

The trunk is not a "dressing case" filled with lotions as my grandmother has claimed, but is filled instead with her potions. One letter can make a great difference, can it not? Sadly, some of the bottles holding her potions were broken when the trunk was last moved, and I can only imagine her "eye of newt," or whatever it is, has caused that deadly odor. I now hold out only a vague hope none

*of us is overcome by it, or—as is more likely—turned into
some sort of goat or toad.*

*Before I send the trunk, it must be cleaned, aired, and
left to dry. When this is done, I will send it by private
courier.*

*Meanwhile, inform my grandmother that her "case"
will be there forthwith. (Note: As she cannot measure
"forthwith," I trust this will end this unnecessary
correspondence.)*

HRH N
November 14, 1824

Chapter 1

Castle Leod
The Small Study
November 17, 1824

"What do you mean, she's 'gone missing'?" Lady Ailsa Mackenzie put down the letter she'd been reading and eyed her grandmother with disbelief.

Lady Edana MacGregor Mackenzie, the Dowager Countess Cromartie, fluttered her lace handkerchief. "I mean what I said: the duchess is nowhere to be found." Dressed in black, a color Lady Edana had assumed on the death of her husband, the late earl, more than ten years earlier, she made an impressive figure. Tall and willowy, with carefully crafted dyed-gold hair that echoed the true color that had faded years ago, Edana fought valiantly to keep age from robbing her of the famed MacGregor beauty. "Ailsa, I am *deeply* concerned. Poor Natasha does not know the dangers of our highland countryside."

"Perhaps Her Grace is oot in the carriage, or going for a ride, or . . . whatever it is she wished to do."

"Dear, it's 'out,' not 'oot.'" Edana sighed heavily. "I do wish your father had sent you to a proper boarding school."

"I needed to be here with Mama after she grew ill. I would nae have missed those moments for anything."

"And now she's gone, your papa is never here. It's as if I lost both of them at one and the same time." Edana gave a fretful sigh. "Your papa is neglecting us all. He should have seen to it that you went to a proper boarding school and had at least one season. You might have married by now, the way your sisters have."

Ailsa refrained from pointing out that while her sisters had inherited Edana's famed MacGregor beauty, Ailsa had taken after the bold Mackenzies. Where her sisters had golden hair, blue eyes, willowy figures, and perfect noses, Ailsa's hair was a darker, less noticeable ash blond, her eyes gray, her form stalwart, while her nose could only be called "prominent."

It was an unfortunate blend of traits.

Not that it mattered; Ailsa was twenty-two now and had no desire to be displayed on the marriage mart among a group of mindless seventeen-year-olds who would drive her mad with their empty chatter and breathless gossip. She was happy to have been left at Castle Leod, where she could hunt, ride, fish, and—when the mood suited her—throw a cloak upon the ground under a tree and read to her heart's content. There were a thousand amusing things to do here in the highlands, and she loved them all.

She was content with her life, especially now that

Papa had left the castle and estate in her care. It was a big responsibility, and she was still learning how to answer the challenges presented, one of which was keeping up with her grandmother's elderly, and at times quarrelsome, houseguest. "Why precisely do you think Her Grace is 'missing'?"

"We were to meet for breakfast almost an hour ago, and at her request, too, for she wished to visit that shop in the village I told her about, but she didn't appear." Edana sniffed. "I had to eat by myself as no one else was up."

"So the two of you are speaking again."

"La, child, of course we are speaking!" Edana frowned, though she instantly ceased, for fear of deepening the lines between her eyes. "I admit we've had a few arguments—"

"A few?"

"No more than is to be expected." Edana waved her handkerchief, wafting a floral perfume through the air. "Poor Natasha; she's changed dreadfully. She used to be quite lovely. Now . . . well, you've seen her. She's aged forty years in the time we were apart."

As it had been almost forty years to the day since the dowager countess and the grand duchess had last seen one another, Ailsa didn't find this difficult to believe. "Are you certain Her Grace is nae just still abed?"

"I spoke with Her Grace's maid, and she said Natasha left her bed chamber at daybreak. I asked the housekeeper to see if perhaps the poor thing was lost somewhere in the castle, as it can be confusing, but Mrs. Attnee says Her Grace is nowhere to be found."

"Perhaps she went for a ride."

"MacGill says all our coaches and horses are accounted for. Ailsa, I'm certain Natasha is *missing*. We *must* send a search party."

"But the carriages and horses are all here, and you cannae be thinking she left on foot. It's been snowing since late last night."

"Of course she's not walking! She's a duchess, for the love of heaven. But if she's been foolish, then we must stop her from—" Lady Edana clamped her lips closed.

Ailsa narrowed her gaze on her grandmother. "Stop her from what?" When Edana didn't answer, Ailsa added, "I see. You're hiding something."

"Nonsense," Edana said sharply, the faintest hint of a flush showing through her face paint. "I'm just worried."

"Of course. Well, if there's nae more to tell, then there's nae more to do." Ailsa pulled forward the stack of waiting correspondence. "The Grand Duchess Nikolaevna is neither a button that has been misplaced nor a puppy that has wandered off. Wherever she is, she got there under her own power and is where she wants to be."

"Ailsa, *please*! Natasha *must* be found. You can't go losing a grand duchess! Think of the scandal! Her grandson left her in *our* care. He will be beside himself with worry!"

"That, I doubt." From her own correspondence with the prince, and the columns and columns she'd read about him in the papers, as well as the little her father had said of the man on meeting him at some function or another, she was well aware that the duchess's eldest grandson was a profligate, a womanizer, and little else.

She pulled a fresh piece of paper from the center drawer and placed it before her. "Wherever the duchess is, she will return when she's of a mind to." Ailsa dipped her pen into the inkwell. "Now, if you'll excuse me, I have at least ten letters to—"

"Fine! I'll tell you what's happened, but do not blame me if something ill has occurred to poor Natasha while you've been lollygagging about with estate nonsense!"

"'Estate nonsense' is what puts a roof over our heads." Ailsa replaced her pen in the holder. "Tell me everything."

Lady Edana's shoulders slumped. "Do you remember the first night Her Grace was here, and how she flirted so shamelessly with Lord Lyon, who did not look at all comfortable with her attention?"

"I vaguely remember that, aye."

"It's 'yes,' dear, and not 'aye.' Natasha was shameless. And my dear Daffyd—I mean, Lord Hamilton— noticed her affections were not returned. It was quite pathetic, and the whole situation put poor Natasha in quite an ill temper."

"I noticed that. We *all* noticed that."

"Exactly. And things just got worse after Lord Lyon left. Knowing how Her Grace taxes me, Hamilton said that he wished he could brighten her mood, just to be of service to me, of course. Which got me to thinking that perhaps what Natasha needed was a distraction."

"A distraction? What do you mean— Och, you dinnae!"

"I did and it was brilliant!" Lady Edana beamed. "I asked Hamilton to ply her with attention. It worked, too, for she was in a much better mood after that, although"—Edana's smile disappeared—"had I known then what I know now, I would never have been so charitable."

"And what do you know now— Ah! Has Lord Hamilton come to care for Her Grace?"

"Don't make me laugh!" Lady Edana said sharply. "He's been playing a part, that is all. And at *my* request. It's Natasha who's made the mistake of caring, not Hamilton."

"Really?" Ailsa considered this. "It seems much more than that to me. He sat near her at dinner last night, dinnae he?" Ailsa squinted at the ceiling, trying to remember all the places she'd seen Lord Hamilton with Her Grace. "And at the picnic and at the musicale and at—"

"Yes, yes." Edana drew herself up, a firm smile now plastered on her lips, although it didn't reach her eyes. "Naturally Hamilton went beyond my request, but only because he knew how much I was suffering from Her Grace's moods. He's been in love with me for so many years—I truly feel sorry for him."

"I know all aboot Lord Hamilton. He eats dinner here so many nights of the week that he has his own bedchamber."

"Then you don't need me to tell you how concerned I was when it dawned on me that Natasha was beginning to believe Hamilton's kindness as something more. Naturally, I warned her not to mistake Daffyd's attention as anything other than politeness. You'd think she would have thanked me for taking the time, but no!" Edana's jaw firmed. "She laughed and said I was jealous. Me! Jealous of an old woman like her!"

"I see. Did you mention your concerns to Lord Hamilton?"

"Of course. I warned him he was in dire danger of being put upon by Her Grace and that her feelings were unnaturally strong. He was much struck by my observations, and asked me several times why I thought such a thing. It's laughable, I know—Daffyd and Natasha!"

Ailsa wisely didn't say a word.

Her grandmother gave a hearty laugh that sounded oddly hollow. "Why would any man pay attention to *her*? She cannot be bothered with keeping out of the sun to prevent freckles, or with wearing something that fits. Like you, she refuses to maintain her appearan—" Edana closed her lips over the rest of her sentence. "You know my feelings on the subject."

"Och aye, I know them well. Too well, many might say. When did you tell Lord Hamilton your suspicions aboot Her Grace?"

"'About,' not—" Edana caught Ailsa's expression and hurried to add, "Yesterday after lunch. He said he would speak with her immediately. Poor Natasha must have been devastated: two men in a row rejecting her. I fear she just up and left us, unable to bear the thought of facing such embarrassment."

"But none of our coaches are missing." Ailsa tapped her fingers on the desk. "When you asked MacGill if any of the coaches and carriages were missing, did you inquire after Lord Hamilton's coach and horses, or just our own?"

Edana stiffened. "You *cannot* be suggesting that Daffyd and Natasha have— No. I will not believe it."

"We must find oot." Ailsa turned to the long, fringed bell pull and tugged it firmly.

"You are wasting your time." Lady Edana sniffed.

An awkward silence filled the room until a soft knock heralded the entry of the housekeeper, Mrs. Attnee. A plump, motherly woman, she wore a beaming smile that dimmed on seeing the Dowager Countess. "Guid morning, my lady." The housekeeper dipped a quick curtsy, her expression softening as she turned to Ailsa. "Lady Ailsa, you rang?"

"I understand you assisted in the search for Her Grace."

Concern creased Mrs. Attnee's forehead. "Aye. She is nae to be found. We searched the house top to bottom, too."

"And Lord Hamilton? Do you perchance know where he is?"

"Lord Hamilton left verrah early this morning."

"*What?*" Lady Edana blinked. "Are you certain?"

"I saw him myself, I did. I'd just sent the upstairs maids aboot their dooties when he came sneakin' doon the stairs."

"Sneaking?" Ailsa asked.

"I would nae call it other, fer he was bent o'er and walkin' like this—" She hunched her shoulders and mimicked someone tiptoeing.

"Nonsense," Edana announced, her neck a mottled

red. "Hamilton would never move in such a-a-a sub-versive fashion!"

Ailsa ignored her. "Did Lord Hamilton say anything?"

"Just 'guid morning.' He'd just sent one of the foot-men to have his coach brought round, though. I dinnae think aught of it as he sometimes leaves early for Caskill Manor if he's plannin' on going huntin' and such. 'Twas obvious he dinnae wish fer company, so I left him in the foyer. When I came back later, he was gone."

Ignoring the strange hissing sound now coming from Edana, Ailsa smiled comfortingly at the housekeeper. "So you would nae know if he left *with* someone."

"Nae, I—" The housekeeper gasped. "Lord, do ye think he's run off with Her Grace?"

Edana made a strangled noise while Ailsa said, "I think 'tis possible Her Grace decided to visit Caskill Manor at Lord Hamilton's invitation."

"Ah!" The housekeeper pursed her lips. "I thought there might be some courtin' goin' on, what with all the whisperin' and such, although I never imagined they'd elope—"

"That is *quite* enough!" Edana snapped, her eyes blazing. "Mrs. Attnee, I will thank you for not spread-ing vile rumors!"

"There, there," Ailsa said soothingly. "The truth does nae always come in a neat box. Sometimes 'tis a messy package, best opened when fortified by drink."

Mrs. Attnee nodded wisely. "I'll pour some sherry." She made her way to the small stand near the window, poured sherry into a small crystal glass, and brought it to Lady Edana.

Lady Edana took the glass gratefully. "That *harpy*! I cannot believe Daffyd would—"

An abrupt knock on the door heralded the entry of MacGill. Tall and gaunt, the butler looked abnormally pale, his eyes wide. "My lady, a message has come from Caskill Manor."

"No!" Edana threw up a hand. "Do *not* say Lord Hamilton has eloped with Her Grace!"

Mr. MacGill looked shocked. "Nae, my lady. Nae that. The steward at Caskill sent word. Mr. Grant says Lord Hamilton sent a note last night that he and a guest were to be expected early this mornin' and his lordship requested a sumptuous breakfast fit fer a queen—"

Lady Edana choked, and then held out her glass for more sherry, which Mrs. Attnee instantly brought.

MacGill cast a cautious look at the countess before he continued. "His lordship and his guest never arrived."

"What?" Ailsa asked, and for the first time, a true flicker of worry pinched her.

"Grant sent a footman here to ask after Lord Hamilton. On the way, the lad found his lordship's carriage left on the road, blocked by a felled tree. The groom, both footmen, and three outriders were wounded, whilst one outrider was naewhere to be seen."

Ailsa's hands trembled, so she gripped them together. *How could this be? Our guests, abducted?*

"There's more," MacGill said in a grim tone. "The side of the coach was peppered wi' bullets."

Mrs. Attnee gasped while Lady Edana went pale. Ailsa found herself on her feet. "The duchess and Lord Hamilton were nae—" She couldn't say the words.

"Nae, my lady. There was blood on the carriage seat; only a few droplets, nae more." MacGill's brows lowered. "But Lord Hamilton's men found a wee rip of tartan pinned under a wheel. The *Mackenzie* tartan."

"That's ridiculous!" Lady Edana exclaimed. "We would never harm Lord Hamilton!"

"Mr. Grant knows tha'," MacGill said. "But nae matter wha' Grant thinks, he has nae choice but to send word of the abduction to Lord Hamilton's brother."

Ailsa had to bite her lip to keep from saying aloud how unjust that was. The Earl of Arran and her father had never gotten along, fighting for decades over various property lines and estate boundaries. If Arran thought them responsible, he would call for retribution. Aware of the servants' anxious gazes now pinned on her, Ailsa tucked her fears away. "MacGill, was a note left? A ransom request?"

"Nae, my lady."

Lady Edana put down her glass. "Cromartie must come home at once and deal with this."

The two servants looked at Ailsa, their gazes questioning. *Are they hoping I'll send for Papa?* She dropped her hands back to her sides, fighting a very real desire to do just that.

It would be easy to send for Papa and let him deal with this crisis, but in doing so she would be admitting she was unable to manage the situation herself. Ailsa wasn't willing to do that. *She* had been left in charge of Castle Leod and all that entailed, and that included the well-being of her guests. "This is my mystery to solve," she said briskly. "And solve it, I will. We must find Lord

Hamilton and Her Grace." Which was a long shot, but her only option. Whomever had organized this little charade would hide their prisoners well.

Lady Edana frowned. "Are you sure? Your Papa—"

"—is busy. I can handle this." Ailsa said the words as confidently as she could, hoping against hope that her grandmother would agree.

To her surprise, Edana sighed, and then shrugged. "Fine. I just don't understand one thing. Hamilton's value is obvious, but why would someone take Her Grace? She's not particularly wealthy that I know of."

"Perhaps she was where she wasn't expected—in Lord Hamilton's coach." Ailsa spread her hands on the desk and leaned forward. "MacGill, have a horse readied; I want to see this carriage and the 'proof' left behind. Inform the gamekeeper he will be accompanying me. Mr. Greer is an expert tracker and I will have need of his skill."

"Verrah guid, my lady." Looking much heartened, MacGill bowed and left.

Lady Edana sank back in her chair. "Lud help us all; the world is upside down!"

Ailsa managed a firm smile. "All will be well. I promise."

Her grandmother seemed comforted by Ailsa's words, but to herself, Ailsa had to wonder if someone was trying to start a clan war. Was it possible that Arran, tired of being put off from grabbing more of the Mackenzie land by his brother's friendship with Lady Edana, had orchestrated this little escapade? It seemed the only answer, and yet the maneuver was so blatantly obvious that it made her wonder if something more complex was afoot. But what?

When she found the prisoners, she would have her answers. Her gaze landed on a small stack of notes resting on the corner of her desk and she grimaced. She supposed she needed to inform the prince of the current situation. Her Grace was his grandmother, after all.

Ailsa hated to do it—just exchanging a few notes about Her Grace's missing trunk had been far too much contact with the man as it was, but there was nothing for it. Like him or not, Ailsa had a responsibility to keep him apprised of the situation. Had he been a man of substance, she might have worried he would take it upon himself to arrogantly barge in, interfering with her efforts to contain the situation and find the prisoners. Fortunately, she doubted he'd do more than demand an accounting. And that, she hoped to be able to provide, and soon.

Sighing, Ailsa sat back down, pulled a piece of foolscap her way, and began writing the necessary note.

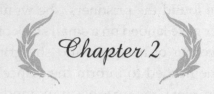

Chapter 2

Holyroodhouse
Edinburgh
November 22, 1824

Count Fyodor Apraksin handed the letter to the master of the honor guards, Vasily Rurik, a large bearded man who had the look and fearless courage of a grizzly. "*You* take it to him."

Rurik promptly handed the letter back. "*Nyet.* I'd rather face a thousand Cossacks than deliver that damned missive to His Highness."

"*Someone* must deliver it." Unlike the rest of His Highness's entourage, Apraksin was not a soldier, but a courtier. And under normal circumstances, delivering a letter would indeed be his responsibility. But not this one.

He held it at arm's length, as though it were a snake about to strike. "What can that Scottish harpy want now? We sent Her Grace that blasted trunk."

"Every time the prince gets a letter from Lady Ailsa, he snarls for hours. Sometimes days."

"He has been in an especially surly mood of late."

"So I've noticed," Rurik said in a dry tone. "Something is on his mind."

Apraksin sent the head guard a curious look. "I forget you know him better than any of us." The royal family's honor guards were made up almost completely of the younger sons of the nobility, and Rurik's family was especially close to the prince's.

"I used to be," Rurik said shortly. "But now, like you, I don't even know why we're here. Has His Highness told you anything?"

"Nyet." Apraksin glanced at the half-open door and, determining no one was listening outside, said in a low voice, "It's a mission of some sort, but that's all I know."

Rurik shrugged. "I suppose he'll tell us soon enough. The only reason he would stay here at this time of the year is for a mission, not when we could be in Italy, where it is warm and the women . . ." He kissed his fingers to the air.

"Don't remind me," Apraksin said sourly. There was a widow in Milan for whom he'd have given his right leg to spend just two hours in her company. "He won't admit anything's afoot."

"He is not a talker, this prince of ours. Not to us."

This was true. When it came to developing what seemed like close friendships with various foreign dignitaries and powerful nobles, or seducing information from the wives of those same men, there was no more affable, personable, talkative man than their prince. But when he was no longer onstage, he became himself—direct, no-nonsense, and sometimes chillingly civil, especially if a particular situation did not please him.

Apraksin looked at the letter in his hand and grimaced. "Perhaps we can get Menshivkov to deliver this. That braggart is always saying he is the prince's chief aide-de-camp, a title he made up in his own mind."

Rurik, who'd been looking rather dour, brightened. "*Da!* If Menshivkov wishes to be a true aide, then he can give His Highness the letter after di—"

"What letter?"

The deep voice sent both Apraksin and Rurik spinning on their booted heels to face the door that was now standing wide open, a tall, uniformed figure framed within it.

"Your Highness." Apraksin clicked his heels and bowed sharply, Rurik following suit.

"We did not hear you," Rurik added unnecessarily.

A single black brow rose at this. It was a simple movement, the raising of that black eyebrow, and yet that, combined with the icy stare of its owner, made Rurik and Apraksin gulp silently.

Without sparing them another glance, Prince Nikolai Romanovin closed the study door behind him. At six foot four, he was taller than most men. An imposing figure with broad shoulders, thick black hair, and green eyes so dark they appeared almost black, he was not a man easily overlooked. In front of society, he took the character of a man of town, charming and easily amused, flirting with women one after the other, and never speaking of anything political or of consequence. Indeed, most of Europe believed him a wastrel of a sort, a reputation he had carefully cultivated.

In public, he'd been called "a womanizer," "frivolous,"

and "an utter rakehell." In private, he was well educated, knowledgeable, forceful, unyielding, a brilliant tactician, and a tenacious negotiator. This dichotomy had stood him in good stead during negotiations of all kinds. Only Oxenburg possessed a prince such as Nikolai Romanovin.

Apraksin inclined his head. "Your Highness, a letter arrived from Castle Leod."

The prince's mouth thinned. "Bloody hell, I thought that damned trunk would be there by now."

Rurik offered, "We sent it in our own coach, escorted by the head groom."

Apraksin added, "Perhaps Her Grace has discovered another missing case?"

The prince held out his hand.

Biting back a sigh, Apraksin handed him the letter.

Nik opened it. Composed in now-familiar neat handwriting, this note had been written in far more haste than the previous ones.

To: HRH Nikolai Romanovin

Your Highness,

I am writing to you so that you may learn of this news from me, and not from the idle gossip of strangers. Your grandmother has gone missing. She left yesterday with Lord Hamilton to visit his seat at Caskill Manor, but neither arrived. We are currently searching for Her Grace, but I believe she may have been (and I dread using this word, for I know it will cause you distress) abducted.

I will explain more when I have news. In the meantime,

*my men and I are actively searching for her. I promise that
if Her Grace and Lord Hamilton are not found soon, I will
call in the local constabulary. Rest assured no stone will be
left unturned in our search. We will find your grandmother
and she will be returned to you hale and hearty.*

Yours sincerely,
Lady Ailsa Mackenzie
November 17, 1824

P.S. The trunk arrived this morning.

Nik crumpled the letter in his hand. "*Ehta prost
nivazmosha!*"

Apraksin and Rurik stiffened to attention.

Nik ignored them, the paper crinkling noisily in
his tight fist. Though his grandmother gave him grief
whenever she could with her ceaseless demands and
often ribald comments—truly the woman's sense of
humor was as unchecked as a youth's—he loved her
dearly. More, perhaps, than anyone else.

He rarely admitted that to anyone, for he'd witnessed
others being exploited for their familial and romantic
ties by unscrupulous foes trying to change the tide of
various negotiations. He himself had once almost fallen
victim to that ruse.

Once.

So the question was this: had someone abducted his
grandmother in order to change his position on the current negotiations? Or was she a victim of another plot,
one unassociated with him and his efforts here?

He uncrumpled the letter and read it again. It was

obvious Lady Ailsa had already decided that Tata Natasha's disappearance—and that of this Lord Hamilton—was an abduction. *If someone were trying to reach me, why would they take this Hamilton? That makes no sense.*

A small flare of hope warmed Nik. He re-crumpled the letter, aware of the gazes resting on him. It was a relief to be with his men and not have to pretend to be an empty-headed, idle fool. It was taxing, keeping up such a façade, though the benefits were beyond counting. It was amazing how many times men of great importance revealed pertinent information in front of someone they thought a lackadaisical, inattentive creature.

And in Nik's life, nothing was as valuable as information.

"My grandmother has gone missing," he announced shortly. "Lady Ailsa believes Her Grace to have been abducted."

Apraksin's mouth dropped open.

"Someone took Her Grace? *On purpose?*" Rurik said in obvious disbelief.

"I daresay they regret it now, but *da.*" Nik's jaw ached from where he ground his teeth. *Tata Natasha will not accept such an ignominious fate as being abducted, which could leave her open to abuse. She had better be well or I will—* His hand tightened over the paper. "She must be rescued. But at the same time, I cannot leave or those here will realize something has happened. I cannot have a scandal. *Oxenburg* cannot have a scandal. Not now."

Apraksin's dark eyes gleamed. The slender courtier was at his best when a scheme was at hand. "You *are* on a mission, then."

"*Da*, and it is tenuous at best, but bloody important. A disruption could ruin everything." He tapped the letter. "Lady Ailsa has said she will call in the constabulary if my grandmother is not found soon. We cannot allow her to do so."

"Of course," Apraksin said. "I will go to Castle Leod and—"

"*Nyet*. Tata Natasha is *my* responsibility. I will go."

Rurik nodded. "It is honorable you feel so. Whoever goes to Castle Leod must find her and bring her home quickly and quietly."

"But . . . the mission?" Apraksin said. "Can you leave?"

"I must," Nik said grimly. "But I don't know how to arrange it. If it's revealed my grandmother's been abducted, those involved in the current negotiations might fear our secrecy has been compromised and refuse to continue. We must keep this incident quiet."

"You think Her Grace's abduction is linked to these meetings?" Apraksin asked.

"I don't know, for we have been very careful. Plus, another person of importance was taken with Her Grace—a Lord Hamilton, who has no association with what we do here. Knowing my grandmother's propensity for meddling in what does not concern her, it is possible she is cooking in a soup of her own making. Something totally unrelated to anything here."

"That would be unsurprising," Rurik admitted. "When do we leave?"

"The sooner we leave, the quicker we can return. No one can know I'm gone, which means I cannot take the guard."

"What?" Apraksin gaped. "You cannot travel without your guard!" He looked at Rurik. "It would not be safe."

"*Nyet*," Rurik said shortly. "Your Highness, if it is discovered you are traveling without protection, you will become a target. The only way—" He broke off, frowning.

After a long moment, Nik snapped, "If you have an idea, then say it. I do not have all day."

Rurik's face reddened while Apraksin sent Nik a surprised glance.

Nik ignored them both. At one time, when he'd been a youth, he and Rurik had been close, but those days were long gone. Nik couldn't allow anyone close now—his life was not his own. "Speak, Rurik. What are your thoughts?"

Rurik's mouth had been white, but now he shrugged. "It might be possible to make people believe you are still here."

"How?"

"An illness, perhaps. One that would keep you in your bed."

Nik looked at Apraksin. "Is this possible?"

Though he looked far from pleased, the courtier's face folded in thought. "It can be done, I think." He absently played with the lace on his wrist before finally saying, "Later tonight, we will announce you've fallen ill, perhaps from the food at last night's ball. Many were complaining about it."

Nik considered this and then nodded. "Very good. But I will need three, maybe four weeks. Will this ruse work that long?"

"I think so, *da*. After a week, we will announce you are better, but then you will suffer a relapse, worse this time."

"Good. Meanwhile, you two will announce you're traveling to Castle Leod to see my grandmother. I will follow, but dressed as a groom. I'll make certain no one sees me leave."

Apraksin raised an eyebrow. "And once we've rescued Her Grace?"

"We will take her to Inverness and put her on the fastest ship to Oxenburg. It is fortunate I have these few weeks open in the negotiations; one of the key participants has been held up by early-winter storms. It will be three weeks, and likely longer, before he arrives. Nothing can be done until then anyway."

"Who is this person?" Rurik asked.

Nik hesitated. He'd worked so hard to get the fool to the bargaining table—years, in fact. But Nik supposed he had no choice; everyone would know soon enough. "The tsar of Russia."

Apraksin swore under his breath while Rurik gave a silent whistle.

"As I said, 'tis serious," Nik confirmed.

"I'm surprised he dares leave Russia," Apraksin said in a grim tone. "There is such unrest."

"That is the reason we are having these negotiations. He has ignored all advice and has repressed his people to the point of— Well. I need not tell you. But now he wishes our help and that of other countries in quelling this revolution he's started. If Russia falls to the scourge of anarchy, Europe could follow. While Oxenburg is in no danger because of the concessions we've made to ensure our subjects are well taken care of, some of our neighbors aren't in such a harmonious position."

"And with the treaties we signed after the war, if one country falls to unrest, then the rest of us must be involved." Apraksin took a steadying breath. "I can see why you're determined to see these negotiations through. We will find your three weeks. I will have one of the men announce you've fallen ill later this evening, right as dinner is served."

Rurik added, "I'll set a guard outside your bedchamber to keep out the inquisitive."

"Good."

Apraksin pursed his lips. "Menshivkov can stay in bed, covered by blankets, when the servants bring food, in case someone is watching. His hair is about the same color as yours, and while he's not the same height, he is close enough that we can mask it. I will have Doubrovnik ride to Castle Leod with word once the tsar has arrived for the negotiations."

"That will work," Nik agreed.

Apraksin continued. "Rurik and I will go now and tell everyone who will listen that we are bored and have secured permission to visit Her Grace. We will say we are delivering personal letters. A number of those were delivered just yesterday, so that detail can be confirmed."

Nik nodded his approval. "Once it is dark, I'll find a horse and meet you on the other side of the bridge."

Rurik's heavy brows lowered. "I am uneasy that you are taking such a risk."

"I have no choice. Besides, you will be on hand to keep watch."

Rurik didn't look pleased, but he nodded. "Your Highness will need a groom's clothing. I'll procure some from the servants. I'll tell them it's for one of the guards who wishes to sneak out undetected to court a housemaid."

"*Spasiba*. Bring the clothes to me here." Nik waved them toward the door. "Now go. You know what must be done."

The two men bowed and then left, the door closing behind them. Finally alone, Nik turned to the fire and threw the crumpled letter on top of the smoldering log.

He watched silently as the red-hot flames flickered to life, greedily reaching for the paper, blackening the edges before crackling hungrily and consuming the note in a heated blaze. He had to find Tata Natasha and stop the indomitable Lady Ailsa from alerting the authorities. There was too much at stake to involve anyone else, especially a sharp-witted highlander who managed to convey disapproval with every stroke of her pen.

The final bit of the letter curled into ashes, and he turned away, far more worried about his grandmother than he wished to admit.

Chapter 3

Castle Leod
The Small Study
November 25, 1824

Ailsa paced rapidly, her chin tucked against her chest, her hands clasped behind her. *Good lord, what a coil.*

Lady Edana sat by the fire pretending to embroider a rose upon a piece of cream muslin. She sighed. *"Why has someone done this?"*

"We'll know soon enough," Ailsa replied just as she had the previous nineteen times her grandmother had asked the question. Ailsa continued to pace, her slippers silent on the thick rug, her mind whirling with thoughts. On the day of the abduction, she and Greer had ridden to the overturned coach and, after much searching, had located the tracks of the scoundrels and their captives where they'd disappeared into the woods. There, behind a thick cove of brush, Greer had found signs of waiting horses.

Greer had followed the tracks a short distance, but it quickly became obvious that the abductors were not heading toward the main road, but were going ever deeper into the woods, so he'd returned to where Ailsa waited.

After some discussion and a long look at the map Greer had brought, they'd decided that the abductors, burdened by the uncertain weather and two elderly prisoners, would be forced to join a road at some point north. Traveling into the mountains beyond the Rhidorroch Forest was a hardship even a healthy man would hesitate to face. That left one question: Which road would they join?

There were only two choices; the narrow and winding northwest road traveled through steep craigs before eventually leading down across the bogs of Meall An Fhuarain and on to the coast, where a handful of small villages sat. Ailsa's heart sank at the thought, for that road would take the ill-doers deeper into Mackenzie lands, which would make her clan look all the guiltier.

But if the scoundrels instead took the northeast road, which curved over the Strath Brora to Borrobol Forest, they'd end up on the easternmost holdings of the Summerlands. That option was her one and only hope, for the Summerlands were close allies of the Earl of Arran. If she could prove that the Summerlands had orchestrated the abduction, the Mackenzie name would be cleared.

Thus, she'd directed Greer and two of his men to follow the trail as far as they could and send word as soon as they knew which road the abductors had taken. The heavy snows of the last few days had lowered Ailsa's hopes considerably, but to her relief, a note had arrived this morning, hand delivered by Ian Stewart, one of Greer's men.

Ailsa paused by her desk and picked up the much-creased missive.

"I don't know why you keep reading it over and over; the words will not change." Lady Edana's peevish tone raked over Ailsa's nerves like an out-of-tune piano. "It's the worst possible information, for they are deep in Mackenzie lands."

Ailsa returned the letter to the desk. "Aye, but at least we know where they are headed. Greer traced them all the way to the Corrieshalloch Gorge." She paused, sending a side glance at her grandmother as she added in what she hoped was a casual tone, "Greer awaits me there."

Edana looked up, her eyebrows arched high. "*What?*"

"I and some men will go directly over the mountains and join Greer. It'll be more rugged, as it is a much steeper trail, but 'twill be much quicker than Greer's journey, for he was following the abductors, who had to take the longer route because of—"

"No, no, *no*. You cannot do this."

"I'm nae going alone. I'm taking Stewart and MacKean. We're leaving at first light."

"Ailsa, you could get hurt. I won't have it." When Ailsa didn't answer, Edana threw her embroidery upon the seat beside her. "This is your father's fault. He should have never put you in charge of Castle Leod, and so I told him when he first mentioned it. You are too young, and it isn't proper for a woman to carry such responsibility on her own."

Ailsa's jaw tightened. "Have I done so puir a job managing the estate, that you question Papa's decision?"

Edana caught the look on Ailsa's face and winced. "No, of course not. You know you've done well. In fact, things have never been run better, but— Ailsa, please. I cannot bear to think of you being in danger."

Ailsa's heart softened. "I will take care. I promise. But Her Grace and Lord Hamilton were my guests and I cannae leave them in the clutches of these fools."

"Technically, they were my guests."

"Then you know how I feel."

Edana sighed, a tremor crossing her face. "I do. I worry about them, too."

Ailsa went to hug her grandmother, Edana's perfume enveloping them both. "I will find them," Ailsa whispered against her grandmother's thin, powdered cheek. "I promise."

Edana hung on to Ailsa for a long moment; then she straightened, dug out her handkerchief, and dabbed at her eyes. "I suppose I shall have to let you, for I can't think of any other answer to this wretched situation."

Ailsa patted Edana's shoulder and then returned to the desk, more anxious than ever to be on her way. At least she would be *doing* something; the waiting was onerous.

Edana put her handkerchief away. "Do you know the way over the mountains?"

"Aye. 'Tis rugged, steep country. Gregor and I hunted the edge of it just a year ago, and it was nigh impossible to traverse in places. It's infuriating that these louts have taken Her Grace and Lord Hamilton to the farthest reaches of our own property."

Edana picked up her embroidery and placed it back in her lap. "We look all the guiltier now."

"Aye. If Arran comes and all I can tell him is that our men tracked the abductors and prisoners deeper into our own lands and we did naught aboot it, it will nae be guid for us."

"Arran." Edana poked her needle into the muslin with more force than necessary. "I've quite lost my patience with that man. It's just like him to do something reprehensible so he can storm in and steal some of our lands."

Ailsa drummed her fingers on the smooth surface of the desk as she considered this. "But why such an elaborate ruse? If he's merely looking for a fight, there are more ready ways; he could use an auld claim to stir up forgotten hurts, forge documents that make it seem our claim is false, or other things of that nature. 'Tis done all the time."

"He's not content taking our lands—he also wishes to humiliate us. Arran is capable of any evil. He dresses like a commoner, which I find unforgivable for someone of his station."

Ailsa absently rubbed her temples, wishing they didn't ache from nights of too little sleep and the jumbled thoughts of a thousand what-ifs. This challenge was bigger than any she'd yet faced. People's lives were at stake. People she knew and was responsible for.

I will deal with this, she told herself stoutly. *I may not have Papa's breadth of experience, but I have Mama's calm, logical reasoning and it has stood me in good stead time and again.*

"This venture is most unsafe," Lady Edana continued, as if unaware of Ailsa's silence. "There are brigands in the mountains; Lord Elgin himself was robbed while traveling through that area not two months ago. His horses and silver were taken and he was almost shot. It's a wonder he made it out alive."

Ailsa sent her grandmother a wry look. "You're nae helping."

Lady Edana rested the embroidery frame on her lap, her eyes unusually dark with worry. "We should call your father back—"

"Nae. I will nae throw oop my hands and cry 'quit' at the first sign of trouble when—"

A soft knock came upon the door and MacGill entered, looking flustered. "My lady, we've a guest."

Ailsa's heart sank. "Arran."

"Nae, my lady. 'Tis nae the earl, but 'tis—"

"—your cousin," came a familiar voice from behind MacGill.

"*Gregor!*" Ailsa ran to hug her cousin.

Of Ailsa's height plus an inch, and dressed like the man of fashion he strove to be, Gregor Mackenzie accepted her hug with a chuckle and a fond pat on her cheek. "Oh ho, such a happy greeting."

She released him, laughing a little, glad to see a friendly face. "You surprised me, that's all. The weather is nae conducive to casual visits."

"Ah, but I grew up here. A little snow will not stop me." He tugged one of the curls that rested beside her cheek and then went to greet Lady Edana, who embraced him just as warmly.

Ailsa smiled as she watched him. On the death of his parents, at the age of twelve, Gregor had come to live at Castle Leod. Since he was close to Ailsa in age and loved the outdoors just as passionately as she, the two of them had become as close as any brother and sister, spending hours hunting and riding and talking. As Ailsa's sisters were all more than ten years older, having someone near her own age had been a godsend.

Later, when Gregor reached his majority, he'd left Castle Leod to set up his own town house in Edinburgh, where, to her father's chagrin, the youth had set about living the restless life of a man-about-town. Ailsa's father had fumed over what he perceived as his nephew's profligate lifestyle, and had grown colder to the young man as time passed. But Ailsa had never let her cousin's excesses color her love for him. When he'd left Castle Leod, she'd missed him desperately, and she was always glad when he visited, especially during hunting season, when the two would ride the moors and glens for hours upon hours.

His gaze, the same gray as her own, narrowed as he regarded her. "Ah, my littlest cousin, I see you're still running the huge estate from that too-large desk. What is my uncle thinking, letting you dry into dust behind such a mahogany monstrosity?"

"I fit that desk perfectly, large or nae." She smiled as she looked him up and down. "My, how fashionable you have become, Cousin Gregor."

"He looks quite well, doesn't he?" Lady Edana said with obvious approval.

Though short of stature, Gregor was dressed to advantage, not in the exaggerated manner of a dandy, but in a quietly perfect way. From his starched and complex cravat, to his coat of deep blue that fit his frame without a single crease, to his fashionably knit breeches, he was a sight to behold. Had that arbiter of fashion, the infamous Beau Brummell, still held court in London, he would have approved Gregor's tasteful attire without hesitation. It was a pity Papa never understood the difference between a dandy and a man of fashion.

"Why, thank you, my dearest Ailsa." Gregor gave her a flourishing bow that she imagined would not have been out of place at court. "Coming from you, who rarely notice such mundane things as fashion, that is high praise indeed."

"What of me?" Lady Edana said in a wounded tone. "Does my opinion matter so little?"

Gregor flashed a droll look at Ailsa before he said with dramatic earnestness, "Ah, most beautiful of all grandmothers, your opinion matters the most. But first, I must know—what dark magic is this? You are younger every time I see you."

Lady Edana couldn't have looked more pleased. "I've been using a new lotion," she confided, as if conferring a great secret.

"Whatever it is, you look all of twenty-two years of age, and I— Oh! I almost forgot." He reached into his pocket and turned back to Ailsa. "I found this under a rock by the front door. It's addressed to you, so I assumed you'd want it. It must be a bill of lading, left by some careless tradesman. I wonder that MacGill did not already see it."

Ailsa stared at the envelope resting in Gregor's hand. Dirty and creased, her name was scrawled over the crinkled paper. She took the note, a tremor passing through her fingers. *The ransom request. It can be nothing else.*

Aware of Gregor's curious gaze, she forced a smile. "Of course. It must be for the coal. You know how much we use at this castle."

"I shudder to think of it." He turned to address an idle remark to Lady Edana, and Ailsa was left with the note.

She opened it quickly.

Bring two hundred guineas to the Iron Kettle in Kylestrome. The prisoners will be released to you forthwith.

That was all. The handwriting was awkwardly slanted, as if someone had used his or her weaker hand in an effort to disguise their handwriting.

She pursed her lips. *Forthwith, hmm? And not a misspelling to be seen. Whoever wrote this is educated.*

The village of Kylestrome was in the very northern outreaches of Mackenzie land, in the direction the abductors were taking the prisoners, so that made sense. *But why is the note addressed to me and not Arran? It's his brother who was taken, after all. And everyone knows Arran has more funds than all the Mackenzies put together. Perhaps Arran is trying to distance himself from the abduction in order to appear innocent of subterfuge?*

She frowned. She hadn't expected a ransom note— indeed, she could have saved Greer the trouble of tracking the abductors had she thought they'd offer a chance to purchase the freedom of their captives. *Perhaps this isn't an attempt to cause a clan war at all, but a simple case of greed. But only two hundred guineas? Why not more? Or is it— Blast it, I'm more confused than ever.*

Her shoulders slumped as her thoughts swirled and then tangled. She'd been so sure Arran had been behind this abduction and now, in one second, her beliefs had been put into question. *How do I make decisions for the good of all when I don't know enough about—*

"Ailsa?"

She blinked at Gregor and realized she'd been staring at the note for far too long. "Oh. I'm sorry." She forced a smile and folded the note in half. "I was doing sums in my head." She placed the note on the corner of her desk. "You know how distracting that can be." Before he could comment further, she asked, "So what's brought you to us? I thought you were wintering with the Earl of Argyll."

"Ay, yes. Argyll." A shadow crossed Gregor's face as he turned toward the fire, where he held out his hands to the warming blaze. "I left, and rather abruptly, too. I'm sorry I didn't send word I was coming, but there was no time. I rode here; my coach and things should arrive shortly."

Ailsa shrugged. "You are always welcome here; you know that."

"Of course he is," Lady Edana said firmly. "But still, you must tell us about your visit with Argyll."

Gregor looked bored. "There's not much to tell. He's devilishly short-tempered and dresses like a merchant."

"Yes, yes, but his daughter." Lady Edana leaned out to grasp Gregor's hand as if to hold him in place. "What about *her*?"

Gregor flushed as he gently freed his hand from Lady Edana's. "Ah yes. The most worthy Lady Agnes, of whom I'd heard much, turned out to be as pretty as a flattened mushroom and as intriguing as a dried leaf." He feigned a shudder as he turned back to the fireplace, the flames reflecting in his boots. "No, thank you."

"It's not about her prettiness or ability to fascinate." Edana's voice was uncharacteristically sharp. "Lady Agnes's dowry is impressive, and you have need of a fortune."

"I don't care what her dowry might be. If I must be chained for life, then it will have to be to a prettier and more lively post than that or I will die of boredom."

Edana, red-faced, her mouth set in a belligerent manner, snapped out, "If one needs the funds, one must—"

"Of course, of course. And when things get desperate, perhaps I will return to Agryll's house and court his daughter. But not today."

An awkward silence emerged between the two and Ailsa wondered how it was that her grandmother had been privy to the reason for Gregor's visit with Argyll, when Ailsa hadn't realized the import at all. She cleared her throat. "However it was that you came, Gregor, I'm glad you're here."

He sent her a grateful look. "Thank you."

"Of course we are," Lady Edana said, although a bit stiffly. "When you first arrived, I thought perhaps you'd come because of our misfortune."

"What misfortune?" Concern dimmed Gregor's smile. "Uncle is not—"

"Nae! 'Tis naught like that," Ailsa said hastily, sending a dark look at Lady Edana. "'Tis a small situation, but one that will soon be resolved."

"We can only hope," her grandmother interjected. "And it is not small at all. The Grand Duchess Nikolaevna is a *very* important person." Lady Edana turned back to Gregor. "She was here, as my guest, and now she's gone missing."

"Good God!" Gregor turned a worried face toward Ailsa. "You've looked for her, of course."

"Extensively. And we've a tolerable idea where she might be, too." *In a manner of speaking.*

"Tell Gregor all," Edana said sharply. "Now that he's here, he can assist us in the search."

"How?" Ailsa's voice cracked a bit. It was irksome that her own grandmother didn't seem to think her able to handle this situation without the assistance of a male.

Edana waved her hand. "Your cousin hunts as if born to it. Your papa has said so himself many times."

Gregor nodded thoughtfully, as if he'd already given the matter the deepest consideration. "She has a point, cousin. Thanks to the hours and hours I spent tracking hares with Greer, I'm something of an expert."

"I was with you every one of those days," Ailsa said drily. "And I'd call neither of us an expert."

"True, but we're better trackers than most gamekeepers found today. Even your father noted my ability during the hunts we had before the weather turned, and he doesn't care for me."

"Gregor, nae! Papa is quite fond of you."

"He tolerates me." Gregor made a face. "I wouldn't call it more than that."

"You're exaggerating. Papa is nae the most demonstrative of men." Which was an understatement, indeed. As much as she loved Papa, she knew he could seem quite cold to those who did not know him.

Edana nodded wisely. "'Tis true, Gregor. Your uncle went the direction of his own papa, who had too much common sense and far too little emotion for my taste. It was a rare day when Cromartie allowed a smile to pass his lips. As for a laugh, I can think of only a dozen times I heard one."

Gregor's expression softened. "That must have been difficult for you, for you are a burst of emotion and light."

"You flatterer!" Edana sent him an arch look, her earlier irritation already forgotten. "You are too kind. I'm glad you've come. Ailsa and I have been at wits' end to decide how to proceed."

Ailsa's jaw tightened. "That's nae true. I've a verrah guid idea how to proceed." *I hope.* But with Lady Edana's words, Ailsa's nagging worries returned in full force.

Gregor's gaze flickered over Ailsa's face. "So this duchess has gone missing. How so?"

"She and Lord Hamilton were abducted when on their way from here to his house. Their coach was found abandoned, the servants injured or missing."

"Good God!" Gregor's eyes widened.

"Indeed." Ailsa hesitated, wondering if she should tell him everything, but the concern in his gray eyes banished her concerns. "In fact, the note you found by the front door was nae a bill, but a ransom note."

"*What?*" Edana gaped. "We were so sure there wouldn't be one!"

"Well, there is one. And it quite changes the way I think of this whole affair." Catching Gregor's confused look, Ailsa added, "We thought this incident might be of Arran's making. He's been after the grazing lands for decades."

"He's a hawk, too, and enjoys shredding people in his talons." Gregor's brows lowered. "How much does the ransom note request?"

"Two hundred guineas."

He frowned. "I expected more."

"So did I, which confirms that there's some other reason for the abduction."

"Obviously," Gregor agreed.

"Fortunately, I have that much in the safe. I had planned to use it for improvements on the tenants' cottages this spring, but that must wait."

"Where do you deliver this ransom?"

"An inn in Kylestrome, which is far north of here. I—"

The sound of horses trotting up the drive made them all look toward the front window.

"That must be Arran." Lady Edana's voice was heavy with dire prophecy. "I'm still not convinced he's not behind this."

Gregor shrugged. "We'll just explain the facts and he'll be forced to accept it. At least publicly."

"It's worse than you know," Ailsa said. "Someone went to the trouble to implicate us in the abduction. A scrap of Mackenzie tartan was found under one of the wheels. It looks dire."

"Who would do such a— Ah. Arran, trying to cover his intentions."

"I thought so, but— To be honest, I dinnae know what to think. I fear if I showed the note in an effort to prove our innocence, he'd just say we wrote it ourselves. We are damned either way we play this."

"Bloody hell," Gregor muttered, looking dark. "Who has done this to our family?"

"I wish I knew." She looked out the window, where they could now hear men's voices, low and deep, though indistinguishable. "And now we must face the earl. I'd hoped for a week or more before this meeting. He must have been in his home seat, which is surprising, as he usually winters in London."

Gregor strode to the window, twitched back the long velvet curtains, and peered down. "That's not Arran."

"Thank goodness," Lady Edana breathed.

Gregor leaned a bit closer to the window. "There are three men on horseback, but none of them wear the earl's livery. They have extremely fine horses, too, quite unlike the plodders I last saw carrying Arran and that fat son of his."

Ailsa joined Gregor at the window. On seeing the men, she muttered under her breath, "The prince!"

Gregor sent her a surprised glance. "Who?"

"The duchess's grandson, Prince Nikolai—I don't remember the rest of his title." Ailsa had to admit that the horses were spectacular; two bays and a white gelding, all of them heavily muscled and so beautiful as to draw every eye.

Her gaze reluctantly went to the men. The prince

looked just as she'd expected—he was tall, handsome, and wore an elegant fur-lined coat that was open at the neck and wrists to reveal a touch of lace. He sported a neatly trimmed beard and mustache that gave him a slightly foreign air, although the cut of his obviously expensive clothing was definitely not English.

His expression was faintly haughty as he looked about the entry of Castle Leod, but he seemed far less antagonistic than she'd expected after bearing the brunt of his caustic letters. Her gaze flickered to the man riding beside him, who was taller, broader, and more heavily bearded—a bear of a man. Everything about him, from his neat uniform to his short, combed beard, shouted "military." *A royal guard, perhaps?*

She flicked a quick glance at the third man, obviously a groom. Dressed in the rough clothing of a servant, a heavy, worn-looking, and shapeless coat draped over his broad frame, he wore a muffler wound about his head that covered most of his face, precious protection from the cold that his companions hadn't taken advantage of. Taller even than the others by several inches, he sat atop his magnificent white horse with a lithe grace that made her think of a large cat. *A lion, no less. He must be riding one of the prince's horses.* Had she a horse like that, she'd have been loath to leave it behind, too.

The groom dismounted and took his masters' reins while they alighted. One of her footmen met them, and she let out an irritated sigh. "I don't know why he's come; I told him I'd send word once we knew something."

"I daresay he's worried," Lady Edana offered. "Her

Grace spoke often of her grandson. I gather they were quite close."

That didn't ring true with the dismissive tone of the prince's correspondence, but Ailsa kept the thought to herself. "He's here now, so I'll have to speak with him." She looked back out the window. "They are quite handsome, these foreigners."

Gregor's gaze followed hers. "Prussians dress the same; fur-lined clothing, and very military-style fashions."

From behind them, Lady Edana commented, "I do so love a Prussian uniform. Nothing is quite so dashing."

Ailsa watched as the two guests walked toward the house, the groom following one of her footmen and leading the horses in the direction of the stables. As he passed under her window, he glanced up, his muffler falling from his face. Their eyes met and, to her surprise, he didn't look away. Indeed, he stared, boldly and without hesitation.

In her experience, servants did not boldly stare the way this man did. But what a man, though. Thick black hair framed the sort of face only a sculptor could create. Thickly lashed and slumberous dark eyes framed a bold and straight nose, his cheekbones high and proud, his mouth as brazenly perfect as the rest of him. While the others were bearded, he was not, his firm jaw clearly in view where not covered by the muffler.

But it was his expression that held her attention. No one had looked at her in such a direct manner, as if she were a display at a museum created for no other reason than to be gazed upon and then—to her instant irritation—dismissed when he looked away, apparently disinterested.

At Ailsa's side, Gregor tsked. "The groom is bold for a mere servant, isn't he?"

"I would nae know. I was looking at the horses."

Gregor chuckled. "Ah, cousin, such a lie! I— Ah. There comes my coach. I'm glad to see it, as I'm sure our grandmother will insist I dress for dinner."

Gregor's coach, a frivolous thing in shiny black with the Mackenzie crest over the door, and pulled by a matching set of grays that must have been too dear for a man of limited means, swept up the drive and pulled to a halt at the front door. A footman ran out to assist, and a man alighted, dressed in the sober clothing of a servant. "Who is that?" Ailsa asked.

"My valet."

"What? Did Valjean leave you?"

"Valjean had the ill manners to break his leg, so he sent a cousin in his stead. The man is named—" He bit his lip. "Good lord, what is the man's name? I can never remember it. It is something with a lot of 'r's in it."

"He looks more like a prizefighter than a valet."

"He's all thumbs, too. I shudder to think what my cravats look like now. But poor Valjean begged me to take him on, and was almost in tears while doing so, so I could not say no."

"You are a slave to your kindness."

He nodded glumly. "It is a curse."

A knock heralded the entry of MacGill. The butler bowed. "Your ladyship, the prince's advisor and a guard have come to ask aboot Her Grace's disappearance."

Ailsa couldn't keep the surprise from her face. "So that was nae the prince? Is he following, then?"

"Nae, Your Ladyship. Lord Apraksin was sent here by His Highness, who has taken ill and is unable to leave his bed. His Lordship brings with him the master of the guard, a Mr. Rurik, and a groom."

"How rude that the prince did not come himself!" Lady Edana declared. "If I am ever abducted, I hope *someone* from this family will go and see what's happened to me, and not send some sort of servant."

"Never fear on that score," Gregor said gallantly. "I would leave no stone unturned, ill or not."

Ailsa barely heard them. *So the prince is using an "illness" to escape his duties, is he?* She was not surprised and, actually, was a great deal relieved. It was one less complication in a situation already far too rife with them. "Very good, MacGill. Pray bring Lord Apraksin and Mr. Rurik to us here. And ask Cook to serve tea for five in the small sitting room in a half hour."

The butler, looking relieved to have been given some direct duties, bowed and left.

Gregor turned a quizzical gaze her way. "What will you tell them?"

"The truth. Or some of it. I'll inform them we've already set a plan in motion for the rescue, although I'll provide verrah few details. Hopefully, that will be enough."

Gregor didn't look convinced. "Perhaps we should share our information and ask for their assistance? They were both well armed, for I saw high-quality rifles and a brace of pistols strapped to each saddle."

Lady Edana looked up at this. "Oh dear. Do you think there will be *violence*?"

"Of course nae," Ailsa said soothingly, though Gregor didn't look completely convinced. "Now that we have the ransom note, all we'll need to do is deliver the funds to the proper place, and Lord Hamilton and Her Grace will be released." *That's how it usually works, isn't it?* She longed to ask the question, but knew it could appear as a sign of indecision, so instead, she looked at Gregor. "It's best if we handle this on our own." Of that much, at least, she was certain.

He started to argue, but a quick look in Lady Edana's direction made him close his mouth and shrug. "As you wish."

A noise sounded outside in the hallway, and MacGill could be heard approaching. Ailsa smoothed her gown and checked her hair in the mirror over the fireplace. "Come. Let's put on brave faces, for I'll nae have it said the Mackenzies cower."

"Of course," Lady Edana agreed, lifting her chin.

Though Gregor nodded, he still looked concerned, a feeling Ailsa shared.

It would take all her newfound skills to lead the family out of this mad coil, and she was determined to do just that.

Chapter 4

Dusk settled in, dulled by cold gray skies that carried the taste of more snow. Outside the stables, Nik placed his bucket of tools by his horse, D'yoval, who was tied to the paddock fence.

The horse whickered softly as Nik patted the animal's muscled neck. "Look at you, snorting at this cold. Have you been away from Oxenburg so long that you've forgotten how a proper winter feels?"

D'yoval snorted as if outraged at the idea.

Nik chuckled. "I thought not. Well, I found an apple, and you shall have it once Apraksin arrives to report on his findings. Hopefully that will settle your dislike for this damp chill." It would have been nice to be able to meet his men in the stables, for it would have been warmer, but the other grooms were a loquacious group and were too enthralled with the horses—D'yoval in particular—to allow for privacy of any sort.

Besides, despite the cold, both the fresh air and the view were invigorating. Castle Leod loomed at the top of the drive, square and silvery against the dark gray sky. Judging from the windows and the style of battlements, he thought it must have been built in the early or mid-seventeenth century. Three stories in height, narrow and square, the structure had as its centerpiece a fortified tower house.

Though the castle was an ancient fortress, the lack of additions or embellishments led Nik to believe the Mackenzies to be of small means. The neatly dressed servants wore plain brass buttons rather than the gold ones many men of wealth demanded, and the stables, while sturdy and in good repair, housed only the most mundane of cattle. He'd counted six field horses, three hard-going hunters, and two sets of coach horses, one of them a showy set of grays that the grooms had said belonged to Lady Ailsa's cousin, Mr. Gregor Mackenzie, who'd arrived earlier that day. *As the inhabitants of Castle Leod don't seem to be well-funded, it could mean they would be easy to bribe, so if they are not directly involved, they may have allowed Tata to be kidnapped.*

Before arriving, Nik had imagined Lady Ailsa as a dour, prune-faced spinster with gray hair and a permanently displeased expression, but he'd by chance overheard a comment by one of the footmen that the lady in question was none other than the clear-eyed, square-chinned miss who'd been standing in the window earlier. Though she didn't qualify as a beauty in any way, she was much younger than he'd expected, with dark mousy-blond hair, a bold nose, and an unflinching gaze.

The latter had told him all he needed to know about the lady whose strong, annoyingly neat handwriting had so plagued him. In some ways, she reminded him of the castle—small and sturdy, but unremarkable. Had he met her at a dinner party or some such event, he'd have never spared her a second glance. Even now, he was glad he'd have no commerce with her. He had no illusions about the souring effects of female stubbornness. Living with his own grandmother had taught him that much.

D'yoval whickered softly, his breath puffing white. Nik dismissed Lady Ailsa from his thoughts and dropped the comb back in the bucket. That done, he pulled the apple from his pocket. As D'yoval eagerly took the treat, Nik saw Rurik walking down the path to the stables.

The guard looked about him, his dark gaze flickering over the stables, the paddocks, the open fields, and thick shrubs. He stopped some yards away, pretending to examine the horse and ignoring Nik.

Nik supposed it would look more natural if he were performing groom-type things, so he pulled a brush from the bucket and began working on D'yoval's coat. Without looking at Rurik, Nik asked, "So? What have you discovered?"

Rurik leaned against the paddock fence and pointed to the horse's neck, as if giving Nik orders. "Apraksin will join us soon. He has more information than I." He dropped his hand and flicked a careful glance at the stable windows, which were bolted closed. "Is it safe to talk here?"

"The grooms and stable hands are gathered on the far side around a stove, talking and laughing. They won't hear us." He smirked. "Just to be sure they are attached to their pursuits, I left them a bottle of vodka, which they like very much."

"Do they speak Oxenburgian?"

"*Nyet*. I insulted them every way possible and none of them so much as flinched. I— Ah, here he comes."

Apraksin had walked out of the front of the castle, nodding to a footman as if to indicate he didn't need an escort. As soon as the door closed, he casually made his way to where Rurik stood by the paddock.

"That was bold," Nik said. "Won't they wonder why you left?"

Apraksin grinned. "I asked if I could smoke in the sitting room. Lady Edana was quick to send me outside."

"Lady Edana?"

"The Dowager Countess of Cromartie, Lady Ailsa's grandmother." The courtier pulled a small metal case from his pocket and opened it to reveal slender cigarillos. He offered one to Rurik, who took it with a murmured thanks. "I am here, enjoying a cigar, away from the curtains and rugs her ladyship wishes to protect."

Rurik pulled a tinderbox from his pocket and then made a spill of a thick twist of straw scooped from the ground. Soon the sweet cigar aroma caused Nik to growl, "Do you try to torment me?"

Apraksin grinned and, glancing around, placed a fresh cigarillo on the fence rail. "There. One for you to collect after we've left."

"Thank you. That's something, at least."

"We should leave vodka, too, since you gave yours to the grooms." Rurik slipped a flask from his pocket and propped it beside the fence, near the cigar.

Nik grunted his approval. "That will be most welcome. It will be cold in the stables tonight, even with the woodstove." He moved to the front of the horse and absently ran the brush over D'yoval's neck. "So. What have you found out?"

Apraksin answered, "A ransom note was delivered this afternoon. Two hundred guineas were requested."

"For both hostages?"

"So it seems. Our hostess is unhappy about the situation. Concerned, even. As she should be." He cast a glance at the castle, and then added in a low voice, "From something Lady Ailsa said, I got the impression she hopes to pay this ransom as soon as possible."

"A foolish decision," Rurik said around his cigar.

"Oxenburg does not pay ransoms," Nik stated. "If you make one payment, then the abductors have that much more reason to keep their prisoners. And the longer the abductors keep the prisoners, the less likely it is they will survive."

"I said as much." Apraksin made a smoke ring. "But when I suggested to Lady Ailsa that she might wish to rethink her position, she became very . . . adamant." He grimaced. "It is obvious she does not wish for our assistance in this matter."

"She is a stubborn woman," Nik said.

"She is young. Perhaps that is it."

"And inexperienced," Rurik added. "As we have a Romany presence in Oxenburg, we've faced the consequences of paying ransoms and know the usual outcome." As soon as he spoke, Rurik cast a quick glance at Nik. "I beg your pardon if I offend you with such a comment."

Nik shrugged. "My grandmother would be the first to tell you that if you are so foolish as to allow yourself to be abducted, then you deserve to pay a ransom."

"One of the few things she says that I agree with." Apraksin leaned against the fence. "Rurik and I spoke to some of the maids to see what we could discover about this Lady Ailsa. She is the youngest of the earl's children, is unmarried, and has been running the estate on her own for the last year since her mother's death. She seems quite formidable."

Nik patted D'yoval's neck. "Where is her father if he is not running the estate?"

"In London, immersed in politics. For all intents, it seems she is alone."

"Except her cousin," Nik said.

"He arrived today. According to something Lady Edana said, he is only an occasional visitor. It is Lady Ailsa who is in charge of the castle and lands."

"Interesting. What have you ascertained about this abduction thus far?"

Apraksin blew a smoke ring that was quickly torn apart by the breeze. "While Rurik was checking the security of our assigned rooms, Lady Ailsa shared what she knows, which doesn't seem to be much. The coach carrying Her Grace and Lord Hamilton was overtaken on the road between here and Lord Hamilton's house around dawn on—"

"Wait. My grandmother was awake at *dawn*?"

"*Da.* From the expression of outrage on the Dowager Countess's face, I believe Her Grace and Lord Hamilton might have been involved in a flirtation."

Rurik looked impressed. "Her Grace is a vibrant woman."

"Too much so," Nik said shortly. "And?"

Apraksin explained the details of the abduction that Lady Ailsa had shared. He finished with, "All the servants and Lord Hamilton's escort were accounted for except one guard."

Rurik's gaze sharpened at this. "Is he still missing?"

"*Da*. No one knows if he was part of this effort or if he was taken prisoner with Lord Hamilton and Her Grace."

"We know the answer to that," Nik said grimly.

Apraksin hesitated. "There is more. Blood was found on one of the seats. Not much, but I thought you should know."

Nik's jaw hardened. *Bozhy moj, if someone has harmed Tata Natasha—* He fisted his hands, trying hard to regain control over his hot temper. "Where is this ransom to be paid?"

"Lady Ailsa was not forthcoming with that information, though she hinted she'd share it after dinner."

"A stall, eh?"

"*Da*. But as she spoke, Mr. Mackenzie glanced at Lady Ailsa's desk. I wondered if the ransom note might not be found there."

"It could be. It's obvious she's shared the information with her grandmother and cousin, too. If Mackenzie's only an occasional visitor, I wonder why he's here now."

Rurik spoke. "The footman who came to hang up my clothes said Mr. Mackenzie and Lady Ailsa are like brother and sister. Mackenzie lived here as a youth after the death of his parents, and moved away on reaching his majority. He returns now and then to visit, usually during hunting season. Both he and Lady Ailsa are avid riders."

Nik rubbed his chin. "As Lady Ailsa did not offer to share the actual note or the location for the exchange while she was supposedly bringing you up-to-date on the developments of my grandmother's disappearance, we'll assume she won't find it easier to do so after dinner."

Apraksin agreed. "During dinner, Rurik can pretend to be ill and slip off to the study and see what's in that desk."

Nik nodded, trying not to think of his grandmother hurt or frightened. "Find out where this ransom is to be paid. The note will tell us where to begin looking for these fools. We will leave at dawn."

Rurik frowned. "All of us?"

"Of course," Apraksin said, looking surprised.

"It's not necessary. I can watch over His Highness; no one even knows he's here."

"And what should I do?" Apraksin asked in a stiff voice.

"Stay behind and wait for word from Edinburgh. Someone must inform us if the tsar arrives earlier than expected."

Nik couldn't disagree.

The courtier scowled. "We will ask that a courier forward any message that may arrive."

Rurik gave an impatient shake of his head. "Lady

Ailsa may not be in the best of moods once she realizes we've gone on our own to meet these scoundrels. I got the distinct impression she felt the matter best left in her hands."

"Rurik is right," Nik said before Apraksin could argue. "You will stay here. If word of the tsar arrives, you must inform us as quickly as you can."

Apraksin grimaced, but after sending a black look at Rurik, the courtier muttered a reluctant agreement. Scowling, he flicked what remained of his cigarillo to the ground and put it out with his heel. "The lights in the dining room were just lit. We must get ready for dinner."

"Do so," Nik said. "Watch Lady Ailsa's relatives closely. There may be more clues there."

Rurik inclined his head. "*Da*, Your Highness."

"*Asta rozhti!*" Apraksin hissed. "Do not bow to a groom!"

A dull red colored Rurik's face. He grimaced sheepishly. "I'm sorry. I did not think."

Nik scowled. "Obviously."

Still flushed, Rurik ground out his cigar and dusted his hands on his breeches.

Apraksin tugged his collar higher. "Come, Rurik. We must bathe and dress." Without sparing Nik-the-groom a look, the courtier strode toward the castle, the master of the guard trailing behind him.

Nik watched over the gelding's back as his men disappeared into the castle. The woman he'd seen in the window—so calm and self-possessed—had been unflinching when she'd met his gaze. Challenging, even.

What are you hiding, Lady Ailsa? And why? Why would you pay off a ransom so quickly, without first trying to free the prisoners?

The snap of a stick sounded behind him. He turned, and there, standing by the gate his men had just left, stood Lady Ailsa.

Chapter 5

A thick cloak of dark green wool hung from the lady's shoulders and opened as she walked toward him to reveal the outline of a severe riding habit. With a jaunty riding hat trimmed with a feather resting upon her dark blond hair, Lady Ailsa looked like every young lady of fashion he'd ever seen. Only the sharpness of her pale gray eyes gave him pause.

Did she see me speaking to my men? It was highly improbable she could understand Oxenburgian, but he couldn't stop a flash of unease.

He bowed. "Good evening, my lady. You are out late."

"I always ride this time of the evening." She moved closer, her gaze slipping from him to D'yoval, her expression softening. "Och, what a beauty."

Her voice was low and sultry, like a cup of rich, hot chocolate swirled with sugar, a faint trace of a Scottish accent brightening each word. *The silk of her voice is at variance with the sharpness of her quill.*

He inclined his head respectfully the way a groom should, though he watched her through his lashes.

"I am surprised anyone would ride in such weather. It grows cold."

"My horse likes the cold, as do I." Her gaze remained on D'yoval, taking in the animal's powerful lines with an expert eye.

While she looked at the horse, Nik took the opportunity to examine her in return. Her face was scrubbed of artifice and a slight dusting of freckles powdered her pale skin, while her thickly lashed eyes shimmered a silvery gray that shone with intelligence and—was that humor? He thought perhaps it was.

Her profile was in relief, and he had to admit that her nose was indeed bold, which gave her glance a hawkish directness. He wondered if she were really so imposing a person, or if she merely had the look of a Roman empress.

She moved in front of D'yoval, the wind blowing her cloak as she walked. Her formfitting habit was far more complimentary than the gown she'd worn before, and he could now see that she was pleasantly shaped indeed. Her breasts were high and generous, her hips rounded, her waist feminine while not ridiculously thin.

His gaze followed her fitted jacket down to her sweeping skirts, and then on to her riding boots. They were mud-splattered, as was her hem, which suggested a vigorous ride. But he thought her boots told her story more than the riding habit. While her clothing was fashionable, her boots were comfortably worn, the toes scraped, the heels a bit down. A serious rider never gave up a pair of comfortable boots until they were unusable. It took too much time to break in a new pair.

Lady Ailsa was not a fainthearted, balk-at-hedgerows type, but a bruising, leather-to-hell rider. One to be wary of on, and most likely off, the field.

She sent him a glance now, her gray eyes alight. "This beautiful horse. What's his name?"

"D'yoval."

"D'yoval." She murmured the name as if tasting it. "That's as lovely as he." She reached out to pat the horse, but the gelding whickered and nervously moved away.

Nik hid a grin. "He is not so tamed, eh?"

Lady Ailsa shot him a surprised look, a flicker of suspicion in her gaze, and he realized his tone had been far too informal. *I must be careful with this one.*

"I will ride this horse." She turned back to D'yoval.

Nik almost choked. "I beg your pardon?"

"I will ride this horse. This evening I'll ask Lord Apraksin to set a time for me to do so."

"Lord Apraksin will not allow it." *He'd better not, if he knows what's good for him.* "D'yoval is not an easy horse to ride. He is very stubborn."

"So am I. I can handle him."

Her confidence made Nik raise his eyebrows, but, aware of his "groom" status, all he said was, "Of course, my lady." Best to get D'yoval out of sight before Lady Ailsa decided to abscond with him now. Nik untied the gelding's reins.

D'yoval jerked his head, but Nik knew his horse well and was ready for that particular trick. "As you can see, he requires a firm hand."

"I have one."

"And he bites." Catching her raised brows, he hastily added, "My lady."

Amusement warmed her pale eyes to silver. "I bite, too."

She looked so incredibly appealing standing there, her chin at a cocky level, confidence warming her face. Nik almost returned her smile, catching himself just in time. *Perhaps I was wrong before; if I met this woman at a dinner party, I most assuredly would have noticed her.*

He inclined his head politely, using the gesture to sweep his gaze over her. "If you don't mind, I should take the horse to the stables. Lord Apraksin wished D'yoval to be given oats."

She placed her hand on D'yoval's bridle. "In a moment."

Nik's polite smile faded. She hadn't said "when I say so," but it was obvious in her manner. He had to swallow a very real desire to scowl. He was just beginning to realize what a horrible servant he would be. Not only did he dislike it when someone ordered him to do something he didn't wish to do, but he found it almost impossible to pretend he didn't care.

She patted D'yoval, who was now allowing her to do so, and was even whickering softly now and then.

Nik sent a hard look at his gelding. *Traitor.*

"What is your name?"

He realized Lady Ailsa was no longer looking at the horse, but at him. *Bozhy moj, I must have a name.* He grabbed the first one that came to mind. "Menshivkov. I am Lord Apraksin's groom."

Her cool gaze measured, assessed. "Are you a good groom, Menshivkov? A verrah guid one?"

"Of course." He couldn't keep the outrage from his voice. If he ever decided to be a groom in earnest, he would be the best one of all. There could be no question. He realized her brows had lifted, and he hastily added, again, "My lady."

"Guid. Then I will let you see to my St. George."

"See to your . . ."

She pointed behind him to the stable yard. "St. George is my horse. He is tied to the post."

Nik followed the direction of her gloved finger and caught sight of a horse tied to the far fence. He took in the large, rather mule-faced bay with its sour expression and a head that seemed too large for its stocky body. "St. George does not look like a saint."

A choked laugh made him look back at Lady Ailsa. Her pale gray eyes shimmered with humor. They were actually quite pretty when lit thus. They sparkled as if flecked with silver. Framed by thick brown lashes that curled beguilingly at the corners, they gave her a faintly sleepy look that made her very intriguing.

"He is nae a saint, you're right aboot that." She turned back to D'yoval, dismissing Nik with a glance. "Put him away and give him an extra measure of oats, too. He was verrah well behaved today." She didn't even bother looking at Nik as she spoke, but moved closer to D'yoval, cooing to the spoiled animal as she rubbed his shoulder.

D'yoval seemed to enjoy her attention, too. Nik would have some serious words with his horse once Lady Ailsa was out of earshot.

Meanwhile, he had an irksome part to play. He bowed. "I will put your steed away, my lady."

"Thank you. You may leave D'yoval with me."

"*Nyet.*" The word escaped him before he could catch it.

Her brows rose.

He tightened his hold on D'yoval's reins as he hurried to add, "It is cold, my lady, and I'm sure you wish to go inside. I can take both horses to the stables. It is my duty." There. That sounded properly groom-like.

"Impossible. Like all males, St. George is nae fond of other animals, particularly those prettier than he. He would bite this one, and that would nae be guid."

Nik wasn't sure whether he was more amused at the idea of a horse disliking another for its better looks, or irked that she thought that principle applied to "all males."

Before he could decide, she left D'yoval's side and crossed to where Nik stood. She was even shorter than he'd imagined, her head coming well below his shoulder.

She held out her gloved hand.

He raised his brows, waiting.

She shook her hand impatiently. "Give me the reins so that I may hold D'yoval while you deal with St. George."

A well-trained groom would not question a lady. A well-trained groom would do as he was told, even though he'd already warned the lady of the house about D'yoval's less-than-gentle disposition.

Well, Nik might be playing a groom, but no one said he had to be a well-trained one. He set his jaw. "*Nyet. I cannot.*"

She tilted her head back to more fully view his face, her hand plopped on her hat to hold it in place. "Goodness, but grooms from Oxenburg are forward, intractable creatures," she murmured. Without giving him time to reply, she turned and wandered back to the gate where he'd first seen her. "Fine. If you insist, then I will let you take care of both horses."

He'd won, but somehow he found himself remaining by D'yoval's side, watching her warily, and feeling as if he'd missed something. *What would I have done if a groom had refused to do as I said?* He wasn't certain, for it had never happened. But he didn't think he'd so meekly accept it.

"My, my, my. Would you look at this?" She bent and picked up the flask Rurik had left. "Where did this come from?" She looked around as if expecting someone to claim it.

Nik bit his tongue. *Damn it, that's mine!*

When silence met her inquiry, she shrugged. "I shall keep it for myself, then." She unscrewed the top of the flask and took a cautious sniff. Then, to his utter shock, she raised the flask to her lips and took a sip.

Nik's brows rose. There was vodka in that flask. While he loved the Scots' whisky, which they'd aptly named "the water of life," his native country's vodka was a much, much stronger drink.

She lowered the flask, her eyes watering. She coughed, pressing a hand to her throat. "Guid lord, that is strong!"

"It's obviously not a drink fit for a lady." He couldn't keep the smugness from his tone.

Her gaze locked with his. And then, with the utmost deliberate movement possible, as if she'd taken his words as a direct challenge, she lifted the flask once more and took another sip.

This time she swallowed the vodka with barely a grimace. "It grows on you, this drink, whatever it is." Her voice, already a touch husky, had deepened even more, as if she fought the desire to cough.

Bozhy moj, but I have never met such a stubborn woman. If he didn't say something, she would drink all his vodka. "I recognize that flask. It is Lord Apraksin's."

"Is it? I wonder how it got here?"

"Perhaps it dropped from his pocket when he came to see to the horses earlier this evening. I will return it to him in the morning."

A faint smile curled her lips. "Ah, but why make him wait? I will see him at dinner." She slid the flask into her pocket and patted it. "I'm sure he will be glad to have it back. I—but wait, what's this?" She picked up the cigarillo that had been left on the fence post for him.

The vodka had been one thing, for the flask had been in plain sight. But the cigarillo? She had to have seen Apraksin place it there. *Had she? Or hadn't she?* Nik honestly couldn't say. He supposed the edge of the cigarillo had hung over the fence or— *Bloody hell, is she playing with me?*

He was stuck; if he said something and she hadn't witnessed Apraksin putting the cigarillo on the fence, then Nik would have revealed himself. He was left simmering in growing irritation.

She rolled the cigarillo between her gloved fingers and then took a cautious sniff. "Divine. My father smokes this same kind, I think. The scent of the tobacco is just like this—sweet and soft."

Nik managed to say with what he hoped was unconcern, "That is an odd place to find a cigar. Perhaps someone left it there by mistake. Since the flask is Lord Apraksin's, perhaps the cigar is, as well."

Amusement, curiosity, and challenge fleetingly crossed her face, but were quickly subdued behind a shrug as she continued to toy with the cigar. "A cigarillo would be a lovely way to ward off this chill, would nae it?"

He inclined his head, unable to spit out any more polite words.

"Let us see." She bent and picked up some straw that was lodged against a post and twisted it into a spill exactly as Rurik had done. Her gaze locked on Nik. "You. Bring a lantern from the side of the barn. I'll need a light."

She'd called him *"you"*? He'd never been so insulted. Ever. Worse, she was about to smoke his own cigar right in front of him, from a light she was forcing him to provide.

Jaw tight, he tied D'yoval to the fence and retrieved the lantern. He brought it to her, holding it aloft. The golden light spilled over her face in the early-evening gloom, warming her skin and shimmering over her dark gold curls.

She lit the spill and then toasted the edges of her cigar before she lit it.

She knew what she was doing. A woman smoking a cigar wasn't unheard of, especially in Europe, where the rules of society were laxer. But for a lady to do so in this staid country was almost scandalous. *But perhaps Scotland differs from her older cousin, England?* He hadn't bothered to think about such things before now, as his concerns had been so focused on his mission.

The cigar flared, and she drew on it, her lips encircling the cigarillo in a way that riveted Nik's attention. As he watched, the first puff of sweet smoke slipped over her full lips and warmed the chilled air. *Bozhy moj, those lips . . .*

She looked at him through the haze of smoke, amusement rippling through her voice. "You may put the lantern back."

He hadn't even remembered he was holding it. He must look like a fool, holding the lantern while staring at her in such a way. Cursing his inattention, he returned the lantern to the hook by the barn and then came back to the fence.

She'd already turned away and had walked a few steps until she stood in the center of the path that led to the castle, the cigar held at a jaunty angle, a wisp of smoke curling into the fading light. "Before you put St. George away, see to it that he's brushed and fed. We had a hard run today, and he'll need both."

Though it went sorely against his pride, Nik inclined his head and managed to say in a fairly pleasant, if clipped, tone, "*Da*, my lady." Soon she would leave, and he would be free to express himself by kicking the stuffing from a bale of hay.

As if she knew his thoughts, she smiled through the drift of creamy smoke. "Well done . . . Your Highness."

Chapter 6

Ailsa watched her opponent with bated breath. Slowly, like a lion stalking its prey, he left the fence and came toward her, his dark green gaze locked on her face.

She didn't know him well enough to read his expression—caution or irritation or mere arrogance—so his approach made her heart race even through the boldness now swimming through her blood, brought on by the sting of the cigar and the harsh drink she'd imbibed. *What will he do?*

Her brain calmed her galloping heart. *He has nothing to gain by frightening me, and everything to lose. He's here because of his grandmother, and I know all there is to know about her disappearance.*

Ailsa could only thank the fates that had brought her home at such a providential moment, for it had allowed her to witness unseen the prince's conversation with his men. Although she hadn't been able to hear a word of it, there had been no doubting the commanding way this "groom" had spoken to the others, or the respectful bow made by Mr. Rurik, or the hissing warning it instantly won from Lord Apraksin. And now she knew why the groom had looked at her so boldly when he'd first arrived—he wasn't a groom at all.

He stopped before her now and she was struck by his height. He was so tall—taller even than her father, who was over six feet. But it was more than the prince's height that held her attention. If she'd thought this man handsome when she'd first seen him from the study window and thought him a mere groom, she hadn't accounted for the additional impact of his nearness, which brought with it new revelations, such as his green, green gaze and the sensually handsome cut of his mouth.

She kept her smile, although it took all her concentration to fight the urge to whirl on her heel, lift her skirts, and run for the safety of the castle. *He's trying to intimidate me.* The thought stiffened her spine and she rocked back on one foot while leaving the other firmly in place, putting some space between them without yielding ground.

She took a short puff on the cigar, determined to keep the end glowing for the duration of their talk. "I know you're nae a groom. 'Tis as obvious as the nose on my face, and as you may have noticed, I have a *very* obvious nose."

His lips twitched, but he stubbornly refused to smile. "I don't know what you're saying. I'm only a—"

"—prince. Admit it."

Irritation tightened his jaw.

"I am nae a fool, Your Highness." She tapped the end of the cigar, the ash blowing away in the icy wind as if it never existed. "I saw you speaking with your men. They were deferential in their tone and manner; one even bowed to you." She chuckled. "It is quite obvious you are nae a mere groom."

She waited, but he still didn't acknowledge the truth of her words.

Irritated, she added in a faintly mocking tone, "But the biggest hint of all was that you dinnae know how to brush a horse properly."

His eyes narrowed. "I know how to brush a horse."

"For a man who rarely brushes one, you did"—she looked past him at D'yoval and pursed her lips—"fair. But for an experienced groom, it was a sad job indeed."

His jaw tightened, his eyes flashing irritation. It was odd. She'd heard that he was a wastrel, a womanizer, a typical spoiled member of royalty. All the papers (and her father, as well) had said the same thing of Prince Nikolai. How was it that none of the rumors included the phrase "steely-eyed opponent"? And why would a vapid womanizer care if someone believed him capable of brushing a horse?

"What's wrong with the brushing I gave this horse?" He spat the words as if they were sour.

She held back a smile and flicked a finger toward the horse. "To begin with, you only brushed poor D'yoval's back and flanks. His sides are untouched, and half the time you were using the mane comb instead of the currycomb. Of course, if you'd bent down to brush his sides and chest, you would nae have been able to see your men during your nae-so-secret meeting."

He regarded her for a long moment, his slightly deferential manner now completely gone. There was turmoil in his deep green eyes, a quick flicker of thoughts as he made a decision regarding her confrontation.

After a split second, he drawled, "It seems I am found out." To her surprise, he shrugged and then flashed a smile—and a charming, winsome smile it was, too. "You, fine lady, have discovered me."

She could only blink. Ailsa couldn't believe he'd revealed himself; she'd expected him to at least argue. Perhaps he'd admitted his identity because he believes to gain more from this admission. If so, that was a sad mistake indeed.

He captured her free hand and bowed over it, all grace and playfulness. "Allow me the pleasure of an introduction. I am Nikolai Romanovin, Crown Prince of Oxenburg."

The change in the man from cautious, resentful groom to charming, gracious prince was breathtaking. His entire expression changed, his eyes gleaming as if he were fascinated, a teasing smile now playing around his mouth. "You seem surprised, and yet a moment hence, you were confident beyond doubt."

"I'm surprised only that you admitted your deceit so quickly."

"Allow me to point out that my 'deceit,' if you must call it that, was not perpetrated against you."

His hand, gloved as hers were, was warm where it covered hers, and she was far more aware of it than she should have been. She cleared her throat and tugged her hand free. "Then against whom was this deceit perpetrated?"

"I am here in secret for my own security; no one must know I've left Holyrood."

He'd hesitated before he'd answered. It had been a mere half second's worth of a hesitation, one upon which she might not have put weight were it anyone else. But she had the impression that, with this man, every little nuance held a meaning of some sort.

"I see." She pursed her lips, wondering how she should play this new game. She almost preferred the hostile groom to the warm, charming façade the prince now wore, but only because she knew it to be a façade and nothing more. Had they met under other circumstances, she couldn't begin to imagine how quickly she might have succumbed to the warmth of his expression and the charming smile. She nodded as if she agreed. "Safety is important."

He inclined his head and said in a low, almost intimate tone, "If it is not too much trouble, I hope you will continue to pretend I'm a groom. It will be safer."

Safer for whom? He was so tall and so large that she couldn't imagine him being in any sort of danger whatsoever. Added to that, he stood here, without a guard, without looking over his shoulder or in any way displaying the reactions of someone truly concerned for his safety. She managed a noncommittal shrug, as if she could have cared less about his intentions, even though she burned to know them. "Fine. I will nae reveal your presence."

Yet. To punctuate her agreement, and to irk her guest a bit and perhaps tease him into revealing his true colors, she took another puff on the cigar, pretending to savor the flavor.

"You like cigars?"

"Who does nae?" To be honest, she didn't like it, not even a little. It had taken all her considerable powers of concentration not to cough during the few puffs she'd taken, for the smoke tickled her throat mightily. It had been a childish ploy, drinking the prince's liquor and smoking his cigar. But she'd been unable to resist the temptation to shake his composure. Thank goodness she'd had Gregor as a mentor as she grew up, for when they'd been younger, he'd shared both his whisky and cigars, something her father would have condemned, had he known.

Ailsa enjoyed whisky, but she'd never found any joy in smoking cigars. And now her poor throat, already burned by the strong drink in the flask (whatever it had been, it was stronger than whisky), protested each puff she took. Papa always said the only way to appreciate a cigar was with the mouth, and not the lungs. Gregor had laughed at that, and swore that a true connoisseur both tasted the smoke and let it warm the soul.

However Gregor saw it, Ailsa couldn't imagine puffing any longer—between the drink and the cigar, she was feeling distinctly dizzy. "Tell me, Your Highness: what do you hope to accomplish, if you dinnae intend to let anyone know you are here?"

His gaze flickered over her, lingering on her lips in a way that left her breathless. "That's simple, my lady. I came for you."

"For . . . me?" Her voice squeaked oddly on the last word and her cheeks heated.

His smile warmed. "*Da.* I have come to alleviate you of a great burden."

The untruth of his statement returned her composure. So he'd come all this way to help her, had he? *Not
bloody likely.* She managed a polite smile. "Oh?"

"You will tell me all you know of my grandmother's
abduction, and I will find Her Grace and Lord Hamilton and bring them back unharmed."

He made it sound so simple, almost negligently so,
which irritated her like sand between her teeth. She'd lost
sleep over the abduction, had plotted and questioned,
worried and planned. And now here he was, without the
least show of concern, offering to do the deed for her.

"That is good, *nyet*?" He threw out his hands, looking as if he'd just granted her the world's largest favor.
"You will not have to do anything; I will take care of the
issue for you."

He looked so confident that a flicker of uncertainty
brought her up short. Under normal circumstances, she
would have found it amusing for a huge, handsome
man to look at her in such a solicitous manner. But
this situation was different. She'd been deeply alone,
struggling to find her way through this new, dangerous
situation without the benefit of an advisor or even a
sympathetic ear. Part of her wanted nothing more than
for someone—someone who knew more than she, but
who cared just as much—to assist her in making the
difficult decisions. While another part of her refused to
step away from her responsibilities. *What if he and his
men are better suited to lead this rescue attempt?*

But even as she had the thought, suspicion made her
look at him with narrowed eyes. His expression was
one of concern, and appeared quite genuine, but she

couldn't erase from her memory the way he'd talked to his men when he hadn't known anyone was watching—in a bold, arrogant way.

That was not the prince she now faced. She forced a smile. "That is a kind offer, but I already have a plan in place to rescue Her Grace and Lord Hamilton."

Impatience flashed through his eyes. "I suppose your little plan has to do with paying the requested ransom."

My little *plan?* Her jaw tightened, and she didn't answer.

"Because if it does, then you, my lady, are making a great error. Paying the ransom will only encourage those who took the captives to ask for more gold. And then more again." His jaw firmed. "Oxenburg does not pay ransoms."

He said the words as if that one sentence settled matters, which only raised her ire all the more. "What would you suggest, then? Storming in, swords drawn and pistols blazing, hoping Her Grace and Lord Hamilton do nae get injured in the melee?"

His smile faltered and then disappeared. "Of course I would not ride in with pistols blazing. That's—" He broke off, his mouth pressed into a straight line. But after a few moments, he seemed to regain control of himself, for his expression softened. "Come. We should not fight; we have the same goal, which is to save our loved ones. And *nyet,* I would not race in thoughtlessly, as you suggest, for I am not a fool. But paying the ransom is not the way."

"It is worth trying, at least. If it wins back the prisoners with nae blood shed, then we will all be relieved."

"And if it does not, then you have merely encouraged the abductors to think you weak." He bent down and captured her free hand, cupping it between his own. "Please. Let me help you. My men and I know best how to handle this situation."

Though he held her hand so comfortingly, there was a set to his mouth that told her that no matter what she said or did, he would do as he saw fit.

She looked down at where her hand disappeared in his and gently freed it. There was nothing stopping the prince and his men from setting out on their own; she knew that. But she hadn't shared the exact location of the ransom meeting with Lord Apraksin for a reason; she'd wished to keep some of the cards in her own hands. It had seemed overly cautious at the time, and Gregor had even questioned her about it after Lord Apraksin and Mr. Rurik had left the small study, but now she was glad—so glad—she'd followed her instincts.

The prince might know how to handle this situation in Oxenburg, but he didn't know the Scots the way she did. He had no understanding of the complexities of clan relationships, and could never bring this unfortunate episode to anything but a regrettable end.

She and her party would leave in the morning as she'd planned, and the prince and his men could do what they would, although they'd have no idea where to begin their search. She would not forgo caution for bravado.

It was time to put an end to this. She held her hand to one side to drop the cigar to the ground.

Before her fingers could loosen enough to release it,

the prince's large gloved hand closed about her wrist and she was tugged forward, her astounded gaze now level with the second button on his coat. Less than an inch separated them; she could feel the heat from his body through her heavy wool coat.

It would be best if I don't look up, she decided, her heart thundering in her ears, her skin prickling with awareness.

The prince plucked the cigar from her surprised fingers.

"What are you doing?" she heard herself ask in a breathless voice.

He bent closer, his breath warming her chilled cheek. "Taking what is mine."

She knew he was talking about the cigar, but for a breathless moment she closed her eyes, a willful thought scampering unbidden through her imagination. *I wish he were talking about me.*

Surprised at herself, her eyes flew open, and she found herself drowning in his green, green eyes. She tried to swallow, but couldn't, so she lowered her gaze to his chin, forcing her distracted brain to focus on that and nothing else. But that firm chin was attached to a very sensual mouth, and the sight of it tugged her forward.

One small move on her part, and she'd be against him, her chest to his. And if she lifted up on her toes, her mouth might touch his, which would be foolish—

Or would it? Perhaps in kissing him, she could regain some control over this situation, over him. If he thought she'd fallen under his spell, he'd think he'd won, and that would give her the time to figure out how to deal with this new development.

Without giving herself too much time to think about it, she lifted up on her toes and kissed him.

She wasn't sure who was more shocked, for they both froze in place, her body pressed firmly to his, her chilled lips over his warm ones. And och, how delicious his lips were.

Nae, nae, nae! That's enough! One kiss, nae more! she warned herself frantically. She lifted her foot to step back, but the prince's strong arms slid about her and locked her in place.

And suddenly, she was no longer the one kissing, but was the one being kissed. His mouth, warm and insistent, covered hers, teasing and tempting. He didn't just kiss, he *kissed*, bending her back, pressing her lips apart, his tongue brushing hers in a wantonly intimate gesture.

Heat flooded her, overwhelmed her, consumed her. He deepened the kiss, nipping her bottom lip and—

She broke away and stepped back, her breath rapid, her heart galloping madly. Her gloved fingers brushed her burning lips. *That was . . . Oh my.*

He watched her and she caught a flicker of surprise in his green eyes before he lowered his lids and regarded her through his lashes.

"I dinnae mean for that to happen," she blurted.

"Neither did I," Nik admitted. She'd surprised him. He'd expected the kiss to be pleasant, perhaps even sensual, but nothing had prepared him for the searing passion that kiss had ignited. *There is more to this little mouse than I expected. Much, much more.*

Nik wasn't quite sure what he was to do with that information; he only knew it was now a fact—she was a blindingly passionate woman, and under other circumstances, he'd have enjoyed tasting more of her.

She nervously wet her lips, and his body warmed yet again as she said in a breathless voice, "I dinnae know what came over me. That was . . . I should nae have—"

"Please. Kisses are never to be regretted."

Ailsa could only nod. She hoped he was now feeling even more superior than he had, as if he'd already won the day. As if she'd given him the upper hand without a fight. Which was exactly what she wanted.

Still, she couldn't stop looking at his mouth which had just covered hers. At his strong jaw, or the thickness of his lashes over his green, green eyes. Like it or not, the prince was a handsome man. More than handsome. One could even say he was perfect, at least the parts of him that she could see.

Which had the unfortunate effect of making her wonder about the parts she *couldn't* see. And therein lay the danger: the parts of him—both physical and otherwise—that were hidden from view.

Ailsa took a deep breath, pulling cold air into her lungs and trying to calm her scattered thoughts. She'd been so focused on trying to best this man that she hadn't been prepared for her own reactions, and they'd almost escaped her control. *Almost,* she told herself with a deep thankfulness. This man was an impossible temptation for any woman, especially one who'd just taken two gulps of an unnamed burning liquor and puffed on a cigar that was much stronger than any she'd ever tried.

The prince's gaze flickered over her face, his expression thoughtful. "Lady Ailsa, I owe you an apology . . . and my thanks. I came onto your property without notifying you, and then pretended to be someone I'm not. For that, I am sorry."

"I accept your apology. You were worried aboot your grandmother. That's understandable." She raised her brows. "But the thanks?" Maybe he was going to thank her for the kiss, her impulsive, attempt-to-disarm-him kiss that had left her with such weak knees she could only hope she could walk on her own power back into the castle.

A glint warmed his gaze. "Thank you for the cigar, *rasivya*." He placed the cigar between his lips.

"You are welcome," she said in a dry tone. "I will sleep more soundly knowing you and your cigar were reunited."

He chuckled, the sound rumbling deep in his chest.

She watched him from under her lashes, wishing her heartbeat would slow. His lips now rested on the cigar where hers just had. It was a small thing, nothing really, and yet it was becoming increasingly difficult to swallow.

She drew her cloak more tightly about her and rubbed her hands together as if cold. "'Tis frigid oot, and it's getting dark, too. May we continue this conversation first thing in the morning? I've guests to see to, and there's much we must discuss, you and I." When he didn't answer, she added, "I'll nae reveal your presence to anyone in the castle, of course." *Except Gregor. He, I will tell. I could use another opinion in this matter, and he's the only one I trust.*

"Thank you." Nik removed the cigar from his mouth, and though a smile touched his lips, his eyes were cool, assessing her. "I would not have you freeze, my lady. My men and I will wait until morning when you will share your information as to the location of these abductors, but no more. I cannot be gone long from Holyrood or people will realize I'm not there."

"Aye." She hesitated. "Aboot that. How is it that you've slipped away withoot notice?"

"It is as Lord Apraksin told you earlier: His Royal Highness Nikolai of Oxenburg is sick in his bed and was most sad he could not make this strenuous trip."

So that was how they were keeping his absence a secret. "And Lord Apraksin and Mr. Rurik? I take it they are nae secret visitors here."

"They, with a nameless groom, have come to Castle Leod to deliver letters to the duchess."

"Who has been abducted and is nae here."

"Also something not known outside of this small area."

"Ah. So that's a secret, as well."

He inclined his head. "For now."

She nodded, fighting the desire to ask more questions. He was obviously only telling her the barest minimum. *He hides his reasons for his actions, and yet he expects me to openly share all of mine.*

But it was more than that. That blasted kiss seemed to hang between them, coloring everything he said and did. For her, it was as if every gesture, every intonation held some sort of sensual meaning.

Worse, she *hoped*. And with that hope, she *yearned*.

No wonder the man was filled with his own sense of worth—women must have drowned him with attention from the time he was born. Why, he was probably *used* to being kissed unexpectedly. *Which would mean I am one of dozens—no*, hundreds—*who have done so.*

The thought cooled her blood instantly, and she realized it was dangerous, being out here alone with this man. Alone and uncertain of her own reactions and thoughts. "We are settled, then. We will meet in the morning. Shall we say eight? Is that too early?"

"*Nyet*. Eight will do."

She stepped away, turning on her heel. "Until tomorrow." She spoke over her shoulder, noting that her voice seemed breathy, as if she couldn't find enough air.

She marched on to the castle, hurrying until she was almost running, aware of his eyes on her even now.

Chapter 7

Gregor held up the lantern, the light spilling over the snow-covered path that curved behind Castle Leod. The ancient path was a remnant of the castle's past, and led to the old stables, which had long ago been abandoned and were now only used for hay storage.

Ailsa stifled a yawn, her breath puffing white into the black night. It was still dark out, the snow crunching under their boots.

Into the quietness, Gregor asked, "Ailsa, are you certain we should—"

"Shhh!" She peered back at the castle, glad to note no lights had appeared in the windows. "Keep your voice down, and pray lower the lantern. Do you want everyone to know we're leaving?"

"It's four in the morning and everyone is abed, as all men with common sense should be."

"We want them to stay abed, so hide that lantern."

"I will, I will." He moved the lantern so that it was on the side farthest from the castle, the light reflecting off the snow as it fell around them. "I can't believe the prince has come dressed as a groom."

"I explained why he's done so."

"I know, but he's taking a great chance with his safety." Gregor grimaced. "Although if it had been our grandmother, I daresay we both would have been moved to do the same."

"More than likely."

He sent her a side-glance. "I still think we're making a mistake, leaving the prince and his men behind. We don't know who—or what—we're facing. A few extra pairs of large, beefy fists might not be amiss."

"If you'd met the man, you'd know why that's a horrible idea." She swiped her glove over her face where the snow had melted as it hit her skin and left her damp and cold. "The prince has nae concern for anyone's objectives but his own, which is to retrieve his grandmother withoot paying even a nod to the ransom. 'Tis a reckless, dangerous way to approach this situation."

"Who knew Oxenburg never paid ransoms?" Gregor said sourly. "I'd certainly never heard that tidbit of information before."

"It dinnae matter what they do in Oxenburg; we're nae there. It will be easier and much safer for everyone concerned to pay the coin, collect the captives, and return home."

"And if that doesn't work?"

"Then we'll do what must be done," she said quietly.

He nodded. "Do you still think Arran is behind this?"

"I dinnae know," she answered honestly, the clean smell of snow tickling her nose. "We'll find oot when we face the abductors."

"So we will." They were quiet a few minutes, trudging up the steep path, snow hissing as it hit the glass in the lamp.

Gregor finally broke the silence, his breath frosting each word. "I hope the prince doesn't follow us once he discovers we've left. From what you repeated of your conversation, he seems rather determined."

And arrogant and willful and focused on his own needs and nae one else's. "Nothing will keep him from following. But with any luck, he will nae discover we're missing until eight or perhaps even later. We'll be long gone by then, and he'll have nae idea which direction we took."

"He could track us."

"He'd have to know which direction to look. And the snow will cover our tracks well before he's oop." She hoped that was true. Right now, in the icy black cold of morning, she had to force herself not to question every step she'd made. It was such a complex situation, and she couldn't shake the weight on her conscience of those who depended on her.

She glanced uneasily back at the castle, where it loomed tall and forbidding in the icy darkness, and pulled the hood of her cloak farther over her head. It was frigid cold this morning, and she could only be thankful Gregor had lent her a pair of his breeches. "Thank you for sharing your clothing. It will be much easier to ride in the forest withoot worrying aboot my skirts catching on the branches."

"Our grandmother would be furious."

"It does nae take much."

He chuckled. "No, it doesn't." He stumbled a bit, and almost dropped the lantern. "Sorry," he mumbled. "New boots. They're not yet broken in. I told Golitzin to set out the old ones, but he didn't listen."

"Golitzin? Who is that?"

"My new valet. Well, he's my valet until Valjean heals. I made the new man say his name a dozen times last night so I could learn it."

"You dinnae tell your valet we were leaving this morning?" she demanded.

"Of course not! As far as he knows, I won't be dressing until eleven, as I usually do."

She frowned. "Guid. You dinnae know him well enough to share our plans."

Gregor tugged his muffler more closely about his neck. "Brrr. It's cold."

"I know. Thank goodness I'm nae trying to keep warm in skirts. With all the undergarments I'm wearing, the breeches are much warmer. There's nae a draft to be had." That much was true; Gregor's breeches were toasty warm, especially after she'd tugged them over two woolen chemises and a pair of long men's pants Gregor had thoughtfully sent along with the breeches.

The snow grew heavier as they climbed where the wind had piled it thicker on the ridge. "I told MacKean and Stewart you'd be coming, too. They are to have our horses ready."

Gregor made a face. "Did you tell them I had to beg you to allow me to go?"

"Nae, but I'm willing to change my mind, if you keep reminding me of it."

"Lud, no! I'll not say another word, I vow it." He was silent a moment before adding tentatively, "Although I'd think you'd be glad for the company."

To be honest, she *was* glad for the company. More than she could say. She and Gregor used to ride the eastern edges of Castle Leod's estate, a beautiful trail that spanned several lochs, scenic moors, and not a few dangerous bogs. Sometimes, if they planned to be gone all day, Gregor would sneak some of his clothes to her. They were always careful no one saw them, especially Lady Edana, who had no hesitation in reporting to Papa anything she thought unladylike.

Ailsa smiled at Gregor now. "It's kind of you to come. This is nae your fight."

He didn't return her smile. "Does it involve you?"

"Aye, but—"

"Then it's my fight, too." He linked his arm with hers. "Your family is now mine, and when there's trouble, I wish to help."

"That's verrah kind of you. To be honest, I'd thought to leave you here with Lady Edana to keep her calm, so the men and I could rescue—"

He stopped, and to her shock, his voice cracked, sharp and furious. "Ailsa, I am not a child."

"I never said you were. I just—"

"You don't believe I'm capable of helping, do you? Not really."

"I do. It's just that our grandmother worries so much and I thought you could—"

"Stay home, holding Lady Edana's hand like a child left behind, while the adults participate in life's real events. Is that what you mean?"

"*Nae*, Gregor. I just thought—"

"You are just like your father, neither of you willing to give me a chance." Gregor stomped a short distance away, spinning back to face her, the lantern held at his side. "Well, I'm not a child, and I'm not a bloody fool."

Ailsa blinked, her mouth hanging open in surprise. In all her years, she'd never seen her cousin so angry. "I assure you I never think of you as a child *or* a fool." She spread her hands wide. "Truly, I dinnae."

He glared at her, and for a horrible moment, she thought he'd turn and leave her alone in the black snow, taking the light with him. But instead, he grimaced and pressed a hand to his temple. "I'm sorry, Ailsa. I just didn't—I can't explain how this—" He swiped his eyes as if wiping away tears.

"I've never seen you so overset. What's wrong?"

"Everything. Nothing." He gave a shaky laugh. "It's been a long few months. You don't know how—I just—really, it's not you I'm angry with, it's Uncle."

"He's hard on you, I know."

"He never treats me as if I were an adult. And yes, I know that's partly my fault. Over the last few years, I've let him down more than once." Gregor shook his head and came back to rejoin her on the path. "Ailsa, I must tell you something. And it is not pretty." He swallowed, the noise loud in the silence of the night. "I visited the Earl of Argyll at your father's instigation."

"Papa's? But why— Ah. Argyll's daughter."

Gregor nodded glumly. "Last month, I went to see Uncle in London to apologize for—well, for everything I've done wrong. He wouldn't listen; he just kept saying I was a failure and was heading for the poorhouse and how he couldn't keep me from it forever, and— Oh, it was a horrible argument. We both said things we shouldn't have. At the end, he informed me that he and Argyll had made a decision for me, since I was unable to make one for myself. Argyll's daughter, the indomitable Lady Agnes, was unmarried, and seemed unlikely to gain a suitor. And there I was—a hopeless wastrel with no prospects other than my services as a well-bred stallion." He laughed bitterly. "I was to marry her and get her with a child or two, and then Argyll would give me an allowance and I would be free to wander about the world as I wished, unfettered and unwanted."

"Gregor, nae. Papa would never be so cruel—"

"Wouldn't he? Those are your father's exact words. And I, having no pride, agreed. But I just couldn't bring myself to come to point." Gregor shook his head. "When your father finds out, he will cast me off."

"Surely nae."

"It's what he said he would do. And he meant it. He thinks the worst of me, and when he finds out I left Argyll's in such a fashion—" Gregor rubbed a hand over his face. "Which is why I'm so grateful you allowed me to help. This opportunity, this chance to do something right for once, it could make the world of difference. I could prove to your father that I'm not a waste of air."

She slipped her arm through his. "You're nae a waste

of air, nor a wastrel, nor a failure. You're dear, wonderful, delightful Gregor, and I'm glad to have you along. It will make the trip fly by. But I must warn you, Greer said the way is verrah rough. 'Twill nae be an easy journey."

"I don't care; I'll do whatever I must." Gregor sent her a crooked, strained grin. "Dear, dear Ailsa. You're the sister I never had, which is yet another reason I must come. What if these unscrupulous abductors decide to take you prisoner, too? What then?"

"I'd be oot of luck, for Papa is nae nearby, and Lady Edana never has two coins to rub together. But I'm certain I'll be safe. I was never going alone, you know. I'll have Greer and his men, as well."

"If something ill happened to you, I'd find the ransom money, I promise."

"I know it." She patted his hand. "Ah, and here's MacKean and Stewart, waiting as promised."

The two huntsmen stood outside the old stables with the horses already packed with beds and supplies. Ailsa was glad to note that someone had thought to line the bedrolls with furs, to make the trip more comfortable. There was little to say, and as time was slipping away, they mounted up and were soon on their way, the cold morning air nipping at Ailsa's nose and cheeks. There would be more discomfort ahead, she was sure. Much, much more if this wind and the terrain they had to cover were any indication. And at the end of that . . . she didn't know what challenges awaited her there, only that she had to meet them and free Lord Hamilton and Her Grace.

They quietly rode the horses single file across the

ridge above the dark castle, and then on past the stables where the prince slept. To her relief, nary a light showed.

The only sound in the night, other than the occasional blast of wind and the growing rustle of the trees, was the horses' muffled hoof falls on the thick snow. Soon, they were breaking a faint path across the stretch of moors to the forest beyond.

MacKean reached the forest edge and lifted his hand, signaling for everyone to stay close, as it would grow darker in the forest. St. George lifted his head to whicker at the rustle of the trees overhead, but she patted him soothingly to keep him from making noise. She followed MacKean onto the dark path, Stewart close behind.

She'd just let out a sigh of relief that they'd made it, when a horse's loud neigh broke the silence. Heart pounding, Ailsa wheeled about in her saddle to see Gregor fighting his horse, the animal bucking wildly. He got the animal under control, but Stewart was left muttering angrily.

Her breath coming in quick bursts, Ailsa looked toward the castle. But no light shone, and no movement stirred.

Yet.

"Let's go!" she urged, turning her horse down the path and heading straight into the black forest.

⸺∞⸺

*U*nder a tree across the paddock from the stable, Nik patted D'yoval's neck. "For people sneaking away in the middle of the night, they are making a lot of noise."

Rurik grunted. "Aye. Do you think they did it apurpose?"

"Nyet. It was one horse. Something could have startled it." Try as he would, Nik couldn't keep the snap from his voice.

Apraksin eyed Nik with a cautious gaze. "You are angry they slipped away."

"It does not make me happy." Which was putting it mildly, to say the least. He'd been fooled by Lady Ailsa's seemingly innocent kiss and had thought he'd made a conquest of a sort. So it had been a shock when Apraksin had shown up at the stables well after midnight with the unwelcome news that he'd overheard Gregor complaining quietly to Ailsa about having to get up "in the middle of the night."

Nik checked D'yoval's saddle one last time. He should have known Lady Ailsa had some sort of trickery up her very silky lace sleeve; she'd been far too conciliatory by the end of their conversation. "Slipping away in the middle of the night is an underhanded way of conducting this business."

"We were going to do the same," Apraksin pointed out. "It is why we are here now."

That was true. But *still* . . . Nik growled, "She was never going to consult me about her plans."

"And we weren't going to consult her about ours." Apraksin was once again the voice of reason. "I found the note, and we now have the location of the ransom exchange. I fail to see how her actions are any less—"

"That's enough." Nik swung into the saddle and gathered D'yoval's reins even as he scowled at Apraksin. "Why are you even here?"

"I came to say good-bye and good luck." The courtier shoved his hands inside his pockets. "I wish I were going with you."

Rurik shook his head. "You have a duty."

"I know, I know. Do you have the map I found in the library?"

The guard nodded and climbed onto his horse. "We will trail Lady Ailsa and her men, as they will take the quickest route through the mountains. We will join them at the end of the day, when they are too committed to alter their course."

"Why travel with them at all?" Apraksin asked.

"It will be safer to travel in a group. It's been reported that thieves roam the higher trails."

Nik nodded. "Then let us go. We will walk the horses to the forest and stay far enough back that we are not heard."

"Have a care, Your Highness." Apraksin stepped back from the horse.

"Of course." Nik turned D'yoval to a path that led to the ridge where Ailsa and her party had just passed through, Rurik falling in beside him.

As they rode across the moor, the dark woods loomed before them. They were almost at the forest line when Rurik said into the quiet, "Lady Ailsa will not be happy to see us."

"But I will be happy to see her." They had unfinished business, and Nik was determined to see it through.

He remembered again the unexpected passion that had flared at that damned kiss. There had been fire there, a surprising amount, for such a plain woman.

And she was plain, although there were moments

when, glowing from that kiss, her gray eyes had turned silvery bright, and she'd looked almost pretty. *It could not have been false, the passion I sensed. I will not believe it.*

"I hope they do not have a guard posted on their flank," Rurik said.

"They are not soldiers, and do not expect to be followed. We will not be noticed."

They followed the trail where it disappeared into the black forest, the trees reducing the light. Before them in the snowy path, hoofprints gleamed. As dawn broke, the forest came alive around him, and Nik found himself admiring the beauty of it. It had grown colder as they went, snow and ice frosting every green bough, brown tree limb, and waxy shrub with a glistening veil. The scent of pine mixed with that of fresh snow, and a deeper, richer peaty scent that he was beginning to realize was pure Scotland.

Only once did they hear the party ahead. Mr. Mackenzie's voice carried over the others, complaining about the cold, and the pace. Nik reined in D'yoval and motioned Rurik to stillness. After ten minutes the voices faded to nothingness, and Nik signaled that it was time to continue.

Ah, Lady Ailsa, you are in for a surprise. One I look forward to delivering.

Chapter 8

"We'll make camp here." Ailsa glanced up through the trees at the fading sun before she returned her gaze to their campsite. The small clearing was backed on one side by a huge boulder, and was encircled by trees that provided some relief from the relentless wind.

MacKean, the reticent, lean, dark-haired tracker who'd so far led their expedition, eyed the area with a critical look. "It's nae verrah large."

"'Tis large enough," Ailsa said firmly, dismounting. She refused to look at MacKean, but she held her breath until he, too, climbed down off his mount.

She gave a silent sigh of relief. When she'd first taken on the duties as head of Castle Leod, winning the trust of the servants who worked in the castle hadn't been nearly as difficult as commanding the respect of those who worked in the fields and stables. They were unused to taking orders from a woman, and she'd had to start from scratch, especially with MacKean and Stewart, the two gamekeepers escorting their party to meet Greer. Independent by nature, they'd presented a certain challenge, one she felt she'd finally met.

Ailsa put her hands on her lower back and stretched the stiffness from her muscles, the cold wind stirring her cloak as she moved. She'd thought she was a toughened rider, but now she realized that riding the gentle trails around Castle Leod, even for hours at a time, could not compare to riding over such a steep trail. Not only was one jolted about, but time and again, they had to stop to either rest the mounts, or to walk them up a particularly steep portion of the trail.

She threw St. George's reins over a shrub, frowning as she looked around. "Where's Gregor?"

Stewart tied his horse beside hers. Large and barrel-chested like a bear, his red hair shaggy and long, he was an excellent tracker. He jerked his head toward the path they'd just left. "He's comin' oop the path, my lady. I hear his horse now."

And sure enough, a few seconds later, Gregor appeared. He looked as tired as Ailsa felt, not used to the grueling effort, either.

MacKean shot Gregor a hard look. "Got lost, did you?"

The younger man flushed. "I was only lost in my own thoughts and didn't realize you had trotted ahead." He swung down from his horse and rolled his shoulders.

"I'd keep oop, if I were you," MacKean said in a flat tone. "Dangerous men hide in these woods."

"Of course." Limping, Gregor led his horse to where Ailsa stood. "Here. Give me St. George. I'll take care of the animals."

She could see the tiredness in his eyes. "Thank you. I'll set oot the pallets. We'll want that done before it grows dark." She glanced up at the trees waving over-head against the gray-growing sky, the almost bared limbs showering dead leaves now and then. "We've nae much time to set oop camp. We rode all day."

"It feels like it," Gregor muttered, rubbing his back.

Stewart opened one of his saddlebags. "Whilst you do tha', I'll start a fire. I brought some salted beef and dried carrots and such. If you'd like, I can make a bit of stew."

"Aye," Ailsa replied thankfully, glad to hear they'd have a warm supper. "Please do."

They set about their duties, hurrying to get them completed before nightfall. As Ailsa cleared areas for the bedding, she thought about the prince, something she'd done off and on all day.

He'd be furious now, of course, probably cursing her name up one side of Castle Leod and down the other. She had no doubt he'd have followed if he'd known which direction to take. *Which he doesn't, thank goodness. That is not a man whose anger I relish facing.*

Once the fire was crackling, Stewart pulled a metal stake from his pack and jabbed it into the ground by the flames. At one end of the stake was a large hook, upon which he hung a small black pot for their stew.

"That's a useful tool." She nodded to the hooked stake.

"The blacksmith made it for me. It can be used for more than hangin' a pot, too. I've tied horses to it, used it to secure one end of a laundry line, and anchored a tent, as well."

MacKean sent Stewart a disgusted look. "All of which you could do just as weel wi' a cut stick."

"You could nae," Stewart replied firmly. "Nae like this."

MacKean snorted.

Smiling, Ailsa continued unrolling the pallets. She'd just finished placing the final one when a noise on the path caused her to rock back on her heels and look in that direction, her breath held as she listened. *Was that the strike of a hoof on a rock?*

MacKean was suddenly at her side, his rifle in hand. "Stay low," he whispered. "It could be brigands. I'll go east and loop around to the other side of the trail. Stewart, take the west."

Stewart rose from the fire and gathered his weapons, then disappeared in the opposite direction, remarkably quiet for such a large man.

Ailsa whispered, "I'll find a place atop that boulder. If I cannae, I'll use that ridge just beyond."

"Guid. Have Mackenzie set oop behind that fallen log."

Ailsa nodded and MacKean bent lower still and made his way into the woods, one silent step at a time.

Ailsa made her way to Gregor, who was feeding the horses, unaware of their danger. She grasped his arm and pulled him down.

"We've unexpected visitors," she whispered. "Stewart and MacKean have gone to greet them. You're to take position behind that log." She nodded toward it.

"How many?"

"We do nae know."

He freed his pistol from his saddle. "Where will you be?"

"On the boulder over the camp."

He checked to see that his weapon was loaded before sending her a serious look. "Be careful."

"You, too." She glanced at her saddlebag. The money was securely hidden in its lining, but it wouldn't take long for someone to realize the bag was much heavier than it should be.

Gregor found his way to his assigned position. Though not as quiet as the trackers, he did well enough that Ailsa began to breathe again.

Staying low, she moved toward the huge boulder that shadowed their campsite and carefully climbed up one side. It was steeper than she'd expected, but one hand and foothold at a time, she finally reached the top, her boots scraping on the rock as she scooted across the broad, flat top. She stayed prone, tugging her cloak about her, and looked down at the camp. Through the few dead leaves left on the trees, she could just make out Gregor where he hid not far away, his gun trained on the trail. Better woodsmen, neither Stewart nor MacKean could be seen, though she was certain they were there, too.

A rustle sounded close to the camp, like that of a large animal brushing a shrub, and she turned her gaze back to the trail. In the growing dusk, a rider appeared, flickering in and out of sight through the thick leaves. Tall and broad shouldered, he rode as if he were a part of his horse. But more than that, he rode as if he owned the trail, the mountain, and all the trees.

And she knew before she saw him who it was.

⸺∞⸺

$\mathcal{N}$ik pulled his horse into the small clearing, Rurik riding briskly past him. The guard's sharp eyes took in every detail. "Hello!" he called, swinging down from his horse.

Nik did the same, stopping by the pot heating over the fire. "It looks as if we've arrived in time for dinner, *nyet*?"

Rurik sniffed and then frowned. "That does not smell promising."

"It'll be warm. That's the most important thing." He looked about curiously. The area was fairly level, which was unusual in this terrain, and protected on one end by a huge boulder, which would keep the wind at bay. A fire had been made, the pot hanging over it and bubbling cozily. Four thick pallets were spread out around the fire. "This is a good camp."

Rurik nodded.

Nik scanned the woods curiously. "You may come out now," he called. "We have come to join you."

"You, sir, were nae invited," came a testy feminine voice.

Trying not to grin, he looked up where the voice had come from, high upon the boulder. "Lady Ailsa, is that you?"

"You know it is." She called out in a louder voice, "'Tis safe! Just two lost fools. No one of importance." She muttered something else, but it wasn't audible.

Still, it made Nik grin. He'd wished to see the surprise on her face, but for now he'd be satisfied with the irritation in her voice.

A smallish slender man with light brown hair stood up from behind a log, a gleaming pistol in his hand.

Nik almost reached for his own weapon, but Rurik stepped forward. "Mr. Mackenzie. How nice to see you again."

Ah, the cousin. Nik was glad Rurik and Apraksin had mentioned the man.

"Mr. Rurik, isn't it?" The man left the woods and joined them in the clearing. "Bloody hell, we thought brigands were after us. Someone could have shot you!"

Now that he was closer, Nik could see a faint resemblance between the man and Lady Ailsa.

"I am glad you did not shoot us," Rurik replied. "Or I would have been forced to kill you back."

From up above, Lady Ailsa said clearly, "Pah! Men!"

Nik grinned. "What?" he called. "You would not have shot a brigand?"

Stony silence met his query.

"Good evening."

Nik looked down to find Ailsa's cousin at his elbow.

"You must be the prince; you could be no one else." The younger man inclined his head in a formal greeting. "I'm Gregor Mackenzie, Lady Ailsa's cousin."

Before Nik could respond, Rurik's gaze locked on the woods behind them. "Two more come."

And so they did, from different directions and looking as opposite as two men could. One was dark and lean, a cunning intelligence in his face, while the other was huge and red-haired, almost lumbering in his gait and expression.

"Good evening," Nik greeted them. "I see you've already started supper."

Neither man smiled.

After a stiff moment, Rurik inclined his head. "I must refill our flasks. We just passed a stream, so I can do it there." He hesitated and then said politely to the others, "Do you need yours refilled, too?"

The two men merely glared at Rurik.

Once more, Mackenzie stepped into the breach. "I'm sure we do. I'll fetch our empty flasks and we can go together."

"*Nyet*. There is no need; I will take them all."

Mackenzie started to argue, but Rurik raised a brow in his direction.

The younger man flushed. "Fine. I'll gather the flasks for you."

Nik went to stand before the huge boulder. It towered over them all, casting a long shadow. "You may as well come down, *krasavitsa*. I know you're there."

"My name is not Kra— Whatever that was."

"Fine. Lady Ailsa, then. Come. Join us."

There was a long silence.

"The stew will be ready soon, I think."

No answer came, and Mackenzie cleared his throat loudly and called to his cousin, "You might as well join us."

Nik heard a sigh, followed by a scuffling sound. He

waited and was rewarded when, some long moments later, Ailsa appeared around the edge of the boulder.

His brows rose and he found himself without words. Lady Ailsa with her snapping gray eyes and bold nose in her fitted riding habit, her hat jauntily perched on her dark blond hair was one thing. But Lady Ailsa clad in breeches that hugged her rounded hips, a long fur-lined cloak swinging from her shoulders, her blond hair tied in a thick braid that hung over one shoulder, her mouth pressed in an unwelcoming line so that she looked like a Viking maid from days of old—this Lady Ailsa stole his breath as if he'd been punched in the stomach.

The strength of his own reaction left him speechless, even as she strode past him, slanting him a boldly disapproving glare in a way no woman had ever done. She walked to the fire while he tried hard not to stare, her curves so boldly expressed that his mouth went dry.

She stooped beside the fire and held her hands toward the flames, her cloak pooling about her feet. "Why are you here?"

There was nothing welcoming in that cold, clipped tone.

Mackenzie slanted Nik a sympathetic look. "If you'll pardon me, I'll finish with the horses. I was bedding them down for the night when you arrived." He inclined his head and then walked to where the horses were tethered a short distance away, D'yoval and Rurik's mount now with them.

Nik walked to where Ailsa stooped before the fire. He stood on the other side so he could clearly see her expressions, and nodded to the pistol tucked in her belt. "Expecting trouble?"

"These woods are known for harboring violent brigands. You're fortunate nae one shot you. Especially since you were *following* us."

"We are *joining* you, since our end location is the same."

"You dinnae know where we're going," she scoffed.

"We go to meet a man called Greer who is camped at the mouth of the Corrieshalloch Gorge. He has been following the abductors and their captives and will know the strength of this band of ruffians."

Her amusement fled and she scrambled to her feet, her brows knit. "How do you know that?"

"The same way I also know you're planning to meet the villains who abducted my grandmother and pay that damned ransom."

"I daresay you know where I am to deliver the payment, too," she said in a grim tone.

"Kylestrome. An inn." He smiled. "And now you will demand to know how I came upon such a treasure trove of information. I'm more than happy to tell you all, but even you must agree that such stories are best told around a shared fire."

Ailsa had to swallow a very real desire to snap an ungrateful "nae." She supposed it had been naïve of her to think no one had seen them leave. That was a bitter pill to swallow, for it meant she wasn't as good at scheming as she'd thought. But the discovery that the prince and Rurik knew her entire plan was not acceptable. *Has someone betrayed us?*

Blast the man, she'd have to let him stay if she

wanted her questions answered. "Fine. You may share the camp with us. For at least one night."

Stewart, who was once again tending the stew, sent her a glum look, which she studiously ignored, though it gave her a moment's hesitation. *Should* she allow the prince and his man to join them? If she did not, they would go out on their own, and might even reach Greer first. No, it was best to keep these two close by, so she knew what they were doing.

Nik came to the fire and took a seat.

She watched him covertly. His black hair was longer than was fashionable and curled about his collar and face, giving him a rakish look that was augmented by his lack of a shave this morning. Indeed, his face—so clean-shaven just yesterday—was now shadowed with stubble that accentuated the line of his jaw.

Still, dressed in a commoner's clothes, a determined set to his jaw, he didn't look like the frivolous, flirtatious prince he was reputed to be. *Ah, but he is indeed that flirtatious prince, but—I think—only when it suits him.* She had witnessed his transformation once already, and had experienced his seductive powers only the night before. It was easy to see why society had such a wrong impression of the man.

Stewart tapped the iron spoon on the side of the pot and said in a stiff voice, "I do nae know if we'll have enough stew for the two of you."

Nik didn't look the least put out by this. "I don't suppose you'd like some fresh meat for your stew?"

The redheaded Scot brightened, his scowl disappearing like the mist before sunshine. "What do you have?"

"Rurik!" Nik called to his man, who'd just returned with the filled flasks. "Bring the rabbits we caught."

Ailsa frowned. "When did you have time to catch rabbits?"

"We stopped this afternoon. We were coming too close to your party."

As if we were creeping along! Her irritation grew.

Rurik brought an oilskin-wrapped bundle to the fire.

Stewart opened it with a pleased look. "I'll roast these a bit and then shred the meat into the stew." His gaze flickered to Nik. "It should be enough for all of us, then."

"Good." Nik's gaze returned to Ailsa and rested on her lips.

He was thinking of their kiss. She knew it as sure as she was breathing. She silently thanked the fates he'd chosen to sit opposite her and not beside her, where their elbows or knees might have touched. It was taking all her concentration to think calmly. If he actually touched her . . . She shivered, flooded with memories she'd tried all day to forget.

"Are you cold, Lady Ailsa?"

The words purred over her, as if lapping the heat of her memories. She tugged her cloak closer. "'Tis winter," she said flatly.

"So it is." Nik removed his gloves and held his hands toward the fire, his gaze moving back to her. "Your companions know this forest well. There were times we had to work to see the trail at all."

"They do. They are woodsmen, both." She gestured

to the lean, hard-eyed man with dark hair and a suspicious air who was still holding his rifle. "This is Hammish MacKean. He'll be the master game warden once Greer steps aside."

The prince inclined his head. "MacKean."

MacKean nodded back, his expression cautious.

"And this," Ailsa continued, gesturing to the heavy redhead now skewering the rabbits, "is Ian Stewart. We're lucky to have him; I have it on guid authority he can cook better than Mrs. Attnee's cousin, who is the head cook at Castle Leod."

The shaggy redheaded giant placed one end of the spit holding the rabbits in the pot hook and the other between two rocks on the other side of the fire. That done, he gave Nik a small nod.

Nik returned the greeting. "A pleasure, Mr. Stewart." He gestured to where Rurik was hanging the flasks from a tree branch so they would not leak during the night. "I believe you've all met Rurik."

"And you?" Stewart asked.

Nik hesitated and then said, "I am Romanovin."

"Humph. A prince is what Mr. Mackenzie called you." Stewart sent Nik a hard look from under his bushy brows. "We heard him say so as we joined you."

"And so I am . . . when I'm in court, surrounded by fools and idiots." Nik leaned against a tree and stretched his legs before him, looking comfortable there on the ground, by the fire. A faint smile touched his lips, one both personal and disarming. "But here, under the trees and the night sky, where nothing but honest men can find their way? Then, I am Romanovin."

Stewart and MacKean exchanged glances.

"It would be safer for us all if no one knew a prince was among us," Rurik added without looking up from where he was unpacking his and Nik's bedrolls.

Ailsa couldn't argue with that.

"That's true," Stewart said grudgingly.

MacKean shrugged. "Romanovin it is."

Ailsa waited for Nik to say more, but he merely smiled and then held his hands to the flames and soaked in the warmth.

She smoothed her hands over her knees, trying not to give in to a twinge of jealousy. She'd worked hard to gain the trust of her men, and even now could sometimes feel the waver of their belief in her. To see them accept the prince and agree to call him by his last name seemed . . . unfair, somehow. Would they have agreed to call her something so informal? She didn't think so.

But did she wish them to? Did such familiarity mean anything? Could it denote a lack of respect? *It doesn't matter. I should just focus on the tasks at hand; my actions will speak for me.* She looked at Stewart and MacKean. "Who has first watch?"

"I do." MacKean gathered his furs and a flask of water. "I'll take the spot you found on the boulder, my lady. 'Tis a guid vantage point, nae?"

"You can see all the way down the trail, almost to the stream. But the rock is nae comfortable, and it holds the cold, so you're smart to take that fur."

"Aye, although the cold will keep me awake. Stewart, bring me some stew when 'tis done." MacKean disappeared around the boulder, and was soon heard from no more.

"We'll need more firewood." Rurik arose from where he'd placed the bedrolls and moved quietly into the dark woods.

Nik looked around the camp. "This is a good spot for our camp."

She raised her brows at the approving note in his voice, disliking the small flare of satisfaction his words gave her. "When we hunt larger game, there are times we must spend the night in the woods. The game-keepers, I, and my father have added much venison to our winter stores." She hesitated, but then added, "Castle Leod might nae be wealthy, but she's self-sufficient. The lands are large, but much of it is like this—beautiful, but unfarmable. We rely on the game to help us through the winters."

"Her ladyship is a crack shot," Stewart added.

She grinned. "I'm guid with a knife, too, and it seems as if you need those carrots chopped."

"So I do, my lady." Stewart handed her the small bundle of carrots. "Smaller pieces cook faster." He stood. "I'm going to see where Rurik is with that firewood. The fire will be oot if he dinnae hurry." The Scotsman left, lumbering off into the woods.

To Ailsa's chagrin, the prince came to sit at her side.

She scooted away, giving him more than enough room.

Nik raised his brows. "I will not touch you. Not unless you wish me to."

She shot him a side-glance that was as cool as it was unwelcoming. "Then you will nae touch me."

Nik noted the firm set of her defiant chin. She'd been direct and unhesitating, and he recognized the challenge that lurked in her words whether she knew it or not. Until these last few days, he hadn't realized how much he liked challenges, or how rarely he received them. He spread his hands as if in surrender. "As you wish."

She didn't look completely convinced, but she didn't order him to move, either. She busied herself cutting the carrots, sparing him not another glance.

He was beginning to realize that Lady Ailsa was a complex woman indeed. Her bold kiss had given him the impression that passion simmered just under her cool, collected surface, and he wished to know more about that side of her.

He noted how the cold had pinkened her cheeks and nose. "Earlier, you said you wished to know how I knew your ultimate destination. As you've shared your fire, I suppose I should at least answer your question."

She'd finished with the carrots and tossed them into the stew before she shifted so that she could see his face. "Have you been following us since we left?"

"Aye. We saw you, or rather, heard you."

"Gregor's horse." At Nik's nod, she said, "Something startled it as we were departing." She added in a more sour tone, "So that's when you discovered we were leaving."

"We were already loaded and ready to go. Had you left five minutes later, you would have been following us."

Her brows knit. "Who told you where Greer was

located? I cannae imagine my men doing such a— Ah! The note he sent." She pinned him with a furious gaze. "One of your men searched my study!"

"That they did."

"Dammit! That's— How could you?"

He spread his hands wide. "You were not forthcoming; you left us no choice."

Her lips thinned, yet even then, they were plumper than most women's. She really did have the most beautiful mouth.

"I should have locked Greer's missive and the ransom note away." She shot him a scorching look. "Sadly, I dinnae realize there were weasels in my own hoose."

"Weasels?"

"Little rodents that steal things."

"We didn't steal anything. We just looked. Although I'll admit it was rude of us to look."

"I would call it more than rude."

He shrugged. "Perhaps so, *da*. But it is also rude to sneak off when you've promised to meet with a guest."

"Nae a guest; a groom."

"Is that how you treat servants?" He *tsk*ed. "However you wish to see it, I had no choice but to find out the truth on my own."

"I agree that my lack of openness would be an issue if I dinnae think you'd *arrived* with the intent of searching the castle and property, and had probably already done so when I spoke to you by the stables."

"We had not yet done so, but it's true the plan was already in motion. Normally, I would not sanction such an overstepping of hospitality, but this is a crucial matter."

"You think I dinnae realize there are lives dependent oopon this?"

Her expression, diamond hard and unwavering, made him pause.

The words came from both her heart and her head. *The weight of leadership is heavy on this one.* It was a surprising realization, for he'd thought her natural in assuming her position. He narrowed his gaze. "How old are you?"

She blinked. "What?"

"How old are you?" he repeated.

"What has that to do with anything?"

He raised his brows and waited.

"I'm twenty-three," she said stiffly. After a moment, she added, "Almost."

And there it was. He'd assumed she was at least in her late twenties and had years of experience behind her, but now he understood why she was so prickly about her authority. *Good God, what is her father thinking, to leave his estate in such tender hands?*

Her gaze narrowed on him. "How old are you?"

"Twenty-nine." Although he felt older. Much older.

She shrugged. "It's nae age, but the way you carry your responsibilities that proves your character. So my father has always said."

Spoken like a man who's left a good portion of his responsibilities resting on the shoulders of his youngest daughter. "Age is what you make it," he said in a mild tone. "It's obvious you understand the severity of the issue facing us; I can see that. But your method—to appease an abductor by paying blood money—is flawed and will only lead to further heartbreak. I know this. It is not the way to win this battle."

"Then what *is* the way?"

"We find the abductors and we make them tell us where the captives are."

Stewart and Rurik returned with the wood, piling it beside the fire. The Scot dusted himself off and then sat down near the pot while Rurik removed a whetstone from his saddlebag and sat to one side of the fire, sharpening his knife.

Ailsa ignored them, her attention locked on Nik as she scoffed, "You think we'll be able to *make* the abductors tell us what we wish to know? How?"

"There are ways to get people to talk."

"I see. You think the better strategy is to storm in and beat the information from them?"

He heard the sarcasm in her voice. "It is not surprise we seek, but firmness of an answer."

"And what if your grandmother and Lord Hamilton are close by? Couldn't they be injured in such an attack? Could nae the abductors hide behind our loved ones and use them as shields?"

"*Bozhy moj*, you go right to the worst possible outcome. You do not know how this will end."

"I know your strategy is ridiculously dangerous, and could cause the outcome we most wish to avoid—injury to Her Grace and Lord Hamilton."

"You do not know what will happen," he bit out.

"Neither do you."

"But if we plan carefully, and execute the rescue in an organized fashion, then—"

"That will only work if all these abductors want is the money."

He frowned. "What else could they want?"

"We dinnae know, do we? Nae until we meet them and find oot for ourselves. In the meantime, we cannae just storm in and fire off shots, hoping nae one we love gets injured. You *play* with the lives of others."

"And you offer to placate thieves and abductors, and expect them to act as if they were men of principle and honesty. That's foolish!" Nik struggled to control his temper. This tiny woman dared challenge his every word, treating him as if he had no thoughts of anyone but himself.

"*This* is why I dinnae wish you to come with us," she snapped. "You're brazen, bold, and ridiculously impractical." She almost spat the last word.

Stewart sent Nik a sympathetic look, while Rurik seemed to be fighting back a grin.

Nik swallowed his temper and bit out, "We see this situation through very different lenses."

"Aye. I see it with common sense and reason, and am willing to do what I must to keep two innocent people safe, nae matter the cost to myself. You, meanwhile, only wish to ride to the rescue as if this were a play of some sort."

"I do what needs to be done."

"You are forgoing safety for a mere moment of glory. I would nae call that 'doing what needs to be done.'

There's nae harm in paying the ransom. At the best, it will win the freedom of the prisoners, and at the least it will allow us to take a measure of the abductors and discern their true purpose. If you weren't so used to being deferred to because of your birth, you would listen to what I'm saying and agree."

Deferred to because of his birth? The words struck him with the force of a hammer and he stood, glowering. "I'm not here because of my birth. I'm here to save my grandmother, and that's all."

She rose to her feet, too, plopped her fists on her hips, and glared back at him. "If you'd leave us alone, 'tis entirely possible that I'd fetch your grandmother and you would nae have to lift a finger."

Nik had never thought of himself as reliant on his birth for anything. Indeed, the trappings that came with being a member of royalty were stiff with pomp and boredom, unnecessary formalities, and never-ending politeness. He'd been able to free himself by pretending to be an empty-headed fool interested only in personal pleasures and bored with politics. It was an effective dupe and had made him extremely useful to his kingdom.

But now, while he was engaged in doing what he enjoyed the most, dealing face-to-face with an incident that needed a quick and strong response, this woman dared accuse him of being thoughtless, as if the persona he presented to the world was really who he was. "You are wrong if you believe I have no concern for my own beloved grandmother, or even Lord Hamilton, whom I've never met. I do care. But you are naïve if you think paying the ransom will do anything other than empower those fools to demand yet more gold. Meanwhile, my grandmother and Lord Hamilton will suffer."

Lady Ailsa met him glare for glare. "Which is why we must use caution. This is nae a throne room. This is my camp. My camp, and my rescue. If you wish to perform your own rescue"—she gestured to the night-black forest—"then go."

Nik struggled to contain his temper even as he wondered how in hell their pleasant conversation had ended up so furiously wrong. He'd thought to converse with her, one equal to another, and yet somehow she'd made him feel as if he'd been arbitrary and foolish. He was unused to both. Unable to find a way to express himself, he turned to Rurik. "Come. We will make our own camp." He turned, only to find Ailsa's cousin between him and his bedroll.

The slender young man threw up his hands. "Wait. I've been listening—" At Nik's enraged glare, Mackenzie added, "I couldn't help it; neither of you have been very quiet."

Nik supposed that was true. He took a deep breath, more to calm his temper than anything else. "There's nothing more to say. Please move. I must get my things."

Mackenzie turned to where his cousin stood, her arms crossed, her jaw set in mulish defiance. "Ailsa?"

She glared at her cousin. "You heard him. He will nae discuss—"

"I heard him. In fact, I'm pretty sure everyone in the entire forest heard every word of your conversation.

You keep telling me there are brigands about. Do you want them to find us?"

Ailsa jerked her head toward Nik. "Talk to him, nae me."

"You were talking loudly, too," Nik snapped back. *Bozhy moj, what this woman does to me and my temper.*

Mackenzie spread his hands. "Look, there is no reason we cannot help one another. We have common enemies. There must be some way we can work this out. We have at least a week of travel ahead of us, and we'd be safer in a larger party. I'm sure that somehow, during the time it takes us to reach Greer, the two of you can arrive at an agreement of some sort on how to proceed from there."

"And if we don't?" Ailsa asked.

Rurik stood, shrugging as he did so. "Then it will be a race to see who reaches the abductors first. But Mackenzie is right; we should travel together. It is safer."

Ailsa scowled, and then flicked a glance at Stewart.

Nik instantly knew her struggle: she refused to appear weak in front of her own man. But she must have agreed with at least some of what her cousin said, for she slowly nodded. "I suppose it will nae hurt to discuss this more."

Nik almost sighed in relief. He wasn't sure why, for he didn't need Lady Ailsa's assistance in any way. Yet he had no wish to strike out on his own. Mackenzie and Rurik were right; it would be safer to stay together. Besides, Nik was more and more curious about the prickly woman that was Lady Ailsa Mackenzie. He offered in a cautious tone, "Perhaps there is a way to combine the two plans. We should at least try."

Ailsa flashed him a hard look. "One thing first. You said you were going to Greer's camp. He would nae tell you anything, nae unless you forced him in some way. Did you plan to harm him?"

"Of course not. If we could not find your trail, we were going to wait for you there."

"And when we reached our destination?" she asked. "How would you have stopped us from delivering the ransom, if that's what we chose to do?"

"I'd hoped to have made you see reason by then. But if you had not, then we would have left you and struck out on our own."

"And handled the situation as *you* saw fit."

He shrugged. "I would have."

Mackenzie said in a soothing tone, "Come, Ailsa. We've days of travel ahead of us. It cannot hurt to share our journey. And perhaps you will be able to change the prince's mind. As you've told me many times, you have thought this through. Now you just need to convince him your way is the best. When you wish, you can be very persuasive. I have seen the miracles you have performed on my uncle, and he is stubborn beyond any mere prince."

Nik stiffened. *Mere prince?* He didn't like how this conversation was going, for he seemed to be coming off as spoiled, stubborn, and intractable, all horrendous character flaws. But he could not refute the softening of Lady Ailsa's face as her cousin spoke.

"Gregor, you are—"

"—right. And you know it. I've never known you to let pride get in the way of common sense. Now is not the time for that to change."

She looked past her cousin and eyed Nik in a cool, considering way that took him in from head to toe, as if she were measuring his very soul.

He set his jaw and met her look for look, fighting the desire to storm into the night and be through with them all. He might have done so, too, but with a suddenness that was surprising to everyone, Ailsa gave a rueful shake of her head, her thick braid swinging. "You are right, Gregor. I let my temper get the best of me."

"It is a very emotional issue; lives are at stake. It is no wonder tempers are hot." He turned to Nik. "Your Highness—"

"Please, call me Nik. If we are going to be fellow travelers, we might as well do so as friends."

The young man looked pleased. "I'm Gregor, then. Come. The stew will be ready in a bit. In the meantime, do tell me about these horses of yours. I've never seen their like before."

Nik allowed Gregor to pull him aside, but he met Ailsa's eyes over the man's head. Unflinching, she stared back. After a second, her lashes dropped to shadow her gaze, her lips curling in a smug smile as if she were empowered by her newfound belief that she could change his mind. *I am not so easily swayed, little one. Not by you or any other female.*

Over the years he'd met women who had tried to charm him, many who had irritated him, some who'd offered brief respite from the world, but not one had *interested* him. Now, he found himself intrigued by a woman. Intrigued, challenged, and *interested*. She was no social butterfly intent on using his rank to raise her station, nor a faithless soul to be used to gather information about her family or inattentive husband. She was a woman of strength of character and a too-strong sense of ethical righteousness. *Yet still . . . that kiss. I cannot forget it.*

There was something there, something sensual and . . . bloody hell, he had no idea what else, but he was going to find out.

Mackenzie gushed over D'yoval, asking a million questions, which Nik answered as patiently as he could, while he watched Ailsa, who was now adding wood to the fire, the light of the flames flickering over her face as she spoke with Stewart.

And suddenly Nik was imagining all the ways he would kiss away Ailsa's superior smile. *She will not win this battle,* he decided, hiding his own grin. *I have weapons, and I shall use them all.*

Chapter 9

The next morning, they arose, washed in the nearby stream, ate a cold breakfast of dried venison, and then mounted up and left camp. The morning was frigid and damp, and the trail was arduous and growing even more difficult. Though wider than the previous day's, it was also steeper, and they had to get off their mounts and lead them up several long stretches.

Nik found himself following directly behind Ailsa and her cousin as they rode beside one another, and he was treated to several hours of their shared memories, most of which seemed to center around hunting trips, holidays, and numerous family dinners. Nik didn't mind one minute of it. Every tidbit he discovered about Lady Ailsa was ammunition for winning his way in their ongoing battle.

From listening to her speak with Gregor, Nik discovered that because of her mother's long illness, Ailsa had been left on her own from a very young age. That explained her maturity and directness. He also learned that she had no interest in society life, and was quite content buried in the countryside at Castle Leod. That surprised him, for he'd thought a woman of her obvious intelligence would need more to keep her interest.

Her voice warmed when she spoke of her home, and it made him miss his family's home in the mountains, where they often retreated during the winters. Called the Winter Palace, it was far smaller than their home in the capital, and the hall's rugs and walls bore the marks of the thousand and one childhood battles when he and his brothers played with their wooden swords and peg horses.

He shook the memories away, surprised to find himself indulging in such thoughts, for he rarely dwelled on what had been. He had too much invested in the present to waste time on the past. He turned his attention back to Lady Ailsa, and this time he noted how well she rode, and the quality of her mount. What her horse lacked in beauty, it made up for in solid footing, even on slick mountain trails.

They rode on and on, finally coming to a halt in early evening to set up camp. Rurik, who'd ridden ahead, had selected the location on a ridge over the glen below, but protected from the winds by a thick stand of silver-barked aspens.

Nik dismounted with the others and handed his reins to Rurik, who took the two horses to one side of the camp, where he and Gregor began to bed the horses down for the night. Ailsa stretched as she climbed down off St. George, and Nik knew she'd be sore come morning. They all would be.

MacKean claimed first watch, while Stewart quickly

started a fire. Nik watched as Ailsa collected the bedrolls from the discarded saddles and began spreading them out, making certain each area was free of small rocks and twigs before rolling out the furs and blankets.

She was a graceful woman, this Ailsa of Castle Leod. She moved in a way that made him wish to see her on the dance floor. And in his bed.

He found a fallen log not far from the fire and sat upon it, continuing to watch her. Though it was cold, the setting sun lit the campsite and warmed strands of her dark blond hair to deep gold, flickering over her cheeks and tracing the line of her nose.

Her nose said so much about her character—fearless, determined, *bold*. Was her nose the true tell of her character, or her too-stubborn chin? He had yet to find out.

He noticed how she placed his bedroll on the complete opposite side of the fire from hers. Amused at her caution, he held his hands to the blaze.

In the process of rolling out her bed, she rocked back on her heels and frowned. "Pardon me, but dinnae you have something to do?"

"Do you need help?"

"Nae, but there are plenty of chores to be done. You should pick one and see to it."

Tending the fire nearby, Stewart turned a bark of laughter into a cough.

Nik sent him a scathing look under his lashes and then turned back to Ailsa. "I am free to do whatever you suggest." Truthfully, he hadn't thought about helping, but as he looked about the camp where everyone scurried to complete various chores before dark, it dawned on him that perhaps he should indeed be assisting. "Should I get more firewood?"

She nodded. "It's going to be verrah cold tonight."

"Verrah," Stewart agreed.

Nik got back to his feet. "Then I'll fetch some." He had started to walk into the woods when Stewart cleared his throat.

Nik looked back to see the huntsman holding up a small ax.

"You might need this."

"So I might." He returned for the ax, and then left to fetch the wood, a bit chagrined he hadn't thought to help without being chided. Was Ailsa right when she'd suggested that his position had given him certain expectations? Had he become spoiled? It was an uncomfortable thought, but he was soothed by the realization that he didn't mind assisting; he rather enjoyed it, in fact. It just hadn't dawned on him that he should do so.

As he chopped some fallen branches into more manageable pieces, the fresh scent of partially dried wood tickling his nose, he realized that the few times he traveled in the wild, he'd never been without a retinue of servants. They'd cared for the horses, set out the pallets, prepared food, set up watch—they did everything. He rarely thought of it—but now, ax in hand, firewood in a growing pile at his side, he couldn't help but do so.

Perhaps it was good in more ways than one that he'd undertaken this endeavor by himself. He finished chopping the final branch and straightened, enjoying the smell of the fresh wood chips fanned across the ground, and grinning to think what his brothers would say to see him so engaged. Nik hung the ax on his belt, collected the wood, and carried it back to camp.

Ailsa had finished rolling out the pallets and was heating a kettle on Stewart's hook, a small tin of tea sitting nearby.

Nik stacked the wood beside the fire. It took him two trips, and he was rather proud of the healthy stack by the time he finished.

He returned the ax to Stewart and then looked at Ailsa. "Is there anything more to be done?"

She looked as if she wished she could think of something, but finally she said in a rather disappointed tone, "I dinnae believe so."

"Good." Nik took a seat nearby. "I'll have some tea, too, if you've enough."

"I'm making some for everyone." She said the words as if she couldn't imagine not doing just that.

It dawned on him that her approach to leading her men was as opposite his own as it could be. In a way, she saw herself as an equal, but one with responsibilities, rather than their superior. She rarely issued orders, and he had the impression that were one of her men to disagree with her, she would listen and perhaps even change her mind, if the argument to do so were strong enough.

The kettle tapped loudly as the water began to boil, and, wrapping her hand in her cloak, she lifted the kettle and poured steaming water into the waiting cups. He watched as she made the tea, and soon she held a cup his way.

He took it, wincing a little at the hot cup, before he wrapped it in his muffler and settled back with it. Rurik and Gregor came to join them, and even MacKean made a brief stop to fetch himself a cup before returning to his post.

The tea was weak compared to the type Nik and his countrymen typically drank. In the morning, he'd make them some of his grandmother's tea; he doubted they'd ever be satisfied with this tepid stuff again. *Tata Natasha would be proud of that.*

From across the fire, Ailsa saw the prince's face tighten as he stared into his cup, his expression growing as dark as the encroaching night.

She shouldn't care what he thought. She barely knew him, and he'd done nothing to endear himself to her. He wouldn't have done one single chore if she hadn't chided him. Yet she couldn't ignore his seemingly genuine concern. "What is it?" The words slipped over her lips before she realized she was going to say them.

Nik looked up from his cup, irritation crossing his face.

She thought it wasn't with her, but with himself, for allowing his thoughts to show.

He shrugged. "It is nothing."

She raised her brows and waited, but he didn't offer another word.

Gregor asked Rurik about winters in Oxenburg and how they compared to those in Scotland, a topic that gained Stewart's attention. Ailsa noted this left Nik alone with his thoughts. From his expression, she thought perhaps his worries were growing with the darkness.

Worry was like that; it gnawed upon one in the quiet. She should know; she spent a lot of her time worrying. Was she doing enough? Too much? Had she thought of everything? Should she ask for advice more often, and if so, from whom? She worried more than she should, and yet it was because she cared—she didn't just want to do well with Castle Leod, she was determined to do so, no matter the cost.

Thus, she recognized the worry now settled on Nik's face. Ailsa moved a little closer to him. "You are thinking aboot your grandmother."

His jaw tightened. "Perhaps."

She raised her eyebrows.

He grimaced. "Fine. *Da*. I was. But I do not like that you know what I am thinking."

"I worry aboot the captives, too. All the time."

His gaze met hers. "We must rescue them."

She managed a smile, and for a moment, she didn't feel quite so alone. "So we must."

The prince murmured his agreement, and they fell silent, lost in their own thoughts. The night darkened and the men continued to talk, moving closer to the other side of the fire. Stewart reheated the leftover stew, the fragrant smell lifting over the camp.

"I hope she is safe."

Nik's words were so quiet, Ailsa thought for a moment that she hadn't heard them.

He set his empty cup on a rock. "She is very old, though she does not like that mentioned."

"My grandmother cannae stand us to mention that, either."

Nik nodded, his gaze flickering past her to the forest. "I cannot imagine her traversing such rough country. I assume Lord Hamilton is the same age?"

"Aye, though he is verrah healthy. He rides almost every day, but this would be difficult for him, too. Fortunately, the prisoners dinnae use this trail."

Nik's gaze locked on her face. "Didn't they?"

"They took a gentler trail through two long valleys, most likely because the abductors knew two elderly prisoners would nae make it on this path, which is steeper."

"So we take a more direct route. Good. I do not like thinking of her suffering." He picked up a piece of wood and fed it into the fire, sparks crackling and then lifting with the ash in a curl of gray smoke that rose overhead and disappeared in the trees. "Our conversation last night . . . It was unsatisfactory on many levels."

"I would nae call it a conversation, but a regular mill." At his confused look, she explained, "A fistfight."

A faint smile curved his mouth. "*Da*. Neither of us were at our best. We have lost sight of why we are here: to help Lord Hamilton and my Tata Natasha. On that, we agree."

She couldn't argue with that.

"Ailsa." He faced her, his green eyes almost black in the rapidly growing darkness. "We must work together. If in any way our assisting one another helps, then we should—we *must*—do so."

He is right. And yet she found herself hesitating.

Could she trust him? Was this the real prince? Or the charming man who was only saying what he must to get his way? She'd seen both sides of this man—the arrogant, no-nonsense prince who ordered his men about without care, and the feckless charmer who tried to win information from her. She'd be wise to remember that first meeting.

Not that she could forget it; every time he spoke, she remembered that blasted kiss. It had been only one kiss. Just one not-that-long-of-a-kiss, but it was still so fresh in her memory that her lips still tingled from it, and her heart still raced at the mere thought.

She was surprised he couldn't hear her heartbeat; it pounded so loudly in her own ears.

Perhaps it is good we'll be in one another's company for the next week or so; being exposed to him will kill every reaction but annoyance. Last night, he'd been every inch an arrogant do-as-I-say prince. He'd attempted to take over her rescue expedition as if *he* had more of a say in it than *she.*

Ha! She was the daughter of the Earl of Cromartie; she was no one's servant to be ordered about. She could only hope their argument had disabused him of his misconceptions concerning his role in this expedition. No matter how genuine his concern for his grandmother might be, she couldn't allow his preemptory, arbitrary approach to their situation win the day.

He sighed now. "You are still angry. I see it in your eyes."

The last thing she'd wanted was for him to know

how she felt. "I'm considering your proposition. What exactly are you suggesting?"

"Something simple. We will share our information and do what we can to reach the captives."

"And then?"

"Once we have located them, then we will decide which tactic to pursue."

"And how will we decide that? I am nae guid at arm wrestling, if that's what you're thinking."

He shot her a warm, amused look. "If pressed, I could think of several better ways than mere arm wrestling to resolve an argument with you."

She dropped her gaze to the safety of her cup of tea, her face heating even in the cold. Just a few words from this man sent her imagination racing in directions she didn't even know existed. It was a dangerous power, one she hoped he never realized he held.

She cleared her throat. "And if we cannae resolve our difference of opinions?"

"We can do this, *krasavitsa*. We must at least try."

She couldn't argue with trying, could she? "Fine. But we must have a joint plan by the time we reach Kylestrome. We cannae be arguing all the way to the door."

"Agreed." He rocked back on his heels. "We will make good partners, I think."

We might, at that—providing we keep both our lips and our opinions away from one another. She would make certain they were never close enough for their lips, knees, or any other part of them to so much as brush. The opinions might take a bit more work. "We are partners, then. For now."

"Good." He leaned back, his expression still sober, although less dark. "Who do you think is behind this abduction?"

"I dinnae know." She gave a frustrated sigh. "At first I thought someone took Lord Hamilton to stir oop trouble for my family, but now I'm nae so certain."

Nik's brows rose, surprise plain on his face. "You think he is the primary target of this abduction, not my grandmother?"

"Hamilton's carriage was the one attacked. Besides, why would someone steal away with Her Grace?"

"She's a grand duchess, and extremely wealthy." He seemed about to add something else, but then shrugged. "That is enough."

"But the ransom note was nae for a verrah large sum," Ailsa pointed out. "Both Lord Hamilton and Her Grace are worth far more."

"I agree." His brows knit as he considered this. "Interesting."

"If money is nae the object, what benefit is there to be had from taking Her Grace? And why ask for a ransom at all?"

His lashes lowered until she could no longer see his eyes. "I'm sure there are reasons."

"There must be—but you dinnae seem as if you're aboot to share your ideas." She eyed him over her cup of tea. "We are partners, and yet you are already hiding something. I see how you want it: I tell you all, and you tell me nothing."

"*Nyet.* That's not how I wish it. I just—" He scowled, his gaze still on her face. "If I thought I knew something that would help us recover my grandmother and Lord Hamilton, I would share it. But I do not."

"You clearly have a theory of some sort."

"I have nothing but empty suppositions. I will tell you this: I believe there is more to this abduction than meets the eye. I just don't know what."

Whatever he was hiding, she'd find out. *Perhaps I will charm something from you, my kissable prince, and not the other way around.* The thought intrigued her more than she could say.

He raked a hand through his hair, his green eyes resting on her face. "I have a question for you."

"Aye?"

"If you thought there'd be a ransom note, why did you send Greer to track the abductors?"

"I dinnae expect a ransom. Lord Hamilton's brother is the Earl of Arran. He and my father have never been friendly. At one time, tensions were so high it seemed as if we might end oop in a clan war, which would nae be the first time for our families."

"There's a rivalry there, eh?"

"Centuries of it. It was only through Lord Hamilton's friendship with my grandmother that the conflict had cooled off a wee bit. Arran loves his brother dearly, as does anyone who meets him. Hamilton's a charmer, he is." *Much like you.*

He toyed with his teacup. "If you don't mind, can you explain what a clan is? I've heard the term, but I'm not familiar with it."

"Every family in Scotland has pledged to one of the auld families. Those are the clans."

"Ah. And if you get on the wrong side of one clan—"

"—then you get on the wrong side of all those who've pledged to them."

"I see. It sounds very confusing."

She had to fight a smile. "The Scots dinnae care if we confuse you, so long as we win every battle, even the ones we fight between ourselves."

"You're certainly a contentious people."

"Och, now you've made an enemy for life." She tried to look fierce, but had to laugh when he appeared shocked.

Seeing her grin, he gave a reluctant chuckle. "Since the war, the treaties in Europe are just as difficult— everyone is pledged to everyone else until there's a tangle so thick, you cannot sneeze without setting off a wave of discontent amongst your neighbors."

"Aye, it can raise tensions, but it can also provide small families some protections, and that was the original intent."

"But if it leads to war, then no one is safer." He shook his head. "I sometimes think we are too attached to the ideals of what our countries are, rather than to the people who live in them. There's a certain amount of pride involved in any war, a strict nationalism that is as aggressive as a rabid dog."

"If the Scots excel at anything, 'tis pride. We believe in three things: the power of God, the sanctity of the family name, and the strength of our clan vows. If you break faith with any of those, you open the door to a war that could go on for so long, nae one remembers what began it."

"How do you know which clan is which?"

"We've our own histories and tartans." Her smile faded. "Someone left a torn bit of our Mackenzie tartan at the scene of the abduction, tucked under the coach wheel as if someone's kilt had been caught during the attack."

Nik whistled silently. "So someone wanted to point a finger your way. But that's so obvious—unbelievably so. You might as well leave a signed letter. Couldn't you write Arran and tell him all of this? Surely he'd realize how unlikely such a happenstance must be."

"The last words the earl spoke to my father included the phrases 'dirty liar,' 'bloody fool,' and 'treasonous traitor.'" She nodded when Nik's brows rose. "Aye, 'twas an ugly meeting, that. I'll spare you the phrases my father used in return, for they were nae any better. Arran always believes the worst of the Mackenzies. That makes things difficult."

The prince was quiet for a long while. "When you demanded to be left to run this venture, I thought it was because you were—" He waved a hand, obviously searching for a word.

"Difficult?" she suggested drily.

"That, and bossy, and overly concerned with being in charge." He winced at her sharp expression. "I'm sorry. It was not the most flattering thing to think."

"Worse, it was wrong. I am nae a despot."

"I know. I assumed the worst, and the fault is mine. It never dawned on me there might be legitimate reasons you wished to have the operation under your control. But now I see that it's a delicate situation for you and your clan."

She'd never expected to hear such an admission from him. "Which is why I dinnae wish to rush in, pistols blazing. Lord Hamilton has been a friend of our family for decades. He is verrah dear to my grandmother— and to yours, I should add. For his sake, and the sake of peace, we must do what we can to return him to his family unharmed."

Nik rubbed his chin thoughtfully. "From what you've told me, Arran stands to win the most if 'tis proven—even falsely—that your family abducted his brother."

"He'll have a valid reason to attack Castle Leod, and the crown will do naught since they dinnae get involved in what they call Scotland's 'family matters.' Family matters, my arse." She sent him a quick look, her cheeks turning pinker. "I'm sorry. I should nae have said that."

"I was shocked, but I've decided to shed my tears of horror in private."

She shot him a surprised grin and then laughed. She had the warmest, huskiest laugh he'd ever heard, each note a seduction. He was slammed with a powerful desire to slip an arm about her waist and kiss the laughter from her lips.

Collecting his thoughts, he managed to say, "So, do you think this abduction is a plan of the earl's? That he abducted his own brother?"

"I dinnae know." She sighed and pulled her knees close, clasping her arms about them. "Someone else might wish to stir things oop, and it could be that the earl is as much a puppet as we are."

Nik nodded. "So, believing the abduction was a ploy of some type, you sent your best tracker after the prisoners, hoping to locate and rescue them quickly and defuse the situation before it became public knowledge."

She shrugged. "What else could I do? I dinnae wish this known; the quicker it is resolved, the less dangerous it becomes."

He had to approve; it was exactly what he would have done. He frowned, a thought catching him. "In the note you sent me, you said you would alert the constable if you did not find the prisoners soon."

"Och, I only wrote that so you would nae come running to Castle Leod. I thought if you believed the constable was on the verge of being called in, then your grandmother's plight was in guid hands and there was nothing more to be done but wait on the ootcome."

"It only made me come the quicker."

"So it seems. Had I known you were so fond of your grandmother, I would have written a verrah different note." The wind blew some tendrils of her hair across her cheek and she pushed them away. "That missing outrider from Hamilton's coach bothers me."

"That caught my attention, too."

"Aye. He must have helped the abductors, or he would have been left at the attack site like the others." She pursed her lips. "And why take elderly prisoners such a distance as Kylestrome? Why not hold them somewhere closer? I dinnae understand the need for this lengthy trip."

Nik nodded. Was someone trying to draw one of

them out? But which one? And why? Was his negotiation with the tsar the target? Or was this indeed a plot concocted by the Earl of Arran or someone to start a clan war? If so, was there an ambush down the trail, one intended for Ailsa? If the earl wished to truly start a clan war, then a swift retaliation for the taking of his brother would do it. *Bloody hell, the more I find out, the less I know.*

Ailsa sighed, her breath puffing white in the growing cold. "See? It dinnae make sense. And the ransom request only confuses the issue. I cannae accept that a mere two hundred guineas will make all of this right again."

"Yet you still intend on delivering it."

"I have to at least try. Besides, even if it doesn't free the prisoners, the exchange could tell us something." She picked up her cup and sipped her tea, which must have been cold by now, although she didn't seem to mind.

He watched as thoughts flickered over her expressive face. After a moment, she cut him a sharp look. "So, Prince, I've told you all I know, but you have nae shared a thing. You were surprised to find that I believed Lord Hamilton the target of this abduction, which means you assumed it was your grandmother. Why do you think that?"

She *had* shared her thoughts with him, and quite willingly. In all fairness, he should tell her his purpose in being here, that he feared someone was trying to interfere with what he hoped would be a groundbreaking treaty that could benefit hundreds of thousands of people. That he must regain his grandmother's freedom quickly, so that he could conduct the coming delicate negotiations without hesitation or distractions.

But before he opened his mouth, caution stilled his tongue. Those secrets weren't his to share. They belonged to his country and to his title. He'd been taught this over and over as a child, and had lived with it for years and years as an adult. *Never share more than is necessary. It will only bring regrets.*

Still, he couldn't help feeling as if he were letting her down. Finally, he said, "My Tata Natasha has great wealth. Obviously someone knew this."

Her gaze narrowed. "But only two hundred guineas were requested in the ransom note," she repeated.

"I cannot explain that. I—"

"Stew is ready." Mackenzie sat down beside Ailsa and handed her one of the plates he held, steam rising into the air.

She looked over the plate at Nik. "Well?"

He sent a meaningful look at her cousin. "We will discuss this later."

Her brows knit. "Why—"

"Not now, Lady Ailsa," Nik said firmly.

Mackenzie blinked. "I'm sorry. Did I interrupt—"

"Nae, nae." Ailsa picked up her spoon, sending Nik a flat look, as if she knew he was using the interruption to his advantage and the knowledge disappointed her. "We were done."

Rurik brought Nik a plate of stew, and soon everyone was gathered about the fire, the only sound the scraping of spoons on metal plates.

Still, Nik could not forget Ailsa's expression. It

nipped at him, that disappointed look, and made him wish he could share his thoughts. But he wasn't here to make friends, or to tempt an engagingly honest lady into exchanging confidences.

He was here to save his grandmother and that damned treaty, in that order.

And if that meant he lost Ailsa's regard, tentative as it was, then so be it.

Jaw set, he dug into his plate of stew, fighting the urge to look across the fire into the silver-gray eyes he knew followed his every move.

Chapter 10

The next morning dawned crystal cold, the air burning as one breathed it. Buried deep in fur-lined bedding, Ailsa pulled the blankets over her mouth and nose, drawing her knees to her. Even that small movement had her muscles protesting. *All that riding yesterday. Now I'm as stiff as a board.*

Perhaps she should stay still a while longer. She'd just rest until— An odd noise grated in the quiet. Was someone scraping metal over a rock?

She opened her eyes. Stooped by the fire, his cloak hanging from his broad shoulders and pooling on the ground around him, was Nik. As she watched, the morning sun broke through the thick cover of clouds and flooded the campsite with a yellow glow that lit his shoulders and black hair with golden lights.

It was fitting, she decided sourly, for he reminded her more and more of a lion. A large, pompous, opinionated lion.

The clouds converged and stole away the golden light. She glanced about the camp. The other bedrolls were empty, which made her grimace. She should have been first up, blast it. She might not have slept so late had Stewart not snored through most of the night as if he were sawing enough logs to make a shed.

Her gaze moved back to the snapping fire. A pot hung from the hook—porridge, from the smell of it. The flames had been stoked, and they licked at the fire ring. One rock had been moved into the flames until it glowed red, another pot sitting on it, piping out a steady stream of steam. The scraping sound that had woken her must have come from the tin cup now resting in the prince's hand. He set the cup back down, making no effort to muffle the noise.

Apparently "quiet" was not a word found in the prince's vocabulary. *He is nae a "prince" for this excursion, though*, she thought with satisfaction. *Just Nik, a lowly groom.* In no way did the strong, simple name describe this man. He was far too complex, and far more confusing than the name implied.

She watched him through her lashes as he removed his glove and folded it in half, and then used it to pick up a worn kettle. Steam curled from the spout as he lifted the lid and peered inside. As he did so, he glanced in her direction.

She closed her eyes, hoping he hadn't seen her looking at him. The last thing she wanted to do was add to his too-large pride. Still, it was hard not to stare at him. He was just so very *watchable*. Too much so.

She heard the *thunk* as he replaced the kettle on the hot rock, and then silence once again.

What's he doing now? She cracked her eyes open again

and found him still by the fire, his face in profile as he lifted his cup and took a sip.

The steam curled up, a wisp brushing over his face as his lips touched the warm metal of his cup. She found herself remembering those lips on hers, the heat and pressure of his mouth and how he'd slid his tongue over her bottom lip—

She shoved the memory away. If she wished to lure information from his lips—the very ones she'd once kissed—she'd have to keep her wits about her. It was time *someone* stood up to this man, and she was more than happy for it to be her. Why, if she had her way—

"Your eyebrows are knit so tightly I worry you might get a headache."

Blast it! She gave him a sour look. "I never get a headache," she lied. And then she rolled onto her side, turning her shoulder to him, even though the movement made her eyes water with pain from her stiff muscles.

"*Krasavitsa*, if you wish your tea warm, you must rise. It is good tea and will brighten your morning."

The only thing that could brighten her morning would be if she turned back over and discovered that the prince was nothing more than a bad dream. But that was highly unlikely to happen. Besides, she had little doubt that even if he were nothing more than a dream, he'd be one of those annoying ones that lingered long enough to cast a pall over the entire day.

She turned onto her back, biting her lip against the complaints of her legs. "Where is everyone?"

"Nearby. Chores took them away." Nik folded his riding glove once more and used it to pick up the pot as he found an empty cup. As he filled it, his gaze flickered to her. "Are you getting up now? Or do you still pretend to sleep?"

"I was nae pretending; I was stretching my legs under the blankets before I arose." She gritted her teeth and sat, pulling her blankets and furs with her. "I see I'm the last one oop."

"By only a few minutes." Nik grinned, his eyes crinkling. "Your cousin was also a— How do you say it? A bed slug?"

"A slugabed." She pulled the furs closer. She was warmer inside the bedding than she'd be out of it.

Nik held the cup toward her, grinning. "Here. Drink this soon, or the cold will steal its heat."

Which meant she had to rise and put up with her pained legs, the bitter cold, and an annoyingly cheerful-in-the-morning Nik.

She'd lived her whole life in a drafty old castle that, from September to May, was never truly warm. She knew from experience that the best thing to do was to bolt from a warm bed and face the cold quickly.

Holding her breath, she threw back the cover to grab her cloak where it was spread over her pallet. She gasped as the cold air hit her like an icy wall, grimacing as her calves complained.

She tugged the cloak about her and, for good measure, wrapped the top fur over that.

A soft chuckle from the prince made her flash a glum look his way.

He threw up a hand as if to protect himself. "You cannot walk in all of that."

Her first step proved him right; the heavy fur curled about her, holding her feet prisoner. She had to kick, step, kick, step, kick, step her way to the fire. *This is good for my stiff legs at least*, she told herself through clenched teeth.

She knew she must look ridiculous, but she didn't care. Her shivering body refused to allow mere pride to get in the way of warmth.

She sank onto the log Stewart had placed by the fire the night before, and reached for the tea Nik held out.

He placed the mug in her hands, the warmth tingling and welcome, soothing her shivers. His bold gaze swept over her. "Sore, eh?"

"I'm only stiff." She sniffed with what she hoped was queenly dignity. "Thank you for the tea." Her voice was morning-husky and not nearly as repressive as she wished.

"You're quite welcome. Seeing your dance made it worth my while."

She didn't deign to answer; instead she sipped her tea. The instant it touched her tongue, bitterness filled her mouth. "Bless me," she choked. "What *is* this?"

"It's Romany tea, like my grandmother makes. It is not the weak drivel you drink here."

She stared into the cup, thinking it was strong enough to stare back. "I'm surprised it has nae eaten its way through the tin."

"Drink it. It's warm and it's good for your—" He patted his stomach. "When you eat."

"Your digestion. I find that hard to believe." But the tea was hot, so she took another sip and realized that there was a hint of spiciness to it. *That's . . . not bad.* "Does everyone in your country drink this, or only the auld, who've nae taste left in their ancient mouths?"

He chuckled and reached for the kettle to refill his cup. "Everyone drinks it—men, women, children. It is good for you. The Romany live long, long lives."

"If they can withstand this every morning, they must be hearty indeed." She looked around. "Did the others drink some of this, too?"

"Not yet, but they will like it."

"If it dinnae kill them first." She smiled when he sent her a pretend affronted look. "Where is everyone?"

He nodded toward the forest. "Rurik is scouting ahead. Stewart is on watch, while MacKean and Gregor ready the horses. I'm surprised you could sleep through all the noise we made."

"And you?"

He cleared his throat as if about to make an important announcement. "I collected the morning wood for the fire. And without being asked."

"That's kind of you." She meant it, too.

"I'm learning." He looked a little stiff, as if he were about to say something of vast import. "I'm not used to traveling in such a manner, and I fear I am a bit rusty on the etiquette. Thank you for pointing that out."

"You're welcome." She had to smile a little at his uncomfortable expression. He always seemed so certain of everything. It was somehow reassuring to see him offset, though she couldn't help but wonder if he were indeed sincere. She looked at him through the steam that rose from her tea. "How long have you been oop?"

"I arose with the others. Stewart started the porridge before he left." Nik cupped his mug in his large hand, the vessel too small for him to wrap both hands around it as she'd been able to do. "When Rurik and the others return, we will have breakfast."

She nodded, noting how the smoke of the fire created a veil between them. They seemed destined to be on opposing sides, she and this stubborn, pampered, confusing prince. Yet as he sat by the fire, a nicked metal cup in his hand, his face stubbled, his hair mussed from sleep, he looked . . . normal. Like any man might look. *Any man who was devastatingly handsome.* The scruffiness became him, softening the taut line of his jaw and making her palm itch to run her hand along it.

His gaze met hers, a satisfied twinkle in his eyes, and Ailsa was suddenly aware of how she must look— sleep-wrinkled and ruffled, her braid frayed.

She placed her mug on one of the rocks ringing the fire and smoothed back the loose strands that tickled her neck and cheeks.

He watched, a smile curving his mouth. "You look fine, *krasavitsa*. More than fine."

That, she did not believe. "What is this *krasavitsa*? Is it something rude?"

He chuckled. "*Nyet*. It is merely what I call you, as it becomes you. You do not like it? It is a beautiful word."

"I dinnae know what it means, so I have nae opinion one way or the other." She fumbled with her braid, her hair tangled near the tie. She pushed the braid over her shoulder impatiently. She couldn't do anything about it without her comb and mirror, which would require rising and walking, and her legs bitterly protested the idea.

She'd better move, lest she lock into place. Gritting her teeth, she stretched her legs toward the fire, fighting to keep the blanket and cloak over them.

Nik seemed to note her every move. "We covered a lot of ground yesterday. How many more days do we travel until we meet this Greer?"

"Four, five, hopefully nae more. It depends on the weather and the condition of the trail."

She sipped the tea, managing to swallow it this time without scrunching her nose. By God, if he could stomach this brutal drink, so could she. "Last night Stewart said he expected it would warm some today, so the snow will melt and make the trail slick and dangerous."

"That will slow us."

The wind stirred and she pulled the blanket more closely around her and held out her mug. "More tea, if you dinnae mind."

He filled the mug with the steaming brew. "It is not as evil as you originally thought, is it?"

"I'd have drunk molten lead just to warm my fingers. I—"

A rustling in the shrubbery announced the arrival of Stewart. The huge man muttered a greeting and knelt by the porridge, pulling off the lid.

"Is it done?" Ailsa asked. "I'm famished."

"'Tis guid enough," the hunter answered.

She sniffed. "I can smell the cinnamon, and you know how I love that."

The burly hunter beamed. "It adds a nice taste, din-nae it?"

Watching them, Nik found himself intrigued. The smile Ailsa shared with her servant was brighter and more open than any she'd shared with him. In some ways, she concealed her thoughts and feelings as much as he did, but only with him, which irked him far more than it should have.

The leaves crunched as Ailsa's cousin appeared. Neatly dressed, his brown hair combed above his recently shaved face, he looked as if he were ready for a formal hunt rather than a fireside bowl of porridge. He sat beside Ailsa with the ease of long familiarity, groaning as he did so. "I feel as if someone beat me with a log. How are you?"

She shrugged. "A little stiff. Nae bad."

Liar. You don't like to admit to weakness, do you? That was something he should remember.

Mackenzie peered into his cousin's mug. "There's tea!"

"Of a sort," Ailsa murmured, sending Nik a teasing glance from under her lashes.

"It is good tea," Nik said firmly. He fixed a cup for both Mackenzie and Stewart.

Mackenzie grasped the warm cup eagerly, took a bold sip, and choked. "That's—that's—good God!" He wiped his mouth with the back of his gloved hand.

"It's what?" Nik asked in a flat tone.

Mackenzie blinked. "It's—it's quite good, but I'm not used to such—" He pressed a hand to his throat.

Ailsa chuckled. "That's almost exactly what I said on drinking it."

Stewart sent a dismissive glance at young Mackenzie and calmly drank his tea, his broad face expressionless.

Nik held up the pot and asked the younger man, "Would you like more?"

"No, thank you. I still have some." Mackenzie took a sip of what he had left, although Nik suspected the lad merely pretended to drink. "How far will we attempt to go today? Has it been discussed?"

Ailsa answered. "Stewart and I spoke last night. We'd like to camp just south of Loch Glascarnoch, if possible."

"Loch Glascar-what?" Nik asked. The names the Scots gave places and people made his tongue tire. "Had it been up to me, I would have given it a longer, more tangled name, just to keep foreigners from pronouncing it correctly. But Glascar-whatever-that-was will have to do."

Stewart snorted a laugh.

"How long will it take us to reach this loch?" Mackenzie asked, stretching out his legs.

Stewart sent him a glance from under his bushy red brows. "Most of the day. I dinnae think we'll make it as far as the loch, but MacKean wants to try."

"I hope it's safe, with the wet trail," Mackenzie said.

"Aye, and 'twill slow us doon if you fall off the mountain, too, so dinnae do that."

A shadow passed over Mackenzie's face.

Nik swallowed his grin, seeing that Mackenzie's pride had been wounded by the huntsman's barbed humor. "What about these brigands you've mentioned? Should we worry about them?"

Stewart pulled some metal plates from his saddlebag and began to spoon the thick porridge onto each one. "They're here. We've seen signs, but only auld ones."

"I'll keep my pistols primed," Nik said.

Ailsa said, "We'll need a guard oop front and one in the rear."

"Rurik and I can follow behind and provide protection." Nik poured himself more tea and then held the kettle out to Ailsa.

She shook her head and put her empty cup on the ground near her feet. The tea had warmed her, and she was definitely now wide-awake. Bitter or not, it had been effective. "Tell me, have you ever performed guard duty?"

"Aye. Not recently, perhaps, but enough. It would surprise you, all of the tasks I can do if I set my mind to it."

His gaze flickered over her and she instantly thought of several "tasks" a lady should never think of. Fighting her heated cheeks, she said, "I am surprised to hear that."

"My life is not all dress balls and routs, you know."

"But I daresay it has been *mainly* dress balls and routs." She hid a grin at his irritated expression.

All he said was, "Perhaps. Do not ask me to reveal all my secrets."

As if merely asking him would reveal anything. Ha!

Stewart handed her a plate of porridge and she ate, watching the prince from under her lashes as he spoke to Stewart, noting how Nik became more jocular and far less serious as he spoke with the Scotsman.

She wondered how it would have been had they

met in the sedate confines of a ballroom in London or Edinburgh. No doubt he wouldn't have paid her the slightest heed, nor she him. She was not a beauty, nor wealthy, nor politically important, all things that set a woman apart from the masses of husband-seekers who crowded the ballrooms of the world. She would have been politely ignored by him and others, while he would have been fêted and pursued. And she would have been quite content with that.

But here, sitting across a fire in a harsh Highlands winter, they were equals. She was glad she'd met him under these circumstances, dire though they were.

Ailsa finished her porridge and put down her plate as Rurik rode back into camp. Gregor arose to take the guard's horse, and Rurik joined them fireside.

"What did you find?" Nik asked the guard.

"It is steep, more so than yesterday. We'll have to dismount and lead the horses in places."

Stewart grunted in agreement. "It's likely to get worse after we pass Loch Glascarnoch. We have to travel along the slopes of Beinn Dearg, and I hear 'tis straight oop and down in places."

"Wonderful." Gregor sat back beside Ailsa, wincing as he did so.

Her gaze found the prince once again and she wondered that he didn't seem the least stiff from their journey. His physical strength was exceptional. Stooped beside the fire, his breeches stretched over his thighs in a way that showed his muscular—

"An impressive specimen, isn't he?" Gregor's voice was quiet so that only she could hear.

She flushed, but managed a shrug. "Keep your friends close . . ."

He grinned. "And your enemies closer. Always good advice."

Stewart arose. "I'll relieve MacKean and send him for breakfast. We should leave when we can." Without waiting for the others to voice an agreement, he lumbered off.

A few moments later, MacKean arrived and the porridge pot was emptied. Afterward, Ailsa and Gregor took the dirty plates and cups to the stream to wash. By the time they returned to camp, everything had been cleared away, the fire stamped out and covered, and the bedding neatly tied behind the saddles.

She noted that the prince's and Rurik's bedrolls had far thicker furs than the others. Was Oxenburg even colder than Scotland? "Guid lord, what a frigid clime must that be," she muttered to herself.

Gregor, who'd brought St. George to her, raised his brows. "What clime?"

She explained her thoughts and he glanced at the bedrolls with a considering gaze. "Rurik told me it's mountainous there. It would explain why they don't seem the least daunted by this journey." He nodded to where Nik stood talking to Rurik. "Not to be rude, but I keep asking myself, why is *he* here? And if the prince *is* going to be here, why did he arrive the way he did?"

"What do you mean? He cares aboot his grandmother."

"So why didn't he bring his guard? If our grandmother had been abducted and I had an entire squadron at my command, you can wager your last farthing that I'd have raced to the rescue with every able-bodied soldier I could find. I'd ride at their head, sword drawn, and ready to fight."

Ailsa looked over St. George's back at Nik. She remembered now how he'd arrived at Castle Leod to begin with, an entire squadron escorting him and his grandmother for her visit. "That does seem more princely. Instead he snuck in, disguised as a groom."

"And with only two men to assist him. I wonder if he really wishes to find the duchess." Gregor grimaced. "I sound like our grandmother, don't I? Always seeing the worst in everyone."

"You sound nothing like Edana—you have nae made a single comment aboot how anyone is dressed."

Gregor laughed.

"I think he cares for his grandmother; I've seen it in his eyes. So he must have his reasons," she continued. "The question is whether he'll share them with us."

MacKean called for them to mount up, and Gregor sighed. "Here we go."

He bent and cupped his hands, and Ailsa let her cousin assist her into the saddle.

She almost cried out as her sore muscles met the stiff saddle, but she managed to swallow it. Which was a good thing, for at that exact time, the prince and Rurik rode past on their way to the back of the line. As he went by, Nik's eyes locked with hers and he inclined his head, a devilish half smile on his lips.

She nodded and quickly tore her gaze away, even that small, casual encounter making her heart sputter.

She would solve the mysteries that surrounded this man no matter what it took. *But cautiously, for I've no wish to be caught in his charming trap.*

As Gregor mounted his own horse with a grimace of pain, she said, "Thankfully, we've only a few more days' travel to reach Greer's camp. 'Tis but a short distance to the road from there, and it will not be so grueling then."

"I hope so."

"Dinnae fret. Greer and Douglas have nae been sitting idle, so we'll have a better idea of what's ahead."

"Douglas is with Greer? He's a big brute. He makes Stewart look like a mouse."

"Aye. He might come in handy when we go to deliver the ransom."

Gregor started to say something else, but MacKean lifted his arm and they were on their way, filing one by one into the deep forest, the gray sky watching.

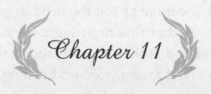

Chapter 11

That day, they rode from dawn till dusk, forced by the steepness of the terrain to lead the horses much of the way. When night began to fall, they hurriedly set up camp beside a small mountain loch. Nik watched Ailsa all day, admiring her fortitude. Even Rurik was stiff from their exertions, and he was a man of iron strength. Everyone complained but Ailsa.

And yet Nik saw the tiredness in her eyes and re-alized she was as exhausted as the rest of them. She almost fell asleep during their early-evening meal, and after picking at her food, set it aside and then eagerly climbed into her bedding.

She was asleep the second her eyes closed, and Nik watched her while the others sat around the fire and told tall tales of their hunting prowess.

She intrigued him, this earl's daughter with the heart of a warrior. If there was an easier but slower route, she chose the harder one. If there was a question to be faced that might assist them in some future moment, she charged at it without a blink. If there was a difficult or distasteful chore that had to be done, she went about

it without complaint and with a stubbornness that
brooked no argument. Contrary as it was, the stronger
she seemed, the more he felt the need to protect her.

Thus it was that this morning he'd risen well before her, and had stoked the fire and made tea. He'd
watched as she'd arisen, sore and aching, tears rising
when she stood, swiping them away in the hopes no
one had noticed.

They all had, though—every jack man of them. Nik
knew from the surreptitious looks the others had sent
her way.

When they'd readied to leave, Nik had to fight the
urge to pull her up in front of him on D'yoval, that she
might rest against him for at least a portion of the day.
She would fit perfectly against him, her head tucked
under his chin.

But he knew she would scoff at such an offer. He was
learning a lot about this woman, things that could be
useful during their future negotiations.

Now they'd reached a less steep but narrower sec-
tion of the trail, and had been forced to ride much of
the afternoon single file, which was not to his liking.
He wanted to talk to her, find out what had given her
such fortitude.

He fixed his gaze on Ailsa's back, her dark blond
braid swinging in a most beguiling manner. The sun
had finally banished the clouds to allow a flood of pale
winter sunlight to filter down through the branches of
the swaying pines. Since it was no longer shivery cold,
the snow now melted in earnest. They were plagued by
water dripping from the tree branches, and occasional

clumps of snow that fell on heads and shoulders. At times, the trail itself was obliterated by melted rivulets that trickled together to form small streams.

As the afternoon went on, they had to dismount time and again and lead the animals over slick rocky inclines. Much like the day before, it was slow, grueling work. From where he rode near the end of the line, Nik watched in appreciation as Ailsa doggedly scrambled up the trail leading St. George. Even his grandmother, with her deep love of the unconventional, could not have faulted Ailsa's stalwart efforts.

She was a damned good rider, too, and dealt expertly with her mule-headed animal. St. George remained calm even on the most uncertain terrain, and never once balked. He did better than high-stepping D'yoval, who disliked the slick trail and had to be reminded more than once who was in charge.

By late afternoon, they were all muddy and tired, everyone showing signs of exhaustion. Earlier on, Ailsa and Gregor had been talking to one another, teasing and joking, while Stewart and MacKean had talked about hunting and the signs they'd seen as they rode. But as the sun sank, all conversation withered.

It was now two hours before sunset, and they were fording a shallow stream one at a time, the snowmelt pure and cold as it rushed over mossy stones before disappearing down a narrow gully. As Nik guided his horse out of the water, he caught sight of Ailsa swaying the tiniest bit in the saddle, one hand fisted into a ball and pressed into her thigh.

St. George must have felt her waver, too, for he

pulled up and then looked back at her, as if questioning what she'd meant by such a motion.

Nik's jaw hardened. "We will camp here," he announced.

Everyone pulled up and looked back at him with varying expressions of surprise.

"Now?" Stewart asked, his brows tight with disapproval. "There's at least two more hours of daylight."

"My horse will go no farther." Nik flicked his gaze from the redheaded Scotsman to Ailsa and then back.

Stewart's sharp gaze went to his mistress and he gave a nod. "Then we should nae press him."

"But—" MacKean began.

"The animals need the rest," Stewart said firmly.

Ailsa frowned. "But we're nowhere close to where we hoped to make camp."

MacKean, after exchanging a look with Stewart, shrugged. "If the horses need the rest, then we cannae continue."

"I fear we were overambitious in our pace," Nik agreed.

"Then we stop." Mackenzie rubbed his lower back. "I, for one, am glad."

Ailsa bent to pat St. George's thick neck, concern on her face. "I suppose we'll only lose an hour's travel, if that. Greer will have to wait."

"He has nobbut else to do than that," Stewart pointed out in a prosaic tone.

Nik stood in his stirrups and looked around, pointing into the woods. "There's a clearing just through that line of trees. It seems level, so hopefully it will do for camp."

"We will go there, then," Stewart said. "'Tis guid to set oop camp a wee bit early anyway, as the wood is wet and 'twill take a bit to start a fire."

Mackenzie brightened at the mention of a fire. "That would be lovely." He looked back at Nik as if to say something, but then his gaze moved on to the trail. The younger man's brows knit. "Where's Rurik?"

Nik looked behind him, not surprised the bearded guard was nowhere to be found. "He must have held back to make certain we weren't followed."

MacKean turned his horse and came down the trail to pull abreast of Nik. "Your mon was there when I looked, fifteen minutes ago or so, so he cannae be far. I'll find him and let him know we've stopped to set oop camp."

"Good. The rest of us will head for the clearing and—"

The sound of a horse churning wildly up the trail caused everyone to turn.

Rurik appeared on the trail, his face grim, his horse lathered. "Brigands."

MacKean cursed.

"They've been closing in for the last two miles. I rode slower and slower, to separate them from the rest of you. They followed, thinking I was still with the party."

"Bloody hell," Mackenzie muttered, eyes wide. Behind him, Ailsa's face had paled.

"Where are they now?" MacKean already had his rifle out and ready.

"I waited until a curve in the trail blocked me from

their sight, and then I guided my horse into the woods and waited for them."

"Och, you challenged them by yourself, eh?" Mac-Kean looked impressed.

Rurik's teeth flashed in his bearded face. "They were very surprised to see me."

"How many?" Nik asked grimly.

"Three, perhaps four. They scattered into the woods like rats."

"Of course they did," Stewart scoffed. "Cowards, all of 'em." He loosened his blunderbuss from where it was strapped to his saddle and checked that it was loaded. "Now they'll nae be so quick to attack, as they'll know we'll be ready."

Rurik gathered his reins. "We should make certain they are truly gone. I would have chased after them, but I thought it more prudent to warn you first."

"You were right to do so." Nik turned D'yoval down the trail. "We will make certain they have truly left."

"Hold," MacKean said. "I'll help Mr. Rurik. My horse is nae so tired as yours." The huntsman glanced at Ailsa as he spoke.

Nik had to fight the desire to grimace. Blast it. If he went after the brigands, it would give the lie to his assertion that D'yoval was exhausted. With no other option, Nik forced a smile. "You are right, of course."

MacKean rode to join Rurik. "You've a plan?" he asked the guard.

"We'll curve to the east for a half mile, and then ride parallel to the trail down to where the thieves and I had our little meeting."

"Mayhap I can follow their trácks from there."

"*Nyet*," Rurik said sternly. "If we allow them to draw us away, those we leave here are unprotected."

Stewart slapped his blunderbuss. "Nae completely."

"But more unprotected than we should be," Nik said. "Rurik has the right of it: do not follow them. For all we know, it could be a trap. Just make certain they're truly dispersed and then return here. And see if you can determine the number. That would be helpful."

Ailsa added, "We will need every able-bodied man at camp for protection, so do nae linger."

MacKean sighed. "Very guid, my lady." He and Rurik rode back down the trail.

"Come. Let's set up camp." Nik turned D'yoval off the trail and led the way over the small, sparkling stream to the flat area he'd spied earlier, scanning the woods as he went.

The sighting of the brigands was unsettling. *Is it possible they know we're traveling with ransom monies? Or do they just want our horses and our goods?* Either way, the brigands would gain nothing without a fight.

Nik reached the clearing and was gratified to find it larger than he'd first thought. Located on higher, and thus drier, land, the small area was ringed by huge pines, the forest floor coated with a thick layer of fresh needles that would make their sleep much more comfortable than the hard ground.

Stewart swung down from his horse, set his blunderbuss over his shoulder, and freed two pistols from his saddle. "I'll set watch a bit farther down the trail. It climbs, so I will be able to see anyone approaching long before they arrive."

"An excellent idea," Ailsa said. "We'll set oop camp while you're gone."

Stewart gave a nod and strode into the woods.

Mackenzie swung down from his horse, groaning, "Bloody hell, it has been a long day." He rubbed his back. "I was never so glad to hear that a horse deserved a rest in my life."

Ailsa agreed. "It is guid we've stopped."

"Indeed." He bent over and touched his toes, and then straightened. "I'll put the horses away. There's a place to tether them over there, just outside this ring of pines."

Nik followed Mackenzie's gaze. "When you return, see if you can find a felled log."

Mackenzie brightened. "Ah, yes. The fire."

"We'll have no fire tonight, not with brigands following."

Mackenzie's face fell. "Then what is the log for?"

"To keep the saddles off the wet ground."

"Very well." Looking disappointed, he led his horse away, collecting Stewart's mount as he went.

Still astride her horse, Ailsa looked at the clearing. The sunlight streaked over her, lighting the gold threads that mingled in her dark blond hair. "This is a guid place to camp."

"*Da.*" Nik tied D'yoval to a tree and began to loosen the saddle. He'd almost finished when he realized that Ailsa was still astride St. George and seemed in no hurry to climb down.

He sent her a curious look. "Are you going to dismount?"

She shrugged. "I'm just thinking."

"You will think better once you've stretched your legs."

"I am fine here."

Nik put D'yoval's saddle against a tree and let the horse wander to a patch of grass. The animal gave it an experimental nibble and then happily settled in for a more thorough taste.

Ailsa watched the horse, her brows knit. "He does nae look exhausted to me."

"You do not know him as I do." Nik crossed the clearing to stand beside Ailsa. As he approached, St. George showed his teeth.

"Don't even think about it," Nik ordered.

St. George huffed and turned his head away.

Nik put one hand on Ailsa's saddle. "Dismount. I will help."

She shook her head. "Give me a moment. I feel as if I'm on a ship with a deck rocking under my feet." She brushed a gloved hand over her cheek to smooth away a silken strand of hair that had come loose from her braid.

Her cheeks were deliciously pink from the cold, which made him imagine kissing them to a warmer shade. *She wears the cold weather well, this ice maiden.* "We rode a long way today, so it is no wonder you feel as if you're at sea. But the sooner you get down, the quicker you'll get your legs back under you."

She didn't answer and he realized that, just as she'd

been doing on the trail, she'd fisted her hand and was pressing it against her thigh. "What is wrong, *krasavitsa*? Is it your leg?"

Ailsa resolutely refused to look at Nik. Her left leg was numb from sitting, while her right thigh had knotted up into one huge cramp. He was being so kind, and the unexpectedness of it made her throat tighten. *I must be more tired than I thought.*

"Come." Impatience colored his voice. He slipped his strong hands under her cloak and grasped her waist. "Let me help you down."

"Nae, th—"

He lifted her from St. George's back as if she were a feather. He did it so quickly that when he set her on her feet, her spasming leg protested, seizing until she was in dire danger of falling down.

She frantically shifted her weight to her other leg, but as it was still numb, her knee buckled. Desperate not to fall flat on her arse, she threw her arms around Nik and held on for dear life.

She stood with her arms wrapped tightly about his waist, her cheek pressed to his rough wool coat, her body flush with his.

For a shocked moment, he stood frozen in place. But then he gave a deep chuckle and slipped his arms around her. "You minx," he whispered in her ear. "All day I, too, have been thinking of this."

Her eyes widened. *He thinks I— He believes I've— Oh lord. What have I done?*

He brushed a kiss to her temple, his breath warm on

her bared skin. Her skin trembled with goose bumps, her body warming to his touch. She closed her eyes and wished she dared loosen her hold, but knew her legs were not yet ready to hold her upright. *No, no, no. I must move. I was just—*

His hands slid from her waist to her back, molding her more firmly to him. That was . . . blast it, it was quite nice. Better than nice. It was warm. And sensual. Every part of her that he touched came awake.

He rubbed his chin across her temple, his whiskers tickling the sensitive skin until she shivered.

She shifted her weight to her spasming leg and quickly went back to the numb one. As long as she didn't put pressure on the cramping leg, it didn't hurt. *Can I stand on the other long enough to reach St. George? If I can, I—*

"*Krasavitsa*," he whispered against her temple. The aching longing that deepened his voice sent her thoughts flying as she shivered in answer.

His arms tightened and he pressed a kiss to the top of her head.

She should step away. *Just move*, she told herself. *As soon as you can feel your leg, move.*

She leaned more heavily on the numb leg and realized she could, indeed, feel it now. At least enough to walk on it.

So she could move.

But there's no reason to be rude. I will move . . . in a minute.

He pressed a line of kisses over her temple to her cheek, each touch a torture and a tease. Her breasts ached with a desire that increased with each feathery touch.

At some point, she'd ceased plastering herself to him, and had moved away just enough to allow him to brush tantalizing kisses over her cheek, to the corner of her mouth.

She waited, eyes closed, their breaths mingling.

"You are smart to take advantage of our being alone, *krasavitsa*," he murmured through a kiss that brushed her bottom lip. "Though I fear it will not last for long."

His voice was deeper than usual, making her think of warm honey and long, leisurely hot baths. *I really, really, really should stop this. I should. And I will.*

A few kisses were not amiss, they warmed the soul, and heaven knew it was cold out.

"Ah, I have thought of this since our first kiss." And then he kissed her again, his mouth covering hers, not as wildly as before, but deliberately, as if he savored the taste of her.

She melted against him, soaking in the feel of his hands, of his mouth, of *him*. God, but he was so sensual, so decadent, this prince of a man. And at this moment, he was kissing *her*.

He broke the kiss as gently as he'd begun it, leaving her clinging weakly to him, her heart thundering a ragged tempo in her ears. "You torment me."

She wasn't sure who was tormenting whom, but she never wanted it to stop. Vaguely, she was aware she should be shaking her leg, trying to work out the cramp that had pained it. But it suddenly seemed more important to pay attention to other parts of her body, like her breasts, which were now pressed against Nik's broad chest and tingled with each breath. Her skin was covered with goose bumps from his hands under her cloak, slowly, slowly smoothing up and down her back, traveling lower with each stroke.

She could feel the heat of that touch through the layers of her clothing. But even more than that, his mouth, his beautiful, sensual mouth, was right *here*, ready for another kiss, another taste, another tease. His eyes, green and shimmering, gleamed with a heat she could feel all the way to her toes.

He cupped her face with one large hand, his thumb making circles on her bare skin as he slowly bent to capture her lips—

"Bloody hell!" She yanked her foot from the ground where she'd accidentally pressed her weight on it, the cramp raging back to life.

He pulled back, his brows snapping together. "What is it?"

She bent to grab her leg. "A cramp," she said through clenched teeth.

"Come. I will—" The sound of horses approaching made him curse.

Ailsa looked over her shoulder to see Rurik and MacKean riding up the trail, their outlines flickering between the trees.

Gregor walked out of the woods, dragging a large log. He dropped it on seeing the guard and MacKean on the trail. "They're back! I'll see if they found anything." He hurried to meet them.

Ailsa took the one step necessary to bring her back

to St. George. Once she reached him, she grasped the saddle straps and held on, balancing on her good leg, as she rested her forehead against the saddle.

"Come," came a low voice near her ear, "we must deal with this cramp that makes your eyes fill with tears."

He was so close that if she turned her head, her lips would meet his again. And while that thought was infinitely appealing, she had no wish to end this kiss like the other—interrupted by their companions. She managed a short nod instead. "It hurts, but it'll get better if I just rest it and—"

He swooped her into his arms and carried her away.

She had no idea why he was carrying her off, away from the camp and deeper into the forest. She should have argued. Or at least protested. It felt rather scandalous, but in what way? They were separated by layers and layers of clothing, which meant nothing truly improper could happen.

She decided not to examine the deep flash of disappointment caused by her own thoughts, and instead looped her arms about his neck and rested her cheek on his shoulder. It was nice being carried so effortlessly. Being held in strong arms. Being protected.

Wanted.

He came to a stop by a stream a short distance from the camp, and gently lowered her to a rock against a large tree. The rush of crystal water over mossy green stones filled the silence. They were close enough to camp should they be needed, but far enough away to give the impression of privacy. She leaned against the tree trunk. It was beautiful here, and romantic—

"Now, you will take off your boot."

She blinked, staring up at him. "What?"

"Your boot must come off."

"Why?"

He sighed. "Do you or do you not have a leg cramp from riding?"

"Och. Yes." So this was really about her leg. Disappointment flooded her and she cautiously moved her foot. It felt better. Much better. Perhaps all she'd needed was to be swept into a large, handsome man's arms and carried away as if she were a princess in a fairy tale.

"Take off your boot and I will massage the muscles so the cramp disappears." Her mouth dropped open, and he chuckled as he reached down and gently pushed her chin back into place. "Come. The boot is restricting. If you take it off, it will allow the blood to flow and ease the cramp."

She should have explained that her leg was no longer so painful. But somehow, she found herself sitting with her boot in her hand and her leg stuck out as if demanding that massage he'd mentioned.

"There, much better." Nik stooped in front of her, so close she could smell him, wood smoke and leather mingled with fresh pine. His hands closed over her ankle. "Where does it hurt?"

She looked at her leg. Most of the pain had been in the back of her calf, right below her knee. Yet somehow, her finger touched above her knee, on her thigh.

"Here?" He placed his hand where her finger had just been, his palm warm through her breeches.

She nodded, mute with wonder in the face of her own daring. She wanted him to touch her, and had wanted him to do so since that blasted first kiss.

The realization was breathtaking. She'd never wanted a man before. Not in this way. But that first kiss had haunted her nights and ruled her days. He was just so damned delicious, and she'd never been able to turn away from a dessert.

He cupped her thigh above her knee, his hands warm through her breeches as he gently rubbed his palm in a slow, slow circle.

The very languidness of his touch made her think of long rainy days reading under a blanket; of the languorous, sleepy warmth of the sun on a hot summer day; of hours of sensual kisses from lips so beautiful they made her moan with desire.

Unaware that she was slowly melting under his touch, he continued. The heat from his fingers traveled all the way through the layers of clothing to her welcoming skin. Her heart leapt with awareness, her hands ached with the desire to reach for him. She gripped them together in her lap, fighting for the control she so far seemed to have lost, if she'd ever possessed it to begin with.

"Your mouth is white. Does it hurt so?"

His deep voice made her breasts throb. Delightful agony was what it was—an exquisite, breathless agony. Aware of his gaze, she swallowed noisily and shook her head, unable to form a single word.

He continued to rub her thigh in a slow circle, tormenting and teasing. "As I increase the pressure, it may hurt more." His gaze traced over her face. "If it becomes unbearable, you must tell me."

He was so close that she could see the golden flecks in his green eyes. And he was *touching* her. Her entire body tightened and tilted. She bit her lip to keep from moaning his name.

He pressed more firmly, and her muscle—so tired from the ride—eased under his touch. She bit her lip and closed her eyes, her hands now fisted at her sides as awareness tore through her, making her want and desire, while her heart raced furiously.

Never had she felt this sort of longing. Was it unmaidenly to experience such raw desire? Did she even care?

All she cared was that Nik never stop touching her. *Ever.*

He pressed a bit harder. "How is that?" he asked, his voice a rumbling whisper in the quiet.

She released her lip and ran her tongue over the bruised surface. She had to swallow before she could speak. "'Tis fine." Her voice sounded deep and husky, as if she'd been asleep.

He continued to rub her thigh above her knee, but every once in a while, his fingers would brush higher. So close . . . and yet so far. She clenched her eyes closed even harder and fought the desire to grab his hand and slide it up, up to— *Good God, I'm so wanton! When did this happen?* How *did this happen?*

"Ailsa?"

His breath brushed her cheek. She opened her eyes and found that he was leaning closer, watching her, his eyes dark with the same desire she fought. Her body leapt in response, and without another thought, she threw an arm about his neck, and pulled his mouth to hers.

She kissed him with all the pent-up longing his touch had rendered, all the stored emotion the trip had caused her, all her concern and worry—everything she had and felt, she put into their kiss.

And he responded, covering her mouth with his own, his hand now gripping her leg instead of rubbing it—insistent, demanding, and sensual.

God, *this* was what she'd wanted. She'd wanted *him*. All six feet four of passionate, delicious, forbidden *prince*. She didn't care if her actions defied prudence. She was here, on an adventure, and she wanted everything that entailed.

His mouth plundered hers, his tongue teasing and tormenting. *This* kiss was demanding and passionate, as if a door had been opened and he was storming through.

She grasped his coat and pulled him forward. His hand slid up her thigh, and he moaned against her mouth, his breath warm over her lips, as he slipped his other hand to her breast.

She gasped in pleasure, arching into him as he kneaded her breast. The heady sensation made her wish for more. She wanted to yank her shirt open, rip off her chemise, and pull his hand to her—

"Ailsa!" Gregor's voice arose from a distance.

Ailsa's eyes flew open, and she froze.

Nik's gaze met hers, and for a long moment, lips locked, they looked into one another's eyes.

Chapter 12

She would *kill* Gregor.

Nik sighed and rocked back on his heels. "Your cousin, he is always close by, *nyet*?"

"Too much so." Ailsa took a slow breath, her heart thudding wildly as she pressed her hands to her heated cheeks. Her mind whirled. "That was—" She shook her head.

His eyes gleamed and he smoothed the back of his hand over her cheek. "There is passion between us."

"So it seems. I never thought I'd . . . But now . . . after all of that . . . It's as if I . . . But then Gregor . . ." She bit back a grimace when she heard herself sounding so flustered. "I will kill my cousin."

Nik laughed, his eyes crinkling. "And I will help you, *krasavitsa*."

Gregor called again, closer this time.

"Good lord," she muttered. "I must go."

"So I heard," Nik said in a dry tone. He cupped his hand over one of hers. "I must say, you kiss very well."

She blinked. *What does he mean by that? Is he sincerely complimenting me? Or is he asking a probing question of some sort? Perhaps he is trying to ascertain whether I've had lots of practice—perhaps even too much?*

Which was ridiculous considering her "practice" consisted of a few hasty kisses with the vicar's son, and a more lingering, but infinitely more awkward embrace with a young peer when she'd been seventeen and left unchaperoned by one of her sisters.

None of those kisses were worth remembering. The kisses she'd shared with Nik were neither gentle nor polite. They weren't questing or uncertain. They were raw. Instinctual. Spurred by a blind passion that she could not resist.

When the prince merely looked at her, her heart leapt, her palms grew damp, her legs felt restless, and she was possessed with a deep hunger for the taste of him. She'd never known this feeling before. Should she avoid him? *Could* she? She *wanted* those kisses.

Pure, unchecked sparks of passion between them flared like tinder to dry wood, and they were growing. Surely there was no harm in indulging in a few forbidden tastes. Their adventure would soon be over, their loved ones rescued, and the prince on his way back to his own country. The very brevity of this mission guaranteed her a certain safety.

And after, she'd be left here, kept warm by some excellent memories and only a few regrets. She could find no fault with that.

"Ailsa?" Gregor yelled. "Are you there?"

"You should answer him." Nik stood, sending a black look in Gregor's direction. "He is like an annoying little brother, always where he is not wanted."

It was such an accurate description that she had to smile even as she hurriedly put herself to rights. She found her boot and put it back on, and then straightened her clothing.

Nik looked back at her. "Wait. There is a leaf—" He plucked a brown leaf from her hair.

She smoothed her hands over her hair, tugging her braid free from where it had been tucked behind her.

"Ailsa!" Gregor's voice was much closer now.

"I'm here!" she called. She made a face at Nik. "We must go. The others will be wondering where we are, too."

"Tell them you were thirsty, and I escorted you to get some water."

"There's a stream by the camp."

"It was muddy because we rode the horses across it."

She shot him a considering look. "You're verrah guid at dissembling." She stood and shook out her skirts.

Nik's gaze flickered down to her leg. "Your leg is better?"

"Aye." All of her was better. Except that she felt oddly lost, as if in allowing this moment to be interrupted, she'd given up something. She peeped at Nik through her lashes. "I did nae expect . . . this." She waved her hand in a general way.

"Nor did I." Nik saw the uncertainty in her gaze and quickly bent to brush a kiss over her temple.

She flushed, looking adorable and womanly, and oh so desirable. The sunlight that filtered from above seemed as enamored of her peach-soft skin as he was.

Her nose and cheeks were pink from the cold, her lips plump and still damp from his kisses. Her braid was mussed where it had rubbed against her cloak, gold and brown curls clinging to her neck and shoulder.

She wore no face paint, no artifice, but looked freshly scrubbed and natural. *Bozhy moj*, how he wanted her. He couldn't remember when he'd lusted for a woman this strongly.

"Ailsa? Where— Ah! There you are!" Gregor appeared through the thick shrubs that grew along the bank of the river. He came to a surprised halt when he saw Nik. "Oh! I didn't know you were here, too."

"Your cousin wished for a drink of water. I didn't think it was a good idea that she go alone."

Gregor's brows rose and his gaze flickered to Ailsa. "You certainly walked a long distance just to get a drink. There's a stream near the camp."

Ailsa waved her hand. "It is muddy from all the horses crossing through it. I could hardly be expected to drink from that."

Nik had to give her credit; she repeated his suggested falsehood so naturally that no one would ever assume she wasn't speaking the truth. *She has many talents, this one.*

She walked over to her cousin. "Did you find a log for the saddles?"

"Two. I've dragged them to the campsite, and set the saddles on them." Gregor looked past her to Nik. "MacKean and Rurik have returned."

"And?"

"No signs of the brigands. MacKean said the trail

was too mucky to read, and Rurik couldn't recall exactly where he'd surprised the louts on the path, so there was no way to find signs there."

Nik nodded. "We will set a double watch tonight, just to be safe." He turned to Ailsa, and inclined his head. "I should return to camp and help set up for the night."

"We'll join you shortly." She watched as Nik left, striding through the woods as if he owned them. For a prince who spent a significant amount of time in the ballrooms of Europe, he was oddly at home in the forest.

She turned to Gregor and found him looking at her with a narrowed gaze. "What is it?"

"Your hair."

She slid her hands over her braid. "Are there leaves in it? I was sitting under a tree—"

"No." Gregor laughed, though he looked at her strangely. "There are no leaves in your hair. I was merely going to say your braid needs to be redone."

"Traveling as we've been, 'tis a wonder 'tis still braided at all."

"It has been a far more difficult trail than I expected." He turned toward the camp, Ailsa falling in beside him. "I fear my back will never be the same."

"My legs will be so sore in the morning. I long for a hot bath."

"So do I." His expression grew serious. "It would be best if you didn't slip away from camp again, not with brigands about."

"I was nae alone."

"I'm not sure that made you any safer."

She came to a stop. "What do you mean by that?"

"Nothing."

She raised her brows.

He winced. "Fine, fine. I suppose I do mean something. The prince is a known womanizer and you've never been exposed to that sort of man."

"I'm well aware of his reputation and I'm nae such a fool as to believe his charm."

Gregor didn't look convinced. "Just be careful. Perhaps I'm speaking out of line, but your father is not here, so it's left to me to tell you to guard your heart around a man like that. The prince is—well, he's a *prince*, for one thing. And if the rumors are to be believed, he's very experienced in seduction. I don't need to tell you how that would give him an advantage, should he choose to use it."

"I appreciate the warning, but I'm nae in danger. The prince and I are on this rescue mission together, but that's all. Once this is over, that will be it and I'm quite fine with never seeing the man again, believe me."

Gregor gave her a searching look and, apparently satisfied with what he saw, nodded. "Good. I've no doubt that rakehell has ulterior motives, and I didn't wish you to be blindsided." He linked his arm with hers and they continued to the camp. "I don't trust that man."

"Neither do I. He's nae telling us everything."

"He has much to gain if he wins you over to his way of thinking in how to deal with this ransom situation, and he is the sort who would use every weapon at his fingertips to get his way."

Ailsa glanced at her cousin. "You think the prince would attempt to seduce me just to win an argument?"

"I know he would. The two of you have different ideas about how—"

"—to deal with the abductors. I have nae forgotten that." At least she remembered it *now*. It was impossible to remember anything when one was lost in a passionate kiss. *Was that why Nik kissed me?*

Surely not. He didn't even bring up the subject, and we had plenty of time to discuss it. Or we would have if we hadn't been engaged in other activities.

She truly believed that, at first, Nik's reason for being solicitous had been to help ease the pain in her leg and nothing else. *She* had been the one who'd turned the moment into something more.

When she thought about it, she was rather proud of herself for that. She'd had no idea she could be so bold.

Gregor's brow furrowed. "The prince is a bit of a chameleon, isn't he? He's different with each of us. I'm sure we're all that way to some extent—I'm less formal with you because I know you well, and less guarded about what I say when I talk to MacKean, as he's a bit of a rougher sort. But the prince is completely different, as if he's trying to win all of us over."

"You're just now noticing that?" she asked, unable to keep the dryness from her tone.

Gregor laughed. "It's as if there are twenty versions of him and he plays the one best suited to the situation."

"So he does. And well, too." Which made her wonder: *What are you after, Prince of All Faces?*

"But it's you I'm worried about. I'd be miserable if anything or anyone upset you."

She patted Gregor's hand. "I'd feel the same aboot you. Fortunately, nothing will happen to either of us."

He let the matter drop, complaining instead of their lack of fire and what a dismal blow that would be for their evening meal.

Ailsa listened with only half an ear. Gregor was right about one thing: she should be more careful around the prince. Only a fool played with fire and was surprised when she got burned.

But that didn't mean she had to give up those delicious kisses. In fact, why couldn't she use them to win the prince over to her way of thinking about the ransom? *It would serve him right if I gave him a little of his own medicine.* The thought lifted her spirits, and she was still smiling when they reached camp.

Chapter 13

Throughout that evening and the next day, Ailsa watched Nik. He was definitely attempting to charm their little group. He was quiet and intent when he spoke with MacKean, louder and jovial when he spoke to Stewart, and then polite and more refined when he spoke to Gregor.

She paid the closest attention to when Nik spoke to her. Then he was warm and flirtatious, his green eyes intent as if she were the only woman in the world and not just the only woman on their expedition. Even though she didn't believe his sincerity for a minute, she couldn't stop her heart from fluttering whenever he looked her way. *So he is flirting with me most likely because he wishes to stave off a future disagreement. Well, my dearest prince, it won't work.*

The realization left her even more determined to use his methods against him. She wasn't disappointed that his seeming interest wasn't real, for she'd had no expectations of—well, anything. And it wasn't as if Nik had changed; on their first meeting, she'd witnessed his rapid switch from stern prince to deferential stable-hand to disarming prince. To be truthful, she found him a challenge. The more he hid, the more she wished to know.

Who was the real Nik? And would she like him? Time would tell. Meanwhile, the attraction between them simmered and grew. They were always together and yet never alone. All day, whenever he'd spoken to her, or helped her on and off her horse, his hands had lingered, his gaze caressed. Each time he'd touched her or even looked at her, her pulse had raced madly and her lips had tingled in memory of their shared kisses.

And that worried her a bit—her inability to hold back her reactions to him. She still found herself imagining his kisses. How his hands had moved over her. Her own wanton response when he'd touched her, tempted her. And he felt the same. She saw it in the way his gaze darkened when he looked at her, at the way his breath quickened when he touched her.

She smiled to herself. Tomorrow she'd do what she could to discover his plans. But she was too tired tonight, still drained from the excitement of the day before, and worn from traveling such a distance. While everyone else finished eating their cold meal of dried venison and apples, she excused herself, climbed into her bedroll, and pulled the blankets over her head, hoping to block out all sight and thoughts of the man who even now watched her, unspoken questions in his gaze.

She slept poorly, awakening at every noise, whether the plop of a large drip on a nearby leaf, the fall of a clump of snow, an animal scurrying in the dark, or the rustle of the wind through the branches. Late at night,

Stewart came to quietly rouse MacKean to trade places as watch. Wide-awake, Ailsa thought about joining the watch, but before she could make up her mind, Nik had risen from his bed, wrapped himself in a cloak, and joined MacKean on the trailhead. She watched through half-closed eyes, listening to them speaking quietly, taking an odd comfort in the deep timbre of his voice, and finally falling asleep.

To everyone's relief, the day had dawned bright and beautiful, the sun warmer and the sky an endless, vivid blue. Though they rode all morning, it didn't seem as much of a chore as other days. In addition to the better weather, the path wasn't steep.

As afternoon approached, the trail began to widen and then dropped until it flattened on a low ridge that overlooked a beautiful loch. The afternoon sun danced across the blue waters, while silver aspen and massive oaks raised their branches from the lush, thick grass to bask in the winter sunshine.

"This land of yours is like no other. Wild, fierce, beautiful."

Ailsa's heart skipped a beat at Nik's voice. She turned and found that he'd pulled D'yoval even with St. George and now looked past her to the loch below.

She ignored the way her skin prickled at his nearness and instead followed his gaze to the sparkling waters. He was right; it was a beautiful land and his obvious admiration allowed her to see it with fresh eyes. "There are reasons my people talk of fairy flags and water spirits. It is hard to see this land and nae believe in the mystical."

"The Scots remind me more and more of the Romany. No wonder my grandmother loves this country." At the mention of his grandmother, a shadow crossed his face.

"It would nae be to anyone's benefit to harm either the duchess or Lord Hamilton."

Nik sent her a surprised glance; he hadn't expected her to guess his thoughts. "I hope that is true."

Her lips curved in a faint smile. "It is." Her gaze flickering over him in a slow, considering manner, coming to rest where his hand lay on his thigh. "Let me see your hand."

"Why?"

She gave an impatient puff and then reached over and grasped his hand. "The Scots have more in common with the Romany than you think. We read palms as well an any gypsy could." Her fingers were warm on his wrist as she turned his hand palm up.

"Do you also threaten to turn people into goats?"

Her lips quirked. "When necessary." She leaned from her saddle and looked at his palm. "Hmm. That is interesting."

Her thumb brushed over his skin as she spoke and a maelstrom of heat roared through him. God, but he wished she would touch other parts of him in such a way. He cleared his throat, his voice understandably husky. "What do you see, all-knowing one?"

"Many things. Some guid, some nae." She released his hand, sending him a look through her lashes. "I daresay I see much more than you'd like." Her voice, silky and lilting, made him want to scoop her out of her saddle and into his lap where he could taste her.

"Tell me everything. I am not afraid." *Much.* Truthfully, caution was merited with this woman. And yet caution was the last thing on his mind as he watched a smile touch her mouth. She had such lush lips, and he wished he believed it would be safe to lean from his saddle and capture those lips for a kiss. It wouldn't, of course, not with D'yoval's uncertain temperament. More than a little irked at his capricious horse, he asked, "What do the lines on my hand tell you?"

"That you are a great leader."

Well. That was something. "What else?"

"You are also wily and should nae be trusted."

He looked at his palm. "Ah. I see what it is; I forgot to wash my hands after breakfast."

She chuckled, the sound as sensual as a touch, but even though she laughed, her eyes did not warm, but remained wary. "Tease as you will, you cannae deny a truth."

"When palm reading becomes a proven window into the future, I'll agree to call it 'truth.' Until then—" He shrugged. "Meanwhile, I am never wily, and I consider myself utterly trustworthy. I never act without a very good reason, one larger than my own wants and desires."

"Even when you kiss someone?"

His gaze rested once again on her mouth, and he had an instant image of her splayed across his lap—to hell with his lap, he wanted her in his bed, tangled in his sheets, her body damp from their efforts. *Bozhy moj, this desire to have her in my bed increases.*

Her fresh-faced beauty was growing on him every day, and he even found himself admiring her commitment to her own cautious take on their mission. But it was the challenge she presented that intrigued him the most. Women always watched him—he was a prince, after all, and a title drew one's gaze. He knew, too, he was not unattractive, and he often used the attention he received to win information for his cause. But he'd never had a woman look at him the way Ailsa did, as if she were hearing a florid but totally unbelievable compliment.

It irked him more than he could say. "I get the feeling none of this has to do with the lines on my palm."

She didn't correct him, but shrugged. "You've been trying to worm your way into my men's good graces, and with nae other intent than to influence them as we progress."

Ah. So that was it, was it? "I never worm my way anywhere. If I go, I go directly and always with an invitation."

She raised her brows, looking singularly unimpressed. "Directly? Then you have shared all of your thoughts on the abduction?"

He met her gaze for a long moment. "It is not wise to tell you all my secrets."

She smiled, which worried him. "Then I am wise to nae tell you mine."

Bloody hell, what did that mean? He thought of asking, but couldn't do so without admitting she'd caught his interest. Frustrated, he found himself abruptly changing the subject. "When will we reach Greer's camp?"

"If the weather holds, by tomorrow afternoon."

"Tomorrow it will be, then. There's not a single cloud in the sky."

"The weather is nae a certainty here. It changes hour to hour and—"

Bang! The bark on a tree just past Nik exploded as a bullet embedded itself in the trunk.

D'yoval neighed wildly and tried to rear up, and it was all Nik could do to calm him.

"Brigands!" Ailsa yelled. "Disperse!"

The next few minutes were chaos. Men shouting, horses neighing as they plunged wildly through the woods on both sides of the trail.

"I see them!" Rurik could be heard behind them. "To the south!"

Just up the trail, MacKean had turned his horse back and looked at Ailsa, who'd disappeared off the trail, St. George plunging through the shrubbery without hesitation.

"I've got her," Nik shouted, guiding D'yoval off the trail after her.

Another pistol shot rang out. Nik's cloak tugged at his shoulder and he looked down, irked to see that the wool had been sliced as if it had been made of paper.

"This way!" Ailsa shouted over her shoulder.

He urged D'yoval after her, and soon they were away, galloping madly through the woods, the sound of horses' hooves muffled by the damp forest floor.

They rode as fast as they could without endangering

the horses, only slowing when they came to a steep embankment. D'yoval slipped here and there, but good, solid St. George didn't miss a step.

They went a short way farther, and then Nik pulled D'yoval to a halt.

Ailsa started to speak, but he held up a hand, listening.

Deep in the woods behind them came the unmistakable sound of a horse—or were there two?—racing toward them on the trail.

"This way!" He turned to where a thick wall of young birch trees stood. More shrubs than anything else, they clung to one another and formed a small circle. Nik jumped down and turned to her.

Ailsa barely had time to kick the stirrups free before he plucked her from her horse's back and set her on her feet. His face grim, he asked in a quiet voice, "Do you have a weapon?"

She patted her belt. "Two."

"Good. Get in those bushes and hide. I'll join you in a moment."

"What are you going to do?"

"As soon as they pass, I'm going to follow those bastards and put an end to this."

"We," she corrected firmly. "We will put an end to this."

Nik sent her a dark look and tied St. George's reins to D'yoval's saddle and then gave an odd whistle.

D'yoval neighed in answer and then, tail swishing, trotted on down the path, St. George following after, led by the tug on his reins.

"What are you doing?"

"D'yoval will go a few hundred feet away and wait." Nik's warm hand closed over her elbow, and he led her into the shrubs. "Lie down. We must be quiet."

She crept into the greenery, clenching her teeth when her hair snagged on the branches. Once there, she dropped down on her stomach, tugging her cloak about her. Soon, she was hidden deep inside the small sheltered center, feeling as if she were in a cave and not mere branches.

Nik followed and was soon beside her on the damp ground, his pistol drawn and ready before him.

For a long moment, they were silent. They could hear very little of the others—a shout from Stewart to MacKean. The thrashing of a horse off in a distance. And then nothing.

She frowned in the silence. "I don't hear anyone now."

"Neither do I," he whispered back. "But they will come."

She nodded. "It is good D'yoval knows this trick. It will lead the thieves away from us."

"My brother Max is the general of all the armies of Oxenburg and he trained my horse. I— Ah! They come." His gaze locked on the path they'd just left.

She turned her head and heard footsteps and the soft whicker of a horse. One person, leading their mount. Was it one of the brigands come to finish them off? Was he after the horses? Was it possible that was all these bloody thieves wanted?

She thought of St. George waiting down the path and

her jaw set. She'd not give up her horse without a fight.

Nik placed his hand on her shoulder.

She cast him a hard glance, and he shook his head and mouthed, "*Nyet.*"

For a splendid minute, she imagined bursting into the clearing, her pistol drawn as she confronted the filthy brigand who'd dared put her people in danger. She'd disarm the thief and make him empty his pockets, shame him royally, and then send him on his way, cowed and frightened, never to thieve again.

It was a grand image that took her all of two seconds to realize would work only *if* she managed to get through this thick shrubbery without getting her cloak or hair caught, and *if* her pistol presented enough of a threat to a hardened brigand to cause him to rethink his violent way of life, and *if* Nik didn't interfere. It was a lot of *if*s.

She gritted her teeth and resigned herself to waiting.

The steps came closer, and then went on past. She lowered her head and watched as the boots went by. They were black, and surprisingly new and shiny. *He must have stolen them recently.* She watched as they disappeared, following their horses.

Nik waited until the footsteps were gone before he bent close and whispered, "Stay here, *krasavitsa*. I will be back."

He was going to leave her here? Not while she had breath in her body. She parted her lips to say so, when he covered them with his and gave her a long, hard, possessive kiss.

Her body, already primed by the danger of the last

few moments, shivered against his. She couldn't think when he covered her mouth with his own, when he engulfed her with warmth and passion that only left her craving more of both.

She lifted her arm to slip it about his neck when he broke the kiss. "Ah, you tempt me even now," he murmured against her mouth.

She pulled back. "I'm coming with you."

"Not this time."

"But—"

He stilled her words with another hard kiss and then, before she could catch her breath, was gone. She scrambled to her knees, intent on following him, but her hair caught in a branch. Before she could free it, he was out in the open, exposed for all the world to see.

One noise, and the thief might look back and see Nik. *Dammit, now I must stay here.*

Ailsa wished she'd followed her impulses and stopped the brigand on her own. Now all she could do was watch through the leaves as Nik moved stealthily. . . . A step. One more.

A noise in the distance made him stop, and then he took another step.

He was leaving, walking away from her and toward danger. *Alone.*

She scowled. *Like hell he'll go alone.* He was farther away now, as was the thief. Ailsa rose to her knees and gathered her cloak close. As quietly as she could, she followed him from their hiding place.

As soon as she reached the path, she straightened. Nik's broad shoulders were barely visible ahead as he silently eased his way toward where the horses would be waiting.

Could he see the bandit? She wasn't certain, but knew she had to stay out of sight. It wouldn't do to confuse Nik; he had his hands full as it was.

Nik disappeared into the woods, and she followed, watching where she placed her feet, and using all the lessons she'd learned from years of hunting to stay silent.

Just as she reached a turn in the path, she caught sight of a movement to her right. She froze in place, her eyes narrowing. The brigand had walked this way, Nik after him. But what if the thief had realized he was being followed? Could he have slipped to one side to set up an ambush?

She crouched low and stepped in the direction of the movement.

A man rested on his haunches behind a fallen tree, his cloak mud brown, the sun flashing off the barrel of his rifle. It was aimed toward the spot where Nik had disappeared.

Ailsa's heart thudded in her ears, her palms damp. She had to stop this man. She stealthily crept forward, getting closer.

Closer.

The man braced the rifle on the fallen log, his head lowering as if to aim.

She raised her pistol, sighting down the barrel and rested her finger on the trigger just as the sun broke through overhead and lit the man's hair—

"Gregor?" she whispered.

He turned, his face pale in the sunlight that flickered over him. Relief flooded his face as he recognized her, followed quickly by shock when he saw her pistol pointed in his direction.

She lowered her weapon and he took a grateful breath before gesturing for her to join him.

As quietly as she could, she made her way through the brush, stooping beside him behind the fallen log. "Good God, I could have shot you," she whispered.

"Thank God you didn't," he whispered back. "The brigand came this way."

"I saw him go by. Nik sent the horses ahead, so the thief is following their trail. Nik is hard after the ruffian."

A startled look flickered over her cousin's face. "The prince is out there, too? Bloody hell, I could have shot him by accident." Gregor had already lowered the rifle, though the barrel still rested on the log. "I'm glad you came when you did," he said in a fervent whisper.

"Me, too," she whispered back. "I wish we could do something, but I fear we'd only make the situation worse for Nik."

Gregor slanted her a side look. " 'Nik,' is it?"

She ignored him and settled in to wait, both of them scanning the woods for movement of any kind. The wind stirred the branches overhead, and brown leaves drifted down, but that was all.

The minutes lengthened, and the sun began to slant into their eyes. Ailsa's heart ached with each beat. As the seconds wore on, her imagination came to life. Where the hell was Nik? Had the thief ambushed him and left him for dead? Was he even now struggling to crawl to the path for help?

She raised up and peered into the woods, straining to see something—*anything*. Beside her, Gregor stirred uneasily and she glanced at him, stiffening when she saw him brush his hand under his nose, his eyes watery. He looked as if he were going to— Oh no! He couldn't, not now when—

Achoo!

The sneeze echoed loud in the silence of the forest.

"Gregor!" she whispered furiously.

"I couldn't help it!" Gregor returned, looking miserable.

Ailsa peered toward the woods, her heart thundering in her ears.

For the longest time, there was no sound. But then, just as she'd started to relax, the brush rattled and she saw the flicker of a figure between the trees.

"Someone is coming," she whispered, pistol at the ready.

Beside her, Gregor lifted his rifle into place.

Nik appeared between the trees, leading the horses.

"*Thank goodness!*" She lowered her pistol and stood, peering behind him. "Did you find him? What happened?"

"Nothing." Nik sent a sour look at Gregor. "That was your sneeze, was it?"

Gregor flushed. "I'm sorry. The sun got in my eyes. I always sneeze when that happens."

"What happened to the thief?" Ailsa asked again. "Did you get a look at him?"

"*Nyet.* He was on the other side of the horses." Nik frowned. "He wasn't moving at all; it was as if he were waiting for someone. But when Mackenzie sneezed, the blackguard turned and bolted into the woods. By the time I got around the horses to reach him, he was already gone."

"Do you know which direction he went?" Gregor asked.

Nik shook his head. "The thick pine needles made it impossible to follow."

"Perhaps I can find the trail," Gregor said, clearly eager to remedy his error. "I'm used to tracking on this surface and know some tricks."

"It would not be safe. We must stay together."

Gregor looked disappointed, but he refused to give up. "You and I can go, then, and Ailsa can return to the trail. The others will be waiting by now."

"I'll not leave her alone."

Ailsa shrugged. "I'll be fine—"

"*Nyet.*" His tone and his expression brooked no argument. "I do not understand these thieves. Two perfectly good horses right there for the taking, and he chose instead to disappear into the woods. That does not make sense."

"Do you think he knew about the gold, but was nae certain where it was?"

"I don't know. But we must be careful." Nik handed St. George's reins to Ailsa. "Take your horse. He's tried to bite me twice."

She patted St. George's neck. "I wish he'd bitten the thief."

"So do I," Gregor agreed. He stared down the path behind Nik, and then frowned. "Perhaps these men have their own mounts and are looking for something more portable, like gold and guns."

"Perhaps." Still looking perplexed, Nik fished a withered apple from his saddlebag and fed D'yoval. "We should find the others. Have you seen any of them?"

Gregor shook his head. "When the shots began, I plunged into the woods and hid, and then, once things grew quiet, I went after the two of you. I haven't seen anything of the others."

"Let's return to the trail, then. I will lead." Nik gestured to Gregor. "Keep your rifle at the ready and guard our flank."

"I'll keep rear guard," Ailsa protested. "I have a weapon—"

"Pistol," Nik corrected. "Which doesn't shoot as far as a rifle."

"Oh." He had her there. "Fine."

He sent her a lopsided grin and she realized that, were Gregor not nearby, Nik would have given her another kiss.

She bit her lip. What had those kisses meant? At the time, all she'd thought was that they'd felt so *right*.

"*Krasavitsa*, we must go."

She realized she'd been staring at his mouth, and her face heated. She was glad Gregor was behind her and hadn't witnessed her foolery. "Of course," she managed. "I hope the others are close by."

Nik's gaze flickered from her to Gregor and then back. "So do I," he said politely, and with utter insincerity. With a final heated look, he turned and led the way back to the trail, leaving her to follow, her mind racing with thoughts of brigands, the safety of their horses, and the confusing feelings caused by a pair of demanding kisses.

Chapter 14

The object sat on the palm of Ailsa's hand, as smooth and round as a rock. She took a cautious sniff, but could find no trace of the yeasty scent she associated with bread.

"Ow!" Gregor glared at his roll while he gingerly rubbed his tooth. "Whatever you do, don't bite into it."

Rurik chuckled. "Silly man. You eat it like this." He flattened a roll into a disc, and then tore it in half, and then in half again. Once he had a piece that would fit in his mouth, he popped it in, and took a swig from his flask.

"Ah. You soften it with the water, eh?" Gregor picked up his flask.

"This is vodka. It will soften the bread. It will also soften dried beans, leather, and perhaps even your brain, if you wish it."

MacKean, who was nearby leaning against a tree, his rifle loosely clasped in his arms, snorted a laugh.

Gregor flushed, but managed a weak laugh as well.

It was early evening and the sky burned a bright red, clouds scattering as if afraid. Ailsa shivered and tugged her cloak closer. "The weather is turning."

"Aye. It will rain come morning." MacKean finished his bread and then opened a pouch and handed out what looked like pieces of bark.

Gregor sniffed his.

"Dried rabbit," Ailsa told him. She sat beside him, cross-legged. She was still sore from traveling, but not as much as she had been.

"Vodka will soften that, too," Rurik said, obviously amused when Gregor reached for a flask.

Nik looked up from the map he was studying. "Do not let Rurik tease you. Vodka will soften the bread, but the rabbit needs no such help."

Ailsa was glad to hear that vodka would not be necessary for her to digest their simple dinner. The one time she'd taken a few swallows of that potent stuff, it had given her the kind of brazen courage that usually led to massive errors in judgment. She was certain she made enough of those without the help of vodka.

She tore her bread as she'd seen Rurik do, and managed to eat a small piece. The rabbit fared better, for it was indeed more tender than the bread, and tastier, too.

The wind rustled overhead, and they all instantly raised their gazes to the sky, Gregor and MacKean reaching for their weapons.

Ailsa managed a dry chuckle. "We're a bit jumpy, we are. But we should nae be, for Stewart is on watch and he has sharp eyes."

Nik settled back on his heels and nodded, though his gaze never stopped moving around the forest. "It has been a long day."

"Too long," Gregor agreed fervently.

MacKean relaxed visibly, pausing to swallow a piece of bread. "The rain will slow us."

"Nae as much as snow," Ailsa said. "Can we still reach Greer's camp tomorrow?"

"Perhaps," MacKean said. "If we travel fast enough."

Nik folded the map. "We must reach it. We will be safer out of these woods."

No one disagreed. After their brush with the brigands, they'd traveled as quickly as they could, barely stopping to eat or rest. They'd made it quite a bit farther than Ailsa had expected, which was good. She, too, had had enough of the woods, the steep trails, and the unexpected kisses from a man she shouldn't trust. As much as she wished it otherwise, he consumed her thoughts.

Even now she remembered how agonizing it had been, waiting for Nik when he went to confront the thief. She told herself she'd have been just as worried had it been MacKean or Stewart or Gregor, but the stressful incident had left her exhausted and more ready than ever to be done with this adventure.

Unable to eat more of the hard bread, she tucked the leftover chunk into her pocket in the hopes that St. George might be persuaded to eat it. Then she leaned forward and clasped her arms around her bent knees. "'Tis a pity we cannae have a fire tonight." She couldn't keep the wistful note from her voice.

A small fire wouldn't completely banish the cold, but it would brighten the gloom. As the sun slowly slid out of sight, the long shadows cast by the tall trees spread across the forest floor as if reaching for them.

She rested her chin on her folded arms and found her gaze going to the shoulder of Nik's cloak, where the bullet had sliced through it. She hadn't noticed the tear until they'd reached camp, but seeing it had made her stomach tighten into a hard ball. *So very close.*

She tore her gaze from the rip, fearing he'd see the emotion she couldn't quite conceal. That she was upset was understandable; he was a member of her party, and as this was her rescue, he was under her care. *If he'd been injured . . .*

She shivered and tugged her cloak closer. "We will have a fire once we meet oop with Greer."

"Once we reach him, 'tis a short march to Ullapool," MacKean noted. "There's an inn there."

Gregor brightened. "An inn?"

"Aye. Ullapool is a port town."

Rurik looked up from where he was cleaning his pistol. "How big is this town?"

"Decent sized. They trade quite a bit with the clans of the Western Isles."

"A real bed," Gregor said reverently. "And the food at this inn?"

"I've eaten there before, and would nae mind going again."

From MacKean, that was high praise indeed.

Gregor rubbed his hands together. "A hot meal would be welcome."

"We should have the horses looked to while we're there, as well," Rurik said. "If we have the chance."

MacKean nodded. "There's a blacksmith in town, if any shoes need replacing."

Perhaps I can get a hot bath, Ailsa thought longingly. "We will stay in Ullapool, then. At least one night."

"Good." Nik folded the map and tucked it away, his gaze flickering to Ailsa. "But then we must decide how to proceed, as it's a straight march from there to Kylestrome."

She felt his gaze, but resolutely stared into the growing dark instead.

After a moment, he said firmly, as if in challenge, "We will make some decisions when we reach the inn in Ullapool."

He was right, and she could only be glad he was not pressing for that conversation right now. The day had been wearing and she'd never been so tired and at the same time, fearful that sleep would elude her. Despite her brave words earlier, every time there was the faintest rustle in the woods, her heart leapt to her throat while she waited for a crazed band of ruffians to burst forth, pistols blazing. And somehow, in her wide-awake vision, the ruffians always aimed at Nik.

MacKean took a swig from his flask. "I've been thinking aboot these brigands."

Everyone looked at the usually taciturn woodsman. "And?" Nik said.

"We're dealing with only one mon."

Ailsa frowned at the usually taciturn tracker. "Rurik saw more than one."

Rurik nodded. "*Da.* There were two, perhaps more."

MacKean sent Rurik a hard look. "The attack came from only one direction. If I were a brigand, and I had an accomplice or two, I'd set us oop so tha' we covered all the members of this little party, and nae a one would have escaped."

"So you'd have placed your men on both sides of the trail?" Nik looked thoughtful.

MacKean nodded. "Staggered, so they dinnae shoot one another, but enough to encircle the whole lot of us. Two men could do tha'. Three, for certain."

"We could not have withstood an attack like that," Nik agreed.

"So why dinnae they do it?" MacKean demanded.

Rurik nodded slowly. "You make a good point. At least for this recent attack."

"Now I really wish I'd tried to track that lout," Gregor said.

"'Tis guid you dinnae," MacKean said sharply. "The last thing any of us should do is go oot on our own."

Rurik grunted his agreement. "*Da.* You'd be a lone target and would not have lasted long. It's possible that is what this scoundrel will try when he comes back—he could attempt to lure us out one at a time and pick us off like plump pheasants."

Gregor offered in a mild tone, "Since there's only one thief, perhaps we should attempt to strike a bargain with him?"

"And how would you do that?" MacKean asked, looking astonished. "Do you go into the woods and shout, 'Mr. Brigand, I would like to parley'?"

Rurik snorted a laugh.

"No," Gregor said defensively. "We leave something here, an offering of a sort."

"We dinnae know what he wants," Ailsa pointed out. "It could be horses or weapons or gold."

"But if we offer him a bribe of some sort, it might convince him to leave us be."

"Or he might think we had something of value to hide, like gold, and are tryin' to put him off from the real treasure," MacKean pointed out.

Rurik nodded. "It would only encourage him to come after us. And this time, he might get lucky and kill someone."

Gregor subsided into quiet, looking a little crushed.

Ailsa slid her foot over to nudge his. When he looked up, she smiled. "We'll be with Greer tomorrow and on the main road, and then we won't have to worry aboot thieves."

"They don't attack travelers on the main roads?" Nik looked surprised.

"Nae normally," Ailsa answered. "Most brigands confine themselves to the woods and the more isolated roads."

MacKean finished his dinner and wiped his fingers on his cloak. "I will join Stewart on the first watch. We should keep a double eye tonight, eh?"

"MacKean, stay here. I'll go." Nik stood, towering over them all, his face outlined by the graying sky. "It's my turn."

After a startled moment, MacKean settled back down. "Thank you. I'll relieve you after midnight. Rurik here can join me."

Rurik murmured an agreement and Nik walked into the woods and disappeared among the trees.

Ailsa had to fight the urge to go after him and— *And what?* she asked herself. *Tell him I'm worried for us all? He knows that, and feels the same. It's difficult, knowing how close I came to losing him today.* The thought sent a chill up her spine, and the realization of the danger of their mission rested on her shoulders with renewed weight.

She hugged her knees tighter.

"'Tis getting dark." Rurik reached for his bedroll and spread it out beside the tree.

"Aye." MacKean arose and gathered the other bedding. "We should all get some sleep."

Soon the bedrolls were in place around the fire.

"Guid night, my lady." MacKean climbed into his bed and pulled the furs around his head, Rurik following shortly after.

Soon they were snoring softly.

After several more moments, Gregor yawned. "What a day!" He arose and then climbed between the fur blankets of his bed.

Though tired, Ailsa stayed where she was, her chin on her knee as she looked up into the sky, which had darkened to deep gray. The moon was a sliver, while the stars sparkled wildly.

"Aren't you coming to bed?" Gregor asked.

"In a moment. I need some time to calm my thoughts."

He was silent a moment, before saying in a tentative voice, "It was frightening, wasn't it?"

"I've never been more terrified in my life," she admitted.

"Me, too." His bedding rustled, and she thought perhaps he'd turned her way. "I knew this was a dangerous enterprise, but it didn't dawn on me until today that someone could die."

"I know. I've been so worried aboot Her Grace and Lord Hamilton that I dinnae truly comprehend the danger to this group, nae really. Now I've five more people to be concerned aboot."

"We'll be fine. We are all a part of this journey, and we have a responsibility to one another."

"That we do." She smiled in the dark. "Which is why we should go to sleep, or at least try to. We've a long day tomorrow and, if MacKean is right, possibly a wet one."

"Lovely," Gregor muttered under his breath. But he burrowed deeper into his blankets and, within a remarkably short time, his breathing smoothed and he was fast asleep.

All around Ailsa, the night awakened. Owls hooted, frogs croaked, an occasional tree branch snapped and fell to the ground. Something about today bothered her; something that didn't ring true. But she couldn't put her finger on it.

Whatever it was, it remained stubbornly out of focus, as if it were too far away for her to see. *Or perhaps too close.*

She sighed and noted a smattering of clouds gathering to the west and grimaced to think that MacKean had been right about the rain. With a grumpy mutter, she arose, slipped into her bedroll, and tugged the blankets over her. Then she tried to sleep.

But her thoughts roiled more loudly. *Why didn't the theif steal the horses? And how had something as innocuous as Gregor's sneeze frightened off a hardened brigand? And if it had frightened the man, why hadn't he just jumped onto D'yoval's back and ridden away? It would have been faster, and he'd have had a prize.*

But that wasn't all. Something was not

A footstep whispered through the grass. Her eyes, halfway shut, flew open and she held her breath. A moment later, a boot crunched on a loose stone, and she frantically wished she'd kept her pistol inside her covers. If she reached for her weapon now, she'd call very unwanted attention to herself.

She waited, and finally, a tall, masculine form emerged from the woods, a cape swinging from his broad shoulders, the moonlight threading through his black hair. *Nik. What's he doing?*

As she watched, he crossed the small clearing that made their camp, pausing to pat D'yoval's neck when the horse lifted its head and seemed ready to whicker in greeting. The horse calmed, Nik continued into the camp. He bent by his saddlebags, removed a map from his pouch, and tucked it into his shirt. He turned to go back the way he'd come, but then paused and walked toward her.

Ailsa closed her eyes and held her breath, waiting. *What is he going to do?*

He stopped beside her, stooped down, then carefully tugged her top blanket up over her shoulders, as if he were tucking her into bed. Finished, he rocked back on his heels.

She waited, but he didn't move. He merely remained where he was, looking at her. It took all her concentration not to open her eyes. *What would I say if I did? "Hello"?*

He sighed and she heard the sound of his hand raking over his stubbled chin before he muttered something under his breath, and then arose.

Ailsa peeped through her lashes and watched as he turned and made his way back through the camp and then disappeared into the night, as quiet as he'd come.

She stared into the woods, wishing she'd been able to see his face and wondering why he'd stayed beside her for such a length of time. What had he been thinking? And why had he seemed so pensive? It was a long, long time before she was able to sleep.

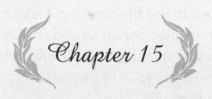

Chapter 15

The next morning they arose early and rode hard, making excellent time. The weather was unusually warm, though a brisk wind lifted from the west, bringing with it more clouds. To Ailsa's delight, although the sky grew darker, the rain held off.

Because of the narrowness of the trail, they were forced to travel single file once more, Stewart in the lead, MacKean behind him, while Nik and Rurik took the rear guard. Ailsa had requested that she and Gregor be allowed to assume the rear position, but Rurik had pointed out that he had the most training, should anything go awry. There had been no arguing with that, though she'd wished to.

Still, she had to admit that the ride today was more pleasant than any they'd experienced thus far. Though they rode along the rim of a steep mountain that offered a dizzying view off the west side, the trail was smooth and flat. Their way was shadowed on the upward slope by pines and aspens, which meant the path was thick with fragrant needles that made her take deep, happy breaths with each of St. George's steps.

She'd have been satisfied to have ridden under these conditions for the rest of their journey. But at noon, when they'd stopped to rest the horses and take a few bites of venison, a chilly plop of rain landed on Ailsa's cheek.

She looked up and grimaced. "Here comes the rain."

Nik followed her gaze to the dark sky. "*Da*. It looks as if it'll be a hard one."

"So 'twill," MacKean said. "Those clouds are getting darker by the moment."

Stewart grunted and began to pack up. "We should hurry, then."

Rurik was already on his horse. "I'll ride ahead and find shelter."

"We'll need it," Nik agreed.

The guard rode off, and the rest of them finished collecting their gear before they mounted up and headed down the trail.

At first the rain fell lazy and sparse, plopping in fat drops, much of the wetness deflected by the tree branches overhead.

Then a flash of lightning, punctuated by a crack of thunder, rolled over them, echoing off the mountains with shocking fury.

The startled horses pranced and balked, and it took a moment to get them under control.

"I hope Rurik finds cover from this rain," Gregor called over his shoulder to Ailsa.

"Me, too," she replied fervently. She glanced behind her to where Nik followed, riding rear guard.

The lightning had spooked D'yoval and Nik was still struggling to bring his mount to heel, the horse shaking his head and prancing wildly. Ailsa pulled St. George to a halt and watched, holding her breath, for there was a sharp drop-off to one side of the trail.

But under Nik's firm hand, the high-strung animal stayed well away from the trail's edge. She relaxed as Nik finally got the horse under his command and nudged the creature to a faster pace to catch up.

There. She turned back in her saddle and realized she, too, was in danger of being left behind. She could still see Gregor, but barely. She urged St. George on just as the skies opened.

The rain poured, sheeted, stormed, and flooded down. It rained so hard, it was difficult to see, blanketing the trail with thick waves of sheer wetness.

Water ran across Ailsa's face, through her hair, and down her neck. Her shoulders and the tops of her breeches were instantly soaked.

Ahead, MacKean shouted something. She couldn't hear him over the howl of rain and wind, but she saw Gregor's eager move forward. *Ah. Rurik must have found shelter. Good!*

She turned to yell the welcome information to Nik, but found that he was too far back to hear her.

With a regretful look at the disappearing backs of the others, she pulled St. George to a halt and waited for Nik, tugging her cloak about her, the wetness already soaking through to her shoulders.

Behind her, Nik peered through the downpour and saw Ailsa waiting, her cloak black with rain, her face wet, tendrils of her hair plastered to her cheeks and neck. *She will be so cold.* He spurred D'yoval to a canter.

Rain pelted Nik's face, soaking his cloak and his hair. He reached up to swipe his eyes just as another flash of lightning cracked, followed by a roar of thunder. Seconds later, there was a crash as a tree came tumbling down the mountainside toward Nik and fell across the trail.

Nik pulled D'yoval back just in time to avoid the worst of the branches, but the animal was beyond calming. Terrified, D'yoval reared and screamed. Nik fought for control, aware that the horse was moving ever closer to the edge of the path.

Her heart thundering, Ailsa stood in her stirrups and watched. The fallen tree blocked the trail and kept her from riding to the rescue, and it was with gasping agony that she saw Nik struggle to hold D'yoval on the path. Another crack of thunder rumbled, and the horse reared and then backed off the steep trail. With a sickening crash, the two disappeared from sight.

"*Nae!*" Ailsa yelled. She cantered to the fallen tree and jumped from the saddle, holding St. George's reins tightly as she looked this way and that, trying to find a way around the obstacle. It took only a few seconds, but those seconds felt like hours, before she found a place where a branch had broken off and she could get through the tangled wall of broken limbs. Tying St. George to a branch, she wiped the rain from her eyes and hurried to where she'd seen D'yoval disappear with Nik. The torrential rain was erasing their tracks even as Ailsa peered over the side of the trail, her heart caught in her throat.

She threw her arm across her forehead to shade her vision from the onslaught and saw where the horse and rider had slid through the undergrowth and thin aspens, breaking branches and carving a wide path, but thick foliage obscured her view beyond that point. Had they stopped? How far did the slope go? Were either of them injured? She prayed there weren't sharp rocks or—

No. I can't think that.

She hurried back to where she'd left St. George, then tied his reins to his saddle and sent him off. As if he understood the urgency, the horse cantered down the trail toward the others.

Throwing her cloak back from her shoulders, she ignored the sheeting rain and ran back to where horse and rider had left the path. Slipping and sliding on mud and wet leaves, she frantically made her way down the embankment.

She finally gave up trying to stay upright and sat down, scooting her way to the bottom of the ravine.

It was laborious, filthy, muddy work, and she was exhausted and shivering by the time she reached the bottom. And there they were.

D'yoval stood in the middle of a stream, nudging at something near his feet.

Nik lay on his side in the small stream, moaning as he struggled to sit, his cloak twisted about him, the rain pelting his face as blood washed from one arm into the water to swirl, whirl, and then disappear.

Chapter 16

Nik woke up slowly, opening his eyes to the blackness that hung above him. Though wrapped in fur blankets, he was cold. So very cold. And yet his shoulder and head were afire, his eyes leaden as if weighted down.

He shivered, and a stab of pain rippled from his shoulder down his arm. He clenched his eyes closed and gritted his teeth as he fought off the searing agony. *Bozhy moj, such pain. What happened? Where am I?*

He swallowed, his mouth dry and hot, and realized he was nude. As that was how he normally slept, he didn't find it odd, but the fact that he was on a hard floor instead of a comfortable bed made him wince every time he tried to shift to a more comfortable position.

His memory stirred and he remembered lightning and thunder and a falling tree followed by D'yoval sliding down an embankment. Now there was such pain in Nik's shoulder—had he landed on a rock? He didn't remember anything after that except icy-cold water and Ailsa tugging him to his feet, urging him to go just a bit farther. And then a bit more. And then—

We found a cave. He'd been so very glad to get out of the relentless rain, and for the chance to lie down. He didn't remember much after that.

He shifted his shoulder experimentally and instantly regretted it. *Bozhy moj, but I hurt.* Every inch of him was bruised, aching, or in pain. Perhaps he should keep his eyes closed and let sleep reclaim him. The thought beckoned, for under his discomfort was a deep sense of exhaustion. He was so very, very tired. So much so that lifting his head seemed too much of an effort.

A faint rustle came from nearby, followed by the familiar *thump-crackle* of a log as it settled into flames. Somewhere close, meat simmered over a fire, the delicious scent making his mouth water. His eyes may be tired, but his stomach growled in demand.

He collected enough energy to turn his head. A fire burned cheerily, a hare on a spit hanging over it. He could just make out a figure on the other side of the fire, but the firelight made his head hurt too much for him to focus.

"Ah. You're awake."

He knew that voice, low and melodic, husky, with a Scottish accent.

"What time is it?" His voice was more croak than words, but Ailsa seemed to understand him.

"'Tis night." A rustle sounded in the dark and then she was kneeling beside him, the firelight warming her skin to touchable peach. "Dinnae move. Your shoulder could start bleeding again."

He lifted a hand to his shoulder and found it heavily bandaged, a large knot tied at his neck. "Is it broken?"

"Nae." She bent over him to examine the knot, her soft braid brushing his hand. When she straightened, she managed a faint smile, though it did not reach her eyes. "I used my chemise to wrap your wound, so 'tis quite bonny, as bandages go."

He looked at her. Her heavy coat gaped open where she bent over him, her thin muslin shirt outlining her breasts. God, but she had perfect-size breasts, just fit for a man's hands.

"Does it hurt?" she asked.

"What? Oh. *Nyet.*" No more than he could bear.

"I can loosen the bandage if you think it'll be more comfortable."

The thought was appealing, for the bandage was tight, but the thought of the pain of untying and then rewrapping the bandage gave him pause. "It is fine. We will leave it."

She sat back on her heels, clasping her knees with both arms. "I'm glad you're awake. It's been a wee bit quiet, having nae one to argue with."

He managed a faint smile in return. "I'll be ready to listen to your nonsense once this headache and my shoulder have ceased plaguing me." His voice creaked as if he'd swallowed a rusty file.

"You've a fever." She placed a cool hand on his forehead. "You've had one since this morning."

"This morning?" He sent her a searching glance. "We have been here a night and day, then."

"Aye."

That explained why he ached so much, and why his mouth felt as if it had been stuffed with cotton. "I need something to drink."

"I'll fetch some water."

"No water. Vodka."

She quirked a brow in his direction. "You just woke oop. Dinnae you think you should try the water first, and work your way to the vodka?"

"It will dull my shoulder ache."

"It will make your head ache worse."

He scowled, though it tugged painfully at a wound on his forehead.

"Do nae look at me as if you'd like to roast me over the fire. Spirits are nae guid when one has a fever. Once you're better, you may have some."

"You should not deny a sick man."

"I can and I will." She placed her hand on his forehead, her fingers deliciously cool against his hot skin. "You've a fever still, though 'tis nae as high as it has been." She removed her hand and he instantly wished she hadn't. "The vodka is in the flask on the other side of the fire. As soon as you have the strength to get up, walk over there, and fetch it yourself, you may have as much as you wish. Or, of what's left of it, anyway."

He slanted her a surprised look. "You've been drinking my vodka?"

"I've been here alone, with you ranting in a foreign tongue. I may have had a wee sip or so." She smiled, her gray eyes warming. "Dinnae look surprised; you'd have done the same had our positions been reversed."

He couldn't argue with that.

"If you're to have some water, you'll need to sit oop a bit. I'll move the saddlebags for you to lean on, but you'll have to help, for I cannae move you by myself."

She slid the saddlebags near him and then slipped an arm under his good shoulder. It took several moments of blinding pain, but he was soon reclining. He shivered when the blanket slipped and the damp, cold air nipped him.

She immediately tugged the blankets back in place, her fingers brushing his bared chest.

He fought the desire to hold her hand there. "I've imagined you taking off my clothes, but never under these circumstances."

She chuckled. "Aye, this is nae very romantic. Your clothes were wet, and as you were soon burning with fever, I dinnae think it guid to leave you in them." She smoothed the blankets, covering him thoroughly, and then handed him an uncorked flask.

He lifted the water to his dry mouth, the taste so fresh and inviting that he had to force himself not to gulp it. Finally refreshed, he lowered the flask. "Thank you."

"You're welcome."

He loved the lilt in her voice, the silkiness of her tone; it teased and soothed at the same time. He took another drink of water. "I shall owe you for this once we are rescued."

"I dinnae do anything you would nae have done for me."

"That is true. Had I found you alone, I'd have definitely removed all your clothes and wrapped you in fur blankets before a fire."

"That is reassuring," she replied in a dry tone.

He grinned. "Where are my clothes?"

"I washed the blood from them, and they're spread oot by the fire. They're almost dry."

She'd taken such good care of him, and under trying circumstances, too.

Impulsively, he caught her hand and lifted it to his lips, pressing a kiss to her fingers. "Thank you."

Their gazes locked and she flushed before she tugged her hand free, her smile disappearing. "'Twas nothing. Really." She moved away. "I should see to our dinner." She returned to the fire where the rabbit roasted.

He watched the firelight play across her face, kissing even more warmth into her cheeks. "You went hunting, I see."

"I used the leather straps from your bedroll and some sticks to fashion some snares. This is all I've caught, though. We'll need more if we stay longer."

His smile slipped a bit. "You haven't heard from the others?"

"Nae, and I doubt we will. Before I followed you and D'yoval, I sent St. George on to let them know to come looking for us, but it was raining hard enough to wash the ground away."

"So there won't be tracks to show where we left the trail."

"I fear nae. I daresay MacKean and the others have gone on by now. Once you're better, we'll join oop with them at Greer's camp. They'll wait for us there."

"Very good." He gingerly touched his forehead. "My head aches like the devil."

"'Tis the last bit of fever. You should go back to sleep. You will heal faster."

She was so matter-of-fact, her tone exactly the one mothers used with ill children, that it annoyed him greatly. Of course, right now even breathing annoyed him greatly. *I am as weak as a kitten.*

A yawn tickled his throat and he suddenly realized she was right; he did need to sleep. He was so very, very tired. "I have been sleeping, yet I'm sleepy still." He couldn't keep the petulance from his tone.

"I would nae call it sleep. It was all I could do to keep you still; I was worried you'd break open your wounds." She sat back on her heels. "You were a stubborn patient. More than once, I thought aboot tying you oop."

For all her bold words, he caught the faintest quaver in her voice, and he realized she'd been frightened. She'd been alone, responsible for his care, and most likely fretting about those she'd left behind, not to mention the worry she had for the success of their mission. "Come here."

She shook her head. "I need to watch the rabbit or it will burn."

"We're three feet away, if that. Come," he repeated.

She hesitated, but then joined him, sitting at his side.

He captured her hand again, only this time he tugged her closer. "Lie with me."

She didn't move.

"It will keep me warm. This is a damp cave." He thought she would argue, but after a second, she did as he asked, though she stayed outside the covers, her head resting carefully on his good shoulder.

She fit against him as if made to be there, and he rested his cheek against her hair. His arm went around her, his hand resting on her hip. "You needn't be so worried, *krasavilsa*. It will take more than a mere fall from a horse to hurt me."

"This was nae a mere fall. It— I've been worried."

"I am fine," he soothed, closing his heavy eyes. *Bozhy moj*, but he could sleep forever like this, her warm, curvy body against him. It was as if they were pieces of the same puzzle, her head on his shoulder, her arm over his chest, her hip pressed to his—

"Do you remember what happened?" she asked.

He opened one eye and glanced at her before closing it again. "Aye. It began to rain and there was a lightning strike, which D'yoval did not like. I tried to calm him but the lightning, it came again, and a tree fell across us. I tried again to calm him, but the reins became tangled, and I could not hold him, and we slid off the embankment."

"All the way to the bottom of the ravine."

A thought occurred to him, and Nik opened his eyes. "D'yoval. Is he—"

"He's fine. A little scraped, but nothing that will nae heal."

Relieved, Nik closed his eyes again, noting that her thick braid now lay over his arm, a comforting weight.

Ailsa toyed with the edge of the blanket where it rested under his stubbled chin. She could see the tiredness already stealing him away. She thought about letting him drift off, but she couldn't. Not yet. "Nik, the reins were nae tangled."

He slanted a sleepy glance her way. "Oh?"

She lifted up on her elbow. "You could nae hold them because you'd been shot."

"Shot?" Nik repeated blankly, his eyes now wide open. "I couldn't have been . . . but—" He frowned. "The pain in my shoulder happened *before* I fell." No wonder he hadn't been able to control D'yoval. "I don't remember hearing a pistol shot."

"I thought it was thunder. Perhaps you did, too."

"The brigands were lucky; the storm covered their attack."

Nik saw a shadow cross over her face, as if she wished to say something more. But after a long moment, all she said was, "I hope we catch them. I—" A log shifted in the fire and sent sparks fluttering through the air. She pushed herself up, her braid trailing across his shoulder as she moved away. "I must tend the fire. I dinnae wish our dinner to burn."

Before he could protest, she was already gone, adjusting the logs with a long stick. It was tempting to call her back, but from the serious expression on her face, he knew the moment was lost.

She had reason to be worried, as did he. *Why would thieves go to so much trouble merely to rob us? Something is not what it should be. We are vulnerable away from the others; we must rejoin our party.* "We will leave tomorrow."

Her brows lowered. "Perhaps. If you're oop to it—"

"*Nyet.* We must go as soon as we can. We've a mission to accomplish and we're not safe away from our escort."

"I'll nae have the wound on your shoulder opening again. It was . . ." She clamped her lips together until they were in a white line and suddenly she became very busy with the fire.

He pressed his fingers to the wadded bandage. He couldn't tell a thing about the wound except that it ached. "Is it that bad?"

She didn't meet his gaze. "Bad enough."

"Is the bullet still in my shoulder?"

She shook her head. "It merely sliced you, although it was a deep cut, and bled so much, I feared . . ." She turned away, the shadows hiding her expression.

"It's a good thing you tied the bandage so tight. There's not a spot of blood to be seen."

"It is healing. And you need nae worry that we're exposed. I have been keeping guard, in case the brigands find us again, and I tied a string across the mouth of the cave and threaded two cups to it, to serve as an alarm."

"And D'yoval?"

"He is inside the cave, near the entrance. He cannot be seen from the outside."

Nik could not imagine his men doing any better. "Thank you for watching after both me and my horse."

She shrugged as if she didn't care one way or the other, though the brightness of her eyes belied her casual tone. "It had to be done."

Nik fought the urge to close his heavy eyes. "Where are my weapons?"

"You rifle's there."

She nodded toward one side of him and he realized his rifle was leaning against the wall, easily within his reach.

"Your pistol is beside it," she added. "They got wet, so I cleaned them. They are loaded and ready, should you need them."

"That is something, at least." He yawned sleepily, noting the way her lips were downturned, her brow knit. "Do not look so glum. It will take more than one bullet to kill me."

"One bullet almost did kill you," she said sharply. "Had I nae seen where D'yoval slid off the trail, you would have bled to death in that stream."

"Perhaps. And perhaps not." He rubbed his hand over his face. His eyelids would not stay open, they were so heavy. He closed them and murmured, "Tomorrow, we leave."

"We'll see," she said flatly.

He thought about disagreeing with her, but sleep began to creep in, stealing his thoughts and lulling him to quiet. After a few moments, he heard Ailsa beside him. She arranged his blankets, tucking them around him until he was once again cocooned in warmth.

The fire crackled, and the pleasant scent of roasting rabbit made the cave seem homelike, especially with Ailsa beguilingly close. *Close enough for a kiss*, he thought wistfully.

With that last, lingering thought he fell back into a deep, deep sleep.

Chapter 17

D'yoval nudged Ailsa's pocket, pushing her a step to one side.

She clicked her tongue, trying not to laugh at the insistent horse. "You are as stubborn as your master, you are."

The horse snorted in protest, then butted his nose against her pocket again.

Laughing, Ailsa fished out the bit of dried apple and fed it to him. She'd found a number of apples in Nik's saddlebags, as well other items that had helped them get through these last few days. But supplies were now low, and she'd had no luck in snaring another rabbit.

It was a good thing they were leaving in the morning to rejoin the others. Had Nik had his way, they'd have left today, but she'd been adamant about waiting. If the brigands found them, they'd have to make a run for it, which would reopen his wounded shoulder.

She glanced about her now. Her pistol was tucked in her belt, just in case they were discovered by someone other than their traveling companions. The peacefulness of the woods eased her tensions for the moment.

She patted D'yoval as he munched happily, running her hand over the scratches on his neck and side. Thankfully they weren't deep. She remembered how close the tree had fallen to the horse and she wrapped her arms around the animal and rested her cheek on his powerful neck, breathing in the earthy scent of his mane and the sweetness of the apple. Overhead, the sun shone brightly and warmed the air while birds sang in the trees. She closed her eyes, the sun delightful on her shoulders.

"D'yoval has charmed you."

She turned to find Nik just outside the mouth of the cave. His legs were planted as if he were standing on a ship, his powerful thighs outlined by his black breeches, his calves lovingly encased in riding boots, while a wide leather belt encircled his narrow hips. His muscled arms were crossed over his bare chest, a coat hanging loosely from his shoulders. With his shadowed beard and torn clothing, he looked more pirate than prince.

Why, oh why had she made the bandage so thick that Nik's shirt would not fit over it? She'd used her chemise to make the blasted thing, too, and there wasn't enough of it left to make another, so they were stuck with him wandering about looking like . . . *that*.

She cleared her throat. "'Tis a bit cold. You should wear your cloak."

"I'm fine, *krasavitsa*." A flash of humor softened his mouth. "Does it bother you that I do not wear a shirt?"

"Och nae. I barely noticed. I just thought that as 'tis a wee bit cold this morning, you might want to cover"—she waved a hand toward his bared chest—"that oop, and your coat does nae work because of the bandage. But if you dinnae wish to use your cloak, then a blanket would do just as well. I can fetch one for you, if you'd li—"

"*Nyet*. I am fine as I am." Humor glinted in his green eyes. "I would worry my nakedness might offend your sense of modesty, but as you took off all my clothes when I first arrived, I need not fear."

"I did nae have time to look. I was too busy trying to stop the blood." Her voice was sharper than she intended, and she swallowed the wave of irritation that had made it so, and then added mildly, "I merely think you would be warmer were you to wrap oop in a blanket. That's all."

He grinned. "But *you'll* be warmer if I do not."

Her cheeks simply could not get hotter than they were.

He added in a smug tone, "I would be perfectly fine if you decided not to wear your shirt, as well. That would only be fair."

"You're right; that is quite fair of you. And lecherous."

He chuckled. "It is normal that men and women should look at one another. Surely you have seen a man's chest before?"

"Of course I have," she said in a lofty tone. "The harvesters who come each summer to bring in the oats and barley often go withoot their shirts. And each year, men from different villages compete in the games in Inverness wearing nothing but kilts and boots." Her father wouldn't let her watch the games, but Nik didn't need to know that.

"Ah, a woman of experience. Then I need have no fear I'm shocking your sensibilities."

To be truthful, it wasn't her sensibilities, but other parts she didn't wish to think about that were affected by him. Nothing had prepared her for the feast before her. He was all sinew and muscle, hard and firm planes that made her fingers ache to touch him.

Somehow, Nik's bare chest was *different* from the few male chests she'd seen. The others had warranted no more than a mild glance, but she could no more ignore this one than she could stop breathing. Over the last few days, Nik's illness had kept all lustful thoughts at bay. But today he'd arisen much recovered, and she felt increasingly vulnerable when he was near.

Unaware of her turmoil, he walked farther into the sunlight, the coat swinging open. Streaks of golden sun flickered across his chest and powerful forearms, and she followed the bars of light down to his taut, ribbed stomach.

She imagined placing her hands on that hard stomach, of the warmth that would soak into her fingers from his heated skin. Of the way she could trail her hands down to—

She yanked her gaze back to his face, trying not to notice his strong neck where his dark hair curled so beguilingly, still damp from where he'd bathed in the stream not an hour ago. "Your hair has nae yet dried. You'll catch your death of the ague."

"It will dry soon enough."

She answered him with a sniff. This morning, after their paltry breakfast of dried venison, Nik had announced his intentions to bathe in the stream. She'd pointed out that it would wet his bandage and potentially reopen his wound. But, instead of seeing the dangers, he'd taken her advice as a challenge.

He'd been in far better spirits since that bath. She, meanwhile, was irked.

She turned her attention back to D'yoval and threaded her fingers through his mane, untangling it as she went.

Nik crossed the clearing to stand in front of the horse, patting the animal's velvet nose. "He is beautiful, *nyet*?"

Ailsa kept her gaze on the horse. "Magnificent. The horse, I mean." *Blast it, why did I say that? Of course I meant the horse.* She hurried to ask, "How long have you had him?"

"Four years. He was given to our country by the Prussians as an apology for their behavior on some border issues."

"I wish someone would make such an apology to me." She smoothed D'yoval's mane and then stood back to admire him. "You are fortunate to receive such extravagant gifts."

"I get many gifts, but few have been as welcome as D'yoval." Nik moved to the other side of the horse and patted its neck. "As my grandmother often says, 'When everything is special, nothing is special.'"

"What does that mean?"

"If you eat off a gold plate, and drink from a gold cup, and sleep in a gold bed day after day after day, there will come a moment when you will find yourself in an inn with a blue crockery plate in your hand, and you will be astonished at the beauty."

"Are you complaining aboot gold plates and cups? Because if you are, I'll gladly help you be rid of them all."

He gave a dry laugh. "I sound ungrateful, and I did not mean to be. I am fortunate, and I know it. But do not think I have everything I wish for, any more than anyone else. That does not happen."

She shouldn't have asked, for they were dancing around some sensitive subjects, but she couldn't help herself. "What sort of things *do* you wish for?"

A thoughtful expression crossed his face. "Before this journey, I would not have been able to answer that. But being away from my men, I realize how much I miss being Nik instead of Nikolai, His Royal Highness."

"What is the difference?"

"Princes do not own. They are owned."

"Surely it is nae so severe as that."

"From the time I was young, I've known that one day, Oxenburg would be mine to rule. I was told by every tutor I ever had that I could not waste time playing, but must be ready to bear the weight of the crown."

"That dinnae sound like a pleasant childhood."

"It was . . . lonely, in some ways." His expression softened. "Fortunately, I have brothers, and where there is a pack of boys, there is laughter and mischief."

"All overshadowed by the dark warnings of your tutors."

"They did what they had to, and they were right. I am the future king. Now, I perform the duties of the future king. I eat and live and breathe as the future king. It is not just what I am—it has become who I am."

He had smiled, though she detected a hint of sadness. "Won't you enjoy being king? It's rewarding to see your lands and people prosper. I cannae think of a happier day than when my father told me he was entrusting Castle Leod to my care."

Nik's dark green eyes measured her. "It can be fulfilling. I do not deny that. But there's a price."

She eyed him curiously. "Which is?"

"You have value, but not as a person. People will try to gain your favor. They will woo you, pretend to like you, act as if they care for you. And all the while, all they want is to throw dust in your eyes so you won't notice their ill intentions."

"That sounds rather horrible." She pursed her lips, unwilling to look away from him. Even half clothed, he had a kingly air. He wore his responsibilities and power without thinking, without being aware of it. A twinge of envy made her ask, "What exactly does a 'future king' do?"

"I build strong alliances with those who can protect us, and fend off the treachery of others."

"Treachery again. Is it really so common?"

His face grew grim. "There is much dishonesty in this world. I have known that since I was young." He patted D'yoval. "It was a painful lesson. I was but sixteen; sometimes the things we learn at that age feel harsher."

Sixteen? Ah. "A woman."

He laughed softly. "What boy of that age thinks of anything else?"

Though he laughed, a shadow had darkened his green eyes.

"Who was she?"

"The daughter of a minor count in the Oxenburgian court. She was older than me, almost twenty." A mirthless smile touched his lips. "That should have been my first clue, for what woman of twenty would have aught to do with a lad barely sixteen?"

One with her eyes on a glittering crown. Ailsa swallowed a flash of anger at this ice-cold woman who'd taken advantage of a tenderhearted youth. "You fancied yourself in love, I daresay."

"Head over heels, as the saying goes. I even asked her to marry me, against my own father's wishes. She seemed thrilled, and—I thought—cared for me just as much as I cared for her."

"But she dinnae."

"Not even a little. A few months after our engagement was announced, I was in the stables seeing to a horse I'd just bought, and she and her father came in from a ride. They didn't see me standing in the back stall with my new purchase and I overheard them speak. My beloved was complaining about my callowness, my lack of conversation, my oh-so-boring declarations—all manner of things." He pursed his lips, a thoughtful expression on his face. "Now that I am older, I admit she had a point. I was a callow youth, a fool, and worse, I was in love. It's a wonder she didn't burst into tears from boredom every time I spoke."

"You are too kind," Ailsa snapped. "She knew exactly what she was doing."

"She did. But she is not at fault. It is how the marriage mart goes: women look for men who can provide well, and men look for women who will decorate their husbands' arms and provide heirs. There is no deceit in that, if one is honest. I just didn't know the rules of the game."

And to think her grandmother had been upset Papa hadn't given Ailsa a season in London. The more she heard about the way people went about finding a husband or a wife, the happier she was out of it. "My sisters had seasons in London and found husbands, but I believe they married for love."

"They are fortunate, then, for that is not always the case."

"My sisters valued character over wealth. None of them have married high, but they are all secure and happy."

"When you are in a position of wealth or power, the rules change. The number of those willing to use the words 'love' and 'forever' without meaning grows with each gold coin. My intended had been trained to do exactly what she did—seduce and marry the most influential youth she knew."

"Trained? Surely her parents did nae wish her to endure a loveless marriage."

"Her father didn't just wish it; he demanded it. When she complained about her boredom, he told her to keep her opinions to herself and to remember that once she was queen and had provided the throne with a prince, she would be free to find more interesting company."

"What a . . . a . . ." She folded her lips. "I have nae words."

"To a sixteen-year-old, it was the worst possible rejection. Of course, now that I look back on it, I realize I was a fool for believing her to begin with." His face hardened. "I've never made that mistake again."

"You mean, asking another woman to marry you?"

"That, and I've never again assumed anyone 'loved' me without a reason. Both decisions have stood me in great stead."

Her heart ached for the boy he'd once been. "What happened to that woman?"

"She married one of my cousins, a duke." A flicker of humor curved his warm mouth. "You may be happy to know she is now very fat and has nine children."

"Nine? Och, then perhaps their marriage was for love after all."

"*Nyet.* My cousin says it is the only way he can keep her home."

She winced. "Now I feel rather sorry for her."

"Why?" He shrugged. "We all make choices and at times, face disappointments. It's inevitable."

"Nae everyone is oot for their own good. Some people are kind and want only what is best for all."

"Not in my experience."

He said it casually, and she wondered if he'd felt this way before that ruinous betrayal. Had such a thing happened to her at that tender age, she'd have been harder, too, and definitely colder. She might also have believed, the way he now seemed to, that every declaration of affection was spurred solely by the desire to gain wealth and power, rather than by love. She couldn't imagine how lonely his life must be. "I'm sorry that happened."

"I'm not. It was a good lesson to learn. It taught me many things, not the least of which is that people see what they want to see—a bit of information that has stood me in good stead."

She frowned. "How so?"

"In parts of Europe, princes are as common as sparrows. And because of the very public and very foolish actions of a few of those princes, many people have such low expectations of a prince's behavior that they expect him to be a half-drunk womanizer, one who thinks his only purpose on earth is pleasure, and is bored by conversation of any consequence. People with secrets and power pay no attention to such a princely fool and will converse freely in front of him, thinking he not only doesn't care, but that he lacks the intelligence to understand anything he may hear or see. So, he comes, he goes, he listens, he sees, and he learns."

And suddenly, Ailsa understood why Nik's reputation was so different from his true character. He *used* those expectations to his advantage, and even encouraged them. She couldn't believe he was sharing this with her. But then again, why not? Who would believe her, if she told them? And whom would she tell? She was confined to the depths of Scotland, and would never leave. "This prince you speak of. That's you. You hear and see and learn."

"And seduce." His eyes glimmered with amusement. "Of all the roles one can don, that offers the most pleasure." His voice purred over the word, caressed it, and made her skin prickle as if he'd touched her. He slid his hand along D'yoval's back, Ailsa's gaze moving with it.

He had the most sensual hands she'd ever seen, his fingers long and masculine. They made her think of being touched, caressed, stroked.

Her mouth went dry and she had to fight not to reach out for his hand, which was so temptingly close. Oh, the things she might have done, had she been a bolder sort of woman.

She cleared her throat. "Thanks to the actions of England's last prince, whose exploits and scandals filled more newspaper columns than I like to remember, I am one of those who have a rather poor impression of princes. I always thought they did nothing more important than dancing at balls, chasing the latest beauties, and attending lavish dinner parties. I assumed a bevy of courtiers saw to the more serious issues."

"When I go to social events, I do not just go and dance and talk to whomever I wish. Everything I do— *everything*—is watched, measured, and recorded. Even when I attend a ball, I am engaged in other activities. When I am dancing with the wife of an Austrian baron, I am confirming an alliance. When I smoke a cigar on the terrace with a Russian count, I am paving the way for a future treaty. When I ignore the ambassador from England, I am sending a message that my country does not appreciate the way they're treating our close allies, the Prussians."

"All that at a simple ball?"

"*Da.* And sometimes more." His smile held a hint of bitterness.

"So that's where you get your different faces."

His brows lowered. "Different faces?"

"You are one way when you talk to some people, another way when you talk to others, and a third way when you talk to me. Sometimes I wonder which is really you."

"*Bozhy moj*, you make me sound atrocious. This is what you said you saw when you read my palm, I think. I do not like it."

He sounded genuinely upset, which surprised her. "I only meant that you are probably quite guid at what you do."

After a moment, he said shortly, "I do what I must."

"I'm glad I dinnae have gold plates and cups and beds, for it seems like a lot of work. Do your brothers also do these things?"

"My brother Max is our general. My brother Wulf— he and his wife have become our best representatives in foreign courts. And Alexsey has undertaken the preservation of our cultural heritage, especially the Romany, from whom we descended. As in most families, we each have our place. I daresay 'tis the same with yours."

"Aye. My sisters are married and have set aboot providing heirs. Papa purchased my brother a set of colors, since the lad was mad for the military. And Gregor . . ." She paused, thinking about her cousin. "Gregor is still trying to figure oot what he can contribute."

"And your father?"

"He is in London, fulfilling his political duties. That is his passion."

"What about you, *krasavitsa*?" Nik's gaze fixed upon her face. "What is your passion?"

"Castle Leod. I make sure there is enough food in the

larder for winters, enough silver in the coffers to pay taxes, make repairs, and take care of our tenants and retainers, and keep my grandmother oot of trouble."

"Do you enjoy these things?"

Enjoy? She'd been honored Papa had put his trust in her to oversee the estate, but she'd never thought of her duties as "enjoyable." "I'm guid at it."

"I'm sure you are. But does it inspire you? Leave you breathless from meeting the challenge? Do you wake up eager to face the new day, ready to *make* something of this opportunity?"

"I love Castle Leod. I grew oop there and—"

"We all love our homes. I'm asking if this is your life's purpose. Do you see yourself doing it your entire life? When you're thirty? Forty? Fifty?"

Fifty? "To be truthful, I never thought that far ahead."

"You should. In many ways, you are the freest person I know. Your family is well situated: no one has a true claim on you or your time. Your sisters are busy elsewhere, your brother is enjoying his commission, and your father's employed in something that absorbs him. *You* deserve that, too. You should find the thing you love to do, and take advantage of that before responsibility steals away your freedom."

"But . . . what aboot Castle Leod and the people? Nae. I'm where I belong."

"What about a husband? Children? A family of your own?"

"I dinnae see me having any of those."

He laughed softly. "There are too many men in Scotland to let a beauty like you walk away."

He thinks me a beauty? "My sisters are the beauties in my family, nae me. Nae one has ever paid me the least heed." At his shocked look, she hurried to add, "Nae that I wished them to, for I've always been happy with my lot."

"*Bozhy moj*, are the men of Scotland all fools? I refuse to believe that. You will be married and with child within the next year, perhaps two, but no more. It is inevitable." He spoke as if he'd just commanded such a thing to happen.

How could he go from telling her he thought she was beautiful one moment, to almost demanding she marry a fictional person who didn't even exist, the next? For some reason, it irked her.

"You, too," she replied hotly. "Don't all princes have to marry?"

"In time, *da*." His expression darkened. "I will eventually marry and it will be to someone who brings wealth, or a strong connection, to our country. Someone trained to navigate the dangerous shoals of court life. But you have no such complications. When you marry, it will be for one reason only: love."

Envy colored his voice. Though he hadn't chosen them, he'd paid for those gold cups and plates, and was paying for them still. Ailsa tried to imagine the sort of worldly, sophisticated woman, who could live in the prince's world, one filled with oily courtiers and false friends. The woman would be beautiful, of course, and intelligent, and knowledgeable about life in court. *A paragon. And yet I'm sure one exists . . . somewhere.* The whole thing was rather lowering.

"What are you thinking, *krasavitsa*? You look sad."

"I'm nae sad." She pasted a smile on her stiff lips. "I was merely thinking that I've had enough lounging aboot. If we wish to leave at first light tomorrow, we should see to packing oop." She turned and walked toward the cave.

He fell in behind her, his boots crunching the dead leaves at their feet. "How long do you think it'll take us to catch up to the others?"

She paused by the cave opening. "Nae more than a day, mayhap two, if they're waiting for us in Greer's camp, which is where I think they'll go. This ravine travels northwest, which is the direction the trail followed, too."

"Good." He glanced up at the sun. "I hope the weather holds."

"So do I," she admitted, her gaze drawn to his stomach as he lifted his hand to rake his hair from his face.

Perhaps it wasn't just his powerful chest muscles that kept capturing her imagination, but something subtler. Like the fine, crisp hair that covered it in such a beguiling fashion, narrowing when it reached his taut stomach, into a thin line that disappeared under his belt in the most tantalizing way.

She wanted to trace her finger down that line and follow it to the forbidden secrets below.

Goodness, where had that come from?

"Bloody hell, you must stop looking at me like that."

Ailsa's gaze locked with Nik's, her face heating. "Like what?"

"As if you wish to devour me whole."

"I'm nae the only one."

"Indeed, you aren't." He grasped her wrist, his fingers warm on her skin. "We have been dancing about this for days now. It is time we stopped dancing."

She looked about wildly, feeling like a rabbit trapped in the seductive gaze of a viper. "I'm nae dancing. I'm just—" Good lord, could she even put it in words? *Should* she?

"You want me as I want you." He gave her that damnably knowing smile that always set her stomach aquiver. "Are you afraid, *krasavitsa*? Now that we've shared our secrets?"

"Of course nae." She tugged her wrist free and, impatient to put some space between them, brushed past him. Outside the cave sat the log that she'd used as a hitching post for D'yoval. She sat down on it, and stretched her legs before her, crossing them at the ankles. She was safe here, for there was only room for one person. "I'll admit my mind has been wandering a bit."

"And your eyes."

"I'm honored, I suppose, that you've been looking back. That's nae something I'm used to."

"You should be." He put his foot on the log beside her and rested his elbow on his knee, so close that his ankle brushed her hip. "To be honest, I've been doing more than mere looking."

"Oh?" she managed to say, though it was more a sigh than else.

"I've been wondering what your bare skin tastes like. How you'd quiver if I touched you a certain way. How much I'd love to see you naked, lying before me—"

"Goodness, I did nae think to hear all that! I was—I

was nae thinking those sorts of things. I was just wondering what it would be like to . . . touch you. Perhaps kiss you once again. But that's all."

Nik noted how she bit her lip after her denial, as if worried it had sounded as untruthful as it was. God, but he loved those lips. Plump and full, they flashed smiles like lightning strikes, and issued quips that could cut iron. Never had he met a stronger or more stubborn woman.

When he'd first seen her, he'd thought her merely prickly spirited, unremarkable in all else. The high-waisted gowns that were so in fashion did nothing to reveal Ailsa's beauty, let alone the fire of her spirit. But dressed in formfitting breeches and a shirt that followed the generous curves of her hips and legs, her waist defined by a belt, her full breasts behind the thin muslin of her shirt, she was transformed from a shy dumpling of a woman into a brazen, brave warrior.

She was unique. Unpredictable. Often annoyingly right. And so sensual, she made him ache with want.

She tilted her head back, the sun warming her dark blond braid where it hung over her shoulder, highlighting the bright gold that mingled with other colors—the darker gold of an antique coin, the lighter brown of a brand-new saddle. There were even some strands the color of the peat beneath their feet. The hues mixed together in a delicious silken tangle that begged to be touched. *Bozhy moj*, but he longed to undo her strict braid and sink his hand into that rich mass of hair. He'd tilt her face to his and kiss those soft lips, which she was biting in such a beguiling fashion.

Somehow, he found himself standing before her.

She looked up, caution deepening the color of her eyes.

"You said we should pack our things, *nyet*?" He held out a hand to assist her to her feet. "We will do it together."

She placed her hand in his.

He pulled her up, careful not to strain his bad shoulder. But as soon as she was standing, he took her place on the log and, in a lightning-quick move, tugged her firmly into his lap. "There," he said, wrapping his arm about her as he pressed a warm kiss to her temple. "Finally, you are where you belong."

Chapter 18

"You tricked me."

"A little." Nik nuzzled her ear—her hair was scented of lavender and honey. "You've but to say the word and I'll release you."

She didn't move, her thick lashes resting on the crests of her cheeks. "I'm thinking aboot it."

"We've been thinking too much, you and I." He traced his lips from her ear to her neck. She was slightly turned toward him, one hand flat on his bare chest.

"Aye, but"—she shivered as he brushed a kiss over her earlobe—"this is a mistake. I should nae—"

"Ow!"

Her gaze flew to his, a horrified look on her face. "Your shoulder?"

"*Nyet*, my pride." He sighed. "I'm not used to women questioning everything I say, especially while I'm kissing them."

Her lips quirked. "It's nae what you're *saying*, but what you're *doing*."

He slid his hand to her hip and pulled her closer. "I'm only doing what we've both been thinking about all day." God, but she had the most delicate neck. It begged for kisses, and he bent to oblige.

She shivered, closing her eyes. "This is . . . verrah pleasant. But . . ." She sighed and pulled away. "Won't this make our situation worse?"

"The situation where we cannot look at one another without imagining doing this?" He slid his hand over her hip to her waist, savoring the way she arched, her breasts pushing toward his chest. "And this?" He cupped his other hand behind her head and covered her mouth with a hard, long kiss.

She opened to him and he slid his tongue between her lips, filling her until she moaned. She gripped his coat lapel, though it was only hanging from his shoulder and did nothing to bring them closer. And yet there was no need, for he was already holding her as tightly as he dared, her full, soft curves delightfully gratifying against his body.

She gasped against his mouth, pulling back as she fought for breath.

He reluctantly stopped the kiss, though his body ached. "I burn for you." Never had he felt such desire. It crackled along his senses everytime she was near.

She leaned against him, her gray eyes smoky. "You are making it difficult to think."

"Then don't think at all. Just *do*. We are alone, in the middle of a beautiful forest, and we cannot go anywhere. Why shouldn't we share a kiss or ten?"

Her gaze dropped to where her palm lay flat against his skin. "I suppose it would nae hurt to have a kiss—"

"—or ten," he insisted.

She laughed softly, her voice husky. "Or ten," she conceded. "You tempt me." She leaned up to brush her lips across his cheek. It was feather-soft, like a butterfly's wing on his bare skin.

The innocent touch ignited the fires deep in his soul and with a huge sigh, he gathered her to him and buried his face in her neck, soaking in the lush feel of her, the scent of her skin and hair. "I would have you, *krasavitsa.*"

"And I, you." She slid her hands down his chest to his stomach and then back up. Seeking, touching, her breath harsh and quick.

Her thick lashes trembled on his cheeks as he bent to taste her lips. Gently at first, but soon he forgot his own attempt at caution as the raging heat that had been simmering under his skin since he'd first met her flared into life. He plundered her mouth, and devoured her ravenously. God, he'd wanted this, wanted it since the first time he'd seen her standing in the window at Castle Leod, proud and intractable.

He tugged at her jacket. "Remove this."

She pulled off her coat and dropped it, leaving nothing but her thin shirt between him and her breasts. All day, he'd been tormented by those full, round globes, how they pressed against her shirt when she moved, her nipples thrust so wantonly against the thin muslin.

He cupped her breast through the thin material, loving how the mound filled his palms with a gratifying weight. He flicked his thumb over her nipple, bringing it to a peak. She gave a soft cry and arched against him, tilting back her head and closing her eyes.

He flicked her nipple again and again, watching as she gasped and writhed with pleasure. He then bent to press his lips over her puckered nipple, swirling his tongue over the wet material so that it clung to the sensitive nub.

She buried her hands in his hair and pulled him closer, pressing her breast into his mouth until he could take no more.

She is, for this moment, mine.

The words echoed in his head—*mine, mine, mine.* He couldn't think the word enough.

He lifted his mouth from her breast and trailed kisses up to where her shirt parted at her neck. "Undo your braid," he whispered against her skin. "I would see your hair loose."

She lifted her arms, her wet shirt clinging to her breasts as she untied the braid. With hands that shook, she tossed aside the ribbon and began to untwine her braid.

Impatient, he speared his hands into her hair and dragged free the silken strands, spreading them in shiny waves over her shoulders. Mingled golds and browns met his gaze, like the beauty of a field of golden grain lit by the sun and furrowed in rich peaty soil, as pure and perfect as she.

Ailsa barely noticed the weight of her hair on her shoulders. Her body hummed from his touch, and with every breath she took, her nipples scraped the wet muslin of her shirt. Her legs were restless, her heart thudding wildly, her lips tender from his kisses. Desire as she'd never known it flooded through her.

And all she could think was that she wanted more. Needed more.

Now.

She gasped as Nik slid his hands from her hair to frame her face. He kissed her again, filling her mouth with his tongue, tasting and testing. She shed her final lingering doubts and gave herself to the passion between them, kissing him with heated fervor.

Never had she given herself to such wildness, and she reveled in it, in the freedom of releasing her feelings completely.

He moved his warm, seeking lips to her ear, nipping and teasing, leaving a damp trail that his warm breath turned into a torment.

She caught her breath as he nuzzled the crook of her neck, her hands splayed over his broad chest, his skin hot under her fingertips. She slipped her hands across him, threading her fingers through his crisp hair, savoring his rippling muscles as they warmed her palms. She was enthralled, captured, her imagination roaring ahead of her hands.

She wanted more of this. More of him.

And then more. And more again.

It was as if she'd been starved and hadn't realized it. As if deep inside, she'd longed for this but had been afraid to admit it. And now here he was, temptation embodied, and she couldn't kiss him enough, touch him enough, *feel* him enough.

She moaned as his hands ran down her back and then cupped her bottom in a deliciously firm grip.

She swung one leg over his knees and sat facing him, her legs parted over his muscular thighs. She slipped her arm over his good shoulder and pressed against him, and this time she was the one doing the kissing, the stroking, the touching. And did it, she did.

Nik was enthralled. Just when he thought his passion was at its height, she proved him wrong. He tugged her shirt free of her breeches, sliding his hand underneath, savoring her soft, warm skin. He loved her curves, and the luscious softness filled his hands and made him ache to dive into her.

He ran his hands higher, tugging her shirt up. Finally, he lifted her arms and pulled the shirt free. Enthralled, Nik's gaze locked on her creamy skin, roaming over her soft shoulders, down to the delicate shadows of her dimpled arms, and on to her full breasts. Plump, with large, blush-pink areolas that made his mouth water, they were perfection. And now they were bared to him, moving with her every breath, tempting him beyond thought.

God, he'd never seen a more beautiful sight. He pulled her closer and rubbed his chest against hers, knowing his hair would abrade her delicate nipples to new sensual heights.

She gasped and gripped his arms, throwing her head back and baring her neck for his kisses.

He kissed a heated trail to her ear as he slid a hand over one breast and rolled her nipple under his palm. Gasping wildly, she arched against him, her lips parting as he leaned forward to capture her lips and—

"*Nik!*"

She'd gone completely still, her eyes wide.

It took all his concentration to regain the ability to think. After a moment, he was able to say in a hoarse voice, "Yes?"

"Did you hear that?" she whispered. "Toward the stream."

He dropped a kiss on her shoulder, his groin aching with the heat growing between them. "I didn't hear a thing; my blood is thundering in my ears. I—"

She stood, giving him an agonizingly beautiful eye-level view of her breasts.

But only for a second.

"There! I heard it again."

She crossed her arms over her chest and stared into the woods.

D'yoval suddenly raised his head, his ears flicking forward as he stared into the woods in the same direction as Ailsa.

Nik frowned. *Bozhy moj, someone* is *coming.*

As if in answer, a twig snapped in the distance.

Ailsa scooped up her shirt and yanked it over her head, and then reached beside the cave and found her pistol.

Still hard with lust, Nik swallowed a bitter curse, and came to stand beside her. "My rifle?"

She jerked her head toward the cave. "Beside the opening."

He ducked into the cave and returned with his weapon. He checked that his weapon was loaded, and then stood beside Ailsa, listening intently.

Silence met them, the only sound their still-rapid breathing.

"No birds are chirping," she whispered.

He nodded, his attention finally on something other than the woman beside him.

The silence lengthened and grew. Finally, Nik lowered his weapon. "An animal, perhaps. Or a—"

The shrubs rustled and a man appeared, the sunlight glinting on the barrel of his pistol.

"Rurik!" Relief swept Nik. "I was beginning to wonder where you were." He'd started toward Rurik but Ailsa stepped in front of him, her gaze locked on the guard.

"If you wish to speak with him, then put doon your weapon," she told his guard.

Nik chuckled. "*Krasavitsa*, it is Rurik. He comes to escort us to Greer's camp."

She didn't look the least convinced. "Then why has he drawn his pistol?"

"Because he . . ." Nik turned to Rurik. "Why *do* you have your pistol drawn?"

The guard's thick black brows rose, but the pistol remained where it was, level and pointing at Nik's chest.

Nik's smile faded. "Rurik, what is this?"

Rurik's gaze flickered to the woods, an almost regretful look entering his gaze before he lowered the pistol and tucked it into his waistband. "The brigands."

Nik looked around, instantly on alert. "Did you see sign of them on your way here?"

"*Da.* It's good you're armed. But what happened to you? You've a bandage."

"A minor wound, nothing more. Lady Ailsa says it's only a—"

"*Ailsa!*" The yell echoed loudly.

Everyone looked in the direction of the voice.

"*Ailsa, where are you?*"

"Gregor?" Ailsa called out.

"You brought the whelp with you?" Nik asked Rurik.

"Not by choice." The broad-shouldered guard shook his head ruefully. "You can hear that man a mile away—he crashes through the bushes like a drunk deer. That was why I had my pistol drawn. With him thrashing through the woods the way he does, I was certain the thieves would find us all."

Ailsa said, "But you're nae traveling with him. You came from one direction; he's approaching from another."

The guard's gaze flickered to Ailsa. "Your cousin has been most annoying since you disappeared. Talking, talking, demanding we *do* something, but having no idea what. It was decided I should be the one to find you and escort you to where Greer and the others wait, but your cousin decided to strike out on his own."

"He can be verrah insistent."

The brush moved and then Gregor appeared, leading his horse, his pistol at the ready just as Rurik's had been. On seeing Ailsa, his eyes lit. "Good God, cousin, where have you been?" He replaced his weapon in its holder and tied his horse to a shrub. "Never disappear on me again! I've been so worried, I can't even—" Gregor had walked toward them, but now he stopped, his gaze going over Ailsa's loose hair, her untucked shirt. He turned to Nik, his eyes widening at the bare chest that met his gaze. "Bloody hell! What's going on here?"

Ailsa sighed. "Can you nae see the bandages, Gregor?"

"Oh. That. I didn't— And I should have— I'm sorry. That must be why— And then Ailsa helped— There's lace on that bandage, so I'll assume it's—"

"Gregor, please." Ailsa, holding back a quiver of a smile, held up a hand. "Enough!"

Rurik crossed his arms over his chest. "You see what I mean, *nyet*?"

Gregor's face was so red it appeared he might burst into flames. "I hope you weren't— Not that it would be any of my business if you did, but—"

"Careful, Gregor!" Ailsa sent him a warning look as she tucked her hair behind her ear. "As you noted already, he's been injured. The bandage is too thick for him to wear his shirt over it."

Gregor brightened. "Ah! Good, then!"

"I'm glad you're so pleased," Nik said tersely.

Rurik came to stand with Nik, his brows lowered. "I found where D'yoval slid off the trail. It's a wonder your arm isn't all you injured."

"I didn't hurt my arm from the fall. I was shot."

Gregor, who'd been walking toward them, came to an abrupt halt. "*What?*"

"You heard what I said."

"I know, but . . . I *knew* something had happened. You ran into the brigands after the storm, didn't you? And with only one horse between you. I was worried sick about you, and with reason."

"You should nae have been," Ailsa answered. "Nik

was shot during the storm. Someone fired under cover of the thunder, for I never heard it and I was looking right at him when it happened."

"Bloody hell." Gregor looked contrite as he turned to Nik. "Are you able to travel?"

Nik gave a dismissive wave. "Perfectly able. We would have already joined you, but your cousin was worried my wound might reopen."

"Ah. She's been babying you, has she? She does that."

Ailsa scowled at her cousin. "Only when 'tis warranted. I take it you found Greer, and all is well?"

"Aye. He's waiting with the others at the inn in Ullapool." Gregor gave the guard a hard look. "Hello, Rurik. Surprised to see me?"

"*Nyet.* I've heard you these last two miles, if not more."

Gregor's mouth thinned. "You should have waited for me."

"There was no need." Rurik grinned, his teeth gleaming in his bearded face. "I thought it best to find our lost members quickly. Traveling with you might be noisy, but it is not quick."

"I wouldn't have slowed you—"

"You would have. We both know it." Rurik turned to Nik. "We must reach the main road before nightfall. We can travel much quicker then."

"Let us go, then," Nik said. But inwardly, he sighed in disappointment. Ten minutes ago, he'd thought the world fit into the palm of his hand—or at least a delicious bit of it.

Ailsa frowned. "But your shoulder—"

"—is fine." He gave her a lopsided smile. "It is well enough, as you have seen."

Her face pinkened, but she gave a short nod, and then went to collect their things.

Nik was surprised at the wistfulness that pressed upon him as he watched her disappear into the cave. This had been their little oasis away from their quest, and he would miss it.

Stifling a sigh, he went to saddle D'yoval.

Chapter 19

Ailsa took a sip of her whisky. The smoky gold flavor slid over her tongue and warmed her throat. She smiled and stretched her booted feet toward the fireplace. The inn in Ullapool was small but comfortable. She was sitting in an overstuffed chair in the common room, a toasty fire at her toes, a glass of good whisky in her hand—and she sighed with pleasure.

After Rurik and Gregor had appeared, she and Nik had followed them out of the forest to the main road. With only three horses among them, Nik had insisted she ride before him. Her cousin had protested, but Nik had put an end to it by pointing out D'yoval's superior strength. It had been pleasant, riding tucked against Nik's broad chest, his heart in beat with her own.

Primed by their kisses, she was constantly aware of him—of his strong arms where they wrapped about her, of the ripple of his muscles when he guided the horse around a deep puddle in the road, of his powerful thighs where they rested against the back of hers.

Though they made excellent time once they reached the road, it grew dark quickly, and they had to camp one last night in the woods. There'd been a brief argument between Rurik and Gregor about who would stand guard, settled when Nik flatly ordered Rurik to let Gregor do his part.

Gregor had been elated, although he'd faced this morning bleary-eyed and sleepy. She thought he was as grateful as she was when, shortly after noon, they'd finally reached the inn where the others waited.

She'd never been so glad to see an inn, even though it marked the final stage of their journey. It was odd, but she both longed to be away from Nik and dreaded it. There would be no further opportunity for them to engage in their flirtation, as once the captives were recovered and they returned to Castle Leod, their adventure would be over.

Finished.

That was better for them both, and she knew it. But the realization left her feeling wistful and . . . not sad, for she'd tasted only a bit of the passion he offered, but . . . lonely. Yes, that was it. Lonely. And for the first time, she found herself wondering if Castle Leod was indeed her final destiny, or just a stop along the path.

So it was that her final ride in Nik's arms had been dampened by her conflicting thoughts. The only good thing that had come from the long morning's ride was that Rurik and Gregor seemed to have healed the breech between them, for they'd spent the better part of the ride engaged in a low-toned earnest conversation.

That had left her free to talk with Nik, though they'd said very little. Instead, she'd soaked in the feel of him, the nearness, refusing to think about how it would soon be over. She wasn't sure whether it was her imagination, but once or twice she thought she felt him press a kiss to the top of her head.

She sighed now as she crossed her legs at the ankles, enjoying the warmth of the fire as it soaked into the bottoms of her boots. *I need to focus on the ransom exchange and nothing else. That is where my thoughts should be.*

"It's good to be indoors, isn't it?" Gregor stood in the doorway, his riding gloves in one hand, watching her.

"It seems shamelessly luxurious."

"The inn?"

"The whisky. 'Tis heavenly." She gestured to a nearby bench. "Would you like a wee dram?"

"I don't mind if I do." He left the doorway and crossed the room to slide onto the bench, dropping his gloves on the table. "Thank you for sharing with me."

"Why would I nae?"

"Because it will appear on *your* bill of lading." He gave a rueful smile as he picked up a glass from the small tray at her elbow. "I'm woefully short of coin."

"As ever." She smiled at him fondly, sliding the bottle toward him. "Have however much you wish. I owe you more than a few glasses of whisky for riding to my rescue." Although she wished he and Rurik had been a little slower in finding her and Nik. She was just getting to know him, and what she'd found out had surprised and intrigued her.

And then there were those kisses.

She fought a shiver, well aware that her thoughts were in such turmoil because she and Nik had left their explorations at such an unfulfilling point. Several times during their ride here, she'd had to fight the desire to turn in the saddle and draw his mouth to hers and demand that he finish what they'd started.

Nik must have thought the same, for when they'd finally arrived at the inn, he'd dismounted and then reached up to assist her. As his hands had closed around her waist, he'd stayed in place and looked at her as if he would like to drag her all the way to the ground and take her there, as if there were no other people in the world but the two of them.

Just the memory of that look made her mouth go dry. She took a bigger sip of the whisky, coughing a bit when it burned her throat.

"Easy, lass!" Gregor chuckled. "'Tis not water."

"According to Papa, it is the water of life."

Gregor poured himself a bit more whisky, then replaced the stopper in the bottle and slid it back her way. "I was so glad we found you yesterday. I was beginning to fear I might never see you again."

"We would have caught up with you before long. We'd already agreed to set oot first thing in the morning." The fire crackled, a log settling into place, putting off a new wave of delicious warmth. "But it was kind of you and Rurik to search for us."

"You must have known I would. Although Rurik wasn't happy about it. We had quite a row over the whole thing. He wished to go on his own, saying he could travel faster and quicker alone, but I thought it best if at least two of us went, so we could cover more area. We had no idea where you were, and only the vaguest notion where to begin searching. We saw the felled tree, but we didn't know if it had fallen before or after you'd passed, and the rain made tracking an impossibility."

"I should have marked the place Nik slipped off the trail."

"It was raining so hard that day, it would have washed away any sign you might have made. I don't know what it is about Scottish rains, but they're wetter than others."

She agreed. "And more fierce."

"That too. After the rain stopped, Rurik raced back down the trail, hoping to find the two of you. I tried, too, but was no more successful." Gregor shook his head. "That's when Stewart and MacKean decided to take St. George and the ransom monies on to Greer's camp for safety."

"And when you and Rurik had a falling-out?"

He nodded glumly. "Rurik decided I was to go with the others, but I couldn't. Your safety is my responsibility."

She patted his hand and smiled. "I came to nae harm. And I'm glad both you and Rurik came to find us. Had Nik been injured worse, I might have needed both of you to get him here."

Gregor put his hand over hers and squeezed it. "I was never more glad to see anyone as when I saw you standing in that clearing."

"And I was never so glad as when I arrived in this inn and discovered we'd have real beds and hot meals."

He chuckled. "One never truly appreciates things until they're gone."

"I'll certainly never again sit at the bounty of the table at Castle Leod withoot remembering dried venison and hard rolls."

He shuddered. "Don't remind me!"

She settled back in her chair. "A bed, Gregor. With blankets and nae rocks poking us in the back. I will nae be able to sleep for the happiness of it."

And the disturbingly tantalizing memories of Nik's kisses and insistent hands. She found her gaze flickering up to the ceiling. Overhead were four bedchambers, all of which they'd bespoken. Nik would have one, she another, Gregor the third, and Rurik, as guard, would take the fourth room directly off the stairs. The rest of their party were bedding down in the grooms' quarters off the stables.

Thus it was that her bedchamber and Nik's were only a few steps apart. It was tempting, those few steps . . . if she dared. She found herself staring at the ceiling, her heart thudding at her own boldness.

But no, her common sense warned. It was already difficult being near him without betraying herself. If they went farther down this dangerously beguiling but tricky path, she wouldn't be able to hide her desires from anyone. She returned her gaze to her glass and took a fortifying sip. "I must win Lord Hamilton and Her Grace's release as soon as possible."

"It's been a wearisome adventure, but it should be easier from here on out," Gregor said, in a preoccupied tone.

He was absently tracing his finger around the edge of his whisky glass, his uncharacteristically somber gaze on the amber liquid.

Ailsa pinged the edge of his glass with the flick of her finger. "Oot with it."

He started. "Out with what?"

"Something's bothering you. I know you too well, Gregor Mackenzie, nae to know when there's a weight on your mind."

He shook his head. "It's nothing. A mere thought, best left unsaid."

"Either you tell me, or"—she slid the whisky decanter out of his reach—"nae more."

"You're a cold, cruel woman, Ailsa Mackenzie."

"Only when forced. Now, what has you staring into the bottom of your glass as if you can see the end of the world."

He sighed. "I will tell you—but you must promise to hear me through before you react."

"You're afraid I'll stop you?"

"I'm afraid you'll throw what's left of this lovely whisky into my face."

"Then you dinnae know how I feel aboot whisky."

He laughed, though it didn't reach his eyes. "Fine. I'll tell you, but I'm holding you to your promise not to throw your glass or anything else at me for saying my thoughts aloud." He fixed a level gaze on her. "I think it would be best if you returned home."

She blinked in disbelief. "Are you serious?"

"Very. Now, hear me out," he said when she straightened in her chair, ready to tell him what she thought of such an asinine idea. "It's the only thing Rurik has said that I agree with, and that's that from here on out, things could get deadly very quickly."

"I cannae believe you'd dare suggest such a thing, after all we've been through to get this far."

"I know you want to see this through, but we're facing an unknown enemy, someone who possibly intends us harm. And to be frank, you'll be a distraction."

"*What?* A distraction to whom?"

He flushed. "To everyone. You're a woman, and naturally we'll all wish to protect you."

She had to force herself to breathe. "Other than you and Rurik, who else has agreed with this ridiculous idea?"

"It may also have been a topic of conversation earlier today with Greer and MacKean."

"I see. So while I was nae in the room, the lot of you decided I was a 'distraction' and nae capable of dealing with the coming dangers. Lovely. Fortunately, I am here, and I am nae leaving until we've rescued Lord Hamilton and Her Grace."

"Ailsa, just think—"

"I *am* thinking! Within the next day or two, we'll be delivering the ransom, and our quest will be over. There may be dangers, I agree, but I came this far to face those dangers, nae to run from them like a frightened hare."

Gregor looked miserable "Please. We just want you safe."

"I'm nae leaving, and that's that."

"But—"

"She said *nyet*, Mackenzie," came a deep, rich voice directly behind them. "Now, leave her be."

Nik stood in the open doorway, his arms crossed over his broad chest, his cloak hood cowled about his shoulders. Shortly after they'd arrived, he'd changed his clothes, appearing with a fresh, less bulky bandage that fit well under his loose white shirt. With his coat unbuttoned, his shirt untied at the neck, his pistol tucked into his wide leather belt, a knife hilt protruding from one of his boots, she thought once again that he looked like no prince she'd ever imagined, but more like a highwayman, or a pirate. Powerful, untamed, and lethal.

Ailsa's heart fluttered as he shoved himself from the doorframe and walked past them to stand by the long, low table that sat against the farthest wall. "Ailsa has come this far—it would be foolish for her to quit now." His gaze rested on her for a long moment. "She is many things, this one, but foolish is not one of them."

"Thank you," Ailsa said. *I think.*

Gregor muttered something under his breath, but he didn't offer a challenge.

Footsteps sounded in the hallway, and Rurik entered, joined soon by Greer. Rurik went to the table where Nik had spread some maps, while the small, wizened-faced huntsman stopped near Ailsa and Gregor. The older man's face brightened on seeing the decanter of whisky.

Ailsa obligingly slid it his way.

He poured himself a glass. "Thank you, my lady."

"Of course." She forced a smile.

Greer tasted the whisky and smacked his lips. "Ah, that hits the gullet like a feather, it does."

She pinned him with a direct gaze. "I heard it has been decided I might be a distraction to the rest of you were I to continue on from here."

Greer sent a hard look at Gregor. "Who told you tha', I wonder?"

"It does nae matter. Do you believe that?"

Greer took a drink of the whisky, obviously stalling for time. Finally, he said, "I think you'll do what you know to be best, my lady."

"What I know to be best is for me to continue this journey, and the rest of you nae make fools of yourself thinking I'm too soft to handle my own pistol."

Greer flushed. "Nae one said you could nae handle yourself. We just thought—"

"You dinnae think at all," she said sharply. "I dinnae want to hear another word aboot this ridiculousness. And if any one of you finds yourself distracted from your duties because you're so silly as to fear for my safety over your own, then you should return home before your lack of wits causes someone to be killed."

"Aye, my lady." Looking miserable, Greer put his half-finished glass on the table. "You're right, of course. We should nae blame anyone but ourselves if we cannae keep our heeds on our own shoulders."

"Guid. We have one purpose here—to secure the safe release of the prisoners. We cannae become distracted."

"Aye, my lady. I'll remind the others." Greer inclined his head and sidled away from the table, making a break for the other side of the room, where he joined Nik and Rurik.

From where he stood, Nik inclined his head as if silently congratulating her, a smile curving his lips.

She fought the urge to return his smile, and instead turned back to Gregor, who was looking shamefaced.

"I'm sorry," he muttered. "I knew I should have kept that to myself."

"Dinnae be sorry. 'Tis guid I know what's being said so I can nip the head off any malcontented muttering before it blooms into something more."

"It's difficult to win someone's esteem."

"And harder to keep it."

Gregor looked across the room to where the three men were now bending over the map. "I do not think your prince holds me in much esteem."

She frowned. "He's nae 'my' anything."

Gregor slanted her an amused look. "Then perhaps you're 'his.' All I know is, he seems very possessive of you."

"You're imagining things." And yet Ailsa found herself watching Nik from under her lashes, an odd warmth stealing over her at Gregor's words. She supposed she did think of him as hers. At least a little. And why not? There were no other women on this journey, so without competition, whose else would he be? But knowing the little she did of Nik's past, it was very unlikely there would ever be a "his" for the prince. Such a thing would take more trust than he could give.

The thought depressed her, but it was good to admit the truth before her imagination went places she could never follow.

"Lady Ailsa?"

Nik gestured to the map on the table. "Come join us. We must decide on our movements from here on out."

"Of course." She rose and crossed to the table, aware of a faint sense of dread. The time had come.

Gregor collected his glass and followed.

Greer moved aside so she could see the map. "What are you thinking thus far?" she asked.

Rurik placed his finger on the map. "We're here. The inn at which we're to meet the abductors is here." He slid his finger along a road to a place farther north. "If we leave in the morning we'll reach the inn within a day, perhaps two."

"More travel," she murmured, trying not to grimace.

"*Da.* We are all tired of it." Rurik pulled a flask from his pocket, took a drink, and then offered it to Nik.

"But we've the element of surprise. Even with the few days we lost because of the brigands and the rain, we made guid time getting here," Ailsa said.

Rurik agreed. "Those fools won't be expecting us quite yet. It should have taken us another three to four days, at the least."

"So we've surprise on our side. Or we do unless the abductors have eyes in Ullapool."

"Och, I had nae thought of that." Greer scratched his chin. "But it makes sense. If I thought to meet someone at a specific spot but dinnae know for certain when they'd arrive, I'd set someone to watching for them doon the road, too."

Ailsa nodded. "But . . . would you post those eyes

here, in Ullapool? Or in Kylestrome, where we're to make the exchange for the prisoners?"

"Kylestrome," Nik answered, tapping his fingers on the map. "Ullapool is too far removed to make communication convenient."

Ailsa nodded. "Which means the watchman might be in Kylestrome now."

Nik sent her an amused look. "You think we should send someone to find out?"

"Immediately."

Greer nodded. "I'll go after supper."

"Verrah guid," Ailsa said. "Take Stewart or MacKean in case there's a run-in. We dinnae know anything aboot these people other than they're willing to take poor elderly people hostage."

"I will, my lady. If we're lucky, mayhap we can track these blackguards back to their camp."

"If you can follow them without anyone being aware of it, we could attack them there." Nik nodded thoughtfully. "That would be the best way—"

"Nae."

Everyone looked at Ailsa.

She straightened her shoulders. "We will nae take chances with the lives of the hostages. Greer, if you find the camp, we'll use the information only if the delivery of the ransom monies does nae satisfy these thieves."

Greer blew out his lips in a blustery puff. "My lady, you cannae hope to negotiate with these bloody arses."

"I'm nae going to negotiate. We're going to pay the ransom, retrieve the captives, and then get home as quickly and safely as we can. That is, we will do so *if* the abductors do nae do anything foolish."

Greer chewed his lip, while Rurik's heavy brows snapped down and his jaw tightened. Even Gregor, who was trying to look supportive, but failing miserable, revealed all with his expression. Only one person at the table was successfully hiding their thoughts, and Ailsa realized with a sinking feeling that she valued that opinion the most.

Gregor sighed. "I fear we could end oop with neither the money nor the hostages. It would be a more sensible plan if we found this camp and attacked it while the abductors are off guard."

"How would we do that, Gregor, and keep the captives safe? Are you going to storm in as if we were putting a castle under siege, guns blazing and cannons firing, and leave it to luck and hope that an elderly man and woman will find safe cover?"

"If that's what it takes, aye."

She gave a frustrated "Nonsense!" and then added, "That would put the lives of the captives in extreme danger. I will nae have it until 'tis our only recourse."

Gregor slid a look at Nik. "What do you think?"

Nik felt the weight of Ailsa's gaze, and recognized the flicker of hope in her eyes. She wanted his support here, before her men. And God, how he wanted to give it. He wanted to see those amazing eyes light up, see her full lips part in a smile that was for no one but him.

But he had to tell the truth. "I cannot agree with paying the ransom."

Her jaw tightened. "But—"

"It is not a good policy. If we locate the camp where the prisoners are being held, we should attack as soon as possible, before those fools have time to flee with our loved ones and leave us with naught."

Ailsa's brows lowered. "This is *my* rescue effort. You joined me and my men, nae the other way around. Things will proceed as I say. We will nae participate in a raid until we know for certain if paying the ransom will yield results."

He would have given his left arm to be able to agree with her. He could see from the tension in the stiff set of her shoulder, the tightness of her jaw, that she was heels down on this idea.

But all of his experiences, all of his instincts told him she was wrong. "*Krasavitsa*, we are speaking about my grandmother. I must do as *I* think best."

"And what makes you think you know best?"

"Because just as you have more experience with brigands, I have more experience with abductions."

Her gaze narrowed. "How many abductions have you dealt with?"

He silently counted, then said, "Sixteen that I can think of. I'm sure I've missed a few."

"Sixteen—I cannae believe that."

Nik shrugged and took a drink from his flask.

"Ailsa, it's possible he's telling the truth," Gregor offered cautiously. "I daresay members of royalty are more often the target of abductions and worse than the rest of us."

Nik put the top back on the flask and handed it to Rurik. "Whoever took Lord Hamilton and my grandmother did not make up the term 'abduction.' It has happened since ancient times. And it happens far more often than you might imagine."

Ailsa frowned. "It costs us nothing but effort and some gold to pay the ransom. If we do, and the prisoners are nae released, *then* we can attack these fools in their camp."

"But paying that damned ransom costs us much more than that," Nik replied. "If we pay the ransom, we lose our chance for true surprise."

"It's worth the risk. You forget that it is verrah possible someone is trying to push my family into a clan war. I cannae allow that. We *must* free the captives and bring them home safely. 'Tis a sad plan if all you can think to do is attack the camp and hope our own people are nae hit by stray bullets or have their throats slit before we can reach them!"

Nik bit back a sharp reply. She was strong and passionate in her beliefs, and God help him, beautiful when her ire had been raised. Beautiful and as sharp-edged as a new knife.

Keenly aware of their audience, he picked up his map and folded it. "Let us think on this some more. We will discuss this again once Greer has returned from scouting the location where the ransom is to be delivered. We'll have more information then." And hopefully cooler heads. He met Ailsa's gaze directly. "Agreed?"

It wasn't a satisfactory answer, and he knew it. But to his relief, after a stilted moment, she gave a curt nod.

A noise came from the hallway, and the innkeeper

arrived to announce that food would be served shortly, a hearty soup and fresh bread made only that morning.

Greer went to get the others from where they were settling into their quarters off the stables, and Gregor pulled Ailsa back to the long table near the fire, where he spoke to her in a low voice, obviously attempting to cheer her up after the tense discussion. When Rurik started counting through the weapons they'd need for a possible raid, Nik listened with only half an ear, distracted by Ailsa's concerned, disappointed expression. He wished with all his heart he could change her countenance from dark to light, but he couldn't. Not when his grandmother's life was at stake.

Across the room, his gaze met Ailsa's, and he inclined his head, hoping she at least knew this wasn't a matter of trust or regard, but rather of expediency and experience.

To his deep disappointment, Ailsa merely turned away and did not look back.

Chapter 20

Hours after retiring, Ailsa found herself wide-awake. Her bed was a poor excuse for comfort. The feather pillow was flat, and the straw-filled mattress was so hollowed in the center that she couldn't sleep anywhere but the dead middle of the bed.

Worse were the thin sheets and blanket. Not only did they provide no warmth, but she was fairly sure that if she moved with any suddenness, her feet would poke through the threadbare muslin. She thought about fetching her bedroll from the stables, but the floor in the hall was too creaky, and would wake the others.

She flopped to her back, and stared at the ceiling. The inn was pitch-black, for everyone was asleep. *Except me*.

She sighed and crossed her arms under her head. Perhaps her wakefulness was due to more than the discomfort of the bed. It could have to do with how she was irritated over a number of things.

When she'd started out on this trek, she'd known it would become a test of her ability to lead her people. She was the lady of the manor, and at one time, she'd assumed that gave her complete say over their rescue mission. But that was before she'd somehow been outranked by a too-certain-of-himself prince. Worse, the farther away they got from Castle Leod, the more things changed. Her men were far more willing to challenge her.

Perhaps that was the normal way of things. They'd faced extremely difficult situations on their travel here, which had changed all of them in one way or another.

She, for one, had a newfound respect for her men. She'd always thought them capable, but had no appreciation for Stewart's dry wit, MacKean's quickness, or Greer's willingness to take on the more difficult chores. From her desk in the study at Castle Leod, she would never have known their abilities. It was only when she worked side by side with them that she truly saw what they were capable of.

Perhaps one of the gifts she would take away from this venture was the realization that she'd been unwittingly isolating herself from her people. She would find a way to address that issue when she returned, for it would make Castle Leod more successful.

She loved her home and her charges. For now, at least, it was who she was, what she was meant to do.

She shifted restlessly in the hard bed, her thoughts settling on a far more troublesome issue—Nik. He was a very pleasant, amazingly sensual diversion, but that was all. From the little she'd garnered, it seemed his life was too complicated to be shared. It saddened her that he believed everyone in his world had an ugly motive for being there. She thought—

A creak sounded in the hallway. She lifted her head

to stare through the pitch dark at the closed door. *Was that a footstep?* No other sound could be heard.

But as soon as she relaxed her head on her flat pillow, she heard it again.

Someone was in the hallway.

Her heart gave a sickly thud. Twice now someone had tried to rob them, and both times Nik had been injured. What if it happened again? What if he was, even now, bloodied upon the floor of his bedchamber?

She threw off the covers and arose, her chemise offering scant warmth. Although it was made of soft wool, her skin prickled with goose bumps as she found the chair she'd placed at the side of her bed, where her pistol rested on top of her clothes, ready for the coming morning.

The weapon was cold and heavy as she carried it to the door. There, she pressed her ear to the cold wood and waited.

She waited, breath held, listening. There! Another creak, this time near the stairwell. Only she, Nik, Gregor, and Rurik were on this floor. *Had someone slipped up the stairs to do mischief?*

She remembered the bitterness in Nik's gaze when Gregor had mentioned in such a matter-of-fact tone about royalty being abducted "and worse."

She tightened her grip on her pistol and slowly turned the doorknob. It opened with a faint click.

She waited, but no sound answered it.

Thank goodness! She let her breath out in a faint sigh, then peered into the hallway. Nothing but blackness met her gaze. When she'd come to bed earlier in the evening, she'd noted that the hall floor had creaked loudly near the steps. If she stayed near the wall, the creaking should be much less. First, though, she held her place, waiting. Somewhere outside, she heard a low noise, but nothing else.

Perhaps she'd imagined the footfalls. Or perhaps—more alarming—whoever had been in the hallway had completed their evil task.

She looked in the direction of Nik's door, but she was too far away to hear anything.

If she listened at his door and heard him breathing, she'd know he was safe and her alarm nothing more than her own overactive imagination. She stepped into the hallway and quietly made her way to his door.

There, she pressed her ear to the rough panel, listening intently.

No sound met her efforts. Shouldn't she be able to hear him breathing, at least? She put her hand on the knob, wondering if she should chance a peek. Her heart beat rapidly. Perhaps something was indeed wrong. She had to find out or she'd never sleep.

She turned the knob as slowly as she could. Just as she went to push the door open, it swung back, and in one swift, blinding move, her pistol was jerked from her hand, and she was pinned chest out against a warm, hard wall, a hand over her mouth. "Shhh," Nik whispered into her ear.

He needn't have worried; her tongue was as frozen as her mind.

He quietly closed the door and then eased his hold, bending to whisper, "You heard it, too?"

She grasped his wrist, pulling his hand from her mouth. "Who was it?"

"I don't know, but they are out in the courtyard now. I heard the front door below my bedchamber open and close."

"Did you see anything?"

"Someone was near the stables. But it's a new moon and I couldn't make out who it might be."

"Should we go see who it is?"

"*Nyet*. I don't hear anything now. Perhaps it was Rurik or your cousin searching for the outhouse."

"Oh. I had nae thought of that." She paused, aware of how warm his skin was against her chemise. "I . . . I should return to my room, then."

But she made no move to do so.

And he made no move to release her.

Instead, he lowered his head, his breath sweet and warm on her cheek. "Why did you come here, *krasavitsa*?"

"I heard the footsteps and wished to make certain you were well."

"I am honored, but . . . that's all? You weren't slipping into my room in the hopes of joining me in my bed? I'm disappointed." As he spoke, he turned her so that she faced him, sliding his hands over her, from her hips, to her waist, and then up her back, molding her to him.

She shivered, pressing against him.

His hands never stopped roaming and tugging, pulling her closer. Soon, she realized he'd untied her chemise.

"Take it off," he growled in her ear, easing his hold.

She could have argued. And he would have listened, too.

But her breasts were already heavy with wanting, and she realized that if she left now, without embracing her desires for him, she'd have naught but regrets. She slipped the undergarment from her shoulders and let it drop to her feet.

She stepped out of the pool of clothes made by her chemise as Nik's arm tightened about her waist. With one easy movement, he lifted her to him, over his glorious expanse of bare chest. She let her hands wander, tracing his ridged abdomen, his muscled arms, the strong column of his throat.

His ragged breath met her explorations, and with a swift tilt of his head, he captured her mouth with his, his hunger and wildness as evident as her own.

She pressed into him, her bared breasts to his unclothed chest, her naked hips to his powerful thighs, shifting against him, wordlessly inciting him to do more.

He cupped her breast, his thumb flicking over her nipple until she gasped and squirmed against him, lifting her legs around him.

He held her there, her womanhood against his hip, his erection captured between them. She clenched her teeth against a wild moan. God, how she loved the feel of him against her.

She pressed against his thick shaft, gasping as wanton heat flooded her.

He growled, and rocked back on his heels, thrusting his hips forward as he trailed hot, openmouthed kisses down the line of her throat, over her collarbone, sending spirals of heat through her.

She rocked her hips against him, and he broke the kiss, his hot breath tickling the trail left by his kisses.

He took two steps and then found the bed. He lowered her to the edge.

She started to scoot back, but he placed his large warm hands over her thighs, holding her in place. "Stay."

She did so, her heart pounding furiously. *What is he going to do? How do I—*

He knelt, and she gave a startled gasp as he pressed her legs apart, bending forward to capture her mouth in a demanding kiss. When her objections had been quelled, he left her swollen lips and trailed his lips over her jaw to her neck, kissing and nipping as she splayed her hands through the crisp curls on his chest.

His mouth went lower, to her breast, where he captured a tortured nipple and twirled his tongue over it.

She sank her hands into his hair and arched toward him, half mad with desire.

Though she couldn't see a thing, the darkness sharpened her other senses until she was filled with them. He smelled of sandalwood soap and leather; his skin so warm that she wondered if he still had a fever. His breathing was rapid and harsh, which delighted her to no end. She ran her fingers through his hair, arching her back, pressing her breast more fully into his mouth.

He obliged her unspoken demand, twirling his tongue over her nipple, rolling it between his teeth until she shook with need.

He released her and sank lower, dropping heated kisses down her midriff.

He pressed her back on the bed, his broad shoulders opening her legs.

She panted as if she were running with all her might up a steep hill. Sensations flooded her; her body ached and yearned. She couldn't keep her legs still, couldn't stop moving against him, like waves thrusting upon a shore, seeking land upon which to rest.

He shifted, his weight moving down, spreading her legs until she was fully open before him, her most intimate part level with his stubbled chin.

He raked his chin over her wetness, and she dug her fingers deep into the blankets to keep from crying out.

He did it again, and then again, each time listening to her panted whimpers. He flicked his tongue over her damp curls.

She clenched her eyes closed and dropped her head back as he teased and taunted with his tongue. In, out. Up, down.

She reached for him with one hand, her fingers threading through his hair as she pressed his face to her, urging him to keep kissing, keep stroking, gasping his name as her hips lifted of their own accord. He slipped his hands under her bottom and held her up, angled now for his pleasure as he plundered her.

He was unrelenting and ruthless, tasting her with a thoroughness that left her writhing under an assault of feeling so intense, a tear slid down her temple to pool in her hair. She anchored him in place, holding him to her, pressing herself to him.

He cupped her cheeks tightly as his tongue filled her and, with a cry, she arched wildly as her senses tumbled, gasping his name over and over while her body spasmed with pleasure.

Her cries seemed to inspire him, for he increased his ministrations, lapping at her until she was lost, quivering at the wildness that was her body.

Finally, she could stand no more and she whispered a broken, "Please, dinnae—"

He stopped instantly, and arose to slide an arm about her waist. He pulled her to the center of the mattress, covering her body with his.

His erection rested against her hip, and she turned toward him, kissing him fiercely. Now she was the one tempting and teasing. She splayed her leg over his hip and reached between them, her fingers encircling his hot shaft—

He groaned and lifted on his elbows, positioning himself between her thighs. With an insistent push, he pressed into her. His ready cock filled her slickness with a thick, velvet hardness. A momentary pain made her gasp, but then he was moving, his hips thrusting against hers, her body aching with the sweetness.

She closed her eyes and met him thrust for thrust, as he rained kisses down her neck, his harsh breath spurring her onward as she planted her heels on the mattress, lifting her hips to meet his.

He murmured her name, gasping harshly as he took her with a wildness that stole her breath. Their passion built until she gasped and arched against him, losing herself in another wave of pleasure. As if in answer, he gave a final thrust, pulling free just as his own passion erupted.

Chapter 21

Ailsa slid her foot into her boot. The inn was abuzz with voices and noises, while outside in the courtyard arose the whicker of horses and the thud of boots scuffling across the flagstones. The scent of ham and sausages wafted upstairs, and her stomach growled in return.

The whole world was now awake, which was very different from late last night when she'd gone to Nik's bedchamber. She couldn't help but smile. *What a glorious, glorious night. Whatever happens, I will have that memory.*

It was a bittersweet thought, one she'd avoided thinking about all morning—that a memory was all it ever could be.

And that is fine, she told herself, ignoring the lump in her throat. *I knew that from the beginning. Perhaps that is why I felt bold enough to do as I've done. There can be no complications.*

Can there?

She'd awoken this morning to find herself scooped against Nik's broad chest, his steady breathing warm against her ear. She'd never felt more comfortable or safe, resting in his arms.

But feeling safe and being safe were two very different things and she'd quickly arisen, put on her chemise, and slipped back into her own room. There she'd waited in bed until she heard Rurik and Gregor speaking on the stairway before she arose and rang the maid for a bath.

Now, bathed and dressed, Ailsa felt as if she owned the world. This venture had been freeing in many ways. Smiling, she turned her face toward the morning sun that poured through the window, and basked in its warmth. She supposed she should feel some sort of loss for having given herself to Nik last night, but all she could dredge up was a relaxed, sated sigh. She'd never dreamed she could be so forward or wanton. And it had been obvious that Nik had enjoyed her efforts, which only confirmed her decision all the more.

She stood, pushed her still-damp hair to one side, and stretched, as languid as a cat basking on a windowsill. *So this is what a woman of the world feels like the morning after indulging herself.* Truly, other than a faint tenderness to her nether regions, which the bath had already eased, she felt stronger and more capable than ever.

Nik had the right of it—he never worried what other people thought or said. Perhaps it was time she did the same. This morning, she felt as if she could conquer the world. She even found herself wondering if the huge desk at Castle Leod was big enough to challenge her forever. Was it was possible she'd now want more than it could offer? It was a thrilling thought.

She stepped around the small tub the maid had carried in earlier and had just picked up her comb when her door flew open. "What—"

Nik stood in the doorway, his black hair falling over his brow, his green eyes cold with fury. In his hand, he held a sheet. He stalked in and slammed the door behind him.

She blinked. "What's wrong?"

"This." He shook the bedsheet, and she saw a small, reddish stain in the center.

Her face heated. "Oh. That."

"Yes, *that*. You are a virgin." He said it as if it were the worst thing she could possibly be.

"Well, I *was* a virgin, but now, nae longer." She tugged the comb through her hair.

He watched her with a stunned expression and then threw the bedsheet to the floor. "Bloody hell, do you not know what this means?"

"Aye, it means I'm nae longer a virgin, something I discovered last night around two. Or I think it was aboot two; I'm nae certain as to the exact time."

"This is not a laughing matter!" He stalked about the room, as if in a cage. "You could be with child."

"We took nae precautions," she pointed out matter-of-factly. "You withdrew, if you remember."

His face turned red. "This is my fault."

"It is *our* fault," she corrected sharply. "But rest assured aboot that; 'tis nae the proper time of the month for such."

"Are you certain?"

"Verrah. I've sisters, you know. More than one."

"That's good, I suppose. But, dammit, you should

have told me before we—" He raked a hand through his hair.

"Why? Would it have mattered?"

"*Da*," he said grimly. "I wouldn't have touched you."

"Then I'm glad I dinnae tell you, so that I was able to enjoy the best half hour of this expedition thus far."

When he didn't smile or even agree, she threw the comb back on the dresser. "Fine. You and I agree it would be unfortunate if I were with child. But I doubt it would happen after one time, especially at this time of the month, and that my first attempt, too."

He eyed her with a dark look. "You are damnably calm about this."

"To be honest, I'm relieved."

"Was your virginity such a burden?"

"Nae, but my curiosity was." That was true, especially after she'd met him. "Now I'll nae longer wonder what I have given oop by being my father's estate manager. And dinnae say I might still wed, for nae one visits Castle Leod other than my family."

His mouth tightened. "So last night was nothing; you were merely sating your curiosity and nothing more."

It was more than that. Much more. But she hadn't allowed herself time to consider what. And now, facing the unmistakable fury in Nik's eyes, she found it even more difficult to do so.

Why was he so angry? There was no reason for him to be so unless he'd thought she— Her gaze flew to his face. "You thought I was planning on using my loss of innocence against you."

"Of course not."

But she saw the way his expression shuttered, as if to keep her from reading his expression. *Bloody hell, that's exactly what he thinks.*

Up until now, she'd been sympathetic to the bitterness that encircled him. She knew why he was so distrustful of those around him.

But when he turned those uncharitable thoughts on her, and after such a beautiful experience, she felt nothing but anger. "I am nae the sort of person who would use such a despicable method to win a husband—*especially* nae one who spends all his time suspecting the worst oot of everyone he meets."

Nik winced at her bitter words. *Bozhy moj*, what had he done? This morning, his first thought had been of Ailsa and their passionate tryst. Their time together had been special—heart-wrenchingly so, and he knew it.

Perhaps that was why, when he'd found the bloodied bedsheet, he'd grown instantly and blindingly furious. Of all the women in the world, she was the last, and perhaps the only, one he'd thought he could trust. To think even for a second that she wasn't, that she was no different from all the others, had burned him with righteous fury. He hadn't been angry so much at her as at himself for falling so thoroughly under her spell that he hadn't questioned a damned thing when she'd arrived unbidden at his door in the middle of the night. Had any other woman done so, he'd have suspected a trap, and looked for it. But with her?

His heart tightened with a heavy ache. He could see the truth in her eyes, and could feel the weight of his error, horrid that it was. He spread his hands. "I was overly suspicious, I admit it. But you must understand, It would not be the first time such a thing has been attempted."

Ailsa's fury was so strong that it burned her tongue. "Then lock your cock in a box and throw away the key. But dinnae come here and accuse me of doing anything other than enjoying what you freely offered. And until now I thought I had enjoyed it. Now I wish it had never happened."

He winced. "Ailsa, none of this is what I meant to say. I was just—worried, that is all."

"You're worried someone might find a way to slip under that shield you've put between yourself and the world. Well, Mr. High-and-Mighty Prince, you've met one woman who won't even bother to try—me."

His expression darkened. "Are you done yet?"

"Nae. You pretend to be this person, and that person, and never are you just Nikolai. Ever. It must get wearisome, trying to remember which person you're pretending to be at any given moment. Who were you last night whilst we were together? For 'tis obvious to me now that it was nae you."

"You can't say these things without—"

"I will, and you'll listen." She marched to him and poked him in the chest. "Rest easy, for I've nae intention of marrying you. Nae if you were the last mon on earth. Nae a mon who believes the worst of everyone around him, including me. So you're safe. I want nothing of you, nae matter the circumstances."

She turned on her heel and stomped out, making certain her boots thudded hard on each and every step.

The nerve of that man, acting as if she'd tried to trick him! She'd thought those moments had been special, cherished even.

She reached the door of the common room, and had to stop in the hallway to fight back a sob. It took her some minutes before she could relax her face into a smile without also letting angry, furious tears slip from her eyes.

Finally, after numerous swipes at her eyes, she took a deep breath and joined the others.

She was welcomed with a smile from Gregor, respectful nods from her men, and a cool greeting from Rurik. After fixing herself a plate from the food at the side table she sat down. But her stomach, which had growled with hunger at the smell of sausage and bacon not twenty minutes ago, was now too full of anger for her to eat.

"You should try the eggs."

She looked up to find Gregor smiling at her. "I will. I'm just thinking about Greer. He should be back soon. I hope he's found something."

"Me, too." Gregor's gaze moved over her face. "You didn't sleep well, did you? Neither did I. My mattress felt as if it was filled with rocks, and every time I turned over, my bed creaked. I finally got up and fetched my bedroll, and took it to the stables to sleep with the others."

Rurik, who was sitting close by, looked up from his plate. "You were up last night?"

"Aye."

"What time?"

"Two, perhaps three."

"I did not hear you." Rurik sounded almost accusatory. As if he realized it, he grimaced. "As the guard, I should hear everything. The prince is my responsibility."

"Did you sleep better in the stables?" Ailsa asked Gregor.

"Much."

Rurik nodded. "The hay makes a good bed."

Ailsa agreed. "I heard you get oop."

Gregor looked surprised. "I'm sorry if I woke you. It was bloody cold outside, I can tell you that." He hesitated. "The strangest thing happened, too. When I went outside, I heard two men talking. Or I think I did."

"Near the stables?"

"Behind them. In the woods, perhaps. And they weren't speaking English, either."

Rurik leaned forward. "So you do not know what they were saying?"

Gregor shook his head. "But I could have sworn I knew one of those voices." He frowned. "Perhaps both. I'm not sure. I just—"

The door opened and Nik appeared. He looked directly at Ailsa, who studiously ignored him. Everyone else called out greetings, and he was soon seated with Rurik, a plate before him.

He sat dark and quietly brooding, and she was uncomfortably aware of his gaze on her many times.

They were just finishing their meal when a horse clattered into the courtyard. Stewart leaned to one side and peered out a window. "'Tis Greer."

"And MacKean?" she asked.

He looked again. "Nay. Only Greer."

Moments later, the small, weathered huntsman hurried in the door, his pale blue eyes alight. "We found 'em," he said gleefully. "And they're nae far from here at all!"

---

 *G*reer unfolded the map Nik had just handed him. "Lady Ailsa, you were right; the blackguards were watching the inn in Kylestrome. They had two men, one inside and the other oot. First thing this morning, a new mon arrived. He exchanged places with the one who'd stayed ootside, hidden in the bushes. We followed that one back to his camp." Greer smirked. "He dinnae know we were there, so we were able to track him the whole way."

Rurik muttered something under his breath.

Nik nodded. "We can surprise them."

"Aye!" Greer rubbed his hands together. "They think they're as safe as a baby in her mother's arms."

"Where are they hiding?" Gregor asked eagerly.

Greer pointed his finger at a spot on the map. "Ardvreck Castle. 'Tis an auld ruin, at the southernmost end of Loch Assynt."

"That is verrah close," Ailsa said, pleased.

Greer nodded.

"Do we know anything about this castle?" Gregor asked.

"'Tis a ruin, nae a functioning castle, but the walls are strong and there's shelter from the elements."

"Did you see the duchess?" Nik asked.

"Aye. There was a tent, and Her Grace and Lord

Hamilton were sitting underneath, playing chess as if 'twere a garden party."

"You're certain they were nae in distress?" Ailsa asked.

"I got close enough to hear them. Lord Hamilton looked much as the last time I saw him. Unshaven, but that's all. He was unhappy he'd just lost another game to Her Grace."

"And Her Grace?" Nik asked.

"In the few moments I was close, she complained aboot the weather, the fact she'd been forced to look at the same view for days on end, and the lack of cushions in her chair."

"Well," Ailsa said in a dry tone, "it sounds as if they are both well, then."

Nik agreed, clearly relieved beyond belief. "My grandmother will yell at us all for not coming sooner."

Gregor straightened up from looking at the map and sent a cautious glance at Ailsa. "What do we do now?"

"Greer, where's MacKean?"

"I left him to watch the camp. I saw four men, and two waiting at the inn in Kylestrome; there might be others oot hunting and such. MacKean's to watch and let us know."

"Verrah guid," Ailsa said. "I'll go to Kylestrome and see if delivering the ransom will be enough to win back the duchess and Lord Hamilton."

"I'll go with you," Nik said.

"Nae one will go with me," she said sharply. "While I'm gone, the rest of you will keep watch over the camp and make sure there's nae foul play."

"I will go with you," Nik repeated, his jaw set.

She ignored him. "If the ransom does nae work, then—" God, she hated even saying it, for it seemed like such a risky proposition, but there was no other way, especially as they now knew where the prisoners were being held. "Then we'll try the prince's suggestion and rescue the prisoners ourselves."

Greer shook his head slowly. "My lady, I have to disagree with you tryin' to deliver the ransom at all. The mon ootside the inn was nae there for pleasure. He had a rifle. And while MacKean and I were watching, someone came doon the road and he lifted oop and drew a bead on them. He was nae on guard, but on the hunt, waitin' for his prey."

She frowned. "You think he's there to shoot whoever comes to deliver the ransom? What would be the point of that?"

"I dinnae know, but 'twas obvious he was nae going to greet them with flowers and a hot toddy."

Rurik made an impatient gesture. "Perhaps he is merely protecting his fellow inside the inn. It is dull, dreary work, standing watch. It could be he only aimed his rifle to pass the time."

"Nae," Greer said stoutly. "I know a mon who is huntin' over one who is nae. And this mon was on the hunt."

Ailsa didn't answer, and Nik could see she was lost in thought. *What are you thinking, little one?* He wished to hell he could just ask her. Had he not insulted her like the veriest fool this morning, he could have done just that.

The taste of their argument still rested on his tongue,

a burning, bitter pill. All the wrong words he'd said, all the wrong thoughts he'd harbored prickled at his conscience and left him restless and disappointed in himself.

He was a lout. There was no other word for it.

But Ailsa . . . she'd been magnificent, all flushed fury, poking him in the chest and accusing him of allowing his overblown caution to keep everyone who cared for him at bay. It was a ridiculous charge, and yet, deep inside, he wondered if she'd seen something he hadn't. Was it possible he'd lost a part of himself as he'd sunk deeper and ever deeper into the mire of court intrigues, and hadn't realized it?

It wasn't until he'd seen himself reflected in her clear gaze that he'd realized the prize he might have paid for it.

"Weel, miss?" Stewart cocked a red eyebrow, his deep voice rumbling and heavy. "Do we deliver the ransom and see what comes of it? Or do you have a different plan in mind, now that we know more?"

She sighed and, to Nik's surprise, said, "We go to Ardvreck and win the release of the prisoners."

"'Twill be a battle," Greer warned.

"I know. But I trust Greer's instincts. The ransom is merely a trap. Gregor, fetch some paper and ink from the innkeeper." She turned to Greer. "We'll need a map of this camp, so we know exactly where the prisoners are being held and where the watch is stationed."

Rurik muttered something under his breath and then leaned closer to Nik. "She's allowed that old fool of a huntsman to change her mind. I do not like this."

"She listens to her men and trusts them." *The way she trusted me when she came to me last night, before I—* He couldn't even finish the thought, his conscience weighed so heavily on him.

It was lowering to realize he had become so callous, so filled with fear that someone might take advantage of him, that he no longer knew how to trust.

As Greer began to sketch the layout of the camp, Nik reluctantly put his thoughts behind him and leaned closer.

After they'd rescued Tata Natasha, he'd examine his soul for answers. Right now they had more immediate matters to attend to.

Chapter 22

An hour later Nik was on D'yoval, ready to ride, Rurik nearby. The day was turning gray, a low mist swirling between the purple hillocks, the scent of snow high on the wind.

Ailsa stood in the courtyard, St. George's reins in her hand as she spoke in a low voice to Mackenzie. They were arguing, for her cousin kept shaking his head, his mouth set in a mulish line.

Finally, she said something that made him grimace and then nod. After a few more words, he left her and crossed the courtyard to where his horse waited.

What was that all about? Nik wished he knew.

Seeing Ailsa was ready to mount up, Stewart went to help her into the saddle. Then he brought his own horse over from where it waited by the inn door.

Ailsa looked around. "Are we ready?"

"Aye," Greer said.

Mackenzie gave a short laugh. "I'm as ready as I can be."

Greer turned his mount and headed out of the

innyard, the others following. They were to ride within
two miles of Ardvreck Castle and then dismount and
encircle the castle on foot. Nik couldn't help but remember Ailsa's husky voice as she cautioned everyone
to aim true as they, themselves, could easily shoot the
hostages. He would be a fool not to worry, but he knew
his grandmother. Natasha was not the sort to sit and let
things happen. Once she realized someone had come to
rescue her, she'd make certain she was in a safe position
and would assist them if possible.

They rode into the woods, Greer following a path
only he seemed able to see. Everyone was unusually
quiet.

Nik found himself watching Ailsa's trim form as
she rode ahead. Memories of her sweetness filled his
mind, the recollection of her surprising passion even
now made him shift uncomfortably in his saddle. He remembered their argument, too. No one had ever dared
rail at him the way she had.

But then again, most people didn't know him well
enough to do so. This adventure he and Ailsa had
shared had brought them closer than he'd realized. In
fact, now that he thought about it, he'd shared things
with her he'd never shared with anyone else.

Why was that? Why had he told her so much?

She beguiled in ways that irritated the hell out of
him. And he found it impossible to fight his own devilish impulses when she smiled at him. Long gone was
his first impression of her as a plain, dragon-like ter-
magant. Now he couldn't look at her without thinking

of those plump lips against his, her lush curves fitted against him, her lavender scent teasing his every breath.

It was that first kiss, he realized. He'd cursed himself with that kiss. Cursed himself with the taste of what he could never have. His life was not his to share with someone whose heart was so open, whose every thought was clearly expressed on her face. He'd been a fool a hundred times over and had allowed his distrust to overcome his good sense. He wouldn't blame her if she never forgave him.

He clenched his jaw and hoped they'd soon be done with this journey. It had cost him more than he could say.

After an hour's ride, Greer finally put up his hand and they slowed to a halt. The small, wizened man swung down from his horse and tied it to a bush. "We must walk from here."

Ailsa added, "According to the map Greer drew for us, the castle sits on the western shore of the loch. Stewart and Greer, you two will join MacKean at that northern point. Be sure you are well hidden, as you'll be the closest to the castle."

The two huntsman nodded.

She turned to her cousin. "Gregor, you and Rurik will go to the south and slip oop the shore, while the rest of us will make our way to the west side of the castle to provide cover."

The rest of us. She wouldn't even say his name. Nik's soul burned at her omission. He would be glad when this event was finally over and he could clear the air between them. *If I can.*

"Greer, once you've given everyone time to get in place, and you have located the duchess and Lord Hamilton, give the signal to begin our attack—three pheasant's trills in a row." She smiled. "I've heard you trill like a pheasant on many a hunt, and 'tis indistinguishable from a live one."

Greer flushed. "Och, 'tis verrah kind of you to say so, my lady."

Ailsa's gaze turned to Nik. "Everyone else will charge but us. We're to stay in place and provide cover as the others take the captives to safety."

"What?" Rurik shook his head. "I do not like this."

"Then do nae like it," Ailsa said sharply, surprising Nik. "But it is what we will do."

"*Nyet.*" Rurik turned to Nik. "Come, we'll—"

"Wait."

Everyone looked at Mackenzie.

He offered an uncertain smile. "Rurik, you and I should join forces as planned."

"*Nyet,*" Rurik answered, more loudly this time. "I'll go with His Highness. You will go with Lady Ailsa."

The young man's face turned red, but his jaw had set in a way that made Nik realize that the lad was indeed Ailsa's cousin. "The prince would be better protection for her ladyship."

Nik had to admit Mackenzie had a point. "I will go with Lady Ailsa."

Rurik's scowl deepened. "I am your guard; I should be with you."

Ailsa chimed in, "The prince does nae need guarding now. Nae one even knows he's here."

"It is still my duty."

Nik noted how Ailsa's lips thinned, and said in a sharp tone, "Rurik, stay with Mackenzie. Lady Ailsa and I will go this way." He stood back and inclined his head toward her. "After you."

Rurik flashed an irritated look at Mackenzie. "Fine. Keep up as best you can." With that, he turned and strode into the woods, Ailsa's cousin following.

Greer and Stewart checked their weapons and then left, while Nik followed Ailsa into the woods.

They'd only gone a short distance when she paused and then stood to one side. "You should go first."

"Afraid?" he teased.

She shot him a flat look. "Only for the safety of the duchess and Lord Hamilton."

He wasn't sure why she wished him to go first, but he could see her temper was still high after Rurik's challenge. Nik obligingly led the way. They walked in silence for some time, the dense woods keeping them in single file. When they could see the edge of the loch, he turned north, making certain they were hidden within the woods and thick shrubs.

Nik glanced back at Ailsa. "Why did you wish your cousin to go with Rurik?"

"It will be safer."

"For whom?"

"For all of us." She turned away as she spoke, her profile in bold relief. "Gregor is nae the best of shots."

God, but he loved her proud nose. He couldn't see it without wanting to trail a kiss down the bridge of it. As bold and brazen as its owner, he—

A movement caught his attention. He held up his hand and crouched down. Ailsa followed, close behind.

A man walked down the rocky shore of the loch. He carried a brace of hares, his rifle casually held in one hand.

They waited, motionless, as the guard continued on his way, the low mist swirling around his boots. As soon as he was out of sight, Nik rose and gestured for Ailsa to follow. "We must be close to the castle," he whispered, stepping carefully through heavy shrubs and around large white rocks.

He was right. Mere moments later, the castle arose from the mist. Ardvreck Castle was a stately ruin. Several stories tall, a round stone tower lifted high over a set of broken one-story walls that must have once been part of a guardhouse. The tower was still complete, though the roof was no more and the narrow windows were black and empty.

Through a large crack in a broken wall, he caught a glimpse of a tent panel, and he waved for Ailsa to follow him. As they passed the remains of a crumbling wall, the tent came into view, and there sat Tata Natasha.

She was perched on a chair under the canopy and was wrapped in an assortment of furs and shawls, a wine goblet in one hand, a small plate in the other, a thick carpet had been placed at her feet—all signs someone had readied this prison for their noble guests. An armed guard sat not ten feet away, but judging by the way she ordered him to fetch her more wine—and the hurried manner in which he complied—she seemed more like a queen surveying a most unsatisfactory tournament than a woman in dire danger.

A wave of relief hit Nik when he heard her cackle with laughter over something the guard said. He'd been so worried about her, and seeing her sitting like the royalty she was, waving an imperious hand at one of her captors as if she were the one in charge and not he, filled his heart with joy.

"Let's move over there," he whispered, gesturing to a low outcropping of boulders. He led the way, settling in place as Ailsa moved in beside him.

The man who'd brought the brace of hares appeared around one of the far walls. He hung the game over the empty window and then glanced up at the top window in the tower.

Nik followed the man's gaze. "Get down," he hissed. "There's a lookout in the tower window."

Ailsa scrambled closer to him, her shoulder against his. "Just one?"

"I think so. There are two others— Wait. Three more. There's someone in the bottom of the tower, as well."

She peered over the shrubs. "Her Grace looks well. Have you seen Lord Hamilton?"

"Not yet, but perhaps— Ah. Is that him?" An older man, dapperly dressed had his clothes been less wrinkled and carrying a shawl, stepped from the door of the roundhouse.

"Aye, that's Lord Hamilton."

The man carried the shawl to Tata Natasha and helped arrange it around her shoulders before taking the seat next to hers. As he did so, she spoke loudly to the guard, pointing to the hares dangling from the nearby window.

"They have chairs, a rug, plates—I dinnae expect that," Ailsa murmured.

"*Da*," Nik answered. "Whoever this is, they are taking exceptional care of her." *Did that mean they never meant to harm the captives? Does that speak to the honor of the abductor?*

Tata Natasha gave a sharp crack of laughter as she discussed with one of the guards the best way to prepare the hares for dinner.

Ailsa leaned forward, her brows drawn. "What's she saying?"

"She's telling the men to cook the rabbits on a spit, as she likes roasted meat rather than boiled. Can't you hear her?"

"I can, but she's spea—"

A single gunshot rent the air, and instantly, the guards leapt to the ready, the taller one heading straight for Tata Natasha.

"What the hell?" Nik muttered.

"Someone fired early," Ailsa said grimly.

"And alerted the damn guards."

From somewhere north of them, Greer gave the signal for the charge. In answer, Stewart bellowed loudly, the sound echoing off the rocks. He, Greer, and MacKean charged from the brush.

"Fire!" Ailsa ordered, pulling out her pistols and aiming toward the walls hiding the guards. "We must cover them."

Nik half rose and pointed his rifle at the one guard he could see. The man's hand rested on the low wall, his head safely tucked behind it. Nik aimed and shot, and the man yelled as the stone where his hand rested exploded. "I got him," Nik said grimly, noting blood on the topmost rock.

More shots rang out and Greer went down, holding his leg. He dragged himself to a low rock, though he managed to keep firing his pistol. Stewart and MacKean continued their charge, leaping over the rocks and brush.

Mayhem ensued for a moment, but then Stewart reappeared, the duchess tossed over his shoulder as he ran for the cover of the woods, Lord Hamilton scrambling to keep up with them.

Two guards pursued, but Ailsa drew her pistol and caught them as they left their protective wall, Nik doing the same.

She shot one of the thieves in the foot. Yelling, he and the other guard turned back for the safety of the castle as, stumbling wildly, they dived back behind the wall.

Greer took the opportunity to limp his way into the forest after Stewart and the others.

Tata Natasha and Lord Hamilton were now safely away, nowhere to be seen.

"Finally," Ailsa breathed. She lowered her pistol, smoke curling from it.

Nik watched the window where he'd seen the guard. As he'd anticipated, the rifle barrel appeared in the narrow opening, and fixed on something well past them, deep in the woods.

Nik pulled the trigger, and with a pinging ring, the abductor's rifle kicked to one side. Nik chortled and turned, leaning against a tree as he opened his powder horn and prepared to reload. "We have them pinned down."

He opened his bag of shot to pour lead into his hands . . . only it wasn't shot, but gravel.

He could only stare at it.

"Bloody hell." Ailsa grabbed her own bag of shot and poured it out. Gravel met their gaze.

She picked up her powder horn and tipped it. Sand poured from the opening. "So that's what that bastard was doing in the middle of the night."

Nik frowned. "Gregor?"

"Nae Gregor, but—" Her gaze focused over his shoulder, her eyes widening as she went sheet-white.

Nik started to turn. *Bang!* Something exploded against the tree directly over his head, splinters and bark raining down on him and Ailsa.

She threw herself over him, though she was so small, she barely covered him at all. *"Gregor!"* she yelled.

Nik grabbed her and pulled her beside him. "What's—"

Another gunshot rang out. This one was closer, near his ear, more bark and splinters peppering his cheek and neck.

Bozhy moj! He swiped at his face, his fingers coming away bloody as the figure of a man walked toward them.

The barrel of a finely wrought pistol glinted in the mist and swirling smoke, and holding the weapon, a grim look on his face, was Rurik.

Chapter 23

"Rurik?" Nik couldn't believe what he was seeing.

"Who else?" the guard said, his mouth white.

From anger? Or fear? Whatever it was, the pistol never wavered.

"Where are the others?" Ailsa asked.

"Oh, I did not change your plan. Your men are escorting the duchess and Lord Hamilton to safety. They are to wait for the rest of us at the inn just as they were instructed by you. You see, I have no need of them now."

"And Gregor?"

Rurik's smile was more a showing of his teeth. "You set him to stop me, but it did not work. He will not bother anyone again."

Ailsa paled, and Nik grasped her hand where it rested near his and squeezed it. "Ailsa? You knew about—" He jerked his head toward Rurik, unable to say the words aloud.

"I was suspicious. Gregor told me . . ." Her voice trembled, but she pushed on. "He could nae sleep last night as his bed was too uncomfortable, so he went to fetch his bedroll and join the others in the stable. When he walked doon the hallway ootside our bedchambers, I was awakened by the creaking floor. I heard him, but this morning Rurik said he dinnae hear a thing. He is a guard, and his bedchamber was beside the stairs. How could I hear something he dinnae?"

"So your suspicions were raised."

"Aye. Gregor and I investigated. We quickly realized that Rurik dinnae hear anything because he was nae in his bedchamber. When Gregor went to the stables that night, he thought he heard men talking in the woods, but they were nae speaking English."

Nik shot Rurik a hard look. "A late-night planning session?"

Rurik lifted one shoulder. "My accomplices were getting restless, waiting so long."

"Because of your previous failures in attempting to kill me?"

Rurik's mouth tightened. "Perhaps. I had to calm them, and assure them we'd finish this today. You were never meant to make it this far."

"I see. There were never any brigands."

Rurik let himself smile. "I was the brigand, but you— Oh, you are a lucky prince. I came so, so close, but . . ." He threw up a hand.

"I dinnae understand," Ailsa said. "Why make it seem as if there were brigands at all? If you wished to shoot the prince, why dinnae you just do it?"

"I know why," Nik said grimly. "If I am killed by brigands here in the wilderness of Scotland, no one will blink an eye. It is dangerous country, we were escorting ransom money trying to save the duchess—who would question that set of circumstances?"

"And it was your idea to travel alone and concealed," Rurik added.

"Led in that direction by you, now that I think about it."

Rurik smirked. "You are not the only one who can dissemble when the need arises. To make certain I'm never suspected, I made certain Apraksin heard me protest time and again the way you were conducting this mission. I will, of course, fight to save your life today, but will sadly fail."

"You thought of everything, didn't you?" Nik said harshly.

"I don't understand," Ailsa said. "Why pretend to save Nik?"

"I know," Nik said, trying to hold back his anger. "Rurik has big plans. After my unfortunate death at the hands of these brigands, he will escort my body home. Comfort my family. Swear vengeance on these criminals. Perhaps even return and shoot a few of them, declaring honor has been served. And then . . ." He raised his brows and said to Rurik, "Do you wish to finish this sad tale?"

"There's nothing sad to it; it is the most glorious of plans. After I've proven my allegiance to the throne of Ox-enburg and delivered the vengeance they will be thirsting for, his family will bestow upon me wealth and titles, and perhaps even the hand of one of the royal princesses."

"Honors?" Ailsa asked. "For *failing* to protect your prince?"

"Ah, but I warned him not to come, and then was sorely wounded trying to protect him— Did I mention the wounds? It will be a nice touch. It won't need to be much; who would dare ask to peek under a hero's bandages? But my bravery will be much admired as I limp painfully beside my beloved prince's casket at his state funeral." Rurik pursed his lips. "Should I weep at your funeral? Or display a stoic face? I cannot decide which will garner more approbation."

Nik wished he dared charge at Rurik. It might get him shot, but God, it would feel good to die with his hands around that man's neck. Yet doing such a thing could endanger Ailsa, and he would not take such a chance.

Rurik smiled almost dreamily. "Oh, the honors I will receive, most of them because your parents will always think of their beloved son whenever I am near."

Nik's stomach churned. "You know my family well."

"I do." Rurik's chuckle was as cold as winter. "We grew up together. Remember?"

"If you are going to kill me, I should at least know who bought your allegiance."

The guard came closer, and Nik was struck by the icy fury in his gaze. "It does not matter."

"The Prussians, perhaps? They weren't happy with the last treaty and blamed me for it."

"The Prussians do not have the wits to plan something like this."

The wits to plan? Who would— "Ah. The tsar."

Rurik pressed his lips together.

"It must be. He knows why he's been called to meet with us in Edinburgh."

"Perhaps."

Nik sneered. "I should have known that weak-kneed

fool wouldn't attend this meeting without some sort of trickery." Ailsa shifted slightly, and Nik was agonizingly aware of her proximity. His fear grew; he had to get her to safety. But how? He shook his head. "Rurik, please. It doesn't have to end this way. You can change the outcome right now. Put the pistol down and just leave. I won't follow. I promise."

"I do this for me as much as I do it for the money."

"But . . . why? Our families—they have always been so close. And you have been my trusted guard for over a dozen years now. Doesn't that hold any meaning for you?"

Rurik gave a mirthless laugh. "Lady Ailsa, did you know that in Oxenburg, the royal guard is chosen from the best families, the ones closest to the crown, to ensure their honesty and integrity? It is a rubbish heap upon which the nobility can toss their second-born sons who have no other purpose in life."

"I now see it is a foolish custom," Nik snapped.

Rurik's smile didn't reach his eyes. "You can change it when you're king— Oh, you won't be able to do that, will you?"

"Your father would be destroyed to know you are doing this."

"Which is why my father will never know. But because of my father, I made certain Her Grace was well cared for. For that, you can thank me, for she has been naught but a pain."

Nik had to swallow twice to get himself to do so, but he managed a nod. "She is very important to all of us."

"She is a favorite of my father's. Plus, I think she will be particularly kind to me once you've met your demise at the hands of the evil men who abducted her."

"It will not work. Someone will talk, and you'll be discovered. The men who abducted Her Grace—"

"—will not live to see the end of this day. There will be no witnesses. None."

Nik's throat tightened and it was all he could do to keep from looking at Ailsa, though he dared not let Rurik know how much she mattered to him. Good God, how had he so misjudged this man? Was there anyone he could trust?

Ailsa slipped her hand over his, her fingers warm and strong.

Yes. He could trust her. *I was a fool to ever question you.* He gave her hand a quick squeeze. "You have no soul, Rurik."

"I have a soul. One cut to shreds watching you change over the years, always taking, always expecting more. You used to be a good friend, someone I could talk to, and you would talk to me. But now . . ." Rurik sneered. "Sometimes days go on end and you never even *look* at me. Once you became a prince, I became a worthless footstool."

"I've never thought you worthless. Dammit, Rurik. I wish you'd come to me, told me how you felt. I know I should have noticed, but I've been so tangled up in these negotiations that I—"

"Stop making excuses! You never notice anything unless it pertains to one of your precious missions. I'll admit I've changed over the years, too. I used to think you could do no wrong. That you were better than the others. Now? I don't care whether you live or die. How could I, watching you get everything you've ever wanted, while I am left behind? Am I supposed to just stand by, with nothing? Work my fingers to the bone protecting your ass as if mine isn't worth the skin covering it?"

"Rurik, please," Ailsa pleaded. "Think what you are doing! There must be a way for us to solve this, something that does nae involve pistols."

Behind Rurik, a shrub trembled. Nik forced his gaze to never waver from Rurik, but whatever or—please God—whoever it was, moved again, and made their way closer.

And then closer still.

Nik caught a glimpse of a brown head as it disappeared behind the ledge of a rock.

Gregor. Thank God! So Rurik has made one mistake already.

But it was obvious that the lad was too far away to shoot. He needed to get closer, and was trying to do so quietly.

Nik wet his lips. He must keep Rurik talking, at least for another minute. "Perhaps I can make it all up to you. What would it take? Money? A castle? Gold? Horses?"

"Don't insult me. This is about respect and power. You can give away neither of those."

"Fine, then. Would you like more responsibilities? A higher position?"

"All I want is to end this now." The guard raised his pistol toward Ailsa.

Nik stepped in front of her. "I will make this easy for you, but only if you give me your word not to hurt Lady Ailsa."

Rurik lowered the pistol a touch. "Make it easy on me? How could it be easier than it is now?"

"When you shoot me, I will not fall down and die easily. I will come for you, and before I die, I will take your life."

Rurik laughed, this time with real humor. "Good God, do you think you're so high-and-mighty that you can just ignore the effects of a bullet?"

"I can try. So if I were you, I'd shoot me first, and I would take my time and make certain I didn't miss."

"*Nae!*" Ailsa sent Nik a wild look. "Dinnae encourage him, Nik. Dinnae—"

He pushed her behind him as he continued to talk to Rurik. "I'm the reason you're doing this. So do it. Get it over with."

She clutched his arm, trying to push him out of the way. "Nik, dinnae—"

"Enough!" Rurik snapped. "The time for talking is long past. Lady Ailsa, I am sorry you became tangled in this. But sadly, like your cousin, you have become a complication." Rurik lifted his pistol and cocked the hammer. "Ah, Your Highness, how many times I imagined doing this!"

"Nik, please! Dinnae do this. I—I love you!" Ailsa choked back a sob. Her voice was more whisper than else, but her words rang through his mind as loudly as a church bell.

It was a hell of a time for a declaration, but it didn't matter now. It *couldn't* matter now.

Nik's stomach churned, his heart thudding so hard, he could hear it. "Stay back, *krasavitsa.*"

Then he met Rurik's icy gaze, and knew the time had come.

Nik held his hands open to each side. "As you will."

Ailsa gasped. "*Nae!*"

Rurik sited down the pistol barrel.

A deafening roar rang out.

Chapter 24

The wind blew over the lawn of Castle Leod, ruffling the grasses, the dead leaves dancing along the ground. Overhead, the gray skies scattered snowflakes that skittered down the cold stone and stuck to the windowsills in icily beautiful patterns.

"Your Highness?"

Nik dropped the curtain and turned to Apraksin, who stood just inside the library doorway. "The coaches are ready, I see."

"*Da*. It took quite a while to fit all of Her Grace's trunks on the luggage cart, but we managed."

"She always packs enough for ten women. One of her many flaws. But if the trunks have been strapped in place, then we are done here." Nik ignored the sinking feeling that pressed on his stomach as he walked to the fire. "Thus ends a very trying chapter."

Apraksin watched him. "You've had an eventful few weeks."

"That I have." More than he wished to admit. He cut a look at the courtier. "Where is Her Grace?"

"She is in the blue salon saying good-bye to the Mackenzies."

Good-byes. Nik didn't want to think of those. Just the word made his chest ache anew. "And Rurik?"

Apraksin's expression hardened. "He will be in the second coach. I put twelve guards on him, none of them his own. I will be with him as well, and if he so much as moves, I will kill him."

"Keep him in irons. He was so angry with me. I do not think that will change."

Apraksin nodded. "He will face trial the second he reaches Oxenburg. Your father has demanded it."

"He will have to face his own father first." Nik sighed heavily. "I imagine Rurik dreads that more."

"His father is devastated." Apraksin hesitated, and then added, "He wrote a most kind letter to you and the duchess. It arrived this morning."

"He is a good man. He deserved better than this."

Apraksin's gaze flickered over Nik's face. "We all did."

"Any word on the tsar? I saw the messenger arrive earlier."

"The tsar awaits us in Edinburgh. I thought to tell you once we were under way."

"What does he say about Rurik's accusations?"

Apraksin gave a humorless smile. "Naturally, he denies everything and says he is impatient to begin the talks."

"Of course." Nik raked a hand through his hair, suddenly sick of it all—the false words, broken promises, and bloody treachery. They turned his stomach and wore upon his soul. He closed his eyes a long moment, and then said, "I must take my leave of Lady Ailsa and her family."

"We owe them a debt of gratitude."

"We do. Though, if her cousin had been a better shot, we would not have to take Rurik back to Oxenburg at all."

Apraksin smiled. "At least Mackenzie hit Rurik's arm and kept him from harming anyone else. His elbow is shattered and causes him much pain. I find that most satisfying."

Nik might have felt sympathy for the man who'd betrayed him, but the bastard would have killed Ailsa with no more thought than he'd give to slapping a fly.

Nik's throat tightened. *Had she died, what would I have done?* He wished he could stop remembering the moment, but it burned into his mind. Every night since then, he'd awakened sweat-drenched, his heart pounding as if he'd been running from death itself.

He realized Apraksin was still waiting. "One question. There was a bit of Mackenzie tartan left pinned under the wheel of Hamilton's coach when all this first happened."

Apraksin grimaced. "Rurik wished to leave a trail that led far, far from the tsar."

"So he was trying to tie the abduction to the clan war." Nik shook his head. "Go ahead to the blue salon. I will meet you there shortly."

"Very good, Your Highness." Apraksin looked as if he wished to say something more, but one look at Nik and the courtier bowed, and left.

Nik rubbed his hands over his face, tired from lack of sleep, and achingly sad. Rurik's brutal betrayal had hurt in ways Nik didn't yet understand.

He walked to the fire and stared with unseeing eyes at the flames. He had to go downstairs and say good-bye to Ailsa under the watchful gaze of her grandmother and cousin. Say good-bye without sweeping her into his arms, which ached to hold her. Say good-bye without admitting what he now knew was the truth—that he loved her madly, more than life itself.

He propped his elbow on the mantel and covered his eyes with his hand. Why, oh why, had he let her under his guard? She'd disarmed him when they'd first met. Charmed and seduced him as they'd traveled. And then she'd stayed with him after he'd been injured—was that when he'd stopped thinking of himself and started thinking only of her?

He didn't know when it had happened, but she was now a part of his heart. Yet Rurik's betrayal had proved that Nik's life was not his own and never would be.

If he did what he selfishly yearned to do—confess his love and sweep her off to Oxenburg—she would become a part of his mad, bitter, harsh world, one that glittered on the outside, while the inside was black and rotting with betrayals and secrets, manipulations and lies. To survive, she would have to build her own walls, protect herself from others, or her tender heart would be stomped to dust.

And in doing so, she would change, just as he had. *Dammit, I cannot allow that to happen.*

He set his jaw. If it cost him his own happiness, then so be it. He couldn't allow her beautiful spirit to become destroyed by lies and treachery. God knew, they had already killed his.

I must do this for Ailsa. There was no putting it off. He left the library and made his way to the blue salon, trying to fortify his courage with thoughts of how much safer she would be here, tucked away in her castle in the highlands, far from the pain and ugliness that had become his life.

————⦿————

"*L*ady Ailsa, it has been a pleasure." Lord Apraksin bowed over her hand.

Ailsa raised her brows. "Would you truly call it a pleasure?"

He laughed and covered her hand with his. "We can at least agree it was not boring."

"Aye, that we can."

He released her hand with a smile.

Ailsa forced her smile to stay in place, although as the moment approached for Nik to leave, she found it harder and harder. She loved him, and he knew it. She'd hoped for a short time her love meant something to him, but once they'd returned to Castle Leod, he'd done what he could to avoid her.

She didn't know what to think; all she knew was that she was miserable, as if her soul had been brutally ripped from her body. She wished with all her heart she had not so foolishly admitted the truth, but it was too late now. She bit her lip to keep it from trembling.

"Apraksin, *you* may not have found this visit boring, but it was for me," Her Grace announced, thumping her cane for emphasis. "I came for some rest, not to be held at pistol point like a sheep waiting for slaughter. *Bozhy moj*, it took the lot of you a long time to rescue me."

"Your Grace," Lord Apraksin murmured, looking uncomfortable.

Ailsa managed a smile. The Grand Duchess Nikolaeva had returned to Castle Leod in excellent form. Despite her many complaints, she seemed invigorated following her ordeal, and had even suggested she'd eaten better while being held prisoner than she had at Castle Leod, a comment that had left Lady Edana huffing in fury.

"In fact," Her Grace said loudly, "I'm bored right now and would sleep if you would all stop with this senseless chatter."

Gregor, who'd been standing by the window watching the coaches line up, released the curtain and made his way back to their side of the room. His head was bandaged, one eye badly bruised, his nose swollen and cut. He moved slowly, still stiff and in pain. "Your Grace, if you must take a nap, then I will do so, too. After so much excitement, life in a genteel house is indeed quite dull."

Lady Edana's smile grew even more taut and she looked as if, for a penny, she'd kick them all out of her drawing room. "Fortunately for Natasha, she will be able to sleep once she's in her coach, which will be *soon*."

The duchess snorted. "With the state of the roads in Scotland? What do you people do, dig holes at night to discourage visitors?"

Ailsa had to laugh, which relieved her aching heart a tiny bit. "If I thought that would work, I might be disposed to do so."

"At least *you're* honest." The duchess used her cane to poke Lady Edana's slippered foot. "As for you, I owe you an apology. I'm sorry I stole Daffyd from you."

Lady Edana laughed, though it was unnaturally shrill. "Oh, Daffyd and I were never— Really, you are mistaken if you think there was ever anything—"

"Not on his side, I'm sure. But yours? *Da*."

Lady Edana's face couldn't be any more red. "You are mistaken," she said icily. "Besides, I'm certain he and I will return to our usual footing once you've left."

"Oh. About that. He is to meet me in Inverness and we will travel to Oxenburg together."

"He . . . Is he?" Lady Edana's shoulders fell.

"*Da*. It will not last, of course, but it will be enjoyable for a while longer. You, meanwhile, will find another man."

"I—I don't think that's—"

"But this time it must be someone younger. You do not look your age, so I do not know why you wish for an old man like Daffyd. He will do for me, but for you? *Nyet*. You need a younger man."

Lady Edana's disappointed look disappeared behind a flush of pleasure. "Oh. Why I— That's quite kind of you. I do use the best creams and—" She simpered, and patted her hair. "Natasha, do you really think I need a younger man?"

"I know so. Find a younger man, but not too young, or you will be bored. The French have a guide: half your age plus seven years."

"That's . . . Goodness, that's quite young."

Her Grace patted Lady Edana's knee. "You will be able to handle it, I've no doubt."

Lady Edana appeared quite taken with this idea, and Ailsa smiled to see her grandmother so cheered.

Apraksin cleared his throat. "Your Grace, I hate to be the bearer of bad news, but the time has come."

"Pah!" the duchess returned. "I do not look forward to this trip. So many holes in the roads. My arse will be black-and-blue by the time we reach Inverness."

"Quite," Apraksin said in a dry tone. He turned to Gregor and held out his hand. "My lord, I hope you will visit us in Oxenburg soon. The king would be delighted to meet the man who saved his son's life."

Gregor flushed and shook the courtier's hand. "It's been a long, exciting few weeks and I need some rest before I think about traveling. As exciting as my adventure was, I fear you had the worst of it, having to stay here with nothing to do."

"It was terrible. How I wish I'd been with you, eating hard bread and berries and sleeping on rocks."

Gregor chuckled. "There were a lot of unpleasant moments between the exciting ones."

"As with most adventures. I would have gone with you, but I, too, fell victim to Rurik's plot." A shadow passed over the courtier's face. "He convinced both the prince and me that it would be best if I stayed behind."

"He convinced a lot of people of a lot of things," Ailsa said. "He was a guid liar."

"I feel for his poor father," Her Grace said sharply. "He will never forgive himself, I fear." Her gaze went to the doorway. "Ah, there you are! I was beginning to think you'd lost the courage."

"To say a simple good-bye?" Nik strolled in, his eyes so dark they seemed black. Dressed in a fitted coat that clung to his broad shoulders, his cravat perfectly tied, his buff-colored breeches outlining his muscular legs, he was the picture of civility. Ailsa watched him hungrily, clenching her hands together to keep from reaching for him.

He went to Lady Edana and bowed over her hand. "I fear we must leave, my lady."

Must? Or wish to? Ailsa tried to swallow the lump of hurt that filled her throat. *Why won't he speak to me?*

To be fair, she hadn't found the words, either. When she looked into his eyes, she could see the devastation caused by Rurik's actions. She had no idea how to ease that pain. He would have to find his own answers.

Which left her feeling achingly alone, especially when he was in the room, within touching distance.

He turned to Gregor. "You, I owe much."

Gregor laughed, though it was a bit shaky. "I'm lucky I hit him at all. He shot me and then, for good measure, bashed me over the head with his pistol. When I woke up, I had a headache that was so blindingly painful, my hands shook."

"I am lucky you have a hard head."

Gregor laughed and, after a handshake, Nik crossed to Ailsa.

He held out his hand and she placed hers in it, aware that everyone watched.

Nik lifted her hand and kissed her fingers, his lips warm on her skin. "This is not an easy good-bye."

Her skin burned where he touched it, and she ached for more. She wondered what she should say—what she could say. But she couldn't find the words.

She was left stating rather stiffly, "I hope we will see

one another soon." As she spoke, she looked at him with every bit of the hope she felt, praying he would see it.

His eyes darkened and he tightened his grip on her hand. "I—"

She held her breath, waiting.

His gaze swept over her face and for one breathless instant, she thought he would say something, *do* something. But then his expression hardened and all he said was, "That would be nice." He released her hand. "But unlikely." He bowed. "Thank you for your kindness, Lady Ailsa. You will not be forgotten."

He turned. "Tata Natasha, are you ready?"

"*Nyet*, but I suppose you do not care. Go ahead. I know you will wish to make certain your prisoner is well secured. Apraksin can escort me to the coach."

"Very good. Again, I thank you all for your kindness." Nik inclined his head and then, just like that, he was gone.

Ailsa's heart lurched and she dug her nails into her palms to keep from saying anything foolish.

Apraksin offered his arm to the duchess, who took it, and with much groaning, stood.

Ailsa stared at the empty doorway, listening as Nik's footsteps faded away. She wanted to run after him and throw her arms around him and— *And what? What do I want of him? That which he obviously cannot give?*

Her throat tightened, and she had to bite her lip to keep tears from forming.

The duchess, leaning on Apraksin's arm, muttered something under her breath and then looked up at the courtier. "I would have Lady Ailsa walk me to the door. You may meet me in the foyer."

Looking surprised, the courtier bowed. "Of course, Your Grace." He smiled at the rest of the assemblage. "Thank you again for your hospitality." With a warm smile, he left.

"Come," Her Grace ordered Ailsa. "Walk me to the front door. And do not argue, for I've no patience with it."

Though she didn't feel like doing anything but running to her bedchamber and throwing herself on the bed and indulging in a good cry, Ailsa came to assist the older woman. "I was nae going to argue, Your Grace."

"Good. Your family seems much given to it." Her Grace jerked her head toward Lady Edana, who sniffed, but pretended she hadn't heard.

The duchess leaned on Ailsa's arm and together they walked out of the salon and into the hallway.

For several slow steps, the duchess didn't speak. Finally, she announced in an overly loud voice, "My grandson is a fool."

"Your Grace, that's unfair—"

"You are a fool, too," the duchess added sharply.

Ailsa closed her mouth, uncertain what to say about this. She finally settled for a sniff.

The duchess's lips twitched. "We will talk about how much you love my Nik."

Ailsa almost tripped over the rug. "I beg your pardon?"

"You heard me. You love him. I can see it in your eyes."

Ailsa didn't trust herself to answer.

"Some people throw that word around very freely. Others—like you, perhaps—use it too sparingly."

"I've told him."

The duchess looked surprised. "Oh. And what did he say?"

"Nothing. It was at the height of our escapade with Mr. Rurik. Perhaps Nik thinks it was the excitement of the moment or— I dinnae know. All I know is that since we've returned, he's made certain we're never alone."

"I'm surprised you didn't grab him by the ear and make him talk to you." The duchess gave Ailsa a cool look. "You have never struck me as shy."

"I'm nae shy, but I'm nae going to beg. If he wished to be with me, if he loved me, he would tell me so."

The duchess gave a disbelieving snort. "Pah, you are such an innocent!"

Ailsa didn't reply. Her heart was in shreds and the man she loved was getting ready to ride away. "I'm at a loss, Your Grace."

"You shouldn't be. He loves you, too."

Ailsa's heart tripped. "Did he say something, or—"

"*Nyet*. Not yet." The duchess pursed her lips. "As much as I think you would be good for my Nik, he must realize that for himself and be willing to pay the cost. For now, he is too hurt by Rurik's defection to think about anything with logic. Nik will need time." They were almost at the foyer, so the duchess stopped and patted Ailsa's hand. "I must ask for your patience."

"Of course, but patience for what?"

"You will see. When the time comes, one or the other of you will know it, and break the silence."

"It will nae matter. He will be in Oxenburg and I will be here."

"For now." The duchess slipped her arm free of Ailsa's and, cane thumping, made her way into the foyer, where MacGill was handing Lord Apraksin his hat and gloves.

A thousand questions on her lips, Ailsa followed. "Your Grace, please. I dinnae understand."

The duchess took Apraksin's arm. "You will," she promised.

"But Your Grace, I dinnae . . . That is, I never—"

"Oh, I'm sure you did."

Lord Apraksin choked, although no words passed his lips.

"Your Grace?" MacGill opened the door and the duchess and Lord Apraksin went out onto the portico. Coatless, Ailsa followed, crossing her arms to protect herself from the icy wind.

The duchess paused on the first step, her gaze on her grandson, where he spoke to one of the outriders guarding the last coach. She looked back at Ailsa and announced, "I will write."

"Thank you. That's verrah kind of you." *I think.*

"You will write back."

Oh? At the duchess's raised eyebrow, Ailsa hurried to say, "Of course."

"Good." She waved her hand. "Go back inside where it's warm. And do not worry. I will watch over him for you."

Ailsa nodded and with one last, lingering look at the coach door where Nik had just disappeared, she hurried back to the house.

Inside she stood shivering, but it wasn't just the cold that held her in its icy grip. It was also the sound of the coaches as they rattled down the drive, carrying away the only man she'd ever love.

Chapter 25

Max Romanovin leaned back in his large gilt chair, ignoring the creak of the antique legs. "If I must wait one minute longer for my supper, I will hit someone." He sent his brother a thoughtful look. "It will most likely be you."

Nik didn't look up from the letter he'd been writing. "Neither of you were invited here, so you will understand why I do not care if you get your supper or not."

His youngest brother Wulf had been absently paging through a sheaf of papers stacked on the corner of the desk, but now he shoved them aside. "*This* is why we have come, Max and I. You have been like a bear with a sore paw since you returned from Scotland."

"I'm busy. That is all." Nik sent them a stern look. "We should *all* be so employed."

Max's gaze narrowed. "You know we work hard."

Nik did know it. Max oversaw Oxenburg's vast armies, while Wulf served as their cultural minister and was always in the middle of a vast array of events and restorations. Their other brother, Alexsey, was with his beloved wife in the southern reaches of the country, overseeing the construction of a new school for the Romany children so beloved by their grandmother. All three of his brothers worked hard and added much to the quality of life of their subjects. A twinge of guilt hit Nik.

Bloody hell, what is wrong with me that I attack my own brothers? The concern in their gaze made him feel even worse. He threw down his pen and raked his hand through his hair. "*Da*, you all work hard."

"We do," Max agreed. "Look at us now, staying with you here in the winter palace, away from our homes and loved ones."

"I was wrong. It's just . . . I'm tired, that is all."

"You've been 'tired' for five months now," Wulf said. "Are you still angry about Rurik's defection?"

"I have made my peace with it." It still hurt, but his sadness was overshadowed by a bigger loss. *Ailsa*.

Even thinking her name made his chest ache, his legs feel heavy, as if moving were a chore. He'd known he'd yearn for her, but he hadn't expected this hollowness of spirit. He didn't care about anything anymore. Not one damn thing. It was a wonder he got his work done at all. He did, but only because keeping himself busy and forcing himself to think about something other than Ailsa was how he made it through the long, dark days.

Wulf perched on the edge of Nik's desk, his leg swinging gently. "So, what has turned you into such a bear, if it is not Rurik?"

Nik wondered if he should tell them. *Tell them what? That I made the right decision, but didn't realize how much it would cost? And yet, knowing it was—and still is—the right decision, I am damned to accept it?*

And even that did not explain the depths of his emptiness. He picked up his pen and bent over the letter he'd been trying to write. "Whatever it is, the two of you harping at me will solve nothing. Go to supper. I will join you later, *if* I finish this correspondence."

Max looked at Wulf. "We tried. He is too stubborn to listen."

"Perhaps we should take him out into the snow and cool his temper there. I saw a particularly deep drift by the garden wall."

"That would work." Max cracked his knuckles and then dusted them on his shirt.

Nik looked up from his letter and eyed his brothers with caution. *Surely they wouldn't.* But they would, and he knew it. "I will not go easily."

Wulf grinned. "Do not challenge us, brother." Less broad than his brothers, he made up for it with lightning-fast quickness. "It will be cleansing."

"I'll take both of you down," Nik warned.

Max didn't look impressed. "We came to you in peace, offering to help you find your way free of your ill humor, and you've done nothing but bark at us."

"The negotiations with the tsar are still ongoing. I've many things to see to right now."

"Your short temper has nothing to do with that," Wulf said. "Something bothers you, but you will not tell us. It's as if you're ill but don't wish to admit it."

"Who is ill?" Tata Natasha came through the open doors, her cane muffled by the thick rug. Dressed in her habitual black, she eyed her three grandsons, who'd all hurriedly risen to their feet at her entrance. "I've several purges in the trunk in my bedchamber. Shall I send a servant to fetch one?"

"Good God, *nyet*." Wulf backed away a few steps.

"Purging is good for the soul." Tata Natasha tottered to the chair closest to the fire and sat down, leaning her cane against her knee. "I will have vodka," she announced.

Max glanced at Nik, who shook his head.

"*Nyet*," Nik said. "The doctor—"

"—is a fool, and I do not countenance fools." She eyed first Max, and then Wulf. She nodded to her youngest grandson. "You. Bring me vodka."

"You're not supposed to—"

"Either bring me vodka or I will come to your house and stay the rest of the winter. *All* of it."

His mouth opened and then closed. Finally, he said in a slightly frantic voice, "We have a new baby. You do not like babies, for they scream and cry."

"That would annoy me, true, so I would be in a foul mood. But I would stay anyway."

Wulf sent a desperate look at Max and Nik.

Nik growled, "Bloody hell, give her some vodka. If we refuse her, she will just get one of the footmen to do it anyway."

Looking relieved, Wulf made his way to the small table by the window where the decanter and glasses sat. He poured a small amount into a glass and brought it to his grandmother.

She scowled at the glass. "I asked for a drink, not a sip."

"Start with this." He pushed the glass into her hand.

She took a small drink, peering over the edge of her glass at her grandsons. "So. Why are you two here?"

Max replied, "Wulf and I came to see why Nik has been so ill-tempered."

"*Da*, we are done with it," Wulf said.

"I see." She cocked an eyebrow at Nik. "Is this about your Scottish lass?"

Wulf and Max exchanged surprised looks. "Who?" Wulf asked.

"I should have known there was a woman involved." Max turned his chair to face his oldest brother more squarely. "Tell us."

"There's nothing to tell," Nik said firmly.

"I met her," Tata Natasha offered. "She can fire a pistol like a Hessian sharpshooter."

"Murian would like her, then," Max said, looking far too interested in Nik's personal business.

Tata nodded. "This woman can ride a horse, too, like a Mongolian warrior."

"Impressive," Wulf murmured. "She sounds like a paragon."

"*Nyet*. Sadly, she is not the best hostess. Her housekeeping . . . Pah. She will need training, once she comes here."

Nik scowled. "She is not coming here."

"Why not?" Wulf asked.

"Nik, you must tell us more about this woman," Max demanded.

"*Nyet*."

"He will not tell you, but I will," Tata Natasha finished her drink and peered into the empty glass with a disgusted look.

Nik tried not to let his teeth grind too audibly. *Wonderful. Just what I wished to do; hear about Ailsa as if I did not remember every lush, haunting inch of her; as if I do not hear her voice in my head all the time; as if I do not sleep, because when I do, I dream of her in ways that leave my heart aching all the worse.*

"Let me see. What more can I tell you?" Tata Natasha leaned back in her chair. "She is a beautiful woman, this Lady Ailsa. She is tall and willowy, with flowing black hair, and as graceful as a swan—"

"What?" Nik threw his pen on the desk, ink splattering over his letter. "Bloody hell, don't you even *remember* her? She is neither tall nor willowy, nor is she particularly graceful. And you know damned well her hair isn't black, but dark blond."

Tata peered now at the ceiling, her face scrunched as if in thought. "Blond hair? Are you certain?"

"You know damn well I remember her hair color."

"Hmm. You may be right. I do remember this: she is very domestic and mild-mannered, like a sheep. She does nothing but knit, knit, knit—"

"For the love of—" Nik shoved himself back from the desk with such force, his chair almost overturned. "Drivel! All of it."

"Oh?" Tata held out her glass.

Wulf came to refill it, this time much more generously.

"Da," Nik bit out. "Lady Ailsa is stubborn and furi-

ously independent, and she's far more spirited than a pathetic sheep!"

Max and Wulf both looked so amused that Nik wondered if perhaps the snowdrift fight might have been a better idea. The way he felt now, he would not have lost.

Tata Natasha nodded thoughtfully. "She has the pride of caesars. And the nose of one, too."

"She's also ridiculously hopeful, a romantic at heart, and too tenderhearted to ever face the bloody creatures who live here at court," Nik finished in a brutal tone.

"She sounds charming," Max said.

"I would like to meet her," Wulf said.

"You never will," Nik said shortly. He eyed his brothers with profound dislike. "Go to supper. Now."

"First we must find out why this formidable woman is not here," Max said. "Tata Natasha, I suppose you know the answer to that, too."

"Nik fears having such a tender flower living here, exposed to the intricacies of court. He believes they will overwhelm her and turn her into a hardened shrill."

"I never said 'hardened shrill,'" Nik protested.

Tata shrugged. "You used other words, but the intent was the same." She sipped her vodka. "I must admit, the court presents challenges. It can be brutal and disheartening, even to me, and I am quite used to such things."

"It has affected us all and we were raised to deal with such," Nik said stiffly. "I would not have Ailsa changed."

"It is true that all courts are filled with wolves in

wolves' clothing," Tata agreed. "Just yesterday, Count Gorchakov visited me. He brought some honey after I said my throat was sore from the dry weather. I had to excuse myself from the room for a moment to fetch my shawl, and when I returned, I caught the lout going through the papers on my desk."

Max's expression turned grim. "Where were the footmen?"

"On other errands."

"Tata!" Nik groaned. "You know better. I will have a word with the count."

"Be gentle, for I hit him in the shin with my cane. He is limping still."

Max chuckled.

Nik sent his brother a hard look. "It is only funny because we are used to it. Gorchakov bears watching, as does Lady Naryshkins, who has been corresponding secretly with the Russians, while Baron Yusopov has fallen into the clutches of a young mistress with ties to the Prussians, and . . . Bloody hell, we live in a hornets' nest of intrigue and mistrust!"

"True." Tata Natasha nodded, her lace cap flapping over her ears. "All courts are this way."

"Ours is worse," Nik said. "We are strategically placed between giants. Everyone wishes to influence us. And thus we must fight intrigues at every turn."

Tata looked at Max. "Was that your stomach growling?"

He nodded. "I'm starving. Supper was to be served a half hour ago, but this one"—he nodded toward Nik—"would not come."

"Then go eat," she said. "And take Wulf with you."

Max stood. "Aren't you coming?"

She shook her head. "I've a letter to write."

"Fine. Come, Wulf. I believe Tata Natasha has this well in hand. And if that is so, then I wish to leave at first light and return home."

"I will do the same." Wulf stopped by Tata Natasha's chair to press a kiss to her hand. "See what you can do for the Hopeless One. He is miserable when he's unhappy."

"So I've noticed," she said drily. She gave her grandson's hand a squeeze and then waved him to the door. "I will join you once I finish my letter."

As soon as they were gone, Tata Natasha leaned back in her chair and sighed. "Thank God they have left. Talk, talk, talk is all they do."

Nik prudently didn't answer.

She continued, "Your brothers may worry about you, but I know you are fine. A little thinner since we returned, perhaps. And your eyes—it is obvious you are not sleeping well. You are a bit pale, too. But other than that, I see no difference."

"Thank you," he said drily. "You said you had a letter to write?"

"*Da*. It will not take long." She reached into the pockets of her skirts and pulled out a folded missive. "Do you have an extra pen? I must answer this."

"Shall I bring you paper, too?"

"I will not be able to answer this letter without it."

He found a fresh piece of paper and then took it, along with his best pen and a small pot of ink, to where she sat. He pulled the side table forward and placed the supplies upon it. "There."

"Thank you." She unfolded the letter and spread it out.

He glimpsed the handwriting, and froze, his heart giving an odd flip. "That's from Ailsa." His voice cracked the words as if he were throwing stones against a wall. He reached for the letter—

Tata Natasha snatched it up and held it to her chest. "You may not see this. It was not written to you."

He opened his mouth to argue, but better sense took over. She was right. Whatever was in the letter, he would be better off not knowing about it. He thought far too much about Ailsa as it was, and reading a note in her handwriting would only make things worse.

Though it cost him dearly, he returned to his desk and randomly sorted papers, trying not to stare at the missive.

Tata watched him for a moment before she placed the letter back on the table, smoothed out the crumpled paper, and began reading.

Nik picked up his pen, irritatingly aware of the way Tata's lips silently moved as she read.

The clock sitting by the window ticked loudly.

Somewhere in the distance, a door opened and closed.

Nik stared with unseeing eyes at the letter that rested before him. He cleared his throat. "Has . . . has she written to you before?"

"Every week or so. And every week I write her back."

"It would take three weeks—"

"Special couriers," Tata said shortly. She picked up the pen and dipped it in the ink.

"Why does she write?"

"She seeks advice."

"From you?"

Tata couldn't have looked more surprised. "Why would she not ask me? I have a lot of advice to give!"

"Yes, but . . . advice about what?"

"That, too, is none of your business." Tata bent over the table and began to write. "You do your work; I'll do mine."

Seething, but unwilling to seem any more interested in Ailsa than he'd already been betrayed into doing, Nik tried to focus on his work. *But why would Ailsa write to Tata Natasha? Lady Edana is right there, at Castle Leod. Surely Ailsa would ask advice from her own grandmother first.*

He thought about this for a while. *Lady Edana didn't seem particularly capable. Tata Natasha has lived a much bigger life. Given the choice, I'd rather speak to Tata Natasha, too.*

The mystery solved, he tried to keep from staring at the letter his grandmother was now writing. He'd just dipped his pen into his inkwell when Tata Natasha gave a frustrated sigh.

"A pack of drunk monks must have developed the English language, for that is the only way to explain the many discrepancies. The spelling—pah!"

"It is not an easy language to write," he agreed.

"It is frustrating." She tapped a finger on her paper.

"How does one spell 'convenience,' as in 'marriage of convenience'?"

He blinked. "Why do you need to spell that?"

"I cannot tell you. It would betray a confidence. C-o-n-v-" She frowned. " 'I' or 'e'—which is next?"

Bloody hell. He absently spelled the word for her.

"Thank you," she muttered, carefully writing it. The room was silent except for the sound of her pen scratching the paper.

Nik tried to still the ache that was beginning to press on his chest. *Perhaps Tata Natasha is writing about a marriage here at court.* That was a possibility. Idle gossip and nothing more. Two such marriages had occurred in the last four months.

Yes, that is it. Satisfied, he pulled the letter he'd been working on a bit closer, and had just written a sentence when Tata paused again.

"Does 'danger' have an 'e' or an 'a' before the 'r'? I can never remember."

" 'E.' "

She wrote it and then squinted at the word. "It looks wrong, but I will take your word for it."

Danger? Bloody hell, is something amiss?

After several long moments, he was relieved when Tata put down her pen and picked up the letter, waving it gently so that the ink might set. "I think it is ready. Let me read through it one more time." As she held it up, she read it to herself, her voice low so that only a few, faint phrases could be heard. ". . . despair no more . . . marriage of convenience . . . archaic . . . shoot someone if you must . . . trapped like a rabbit in a snare . . . seventy-five is too old a man for such a young—" She frowned. "Nik, for 'maiden,' is it 'ai' or 'ia'?"

"That's it." He threw down his pen and stood. "What in the *hell* are you writing? Has something happened to Ailsa? Perhaps you should go to her at Castle Leod—"

"Oh, she's no longer at Castle Leod. She hasn't been for some time now." Tata Natasha folded the letter. "She is in Edinburgh."

His heart went cold. "This marriage of convenience? And—and this seventy-five-year-old—what is that about?"

"You can see that all the way from your desk? You have very good eyes, Nikki. No wonder you're such an accurate shot."

"Tata. The *letter*."

"I am not going to tell you more. You left her, remember? It was your decision."

"I left her to keep her from coming here, and becoming a part of all this."

Tata Natasha shrugged. "And now she will never be a part of it. Or a part of you."

Nik had to unclench his teeth to answer. "Ailsa was raised in a castle in the remote reaches of a wilderness. She's had very few dealings with the real world. She's . . . good. Honest. Kind."

"But she is not weak."

"*Nyet*. But she *is* tenderhearted. She's never been hurt by betrayals, or dealt with people feigning to be friends in order to get something, or—or—men who would pretend to bring her honey for her sore throat, only to try and steal something." He shook his head. "I couldn't bring her here. It would change her. Hurt her."

"You care for her."

"Of course I care for her! If I didn't, I'd have brought her here and let the world steal away her very soul. I could not do it."

"You will not need to. She will be facing the rigors and treachery of court soon enough."

"Is Edinburgh's court so bad? And is—" His throat tightened. "Is that why you mentioned a marriage of convenience? To a seventy-five-year-old man? Is that what's happened?" Somehow, he was no longer at his desk, but standing before Tata Natasha, his voice raised and demanding.

Tata shrugged. "She is not your concern. You have as much as told her so. You can do nothing about what happens to her now . . ."

"Like hell. I may not wish to bring her here to this bloody rats' nest of intrigue, but I'll not have her throwing her life away on an antiquity!"

Tata stiffened. "Seventy-five is not so old."

"I'm going to Ailsa. I'm going to tell her not to marry whoever it is. She deserves love. Happiness." He'd convinced himself that with him gone, she would find another love; her life would be gentle and blessed. But this . . . "Is her father making her do this? Is that what's happened?"

Tata smoothed the letter on her knee. "It is sad, the things fathers do to their children. They mean the best, but . . ." She shook her head.

"When is this wedding to take place?"

"I would imagine it will be soon."

"I will have a ship readied. We will leave this evening with the tide."

She stood. "I'm to go with you?"

"Of course. Ailsa is . . ." He took a steadying breath. "She may not listen to me, but she may listen to you. We must convince her to refuse her father, no matter the pressure he puts upon her."

"Very good. There's a ship waiting at the docks, so you do not need to order one readied." Tata held up her letter. "The courier was waiting for this. I daresay there may be cabins to be had—"

Nik took her elbow. "How long will it take you to pack?"

"I can be ready in half an hour."

"Then do it. We must go swiftly."

Chapter 26

Urged on by Nik's insistent orders, the lumbering coach made its way to the port. Throwing back the curtains, Nik could see the ship moored to the biggest dock, ready for travel. *Good. We must make haste.*

Across from him, Tata Natasha was bundled in a heavy wool cape, her wrinkled face framed by a thick fur-lined hood. "So. We are on a rescue mission, eh?"

"I cannot allow Ailsa to throw herself away on a marriage of convenience. She deserves better." God, she haunted him. The shape of her face. Her delightfully bold nose. Her silken laugh. Her cloud of dark blond hair. Sometimes, if he closed his eyes and took a deep breath, he could still smell the faint lavender of her scent.

"You pine for that woman. I see it in your eyes."

"I think about her. That's all." *When I'm awake. And asleep. And in between.*

The coach slowed as they rolled onto the cobblestones of the main thoroughfare by the dock. The scent of the ocean rose over the clatter of wagons and the shouts of drunken sailors.

Over the clamor, Tata said, "She's not so pretty, this one. She's not the type of female you usually pursue."

"It has been many months since I have thought her one of the handsomest women of my acquaintance."

"Then I am glad."

"Of what?"

"That we will—" The coach made a sharp turn and she grabbed the edge of the seat and peered out the window. "We arrive. Here. Help me down from this blasted carriage."

Nik swung open the door without waiting for the footman, frowning as he did so. "We are not at the docks."

"We are at an inn. I instructed the coachman to stop here. Before we go on the ship, I would take a moment to refresh myself."

"We should go straight to the ship. The tide—"

"—is not due for another half hour, perhaps longer. Besides, when I said 'refresh myself,' I meant something more delicate in nature."

Good lord, this woman was difficult. He tamped down the desire to point out that she could deal with her 'delicate' issues as soon as they reached the ship, but the stubborn set of her mouth told him it would be quicker to allow her to have her way.

He reluctantly pulled out the steps, waving off the footman as he did so. "Do not take long."

Tata Natasha allowed him to assist her down the steps. "A few minutes, no more. I promise."

"I will wait here."

"Come with me," she said over her shoulder, already

walking into the inn, her cane clicking on the stone walkway. "You will want vodka while you wait, *nyet*?"

He stifled a sigh, every fiber of his being focused on the ship he could see so tantalizingly close. But he might as well have a glass of vodka, as he was sure her idea of "hurrying" would not match his.

He followed her into the inn, a delicious aroma causing his stomach to growl.

She sniffed. "Roasted goose," she said with approval as she headed down the long hallway. "Wait in the front parlor. I will not be long."

With that, she disappeared into a side door.

He stifled a sigh and stepped into the parlor—only to stop dead in his tracks.

Ailsa stood at the far end of the room, her eyes wide in surprise. She was dressed in a plum-colored traveling gown, a thick shawl draped over her shoulders, her hands clasped in front of her. Her hair had been twisted on the top of her head, two fat curls resting on one shoulder.

The raging desire to cross the room and scoop her into his arms, to bury his face in her neck and feel her against him, made his knees almost weak.

He forced himself to remain where he was, near the door. "It seems I have been tricked."

Flushed, she said in a tight voice, "We both were. Your grandmother was to meet me here, nae you."

"She is meddling as ever." He took another step into the room, leaving the door open. "She said there was vodka and a roasted goose." He looked her up and down. "You do not look like a goose."

"Nae, but now that I see what she's done, it explains that." Ailsa pointed to the table by the window set for two. The table was laden with a roasted goose, a tureen of turtle soup, curried rabbit, a dish of basket-weave pastry, prawns in butter sauce, stewed mushrooms, and more. It was a feast.

"Her Grace ordered quite a repast." Ailsa gave a short laugh. "I thought perhaps she wished to welcome me, but now . . . I greatly underestimated your grand-mother."

"We both did. But do not worry, I'm not staying." He shouldn't. And yet his feet remained planted as if glued to the floor. "What will you do now?"

"Me? I suppose, for the moment, I will eat my sup-per. I just arrived in this frigid land of yours, and I'm famished. But you . . . you must leave, of course." She walked to the table, her silk skirts rustling as she took a seat and moved the napkin from the table to her lap.

Nik shifted from one foot to the other. The door be-hind him was open. It would take only two or three steps and he'd be through the door.

She was here and so achingly close. His gaze de-voured her and he noted the almost imperceptible changes since the last time he'd seen her. She, too, was thinner, her jaw more pronounced. She held her shoul-ders stiffly, as if she were ready to spring into action at a second's notice. What should he say? What could he say?

She carved a slice of goose, and put it on her plate. "Before you go, would you mind passing the bread? I cannae reach it from here."

His gaze flickered to the bread that sat at the farthest edge of the table.

He crossed to the table, picked up the bread basket, and handed it to her.

Her hand closed on the other side of the basket, both clinging to their side as if it bridged a huge chasm, and if one or the other of them let go, they would fall.

Ailsa wished she could think of something brilliant and witty to say. Something that would move them past this frozen awkwardness. But her mind was unable to do anything but drink in the sight of him.

Did he have to come in looking so blasted dashing and . . . and . . . *perfect*? His black hair was longer than before, falling to his shoulders, his face leaner, which only served to make him look even more handsome, a feat she hadn't thought possible. Worse, he was dressed in an elegant double-caped coat, his hat perched at a rakish angle on his head, his boots reflecting the firelight.

She wished she could think of something to say but all she could do was fight the tears that threatened to leak.

His gaze moved from her eyes, to her nose, to her lips, and then followed her arm to the basket.

He released it and stepped back. "I suppose I should eat. I daresay I'm paying for it, anyway."

She stared at him blankly as he shrugged out of his coat and tossed it and his hat onto the low settee, before he joined her at the table.

Bloody hell, we're together. The room suddenly seemed too small, and all she could do was remember how he'd touched her, tasted her. Her heart beat in her throat and she glanced at the fire, wondering if it had suddenly blazed up.

He filled his plate, watching her, his expression too complicated for her to decipher.

She blindly spooned some items onto her own plate, wishing she possessed some of cousin Gregor's social acumen.

Nik took a drink from his water goblet. "So. How did my grandmother get you here?"

"She invited me. I'm to be one of her ladies-in-waiting."

He looked at her blankly. "She doesn't have ladies-in-waiting."

"But . . . she made it seem as if . . ." Ailsa bit her lip, and then managed a falsely cheerful, "I'll be the only one, then. She said I would be of great help to her."

"I take it you would stay in my castle."

"I'm to stay wherever she is."

"Which would be in my castle. Which would mean you would eat at one of my tables. And ride one of my horses. And walk in one of my halls."

And sleep in one of your beds. She barely managed to squeak the words, "I see." She did see. *That scheming woman.* "I was told I would have a lovely study in case I wished to read or knit—"

"Do you knit?"

"Nae. I'm nae certain why your grandmother mentioned it, but . . ." She shrugged.

"So I thought. And I'm certain the study she referenced is my own." He lifted a piece of bread from the basket. "You will return to Scotland, of course."

She put down her fork. She'd been thinking the same thing, but when he said it, she was suddenly certain that was not what she would do. "Nae."

"Ailsa . . . you know this cannot happen. I cannot have you invading my peace of mind any more than you already do."

She'd been ready with a hot retort, but now her breath caught at his words. "I've been invading your peace of mind?"

His mouth pressed into a straight line. "You'll return to Castle Leod and stay there, with Lady Edana and your cousin."

"I cannae. Castle Leod has a new estate manager and he requested I leave, and quite rightly, too. The servants are loyal to me, and they will nae accept him if I'm there." She smiled. "You may know the new estate manager, for I hired him. It is Gregor."

"So . . . you've left Castle Leod for good?"

"I could nae stay. I told Papa it was because I was bored, but the reality is that there are too many memories there. Every time I ride into the woods, I remember . . ." Tears dampened her eyes, and she blinked them away. "Gregor is happy now; he finally has a purpose."

"You should go to your sisters. They're—"

"—all married, and have children. I have nae wish to join a household that will relegate me to 'slightly above the governess.' You know how these things happen."

He didn't argue, but said, "Go to your father, then. You could be of benefit to him."

"I could. But Lady Edana has convinced him I should have a London season, and I cannae abide the thought."

Nik's face darkened instantly, and a spark of hope warmed her. Had this separation been as hard on him as it had been on her? She couldn't imagine it had, for he was a man of action. If he'd wished to be with her, he would have been.

Or would he let his stubborn principles keep them apart?

As if in answer, he snapped out, "Go to your father, and have your season. It will be the best thing for you."

She toyed with her knife, turning it over beside her plate. "Nae, thank you. I'm already here. And the more I think about your grandmother's offer to be her lady-in-waiting, the more enjoyable it sounds."

He put down his fork. "I cannot accept this."

"'Tis nae oop to you. I've never been a lady-in-waiting, but Her Grace seems to think I'm uniquely suited for it." Ailsa turned her knife over again. "She promised she would help me find a husband, and that there were all manner of handsome, eligible noblemen in the Oxenburgian court. I have to admit, I have a soft spot for a man with an accent."

Nik muttered a long string of curses.

Ailsa listened with an air of attentive admiration. Once he finished, she said, "You must teach me some of those. I'm sure they'll come in handy."

"I will not. They are improper for a lady to use."

She shrugged. "Then I'm sure Her Grace will do so. I daresay she's familiar with them, too."

Which was probably true, Nik thought in disgust. "You do not understand what you are undertaking. The court is filled with—"

"—tricksters, liars, sycophants, and . . . What was the other thing your grandmother mentioned? Ah yes, seducers. I have been warned, you see."

"It is not enough to be warned. Being near such people, getting drawn into their webs of deceit, their trickery—it does something to you. It's done something to me."

She dropped her napkin on the table. "So I have seen. But I need to know these things, for Her Grace assures me we will be going oot in society often as I search for a husband."

"A husband? You said you were to be my grandmother's lady-in-waiting."

"Only because she thought it a good platform from which to fish for a spouse. She mentioned several men by name. There was Baron Potem— I cannae remember."

"Potemkin."

"That's it! She said he is fabulously wealthy."

"He is seventy-five, and confined to a bed with gout." He was gratified to see Ailsa's face fall. "Whom else has she mentioned?"

"A count known for breeding horses."

"Count Naryshkins."

"Aye! I hope he is nae auld, too?"

"He is forty."

"Excellent. Is he perchance bedridden?"

"*Nyet*. But he is well known for breeding children. He has over two dozen by at least eight women."

"Oh. This may take longer than I expected, but I'm certain it will work out if I put my mind to it."

She pushed her chair away from the table and stood. "Where is your grandmother, by the way?"

"If I were to guess, I'd say she is hiding in one of the back parlors, probably having her own meal and drinking far more vodka than she should."

"I will join her." Ailsa curtsied. "Good day, Your Highness." She turned to leave, her head lowering the slightest bit as she walked to the door. With her hair upswept Nik found himself looking at her exposed nape, one loose strand of her dark blond hair curling down it. Never had any woman possessed such a silken, delicate neck as this woman. Damn, he wanted to smooth that curl aside and kiss her neck, to make her shiver with something other than cold, to taste her smooth skin and—

"Ailsa." Somehow he was standing, his napkin forgotten on the floor.

She stopped and turned, her gaze meeting his.

Stark, raw hunger ripped through him, and he tried to find the words to explain things. To tell her that although he knew she would be safer somewhere else, he wanted her here, with him. That the thought of her with another man was more painful than cutting off his own arm.

But the words would not come, and after a long moment, she turned and continued toward the door.

Once there, she stopped, her shoulders straightening as she took a deep breath. And then, to his utter shock, she shut the door, the latch clicking into place, the noise louder than the thundering of his own heart.

Slowly, she turned. "Nik?" Her husky voice held a thousand questions, and just as many promises.

He crossed the few paces between them and swept her into his arms. All of the passion, all of the fury, all of his feelings poured from the dark place he'd kept them locked in, and flooded through him.

He lifted her against him, covering her mouth with his, plundering her ruthlessly. She returned the favor, grasping his coat and twining her arm over his neck, pressing against him and driving him mad. God, he'd missed her. He'd been so lost, so tormented, and so, so alone.

He slid his hands down her back, cupping her full arse, luxuriating in her rich body. She moaned against his mouth and hooked her leg over his hip, and he held her there, pressing himself to her.

And then they were no longer standing, but lying on the settee, and he was furiously batting away annoying pillows as she slid up her skirts and then found the buttons on his breeches.

They came together with a rawness and desperation that left no room for thought. No room for questioning. It was fast and pure and perfect and right and oh, so missed. Hot and greedy, she pulled him to her, lifting her hips as he pressed himself into her.

"Nik," she whispered, closing her eyes and arching against him.

He thrust again and again, filling her completely. He was so enthralled that he could not stop tasting her, touching her, urging her on. The small parlor filled with soft gasps and desperate moans as he teased and tormented her, desperately trying to show her all the things he could not seem to say.

He moved more fiercely, until finally Ailsa cried out, arching against him in exquisite pleasure. He pressed his forehead to hers, her passion tipping him over the edge of his own. Seconds later, he collapsed against her, burying his face in the crook of her neck as she quivered beneath him.

God, but he'd wanted her, *needed* her.

The realization made him open his eyes. Life without her had been so black, so bitter, that he couldn't face it. When he could breathe again, he murmured her name over and over, pressing kisses to her neck and cheek.

The mantel clock ticked, and their meal grew cold, yet they did not move.

"That was so *guid*," she sighed against him.

He raised himself on his elbow and cupped her face. Slowly, he kissed her lips, her cheeks, her eyes, her forehead.

"I love you." The words slipped from her lips on a sigh, but was loud in his heart.

He dropped his forehead to hers. "And I love you." He groaned. "But I shouldn't."

She slipped her arms around his neck and held him tight, and he buried himself against her, holding her. What he wanted . . . what he needed . . . it was all here. But—

A noise arose in the hallway. Tata Natasha could be heard telling someone loudly that she would eat with her grandson and Lady Ailsa in the parlor.

"Good God, she's coming here!" Nik stood, pulling Ailsa with him. "Here." He handed her the napkins from the table, and they hurried to set themselves to rights.

He'd just rebuttoned his breeches, and Ailsa had just thrown the napkins into the fire and smoothed her skirts into place, when the door was thrown open.

Tata Natasha gave them both a swift look. "It is perhaps better that we finish this now, eh?" She closed the door and beamed at them, her critical gaze locking on Nik. "Your breeches are not buttoned correctly."

He looked down, his face heating as he hurried to rectify the situation.

"And you, Lady Ailsa, should see to your skirt. It is caught in your waistband."

Red-faced, Ailsa tugged her skirt back into place. "Thank you."

"It is nothing." Tata Natasha made her way to the small supper table, where she took Nik's abandoned seat. "I hope you two have solved your little problem. Or am I to find Lady Ailsa a husband?"

"We have solved our problem," Ailsa said swiftly, before Nik could answer.

"We have?" The words flew past his lips before he could stop them. "Ailsa, I can't—"

"Shush, love." She smiled and put her fingers under his chin and turned his face toward hers. "Nik has realized that if I were to be left in court alone, a plump duck with nae teeth, that I would indeed be in danger of becoming a pawn of the evildoers, and perhaps disillusioned by their betrayals. However, as I'll be girded in his love, and protected by his advice, I need have nae fear." She flattened her hand over his heart. "And I will do the same for him. I will watch over him; I will guard him against the evils of those who try to harm him. And when it is necessary, I will remind him that there are those who love him for nae other reason than he is our beloved."

His eyes burned and he wondered what he'd done to be with such a woman. Did he dare accept her? Would it be fair? But as he looked into her eyes, he saw his own loneliness and unhappiness mirrored there. She'd missed him as desperately as he'd missed her. Perhaps she was right, and together they could handle the intricacies of life at court. They had to at least try. His heart full, he captured Ailsa's hand and pressed a kiss to her palm. "It will not be easy."

"I'm well aware of that. Your grandmother explained it all to me, and in great detail. A stronger woman would nae have come."

Tata Natasha found a clean plate and selected a pastry. "She is right; I was most thorough."

He had no doubt about that. He took Ailsa's hand in his. "But what if you decide it is too much—"

"Then I will demand we go to the seashore or the mountains or wherever you go to rest, and we will find a better way to deal with the life you must live." She moved closer, her clear gaze locked with his. "But we will do it together, you and I. Always together."

For a second, his battered soul clung to his fears, but her steady gaze banished them.

There was only one answer. Nik placed her hand on his cheek and held it there. "Lady Ailsa Mackenzie, though I know it will go against the grain of your magnificent soul, will you please, please be my princess?"

"Your Highness." She smiled and pressed a kiss to his lips. "I thought you'd never ask."

Epilogue

The wedding took place seven months later and was a grand affair, filled with dignitaries, royalty, and noblemen and their ladies from far and wide. The grand palace of Oxenburg had been draped from the turret to the bottom floor with long banners of white and gold silk that stirred with every breeze, giving the old building a fairy-tale-like quality. After the ceremony, everyone congregated in the grand ballroom, where a ten-foot-high ice sculpture met them. Made in the shape of the castle, it dominated the huge room, the moat filled with a delicious champagne punch. The orchestra played romantic waltzes, and the dance floor was soon filled with the swish of colorful silk gowns and the scuffle of shiny leather shoes.

Nik watched from across the room with greedy eyes as his brothers took turns dancing with his fair bride. Every time Ailsa could, she'd peek at him around his brothers' shoulders and smile, and the world felt right.

Smiling, he noted that Tata Natasha now sat in a red velvet chair that had been placed by the dance floor so she could watch the festivities in comfort while loudly critiquing both the gowns and the performance of each dancer who swept by. He paused to pick up two flutes of champagne from a servant, knowing Tata would enjoy the refreshment. As he went to her, he was greeted on all sides with congratulations, some of which were sincere, some less so, but none that stole his smile.

"I was about to ask one of your brothers to bring me champagne, but you have saved me the trouble." Tata Natasha accepted the glass he offered. "Although I prefer vodka."

"You may have that as soon as the champagne runs out."

"The way your guests are guzzling it, that will not be long." She sent him a side-glance. "So. You are finally married."

"I am." And to his surprise, it felt right, as if he'd been waiting for this moment his whole life.

"You have chosen wisely. I daresay you've already noticed that Ailsa has not suffered at the hands of the court as you expected and she has been here for quite a while."

"She has done well, but it has not been easy. There were several attempts to lure her into divulging information, and some fake friendships were offered, but she is quite good at seeing through people."

Tata nodded. "In some ways, women have better instincts than men."

He finished his champagne and placed the glass on the empty tray of a servant who was walking by. "There's only one task left."

"Children. You must have a dozen, if not more."

"I was thinking of you. What will you do, now that you've married off all your grandsons? What hobby will you pursue? Painting? Embroidery?" He twinkled down at her. "Knitting?"

"*Nyet.*" She sipped her champagne, holding it as delicately as if she were a lady born. "I have already chosen my next project."

"Oh? Who is it? Or should I ask?"

"I am devoting myself to the good of the country. There are too many bachelors in court, and they are troublesome, the lot of them. Half of them are under the spell of some mistress determined to lead them to treason; and the other half are not fulfilling their duty to the crown to have children and populate the kingdom with loyal citizens."

Nik couldn't keep the startled look from his face. "You are going to attempt to find wives for *all* the bachelors at court?"

"Only the titled ones. I cannot do everything, you know."

"There must be— Good God, I don't even know how many."

"One hundred and thirty nine," she replied, looking satisfied. "I decided it was too late for the ones over eighty. Men of that age do not deal well with change."

"I see." Nik wasn't sure whether he should be happy for the men of the court, or worried. Either way, she was right about one thing: it would keep all of them busy, and her, as well. "I wish you luck."

"Pah. It does not take luck, but talent." She grabbed

her cane and stood, pressing her empty glass into his hand. "I am off to find my first project. Lord Pahlen has been a widower for three years now; it is time to fix that. You go, dance with your new wife. Poor Max has been stepping on her feet, for I have seen her wince twice now."

"I will rescue her." Nik caught Tata's hand and gave it a gentle squeeze. "Thank you, Tata Natasha. We owe you so much."

Her gaze softened, and she patted his cheek. "Just be glad you came around when you did. My next strategy involved a potion made of turtle's feet and a bat's wing."

"Good lord. I begin to feel sorry for the men of court."

She cackled and left, making her way to where Lord Pahlen sat watching the dancers with a sad look on his face. Nik thought about warning the man, but sometimes it was best to let Tata Natasha do her magic. Smiling, he went to rescue Ailsa.

As soon as he saw Nik approaching, Max pulled apart from Ailsa and bowed to her. "Thank you for the dance. I'm sorry about your toes."

"Och, 'twas my fault. I moved the wrong way." She managed a smile, though Nik thought he detected the slightest limp as she turned into his arms.

Max bowed and then went to where his wife, Murian, stood waiting near the refreshment table, her eyes twinkling with laughter.

Nik swung Ailsa around the dance floor. She was a remarkable dancer, light on her feet, and unerring in step. "It was kind of you not to blame Max for his awkwardness."

"Murian warned me he is a horrid dancer, but I dinnae listen. He was so eager to dance, too."

"He always is, but his partner always regrets it. Murien won't dance with him anymore. She says she only has ten toes and she needs them all."

Ailsa laughed, her gray eyes sparkling. She looked lovely, her rose silk gown clinging to her curves, her skin flushed and dewy in the candlelight. And she was his. All his.

He pulled her closer and she obligingly stepped into his embrace. They still danced, but at their own pace, without regard to the music.

He bent and kissed her nose, and then her forehead. "You look tired, my dear. It's been a long day."

"So it has." She leaned closer. "The Austrian ambassador's wife wishes me to ride with her tomorrow. She is quite clever, you know. I think I should go, for if we can get her to encourage her poor befuddled husband to accept the new treaty to limit the tsar's power, we would have enough votes in the coalition to—"

He kissed her. He'd loved every word she'd said, that she was here, in his arms, and by his side. He broke the kiss, resting his forehead against hers. "Before you came into my world, I was alone. I was that way on purpose, thinking it would protect me from the hurts and betrayals that are everywhere."

Her hands came to rest on his, her silver eyes shining with love. "And now?"

"And now, I don't know what I'd do without you.

I love you, Ailsa Mackenzie Romanovin. I love you and I trust you and I will never keep anything from you."

She closed her eyes and leaned against him. "I love you, too. So long as I breathe, you will never again be alone." The whispered words warmed him.

Around them, people danced, talked, whispered, and—yes—perhaps even plotted. But none of them would ever part him and Ailsa. Never.

He bent and picked her up, her silk skirts fluttering over his arm and trailing on the floor. "It's time we retired, my love."

And ignoring the shocked expressions of those around him, and the amused guffaw from Tata Natasha, Nik carried Ailsa away.

Don't miss the first delightful novel in the
Made to Marry series,
from *New York Times* bestselling author
Karen Hawkins

CAUGHT BY THE SCOT

Coming soon from Headline Eternal.

Turn the page for a preview of
Caught by the Scot. . .

Chapter 1

Never had an elopement been so poorly planned or so shabbily executed. Theodora Cumberbatch-Snowe, huddled in a wooden chair hastily pulled up to the fire in the parlor of the Wild Boar, pressed her hand to her uneasy stomach and hoped she wouldn't spoil an already horrendous day by retching.

Though her fiancé—the esteemed and quite handsome Squire Watson—possessed many admirable skills, driving an elopement vehicle was *not* one of them. When not racing haphazardly down the straight portions of the bumpy roads found so frequently in the north, Marcus oversteered the curricle, leaning wildly through each and every corner, the entire equipage swaying sickeningly while the wheels groaned in protest.

Which explained why they were not traveling at this moment.

She'd first suggested and had then demanded he slow down, or better yet, allow her to drive, but Marcus had refused, saying that while he acknowledged her greater skill with both horse and carriage, he was determined to do his duty by "sweeping" her away under his own power "or naught."

Predictably, ever-fickle fate chose the "naught" and one of the coach's wheels gave way and sent them both tumbling in a most undignified manner. Marcus and the curricle had ended up sprawled on their sides in the middle of the muddy road, while Theodora and her portmanteau had landed in a dirty water-filled ditch.

She had kicked at her wet gown where it clung to her legs, wincing at the twinge in her ankle. How, oh how, had she convinced herself that eloping would be a romantic, exciting endeavor? She was twenty-and-seven and well past the age of foolishness, and yet when presented with the opportunity for "romance," she'd leapt at it like a callow girl of sixteen.

"Stupid, stupid, stupid," she muttered to herself and reached for the glass of whisky she'd demanded when she and Marcus had first arrived at the inn, muddied and bruised and riding, in the most ignominious way possible, in a hay-filled farmer's cart. Marcus had done what he could to smooth the situation over—bespeaking the parlor, pulling a chair to the fire for her, and procuring the requested glass of whisky. He'd then hired two of the innkeeper's strongest postboys to return to the curricle to see if it could be righted and repaired.

"This is not how elopements occur in novels," she said under her breath. She shoved a wet curl from her cheek, wincing when her fingers brushed the scrape on her jaw.

That's a reason to drink. She took a sip of her whisky,

the smooth tones soothing the ire bubbling through her veins. Taking a deep breath, she put her feet upon the footstool in front of her chair, struggling to free her uninjured foot from the torn flounce and flinching when her bruised knee protested.

There's another reason to drink. She took another sip and leaned her head against the high back of the chair. She'd first doubted the wisdom of her decision to elope when her erst-while husband had met her at their pre-arranged location in an antiquated curricle that had once belonged to his grandmother. For some reason, Marcus had thought the lumbering, faded orange, silk-lined contraption would add a certain luxurious touch to their pragmatic flight to the border.

Sadly, he hadn't taken into account that the main springs were completely ruined, so that each bump in the road had been more of a thud, while the faded leather seats reeked of hen droppings and moldy hay. Marcus had unwittingly explained these unfortunate circumstances when he mentioned that the creaky contraption had been abandoned in the barn "for some time" until he'd "revived it."

Judging from the odor wafting from the seats, Theodora could only imagine that "for some time" was well over a hundred years, and his "reviving" had not included a thorough airing out.

Which is yet another reason to drink. She took a bigger sip than usual, glad her stomach was no longer protesting.

She realized she was already woefully low on whisky. If she kept this up, she'd have to get up and fetch more, as the decanter was on the other side of the room, a move her ankle would protest mightily.

But it wasn't her fault that the whisky was so welcome. As kind and well-meaning as Marcus was, there were times when he seemed oblivious to simple comforts. *Conner would never have been seen in such a curricle. He would have brought his new cabriolet, or perhaps that sleek blue coach he bought in Bristol just a year ago, or—*

She caught her thoughts and grimaced to herself. As if Conner Douglas would ever plan an elopement. Oh, he'd abscond with someone's wife without a thought, yes. But marry? Never.

Which was why she was here now. Conner Douglas was not the sort of man a gently bred woman would usually meet, and with good reason. Though he came from one of Scotland's leading families, by the time he was twenty he'd firmly established himself as a society outcast. Theodora wasn't entirely certain what he'd done to keep his name off the eligible bachelor list for most of England's acceptable families, but she'd heard whispers of sordid affairs, bare-knuckled brawls, outlandish wagers, and misty-dawn duels. One story held that he'd had a duel over a popular, sought-after actress in the middle of the Duke of Devonshire's ballroom, which had left a mirror shattered and an unsightly ding in a precious suit of armor.

The stories were endless, and while she was certain many of them were embellished, there was enough truth in them to label Conner the rakehell he was.

But to her, he was her brother's best friend, and the

man she'd been in love with since she'd been a young, starry-eyed girl of fourteen.

She still remembered the day they'd met. He'd come to visit her brother, a classmate of his at Oxford. She'd been a leggy, flat-chested, deucedly awkward girl, and he'd been a twenty-year-old, handsome, athletic, slumberous-eyed rogue. She'd been lost the second he'd strode into her mother's sitting room—with his dark hair that fell to his shoulders, ice-blue eyes, and a lithe grace as intriguing as his smile was charming. He'd bowed over her hand and smiled, murmuring some polite greeting.

She looked at her hand now and curled it into a fist. *That's how young girls fall in love—instantly, and with no more reason than a handsome face and a set of broad shoulders.* Of course, Conner never saw her as anything more than his best friend's little sister, and so paid her little heed. At least, he had at first. Eventually, over the years, by dint of always being available to listen whenever he had something to say, never offering a critical comment without adding some sort of helpful addendum, and hiding her always present desire to fling herself into his arms, they'd become friends. As they did so, she was more honest with him, too, which he seemed to appreciate.

But though their friendship had kept Conner returning to her side throughout the years, it had also ended any hopes she'd had for romance.

It had taken her time, but she'd learned to deal with her unruly feelings, and now she could say with believable firmness that she saw him as a friend and no more.

Sadly, no one else had caught her attention with the same fervor, and she'd never married. Lately, she'd realized that perhaps she had been foolish to hope for passion at her age. Perhaps compatibility and the hope for years of pleasant and reasonable discourse were reasons enough to marry?

Thus, last week when Squire Watson had begged her to elope and join him in his beautiful manor house, she'd found herself tempted. The squire was a worthy man, his affections genuine, his character flawless. She could do worse.

And so she'd accepted. And now, here she was, wet, bedraggled, and bruised.

The best reason of all for another sip. She finished the glass and then eyed the decanter from across the room.

She needed more whisky. A lot more. Conner Douglas wasn't an easy man to forget, and right now, after such an uninspiring start to her elopement, he seemed even more attractive than ever. He possessed—something. She wasn't sure what it was, but he could just walk into a room and every woman would turn his way and *wonder.* It wasn't just his looks, which were prodigious. No, it was something else; something dark and dangerous, a make-your-heart-pound-until-you-beg-for-me sort of thing. He was the kind of man most women dreamed about, but never admitted to.

Why, even now, if Theodora stared out the window long enough, she could almost imagine that the man who'd just ridden into the innyard was Conner. The figure swung down from his horse, a bold black gelding with a long, flowing mane, and tossed the reins to a waiting postboy. The man was as tall as Conner, his shoulders as broad, his hair just as dark, and slightly long—just the way Conner wore his. Why, the man was even dressed in a kilt—not odd, as they were riding the North Road to the border.

As she watched, the man raked a hand through his hair, the afternoon sun touching his handsome face—

Theodora bolted upright. *"Conner?"*

Heart thundering in her chest, she set down her glass without noticing that she missed the small table and it went tumbling to the rug as she stood. *Bloody hell, what is* he *doing here?*

It had to be a sad coincidence; her own parents didn't realize she was eloping, and wouldn't until they returned from town next week and found the letter she'd left them. She looked around the small parlor and wished she could hide, but the sound of his deep, lilting voice in the hallway put that thought to rest.

Cursing feverishly, she limped to the mirror and tried to do something with her wet hair, which had long since fallen from its pins, wincing at the sight of the bloodied scrape on her jaw. *Good God, I look a fright!*

The door flew open and Conner strode into the parlor, escorted by the maid, a young lass with red hair who couldn't seem to stop staring at the Scotsman, her eyes full of longing.

Theodora couldn't blame the poor girl. The striking Douglas looks were hard to resist. And today with his face half-shaven, he looked as wild as the pirate he was often accused of being.

His gaze flickered over her now, taking in her wet, muddied gown, her bedraggled hair, and finally finding the scrape on her jaw. His gaze turned icy. "Bloody hell, what happened?" Conner's voice was deadly cold. "If that fool laid one finger on you—"

"Don't be ridiculous. The wheel broke on our curricle and I was thrown out."

His mouth thinned, but he didn't look quite so furious. "I'm sorry to hear tha'. Have you nae dry clothes, lass?"

"Sadly, no. My portmanteau was thrown into the same ditch as I. My gowns are being cleaned and dried now, although it will be hours before one is ready."

"Bloody hell. I expected to find you snug in a parlor, but having tea, nae bloody and shivering." As he spoke, he stalked across the room toward her, his brogue rippling through his deep voice like a velvet stroke. He stopped before her, tugged off his overcoat, and swung it about her shoulders.

"I don't—"

"Pssht. Wear the damned thing; you're shaking fra' the cold."

"Fine, fine. I'll wear it, but it's not in the least necessary." She pulled it more snuggly about her. The long coat reached only to Conner's calves, but it pooled at her feet, the faint scent of his cologne unsettling.

The events of the morning hit her with fresh vigor and she swallowed the desire to both burst into tears and throw her arms about his neck, neither an acceptable reaction. It took several hard gulps, but she managed to say in a voice that trembled only a little, "Would you like some tea?" She fixed her gaze on the gawking maid. "Tea for two, please."

The maid struggled to rip her gaze from Conner, who was oblivious to the young girl. With a long sigh, the young lady bobbed a curtsy. "Yes, miss. Shall I bring some for the squire, too?" The maid's tone was stubborn, and she sent a secretive glance at Conner to see if he was surprised to hear that Theodora was not at the inn alone.

Conner didn't so much as blink, but continued to look at Theodora with intense concern. *He knows.* That was good, wasn't it? She would be spared the need to make explanations. She turned to the maid. "The squire is seeing to our overturned curricle, so I doubt he'll return within the next hour. Two cups will be enough, thank you."

The maid looked disappointed at Theodora's aplomb, but bobbed a curtsy again and, with a last longing gaze at Conner, left.

You poor girl, Theodora thought. *He looks like every hero you've ever imagined, doesn't he? And yet he's far, far from that.*

Conner's gaze slid over her to the floor. He raised his brows. "You dropped something."

She looked down. Her glass lay on the rug on its side. Irritated, she scooped it up. "It must have fallen when I stood. The coach ride made me ill, so I was trying to still my stomach."

His blue eyes, as changeable as the weather, flickered over her, resting for a long moment on her face. Without a word, he reached out and took her chin between his fingers and turned her cheek. He tsked and pulled a kerchief from his pocket and gently pressed it to her wound. "Och. Theodora, what ha' you done to yourself?"

He said the words more to himself than to her.

But the kind words made her long all the more to feel his arms around her. *Which is an understandable reaction. I'm so banged and bruised by this journey that I'd accept comfort from anyone.*

She pulled back, ignoring the warm flush that had rippled through her at his touch.

His gaze flickered over her, taking in the grass stain on her knee, concern darkening his gaze. "Are you injured elsewhere?"

She started to shrug, but the ache on her left side forbade it. She thought of her bruised knee, the ache in her side, and the soreness of her ankle. "No."

"Guid," he said. "For had you been seriously injured by tha' fool's ham-fisted driving, I'd have been forced to kill him."

"How did you know he was driving?"

Conner's expression softened into a faint smile. "I've seen you drive, lass. You'd never send your equipment into a ditch."

She had to agree. "I was much more ill from the swaying of the curricle than I was bruised by the fall. Which is why I helped myself to the whisky."

"Did it soothe your stomach?"

"Some. But that's neither here nor there." She frowned at him. "Why are you here?"

"I'll tell you, but first return to your chair." He tucked

a hand under her elbow and gently led her back to her seat.

She supposed the ring of water around the chair gave away her former placement, but he was right. It was warmer by the fire, and her ankle was already protesting how long she'd been standing.

She limped beside him, and took her seat with a grateful sigh. He pulled a chair close to hers and patted his knee.

"You . . . I . . . I beg your pardon?"

"I want to see that ankle."

"There's no need. Marcus—Squire Watson sent for a doctor. He will be here soon."

Conner bent, lifted the edge of her skirt, and placed her foot on his knee.

"Conner!" she bit out. "I said—"

"I heard you." He kept a firm grip on her calf so she couldn't remove her leg, his fingers strong but gentle. He grasped her toes with his other hand. "I'm going to bend it. Tell me when it hurts."

Slowly, ever so slowly, he turned her ankle in a circle.

"It's fine. Just a little— OW!"

He stopped. "'Tis only a sprain. But you should ha' it oop." He placed her foot back on the ground, pulled her footstool closer to her chair. "There."

"But my gown will—"

"Be covered by my coat. Now, do it."

She did as he asked, trying not to look as sulky as she felt. She couldn't imagine any way this day could get worse. "How did you know I'd—" *Eloped.* Oddly, the word stuck in her throat.

"I stopped by Cumberbatch Manor earlier today. Your brother was there. He knew you'd eloped."

"He must have read the note I left for our parents." She'd have some choice words for her brother when next she saw him. Derrick had no right to open that letter. "So Derrick sent you."

"Nae one sent me. I came on my own."

"You shouldn't have bothered. I've made up my mind about this, and truly, it's a good match. The squire is kind and guid and—"

"Do you love him?" Conner asked abruptly, his gaze locked on her.

She blinked. "I . . . That's not . . . I don't see how that's any of your business."

"Do. You. Love. Him." Conner's mouth was almost white.

Why does he care? She cleared her throat. "Love has nothing to do with it."

Conner's expression eased. "So 'tis a marriage of convenience, then."

"You could say that, yes."

"Guid." Conner arose and went to the sideboard, where he prepared a generous glass of whisky for himself, and then brought the decanter to her empty glass and added a measure to it. "Drink. You're still pale."

"I'm fine—"

He raised his brows, disbelief plain on his face.

She gave an exasperated sigh, but then admitted, "I'm still a bit off."

"And nae wonder. You always get a bit squeamish when you travel on warm days."

"It was more than that; the springs in that blasted curricle were far from satisfactory." She sipped her drink, and then reluctantly set it down. She needed her wits about her.

He watched her over his glass. "So, lass. Why have you decided to elope today, of all days?"

"Why not today?"

He chuckled wryly, as if he knew something she didn't. "But an elopement? That is nae like you to throw caution to the wind in such a fashion."

She fought the urge to tell him that he didn't know what was or was not like her. "I like the squire and he has much to offer, and I hope I'll be a good wife. That's all there is to it. I—"

Her gaze locked on Conner's chin. She frowned. "You haven't shaved today." She then noticed the wrinkles in his fitted coat, the marred cravat he'd twisted about his neck, the mud on his boots. Conner Douglas may be so lost to propriety as to fight a duel in the middle of a ball, but he always, always dressed well.

She placed her hand on his. "What's happened?"

Conner raised his glass to his lips, but Theodora's concerned gaze hit him like a hammer, shattering the thin hold he had on his composure.

He lowered the glass, and found that his emotions had wrapped themselves about his throat like a noose. It took effort, but he managed to rasp out a word. "Anne."

It was all he could bring himself to say.

Theodora's eyes widened, and then filled with tears. "Oh, Conner, I'm so, so sorry. I know how close you were to your sister. What . . . when . . ."

"Five days ago."

Theodora squeezed his hand. "She was to have a child. Was that . . ."

He nodded miserably. Conner's parents had died when he was small, and in one swoop, Anne—ten years older than her three brothers—had become caretaker, confidante, and mother.

Conner looked at Theodora's hand covering his. Although he'd had five long endless days and sleepless nights to accept it, he still couldn't believe he'd never see his sister again.

"The baby?" Theodora asked softly.

"A beautiful lad." Conner's throat tightened again and he took a desperate gulp of his whisky, determined beyond all else that he would not cry. Not in front of Theodora.

People assumed Theodora's brother was still Conner's closest friend. But after Derrick married, Conner found himself seeking out Theodora rather than Derrick. She had a level head, and was always glad to listen and give advice, and she never hesitated to tell him what she really thought. Over the years, he'd come to appreciate her honesty and openness.

Of all the women he knew, Theodora was the easiest to talk to, and she was the only woman he trusted.

Which was why he was here now.

He freed his hand from hers under the pretext of refilling his glass, unable to handle more sympathy.

As if understanding, she pulled back. "Is there anything I can do?"

Conner looked at her over the edge of his glass. "You would help if you could, would you nae?"

"Of course." Her clear gaze met his, questioning but unflinching.

"Guid, for I've a need of you."

She blinked. "This isn't about the baby, is it? I'm—"

"Nae. 'Tis something else. 'Tis the reason I went to your house to begin with. Anne had a will, as you would guess, for she was always thinking ahead. When my parents died, they left the Douglas lands and fortune in Anne's hands until such a time as my brothers and I were ready to assume our responsibilities." He rubbed his chin ruefully. "We have nae been in a hurry to accept tha' burden, or so Anne thought."

"None of you have tried to," Theodora said in a fair tone. "Your brother Declan is besotted with horses and racing, which is hardly a firm foundation for running an estate. As for Jack, they don't call him Black Jack for nothing. He's more of a pirate than yo—" She broke off and flushed.

"Than me," he finished. "I'm a privateer, love. 'Tis nae the same as a pirate. And I've made a guid living at it, too."

Her cheeks couldn't be pinker. "Anne's will. What did it say?"

"She tied oop the Douglas lands and fortune with a stipulation. I and my brothers must marry, and soon, or the entire lot of the Douglas fortune will go to the bloody Campbells."

Theodora gasped. "The Campbells? But they're—"

"Our greatest enemy. Aye." He scowled. "Had she left our estate to charity, my brothers and I would have let it go. Who needs the burden of such? But the Campbells? Tha' is nae acceptable."

"I see. So . . . you must marry."

"And soon. We've only three months to do so, all three of us. And it must be to a lady of quality, too." He leaned forward, resting his elbows on his knees. "As soon as I found oot aboot the will, I thought of you."

"Of *me*?" Her voice cracked on the last word.

"Of course you," he said impatiently. "You know me, and you're a sensible sort, you'd have reasonable expectations." Conner could think of no higher praise. His only concern had been that over the years, she seemed disinclined to marry. Arriving at her home to discover she was eloping had been a shock, but perhaps it was a good omen. She'd admitted she wasn't eloping for love, so perhaps she wasn't as disinclined to wed as he'd thought.

Perhaps all she'd needed was the right offer. "Theodora, lass, enough with this ridiculous squire. You can do better."

"Better? Are you . . . Conner, are you proposing to me while I'm in the middle of my own elopement?"

His smile slipped a bit. "It sounds rather puir when you say it tha' way. I'm making you a better offer, a step oop from your current path."

She stared at him as if unable to grasp his meaning.

With an impatient sigh, he took her hand and pressed a kiss to her fingers. "What do you say, Theodora? Will you marry me?"

Her mouth pressed into a straight line and her eyes blazed. She yanked her hand from his, lowered her sprained foot from the footstool, and stood. Bedraggled and damp, her hair curling wildly about her outraged face, she limped toward the door.

Conner stood. "Theodora, wait! You have nae answered."

She stopped by the door and looked at him over her shoulder. "But I have. Conner Douglas, I would not marry you if you were the last man on earth."

And with those damning words, she left.